Folly:
An I Ching Mystery

Mickey Friedman

i

Red Crow Books
222 Main Street, #741
Great Barrington, Massachusetts
All rights reserved.
ISBN: 0-9904286-3-X
ISBN-13: 978-0-9904286-3-3

DEDICATION

Each book, every film I've made offers it's own unique challenges. Both Douglas Macdonald and Ed Weiner helped me better understand not only myself but the inner worlds of those who unexpectedly decided to surface this time around.

EPIGRAM

"Sometimes an incorrigible fool must be punished. He who will not heed will be made to feel. This punishment is quite different from a preliminary shaking up. But the penalty should not be imposed in anger; it must be restricted to an objective guarding against unjustified excesses. Punishment is never an end in itself but serves merely to restore order."

Mêng / Youthful Folly, the *I Ching*.

PREFACE

This is my second effort with the so very impressive Chinese authors of the *I Ching*. My first, *Danger Times Two*, tackled the intertwined lives of two women. One with amnesia and the other with her copy of the *I Ching* and three coins.

As I wrote *Folly*, I followed the same practice, and so I as the character would throw the coins and consult the *I Ching*: all of us bound to accept the answer and continue down these new roads. Until the next question.

So this continues to be a collaboration. The better parts have come from the astute authors of the *I Ching*, while the mistakes are mine. Again please know because of my stubbornness and/or ignorance I continue to disregard many of the conventions that govern the proper consultation and interpretation of the *I Ching*. Instead, Katie and I pick and choose whatever makes sense to us in the text.

These characters and places are almost entirely mine. I have liberally distorted geography and while you might in your travels stumble upon some of these places I've mentioned you won't find the people I've put in them. And so any resemblance to real persons, living or dead, is purely coincidental.

Mickey Friedman, June 2016.

CONTENTS

ACKNOWLEDGMENTS

My thanks to Deborah Haddock for her very informative "The Dissociative Identity Disorder Sourcebook," 2001, The McGraw Hill Companies.

Thanks as well to Carol K. Anthony's interpretation of 'Shih Ho' found in her 1998 *"A Guide to the I Ching,"* Anthony Publishing Company, Stow, Massachusetts.

I must acknowledge the analytical discussion of DID found in the "Diagnostic and Statistical Manual of Mental Disorders, Fourth Edition," 2000, the American Psychiatric Association.

Thanks much to Iris Tuomenoksa, whose keen eye and shrewd suggestions helped me locate and repair some of my most obvious mistakes.

Again I am indebted to my favorite rendition of the *I Ching:* Richard Wilhelm and Cary F. Baynes, translators, *The I Ching, or Book of Changes,* third edition. Princeton University Press, Princeton, New Jersey, © 1950, 1967 Bollingen Foundation. Reprinted by permission of Princeton University Press, permission conveyed through Copyright Clearance Center, Inc.

ONE

Every night this last week Katie had dreamt of her dead parents, Carl and Theresa. These dreams, nightmares really, were fraught with tension. There she was beside Carl visiting the small coffee growers' cooperative the peasants had painstakingly cut from the Salvadoran jungle.

The owners of the nearby coffee plantation had hired armed thugs to force them from the now useful land they wanted for themselves. As Katie ate beans and tortillas and drank dense dark coffee, she heard stories of fathers and mothers and brothers and sisters who had died to create this cooperative, then heard the workers thank Carl for all his help. She watched as a teenaged boy was carried bleeding to the makeshift infirmary with a bullet wound.

Then somehow she was with Theresa, sitting beside Susan, a Canadian nurse, and Maria, a local nun, organizers of the non-profit Hermanas/Sisters. They were surrounded by fifty indigenous women, legs crossed, sitting in the dirt in the courtyard of the local church in a small town in Guatemala as they talked about their children, nutrition, and economic development. Watching as the Guatemalan army gathered about them.

Even in dreamland, it was hard for Katie to take this in. She had tried mightily to push all this painful family stuff away: the great stakes that marked the work they did, the risks they took, and the hardships they endured to do that work. And most of all, the violent explosion that ripped apart the van Carl was driving to take Salvadoran refuges to Canada, taking Carl from them forever. These dreams especially hard because they brought the recent murder of her boyfriend Ralph so sharply back to the surface.

Katie had always done her best to keep the darkness at bay. Whether it was the bright colors she wore, the sage she burned to periodically cleanse her house, the daily meditations, or her steadfast determination to manifest the positive in thought and deed. The decision to leave Theresa and Frank behind, to leave the noise and crowds and chaos of Manhattan for the quiet and contemplation of the country.

So she had moved to the Berkshire Hills of Massachusetts, to an old and modest farmhouse on an out-of-the way dirt road in

Ripton, blessed to have been so quickly chosen by Rabbit, her steadfast husky friend. In winter, she had taught herself to chop wood, make jam, bake bread, and in summer to grow organic green beans and lettuce and broccoli and more zucchini than she could ever eat.

Her policeman brother Frank had also come from the city to help her with the great mystery of Penny's amnesia. Along the way he had come to learn, even appreciate a bit what it was she did with the *I Ching*, the ancient Chinese book of wisdom. So Katie wanted to believe that if there was anything good beside the return of Penny's memory that had come from the two deaths in her kitchen, it was that a few months later Frank had decided to take a job as Assistant Police Chief in Ripton and join her in the country. Offering them yet another chance to regain the closeness of their earliest years.

Even as a young girl, even in her waking hours, Katie had the gift of intuition. At first, it was the imperfectly formed and always unexpected images that came to her without asking, the strange and out-of-place intimations. Or sometimes the odd yet undeniable feeling that something was off, or that something important was about to happen.

Thanks to her twice a week, two years' worth of sessions with Dr. Chau, and his patient yet thorough guidance, she was able with the help of the *I Ching* to shape these dreams of night and day into more comprehensible visions. Consulting with the *I Ching* to provide context and some clarity to what often seemed vague or random. Until over time, she felt comfortable enough to share her work with the *I Ching* with others. Fostering a creative collaboration between the questions her clients brought to her, their coin tosses, the answers the oracle offered in response, and the very personal, often idiosyncratic interpretations she added to the process.

Modest to the point of self-deprecating, Katie was sure that those more skilled in the mysteries of psychotherapy, more knowledgeable about the most recent discoveries in brain chemistry, or those privy to the ways of the ancient augurs and soothsayers understood and could explain this still mysterious practice far better than she ever could. At her best she was more a combination of shepherd, coach, and spiritual instigator, than an expert in anything specific.

Nevertheless, over the years Katie had helped a great many people with a variety of problems: from finding pets to finding love, or leaving dead-end jobs and abandoning destructive relationships. Of course, there were consequences small and serious associated with all that work. But nothing compared to what her work with Penny had wrought: the murder of boyfriend Ralph, and the death of his killer before her very eyes. So now she was slowly beginning to step back far enough to fully acknowledge her great pain, and the lingering sense that she had failed. Because, despite the repeated warnings of the *I Ching*, she hadn't clearly seen exactly how great a danger Penny had faced or how it would impact those around her.

Frank had several times tried to reassure her, to remind her that always when you dealt with human beings you had to expect the unexpected. That as much as we wanted, maybe needed to assume we could control a situation, we were far more ineffectual than we were ever prepared to accept. His years working on the streets of the city had many times reminded him that it was best to acknowledge the likelihood of failure. And then to cherish the unlikely but occasionally astonishing success.

As she recovered from the horrors Penny's brother-in-law, Donnie Kean, had inflicted, Katie had come to appreciate even more her hours at "Books, Books, and More Books," and the complete freedom Anne Faber offered her. "Books" provided peace and tranquility, a sweet simplicity. She had sorted and re-sorted and then moved thousands of used books from Anne's barn to the front store, and yet there were still more books arriving every day from the estate and tag sales Annie scoured, a chaotic mix of fiction and non-fiction, of table-top books, hard covers and paperbacks, books meant for the young and the old.

When she fell into the spell of this work, she could for many moments at a time erase the memory of Donnie's pistol, the blood spurting from Ralph's body, Rabbit leaping across time and space, the sound of the shotgun Penny fired, and the sight of Donnie and her dog slumping to the floor.

TWO

Frank Falco lived on Crescent Street, a few blocks from Main Street, and within walking distance of the town's miniaturized downtown. Though the town was officially called Great Barrington, most locals had long ago accepted the fact that it wasn't big enough to be referred to as anything more than GB on most occasions and Barrington when something special was happening.

His apartment was twice as big yet so much cheaper than his old apartment in Manhattan. Danger, his newly adopted Quaker parrot, had his own room and small TV.

For Frank, a city-born and city-certified New Yorker, this was a seismic shift. Which began with the completely unexpected job offer from Chief David Paul to work for the Ripton Police Department for less than half of what he made in the city.

It wasn't easy leaving the NYPD: he had put in his time, had made it to Detective and even found a certain kind of peace with Captain Rasch. But the fact was that even though he had yet to admit it to anyone other than his therapist, Dr. Silver, he often imagined a future with Penny Davis. A possibility, not surprisingly, given his meager communication skills and fairly pathetic track record with women, he still hadn't shared with said Penny.

There was as well, considering their past misperceptions, a growing desire to be closer to Katie, his younger sister. Then, still unwilling to acknowledge that his own city days might be coming to a close, Frank convinced himself Danger required a quiet space to recover. A notion reinforced when Dr. Silver, Danger's first foster parent, confirmed with a knowing smile that Post Traumatic Parrot Stress was not to be trifled with. Few pet parrots, she told Frank, had had to watch helplessly as two men died, and a new husky dog friend got shot. Add these reasons together and Frank had a compelling enough case to forsake Manhattan for the country.

Probably because he continued to do talk-therapy with Dr. Silver by phone every Wednesday morning, he no longer dreamt each night of his own dreadful encounter with death, the off-duty shooting on Broadway. It also helped that the family of the fifteen-year-old boy he had shot in self-defense had settled out-of-court.

That the killing had faded from the public consciousness and that the New York newspapers and TV stations no longer cared about him.

Now he was more worried about Katie and Penny and Danger than he was about himself: they were still in the midst of the long and painful journey recovering from the murder of Ralph Parker. Dealing with the stark reality that Penny's quick reactions, her ability to get the shotgun blast off before Donnie's second and third shots had saved them from a most certain death. Still, there was no denying the great trauma they shared as both Penny's brother-in-law, Donnie, and Katie's boyfriend, Ralph, had bled and died before them.

Unfortunately, Frank knew that the act of killing someone, however justified, stayed with you always. And those observers, human or parrot, who were the unlucky victims of and witnesses to the worst of human disorders, were all damaged.

Sadly, as an unfortunate bonus or maybe a sharp, perhaps snide passive-parrot-aggressive reminder, Danger, a master mimic, had added the shotgun blast to his wide repertoire of perfect sounds: telephone rings, zippers zipping, a bevy of assorted beeps and whistles, the back-up sounds of the garbage trucks, and a variety of Frank's coughs and snorts and laughs. At the oddest moments Frank found himself flinching at the sound of yet another phantom shot.

Along the way, after all the work they had done together with the *I Ching*, Katie and Penny had become good friends, bound by a shared grief and the recognition that together they had faced and survived danger and death. Aware always that they were both alive because they were together that day.

Ripton, where Katie lived, and where Frank was now working as Assistant Police Chief, was just a short drive away from GB. Its population of six hundred and forty-two was spread across thirty square miles.

Understandably, Frank was still adjusting to the scale of his new life. Manhattan had more than a million and a half people crammed together on a bit more than twenty-two square miles. A couple of big buildings on his previous beat had more people living in them than all of Ripton.

In the city he was combating crime that took no breaks, depravity that demanded a precinct full of fellow cops, three shifts, twenty-four seven. Now, it was just he and Chief Paul sharing a one-room office on the second floor of the one hundred fifty year old Town Hall. Right next door to the office of the Selectboard, the unpaid three-person elected committee that all too enthusiastically tried to steer town affairs, large and small, in Ripton.

Frank had told Chief Paul he had one take it or leave it demand: he would bring his many skills as a cop to Ripton in return for working in street clothes, much like the urban detective he had become. Wanting never, ever to go back to wearing a uniform.

The Selectboard, Chief Paul told him, was more than peeved but ultimately surrendered. They so liked to see their uniformed policemen standing smartly dressed on Saturdays and Sundays in the very middle of Route 23, directing traffic that didn't need directing in front of the church and the Ripton General Store. If only to reassure the taxpayers and ardent voters, that while their precious Ripton was ever so much smaller than Great Barrington, they were just as safe and secure.

Besides wearing his own clothes to work, just about everything was so very different in the country. Starting with his caseload. Last week, for instance, Frank had responded to a complaint that Andrew Peterson, a resident of nearby Saintsville, had been illegally using the Ripton Town Dump. Some anonymous tipster, thought to be Peterson's soon-to-be ex-wife, Cynthia, must have waded after hours at the town dump through a small hill of rotten fruit and empty tuna cans and some burnt toast to fetch several torn letters all addressed to him. Which the tipster proceeded to mail as evidence of his wrongdoing to Patricia McWhinney of the Selectboard, who in turn seemed quite pleased to deposit it all on Chief Paul's desk.

After a short Saturday drive to Saintsville, Frank learned quickly and regrettably that Andrew Peterson was an attorney-at-law who all too energetically practiced his trade twenty-five miles north in the small big city of Plattsford.

Irate that he had been tracked down and bothered at his sister's home when he had a motion to prepare, Peterson argued with great energy and lawyer-like precision that even had he dumped at the Ripton dump, which he certainly wasn't admitting to, it would have been perfectly legal for him to do so. Because until the divorce was finalized, technically he still lived in Ripton in the longstanding

Peterson family homestead that his despicable, money-grubbing wife was trying so hard to steal from him. Not only that, he proudly insisted, his family had lived in Ripton for two hundred years, and almost all of them could be found residing in the Oak Hill Cemetery. So even if, for a very brief moment in time, thanks to the cruel manipulations of the wretched Cynthia, he now found himself forced to take refuge in nearby Saintsville, well "disposal" was an inalienable right and thus "grandfathered in."

It was, Peterson stressed, a position he was so committed to, he would gladly take the case all the way to the state Supreme Judicial Court. Then, with a vigorous finger wag that came perilously close to Frank's nose, he rested his case with the unnecessarily loud conclusion that Cynthia's people came from Little Falls, Missouri, wherever the hell that was.

Frank, as tempted as he was, managed not to laugh. Instead, he found himself calmly conjuring up a set of words he had never used before in his previous life as a cop: "I'm sure the Selectboard will be glad to take the matter under advisement. You have a wonderful day, Counselor."

Two days later, he was called to assist Fish and Wildlife when they brought in Pete Simpson for killing a deer out of season. Then he found himself corralling three nineteen-year-olds from North Otis who probably because they were very drunk thought it was a good idea to drive eight miles to Ripton to steal a sunfish in broad daylight from a summer home alongside the lake. Making his job even easier when, their coordination slightly impaired, they immediately overturned the sunfish in front of the Fire Chief fishing two hundred feet from the town beach.

As the week came to an end, by late Sunday afternoon he had ticketed more weekenders than he cared to remember for going fifty instead of thirty-five along the flats.

It was then the odd thought came to him that even though he was making half of what he had made in Manhattan, just maybe he was making more money than he deserved. Though there were times he missed the never-ending action of the city streets. Sometimes he even envied the cops in GB their occasional murder and small-scale drug busts.

THREE

Penny had left the police station in Little Pointe, Michigan without saying a word to Peter, the husband who had twice asked his brother to kill her. She left Little Pointe knowing her Potter Road property was in good hands with its caretaker, Juan Castillo. Glad to be giving Henrique's, the restaurant in Detroit, to his older brother, José. While she knew she would be back to visit Juan and José, she was thrilled to leave Little Pointe behind.

That first month, back in the Berkshires, she stayed at Bea Foster's B&B in Brett, returning to her old room, walking each morning to Dom's, the simple yet homey restaurant that had offered her refuge. Like completing some essential circle: coming back as Penny, saying goodbye to Sarah, the name she had taken for herself in the throes of not knowing. Discovering that these people mattered even more to her now than they had during her amnesia.

Deb Spencer had been overwhelmed by her gift of Dom's, slow to fully appreciate that her small acts of kindness had meant that much to Sarah/Penny. Because in many ways, Deb was still much more comfortable thinking of herself as a waitress rather than a restaurant owner. But Jack Spencer was working on it, convinced his wife was born to do business, so much more outgoing and friendly than he was at his garage.

In the meantime, Joey Montano, thrilled that Penny had so willingly overpaid and liberated him from yet another decade of eggs over easy, had quickly agreed to keep the sale of Dom's a secret, running the place while Deb waited tables and slowly began to familiarize herself with buying from the suppliers, balancing the books, and learning Joey's secrets to managing a staff as eccentric and rambunctious as she was.

Penny still loved her occasional shopping trips with Deb and the kids to Magic Mart, Price Chopper, and the Outlet Village. There was so much about her life as Sarah that she admired and wanted to hold onto: the simplicity; the emphasis on necessity rather than excess; and friendships based on true affection not affectation.

After that first month at Bea's, quickly craving more space and some privacy, she found a short-term rental in downtown Ripton.

Now that Penny knew she wanted to live in the Berkshires, she had begun a serious search for a new home. Even though she joked that she had inherited a gazillion dollars, and had just sold her Little Point, Michigan home for more than four million, she yearned for a lot less ostentation, less marble, and a much more modest comfort. Hoping for an old-fashioned New England home with some land and space to roam; a place that Rabbit, Katie's husky, would be pleased to visit. Maybe by the water.

As Sarah, so terribly lost in the fog of amnesia, she had barely understood how Katie managed to find any sense in the complex mysteries of the *I Ching*.

While in Little Point, her memory returning, she had made a concerted effort to learn more about this centuries-old Chinese guidebook. She still had questions about how Katie could see so much, but had certainly gained a greater appreciation for her unique and idiosyncratic insights, and a heightened respect for the powers of the oracle.

The process seemed simple enough: you brought a compelling question to the *I Ching*, a question that couldn't be answered with a simple yes or no, then tossed the three coins six different times. Heads counted as three, while tails counted as two. Then, depending on your mix of heads and tails, you assigned a number to each throw. Even totals like eight, two heads and a tail, or six, three tails, were expressed as a broken line. Odd totals like nine, three heads, or seven, two tails and a head, were expressed as a straight line. Then if you threw either three heads or three tails, this was considered a changing line. A changing line of six, a broken line on the first hexagram, became its opposite, a straight line on the second hexagram you were building. With these six lines you built two hexagrams from the ground up.

Each hexagram told a unique story. And here's where Katie's independent, almost anarchic streak asserted itself. Because you could arrive at a straight or broken line in two different ways – by throwing either a nine or seven, or a six or eight – the purists believed that only certain specific parts of the text truly applied to you. They most accurately answered your question. But Katie, as much an intuitive guide, a psychic or poet, embraced the notion that the entire story, and any possible portion of it, could provide useful and provocative insights. In support of that approach Katie had shared with Penny her father's recurring joke about his always unorthodox choices: "Whatever Happens, That's The Plan."

So Penny, who had benefitted greatly from the process, was even more now than before willing to opt for Katie's eccentric inspiration over orthodoxy.

Penny took a moment to pet Rabbit, who, almost entirely healed from his shotgun wounds, was quietly lying by her feet. She and Katie shared tea and some homemade raspberry scones. Then Penny took a deep breath and began to focus on her question: "What will my new life be like?" She said it aloud and threw the three coins: two tails and a head, seven. Then, thinking once more about her question, Penny threw two heads and a tail, an eight, a broken line above her straight line. Then alternating another eight, a seven, an eight and the last seven. She hadn't thrown any changing lines so there was a single hexagram to consult: "Shih Ho / Biting Through."

Katie began to read aloud:

> The theme of this hexagram is a criminal lawsuit …

Both Katie and Penny couldn't help but think about Penny's husband Peter and his upcoming trial for conspiracy to commit murder:

> Whenever unity cannot be established, the obstruction is due to a talebearer and traitor who is interfering and blocking the way … Deliberate obstruction of this sort does not vanish of its own accord. Judgment and punishment are required to deter or obviate it.

> However it is important to proceed in the right way. The hexagram combines Li, clarity, and Chên, excitement. Li is yielding, Chên is hard.

Unqualified hardness and excitement would be too violent in meting out punishment; unqualified clarity and gentleness would be too weak. The two together create the just measure …

Katie was nodding: "Just measure … For you, of course, and to address the crimes of your husband Peter and brother-in-law, Donnie. Justice for Ralph who would still be alive if he hadn't come to help. So, once again, your reading could easily be mine:

If a sentence is imposed the first time a man attempts to do wrong, the penalty is a mild one. Only the toes are put in the stocks. This prevents him from sinning further and thus he becomes free of blame. It is a warning to halt in time on the path of evil …

There are great obstacles to be overcome, powerful opponents are to be punished. Though this is arduous, the effort succeeds.

"Perhaps there's something else we both need to heed. To clearly see, and acknowledge, and better understand the dark within the light. If the events of the last months have taught us anything it's that the impulse to be kind, the desire to exercise mercy must be joined with the appreciation that wrong-doing over time, or with repetition, can easily transform itself into evil."

Penny sighed, then laughed at herself: "So much for speeding things up and getting on with my new life. 'Arduous' … well that certainly seems that I've got, and if you're right about sharing 'Shih Ho,' that we've both got a lot more work to do dealing with the past, and probably the present, before we inhabit the imagined more glorious future."

FOUR

Alex Beaumont hadn't told anybody except Tom and Susie, his bosses at GB Properties, about Las Vegas. After two years of quiet New England days, it was becoming easier to believe that that particular past life had been lived by someone else entirely: the modeling, the parties, the champagne and coke, the secret relationship with the Congressman's so very handsome son, Justin, but, most importantly, that night. The night Justin turned violent, the night his life was ripped apart.

Men had always been drawn to him, even as a teenager. Always looking older than his years, five feet eleven inches tall, with a near perfect complexion and golden light brown hair. A certain lean swagger and charm and confidence that was really more show than substance. Alex was quick to smile and quick to laugh, his soft brown eyes always warm and welcoming.

But as kind and accommodating and naïve as Alex was, Justin, was sharp-edged, selfish, volatile and violent. While Alex was loathe to admit it, there was something about Justin that frightened him almost as much as it intrigued him. Even though he was just eighteen at the time, he preferred to imagine himself an already experienced Las Vegan, wise to the ways of the Strip. Convinced that fear was something you could effectively transcend with gin, vodka and the best drugs.

There was something dangerous about their sex life, exciting sometimes, but uncomfortable at other times. Yet whenever he expressed concern, Justin's brow would furrow, his jaw tighten. "Fuck it, Alex, stop pussying out on me," he'd bark. "This is Vegas. No risk. No reward." Then when he sensed he had pushed Alex too hard, he'd shift gears, and soften, offering a reassuring refrain of loving "trust me's."

That night at The Rising Sun Casino, Alex had too much champagne. Then much too much coke. Plus the Ecstasy Justin insisted he take. Lying naked, semi-conscious while Justin snorted lines of coke off his midriff. When all of a sudden Justin leaned over the bed to pull out the gun Alex had never seen before. Loading a single bullet, then spinning the chamber. When without warning, Justin pressed the gun to Alex's temple and pulled the trigger. Laughing at the click, grinning, eyes mad wide, raising the gun and spinning it once more. Moving the barrel to Alex's chest. While Alex, completely freaked out at this point, somehow managed to summon what little strength he still had, adrenaline surging past the tranquilizing effect of the Ecstasy and champagne. Able at the last second to raise and swing his right arm, smacking Justin's arm up and away from his body, completely changing its trajectory, just as Justin pulled the trigger. Which meant the bullet missed Justin's heart, not Alex's, but lodged just below Justin's collarbone.

Then unimaginable madness. Justin, bleeding profusely, crazed, screaming like a burning baboon, managed to grab a robe as he fled the room for the hall, yelling to all the world that Alex had tried to kill him. Before he knew what was happening Alex, still in silent shock, found himself pinned down by hotel security, as Justin kept shrieking again and again that Alex had shot him for no reason.

In handcuffs, stuffed into the back of a patrol car. Caged. But because the Congressman knew every major official in both the Las Vegas Police Department and the Nevada State Police, Justin was being safely stitched up by the best surgeon at Summerlin Hospital.

Meanwhile, Alex found himself at the police station, immediately bullied by two detectives who could care less about innocent until proven guilty. Just another gay hustler they assumed.

Everyone knew exactly who Justin was, and so these detectives took great pleasure ignoring Alex's every attempt to explain what had happened, quickly threatening him with a charge of attempted murder and the prospect of many, many years behind bars.

After hours of grueling interrogation, a completely traumatized Alex spent what was left of the night in a LVPD holding tank. As the drugs slowly left his system, Alex began to understand just how completely screwed he was.

His parents, Chuck and Betsy Beaumont were members of that small army of worker bees, the waiters, waitresses, cooks, clerks, laborers and landscapers, the dealers and dancers who kept the massive Vegas money machine in perpetual motion, and like most were but a bad month or two away from being completely broke.

Alex, from the very beginning, was sadly just another burden to the struggling Beaumonts. A cranky baby, he was so less adorable than his older sister, who smiled and gurgled and radiated a near constant appreciation. Alex's relationship with his folks only grew more precarious when he announced to them that despite his best efforts he wasn't at all attracted to women.

Alex, now so unexpectedly and surprisingly plunged into a crisis that required cash, had sadly only managed to save two grand from the many hours he had served pizza and the few hours he earned money modeling.

His first lawyer devoured that in a month. The Congressman, within an hour, had hired Robert Furst, the very best of Vegas' best lawyers to represent the interests of his only son.

Then once Alex's money was gone, he was forced to rely upon a series of underpaid, overworked, and almost completely distracted public defenders, most of whom didn't want an aggressive defense of the Congressman's number one enemy to ruin their chances, however remote, to move up to one of the city's better law firms.

The fact is the Congressman's friends in law enforcement had known for a while that Justin was a complete asshole and a lying asshole at that, because they had several times before been pressured to cover for him. But this time, after the many hours interrogating Alex, their perfunctory interview with Justin at the hospital, and talking to the sweating, trembling, thoroughly unconvincing bellboy witness the Congressman provided, they reluctantly acknowledged how absolutely flimsy this case was. They somehow summoned the collective will to insist that the Congressman settle for an assault with a deadly weapon conviction for Alex rather than the attempted murder conviction he thought his son deserved. Then the police, and Judge Paul DuMont, who often golfed with the Congressman, called this a victory.

His last court-appointed attorney convinced Alex that there was no telling how a jury would react: "You know, because of the tricky issue of sexual preference … you understand what I'm saying" he said several times, "given the climate today." So in his professional opinion Alex would be better off betting on Judge DuMont, because everybody said he was basically more or less fair and maybe was even a little gay himself, though nobody knew for sure.

At the trial that everyone but Alex knew was largely for show, Justin testified that in a flash, and for no apparent reason, Alex had turned insanely jealous, frantically rifling through his pockets searching for evidence of his other lovers. While ranting non-stop that he knew for sure Justin was sleeping with other men and an occasional woman.

Then Justin told the court that in the midst of this irrational rage Alex noticed his gun in its holster hanging from a chair. For which Justin had a permit to carry, by the way.

But then without warning Alex yanked it out of the holster – Justin, of course, had immediately told him to put it back – but before he could do anything about it, Alex was carelessly waving it around, then coming closer and closer, pointing the gun at him, screaming he would teach Justin a lesson he'd never forget. Somehow, overcome with anger, in the midst of all this Alex must have flipped the safety switch. Luckily, Justin told the Judge, he managed to grab onto the gun as Alex fired, which explained why, thank God, he was still alive and only wounded.

It was terrifying for Alex to sit helplessly in the courtroom and watch all this happen. But it only got worse when a bellboy Alex had never seen before testified that he was walking outside their hotel room when he heard Alex screaming: "If I can't have you, he won't either!" Alex wanted to laugh, then wanted to cry, but really everything started to turn completely black for him.

Even though there were several days left to the trial, he plunged into a deep unrelenting despair and could hardly remember anything else that was said. He could barely remember hearing his guilty verdict and the Judge announcing his sentence: six years to be served at Lovelock Correctional Center.

Lovelock was more than four hundred miles from Las Vegas. So even if his parents wanted to visit, and they really didn't, the distance offered a perfect excuse.

It was impossible to describe to anyone else the uniquely excruciating bind of innocence. While most people walked around believing that in America the truth prevailed and that innocence would reveal itself in time, that wasn't Alex's America. If that America existed, he hadn't seen it since that last night with Justin. Because it seemed to Alex that nobody believed him. His attorney hadn't believed him. And, most importantly, the Judge hadn't.

It took only a minute to discover the prison guards didn't believe in that kind of America either. His fellow inmates had given up on the idea; and he was pretty sure even his parents assumed his guilt. Only his older sister, Rosie, believed him from across the country.

Still, unwilling to surrender completely, he tasked his latest lawyer with appealing the verdict, but as one month became another, one lawyer morphed into another.

His fourth or fifth public defender, while confessing he hadn't made much progress, just happened to mention that Justin had recently started a construction company and immediately gained a handful of lucrative contracts with the state. That an acquaintance in the police department let slip that finding and re-interviewing the bellboy might prove impossible because he had left town almost as soon as the verdict was announced.

Unless Justin and the bellboy were somehow magically swept up in some unfathomable, completely uncontrollable born-again impulse to redeem themselves, the truth would remain untold.

So along the way he buried his innocence. With every passing day, that truth seemed to move deeper and deeper within him, and further and further away. Until it seemed utterly irrelevant. The best Alex could do was to resign himself to what incontrovertibly had become his fate, to somehow take it day by day and do and survive the time. Which Alex managed to do. One year after another. But how he did so remained a story untold.

Because once the six years were done it took only days on the outside to realize that nobody he knew, even Rosie, wanted to know anything about the horror that was his prison life: the utter lack of privacy; the dreadful food; and a nearly unbroken boredom accompanied by constant noise. There was the stupidity of many of those he shared this life with; the casual cruelty so often expressed; and the continuing threat of rape. With even the slightest mention of that life, he could see the eyelids closing, the shutting down, like the door to his cell slamming shut.

Each, in his or her own way, silently begging Alex to please not burden them with what it was like to live behind bars. So it was unimaginable to ask them to consider that he had suffered prison for no reasonable purpose.

It took only a few months of failing to remake a Las Vegas life, of failing to reclaim his family, his former friendships, to realize he had to move on.

Luckily, Rosie had a former roommate from her college days at Duke, Susie Ford, who had returned home to the Berkshires to craft a lucrative career in real estate. And because all these years later, Rosie and Susie would still do anything for each other, Susie offered to help any way she could.

Alex left most of his belongings behind and drove his used Accord east across country to reinvent himself, feeling freer with every mile he moved further from Vegas and closer to Massachusetts. A week later he rented an apartment in Great Barrington, and began life again. Susie and her partner Tom started Alex out part-time at GB Properties, organizing the files, then helping to create the info sheets the brokers prepared for every house. He collated the best photos, wrote a succinct description of the property, then listed its price, location, number of bedrooms, baths, square footage, style, the most important aspects of the interior and exterior, and, of course, the yearly taxes.

Susie knew most of the business owners in town, and quickly found Alex several shifts at Little Town Toys and Paulie's Homemade Pizza to supplement his income. Prison life exposes you to some of the worst of human failings; you don't survive without developing second and third skins. So Alex brought a rare patience to the task of serving impatient parents and their all too often spoiled and toy-crazed kids; then quickly refreshed his pizza serving skills. After dealing with the daily psychosis of life behind bars, he found it particularly easy to smile past the often petty complaints of some very picky customers. Given his recent history, Alex regarded their willingness to shift so quickly from reasonableness to annoyance as terribly pointless and pathetic.

Meanwhile, helping Susie and Tom and the other brokers sell homes was like therapy. Because even if he wasn't yet able or ready to own his own house, he was at least engaged in enabling those dreams for others. So he studied for his real estate broker's exam, allowing hope to ever so slowly reclaim some of the sad space within, to imagine a new beginning. For most people, dreaming came naturally. Then to transform imaginings into something of substance. For Alex this was something to learn again. Like soil neglected for years; or a muscle so atrophied it required dedicated rehabilitation.

Being out there with people, engaged in a process so very important to them, was very different than his office work. It didn't take long for him to realize that he was being helped as much or more than he was helping them.

And that slowly he was able to realize something very critical about where he had been and what had happened to him. Because while he had never abandoned the core commitment to his innocence, he had come to accept the irrelevance of hope. That inhabiting that contradiction, every hour of every day, had damaged him in ways he was just now becoming aware of.

It might have been his second or third month in GB when, during one of his first afternoon shifts, he found himself in the midst of a series of Little Town meltdowns. There were two boys, one five, then an hour or so later, another eight, both flinging themselves to the floor, tears transformed to screams because they weren't going to get what they were sure they deserved. Which is when he found himself dreaming about a Bloody Mary.

Then, finally come six o'clock, sitting at the 20 Grant Street Saloon besides Artie Ruberto, who worked the eight to five shift at the local hardware store, and who already had an hour's start and three or four beers on him. Artie loved bars and loved to talk in bars. It didn't take long before Artie was propelled back in time, compelled to share with Alex how taken he was with his ability to survive high school in New York City, extraordinarily proud that he was able to move without being mugged through the most treacherous of neighborhoods, skills sadly that were of little use selling batteries and light bulbs and wrenches or walking the dimly-lit, but empty and completely safe streets of Barrington at night.

"Even now when I take the train from Wassaic to Grand Central, I'm almost completely transformed by the time I hit 42nd Street. My eyes are more like slits, my body is tense and taut. I'm really quite peaceful up here but down there I look like a madman."

It was an odd moment, Artie so entranced with celebrating a most poetical version of the kind of life Alex had found himself forced to live, a life not of choice but persistent necessity. So no amount of alcohol would help him find the heroic in what had been a daily tragedy for him. Then, as Artie was detailing the many places he hid his cash before a New York trip: in both socks, the pocket of his t-shirt, a twenty in his front pants pocket to offer just in case, Alex so very suddenly knew he had to make the exact opposite journey that Artie so enjoyed chronicling, from a constant clenched fear to allowing new possibilities.

Which is why he took great pleasure in his new life in real estate, knowing these houses he was now showing were real dreams made tangible. Some with wide wood floors, old beams, and claw feet tubs; others with snazzy contemporary kitchens, large picture windows with views of the lake, and attached three car garages. Houses as varied as the people who lived in them, or those who wanted to buy them.

Time moved so much more quickly on the outside than it had on the inside. With his two jobs, he had little time to spare. He had dated a couple of guys via the internet, but between his own great reluctance to trust, and the sense that came creeping in after a couple of often unremarkable encounters, that no matter his loneliness, the yawning gap between their vastly different recent life histories inevitably prevailed. Because in so many ways these men all took so much for granted, while he had learned along the way to expect absolutely nothing from life. Which very quickly, if maybe unfairly, convinced him they would never quite get where he was coming from. So he rarely made it past a couple of weeks with any of them, because no matter their chronological age, these men seemed so very young and insubstantial to him.

Alex marked the end of his second full year in the Berkshires with his broker's license, leaving Little Town Toys to devote more energy to GB Realty, intensely aware that with Rosie and Susie and Tom's help, he had done something important for himself.

Gaining each day a greater appreciation for the art and craft of selling homes. Understanding more fully that there was always a story to tell: that this particular house could be the start of something new, or this other house the perfect ending. That each and every house could and should be someone's dream house.

Alex got a bit better at it with every listing: learning more with every conversation he had with Tom and Susie; with every additional client he met; and with every open house he attended.

It was most easy when he liked his clients, but some made it difficult. Many of them were from New York or New Jersey or lately, even Los Angeles, with an awful lot of disposable income and an extra dose of arrogance. It was the potent mix of self-absorption and the arbitrary and unpredictable foolishness that Alex had the hardest time with. Qualities that since his incarceration and those many wasted years he had to work extra hard to ignore.

In many ways this, too, was therapeutic. Putting the newfound skills he had learned in prison to a purpose that transcended making it safely through another long and potentially dangerous day. To building a future. To a day, a month, a year beyond today.

Because a client was a serious investment. If you were good at the job, you spent many hours at it. First, talking to your client/clients to discover what he or she or they were really looking for. Then checking every available house for sale, even those houses you thought might someday soon become available. There were the exhausting walk-throughs, house after house. And here's where the arbitrariness most often reared its ugly head, as the most demanding clients found three things they hated for one thing they loved about a house. Wanting somehow to magically put the best parts of seventeen different houses into the nearly-impossible-to-find-dream-house. Then because these houses existed only in the imagination, successfully weaning them from the impossible to the possible required an enviable, almost inexhaustible flexibility.

So Alex drove many miles and then many more with his clients. There were houses to be seen in towns twenty or thirty miles away. With experience, Alex soon intuited much of what the clients really wanted hours sometimes days before they did; you could certainly predict almost immediately what they wouldn't like. But sadly that never seemed to dissuade his least flexible clients from demanding to see ever more houses he knew they'd never buy.

Once in a while, the process worked to perfection. It had taken Tom only a week to find Katie the Ripton house she immediately bought and still loved, and Katie was always sending people his way. When Katie brought Penny to the office, Tom immediately knew Alex could help her. And Alex had the sense he'd be working with a kindred spirit, someone also ready for a new start.

FIVE

Penny's *I Ching* reading had brought a trinity of tragedies back into sharp focus. Sadly, regaining her memory meant acknowledging she was the only daughter of a serial adulterer and his cold and contemptuous wife. Then, to make matters even worse, the clueless mate of a man who married her only to exact his twisted vengeance on her father.

For it was her father's continuing betrayals of her mother, and the on-going sexual relationship he had paid to have with Peter's mother that proved to be the source of the crippling fury Peter felt for them all, transforming his keen intelligence and impressive ambition into a laser focused lunacy. His obsession, and her naiveté, had made a sham of her marriage. Just as thoroughly as her father's insatiable infidelities had poisoned that of her parents. That these two calamities had converged in a third, the death of Ralph, an innocent, was a disaster she would live with forever.

Despite Penny's urge to accelerate her convalescence, there seemed to be no easy way to zip past the new-found comprehension that her father required an unending string of hired women to service him, and that her husband was so scarred by life's humiliations and his great mistake at the poker table that he would eventually need her dead. That he could so easily ask his younger brother to kill her. That at the end of that dreadful day it was he not her who would die. That she would kill him. It was, most times, unimaginable. And worse, just too much to bear.

The other night, in her dreams, Penny had been back again in Little Pointe at her parents' lake house, sitting upstairs in her favorite stuffed chair, her father's goodbye letter still unopened, when she heard Peter's footsteps. Not understanding why, panicking, she hid the letter in her purse. Instinct overriding comprehension. Aware for the first time ever, that she was uncomfortable with her husband's touch, up from the chair, his hand on her back. As he guided her downstairs, and to the car, driving them home. All the while unnerved, when her body in spasm, she woke in her bed in the Berkshires in terror.

As she contemplated a new start, she realized that she had never really had a home of her own. But more than that, a life of her own. First the growing up years, followed by four years at Ann

Arbor, her budding independence so quickly dimmed by Peter's influence, and then surrendering to her mother's and Peter's united insistence that they live on Lakeview Drive, in the ostentatious and unfriendly marble mansion her mother gifted them on their wedding day.

Penny, as the *I Ching* suggested, working so hard these days to see more clearly the people swirling about her, to push beneath the obvious, to better understand her own imperfections as well as those of others, could appreciate in retrospect why it made perfect sense that Peter never wanted to live where she did, by the lake on Potter Road. Because for Peter, for young Petey, it could only ever be the scene of the crime, the place where he saw Penny's father atop his mother.

It was time now to finally find that home of her own. So she had spent her weekend going through the pages of the Berkshire Homebuyers Guide, looking at hundreds of homes and dozens of potential building sites.

Then, when they met at GB Properties Monday morning, explaining to Alex that looking for her own home was as much about coming to terms with the life she had lived thus far as it was discovering the proper place to begin again. Sharing how she had come to be here, her time at Bea Foster's in Brett, the amnesia, then meeting Katie and working with the *I Ching* to slowly dispel the deep fog of not knowing.

Alex had never begun the house-hunting process with such intimacy or honesty and, for a moment, was a bit flustered. This was certainly not the stuff of his licensing exam, and yet it made so much sense. How else could he find Penny the house that fit?

He, too, had spent the weekend working, checking the online Berkshire County Multiple Listings Service, with information and photos from all the brokers. He had found properties in Ripton, some in Mount Washington, Alton, and a few in Upper Hartsville he thought Penny might be interested in.

"I hope" Alex began, "that looking at some of houses featured on our website and the MLS helped you think more about what you really want and need your house to be. What you may not want."

"The lake and our boat were always an important part of my life in Little Pointe," Penny suggested. "Having spent a bit of time at the lake in Brett, I know we're talking about a very different kind of lake here in the Berkshires, and certainly a smaller boat than our 55 foot Viking, but I'm thinking I'd like to see water from my window."

"Well, that narrows it down, Penny. There's Duck Pond, Lake Monroe, the Oldbridge Bowl, Lake Harrison, and there are a couple of lesser known small private lakes, including one in Ripton. Let's take a look at the computer and make a list of the homes in those areas you'd like to see in person."

With a couple of clicks, Alex brought up the listing for a four-bedroom house on half an acre. The first photo was of the front of the house, a patch of lawn and the small waterfront dock.

Penny asked him to enlarge the photo. "It's a bit too contemporary for me, too stark. It seems to challenge the landscape. I'm more interested in a house that's really at peace with its surroundings. Maybe it's a reaction to all the social events I had to attend, the political dinners, the benefits and the fundraisers, the endless obligations, but I am more than ready for quiet and contemplation."

A half-hour later, as he gathered up his printouts and they got ready to check some properties Penny had liked, Alex was sad. Penny had so generously opened up. And while he wished he had as well, it was clear he still hadn't figured out who he could trust with his story.

SIX

The noisy lake with the loud people, the motorboats, the kids yelling, Brett Lake, was right beside the highway to Plattsville, with the constant whoosh, whoosh of cars and the trucks with the honking horns and tires screeching. With almost all the houses visible from the road.

So even though it was further away, Tyler Deakins preferred to visit the quiet lake in Ripton. Especially those houses he had discovered hidden down Pickwick Drive, the little dirt road beneath the big tall trees, so very dark, almost a secret. So different from the large paved driveways that announced some of the expensive homes that loomed over the lake.

Tyler had spent time in Eighty-Seven, Ninety-Five, and One Hundred And Three, owned by the out-of-towners and kept empty for most of the year. One Hundred And Three his favorite and every time he visited, he covered the GB Realty for-sale sign with a few more leaves. Hoping somehow to keep it his for the now.

Mostly, when he was close to breaking, he'd go there in the late afternoon to calm himself, to sit very quietly on the soft black leather couch in the big living room watching the sun fall behind the hills, his anger slowly melting while the sunset colors sparkled in the lake.

Like this afternoon, resting and relaxing until Abigail came from out of the blue, her loud and bossy voice saying, well more like announcing, that the color scheme was off: "This throw rug, right here in front of the couch, it's way too white. I mean, look, it disrupts the entire living room aesthetic, the whole feng shui of the room."

Whatever that was, Tyler thought to himself, taken aback for just a moment, but silent, long ago having learned it hardly ever paid to interrupt Abigail on a roll.

"What about replacing it with that rug in the upstairs hallway of the Thompson house in Great Barrington? With the red and gold and subtle greens, it's so very out of place there but I'm pretty sure it would perfectly match the leaves we see here. Maybe find a painting to complement the several shades of lake blue.

"Harmony. It's key. Believe me, it's for the best. Then we'll give the Thompson house this odd and out-of-place rug, a proper fit. Better feng shui for everyone concerned."

Tyler knew squat about this feng shui stuff. But Abigail, up late at night, sometimes in the early morning, always online, had obviously learned a whole lot about color and design. So he quickly said he'd think about it.

Which seemed to work because all of a sudden she was quiet and gone. Many times when she got an idea she wouldn't let go of it. Now taking a moment, Tyler's eyes almost to closing, squinting and, so yes, if he tried hard he could see her point. All of a sudden the white rug seemed a bit intense. She might be right.

But with all the talk about the white rug, he managed to miss the sound of the approaching car, then the car doors closing, the key in the front door. He had just enough time to scramble out the back door to the crawlspace beneath the house.

*   *   *

Rabbit continued to make his pilgrimages to the Parker farm, walking the many miles from Katie's to say hello to Ralph's parents. They and the land shrouded in sadness. Missing their murdered son Ralph so very much.

Returning home the long way, stopping to swim in the lake, because that somehow helped.

*   *   *

"Now this might be a bit more contemporary than you're looking for, but I thought it made sense to see what some of the available Ripton lake properties have to offer," Alex began. "There's an old cottage next door with about half an acre that's about to go on the market. So if you're feeling particularly ambitious, it's possible to get both parcels, knock the buildings down and start over."

Penny was moving into the kitchen: "Well, I'm certainly open to the possibility." Thinking the kitchen was a bit dark for her, though there was a comfortable feel to the butcher block island and the tempered pots and pans hanging from above. If the place were hers, she'd certainly build the kitchen out, and brighten it up a bit.

They moved into the living room. "This is the main reason I brought you here, Penny. It's got one of the best views of the

25

lake."

Alex and Penny moved toward the couch.

Tyler could feel them walking on his legs, then up his chest, to his head. He recognized the voice of the GB Realty guy, Alex. He had definitely seen and heard him outside of houses several times before but not the lady customer. Praying Abigail would stay out of sight and silent. Because you never knew with Abigail. She just didn't do well with complications.

Usually the quieter and calmer he was, the less likely it was that Abigail would return. But having people sit on her couch could be very complicated. Imagining the dirt they might have tracked in on their shoes, or how they might be messing up that feng shui stuff? Could be she'd just disapprove; but just as likely she'd make a scene and try somehow to chase them away.

So he took a bunch of silent deep breaths, doing his best not to care so much. Trying not to feel like he did at the home that wasn't really home.

"This is the best spot in the house," Alex said, gesturing for Penny to sit on the couch. "The view of the lake is breathtaking."

Which was when Penny saw Rabbit swimming his way back to shore, smiling to herself, a sign that she was on the right track.

Alex unaware of Rabbit, continued on: "I've only been here during the day, but I imagine it's even more lovely when the sun is setting."

Tyler, beneath them, nodding because the sunsets were the very best here. But then quickly worrying, wondering if they had done anything upstairs that Alex might notice. Trying to remember whether or not Abigail had actually moved that white rug she hated?

He had to do a better job of paying attention, of listening for cars. Because he definitely didn't want to get caught. His friend Leonard had been to jail and he said it was just about the most horrible thing you could imagine. Jail would mean he couldn't get out to visit his houses. And he knew he couldn't spend all his time in one small and noisy place. Guessing jail was just like home.

Penny was trying to imagine herself in this house: "You know, you're absolutely right, the view is its saving grace. But even with the large cathedral ceiling, the living room seems dark. The only spark of light is this odd and out of place white rug, which unfortunately, reminds me of my former house, my mother's stone house in Little Pointe."

Penny paused, "Your suggestion makes a lot of sense, Alex: start over, tear down the house, and reclaim the potential of the land. I can certainly afford it. But it seems like such a waste. So much effort when there are so many people without homes. People who might love this particular house just the way it is. It's almost unimaginable to think of tearing one down only because it doesn't work for me."

Tyler thought that made a lot of sense. There were certainly a lot of different houses he liked that maybe other people wouldn't. Some he didn't like so much. Including some of the very new houses that the really rich people built. Like the place with the long winding driveway and all those big screen TVs. Most of them without soul. Momentary, convenient way stations for him.

But the other thing, different for him than for Abigail and that lady upstairs, was that he liked the dark, such a great comfort. Happy that there were trees everywhere, and that the trees were bent over the roof, keeping the light out.

"Well, there are several other waterfront properties that might work a lot better for you," Alex added. "I mainly brought you here for the view, Penny."

"I love it, thanks."

Tyler was thinking she would like the Stoughton place. But mostly he was very glad that they were leaving and he could go back upstairs, clean up and relax a bit more before he took the white rug over to the Thompson house.

SEVEN

Over a cup of coffee and one of Scott's fresh croissants at the Ripton General Store, Chief Paul asked Frank to check into the break-ins. Members of the Selectboard had gotten an earful of new complaints and were now complaining to him. Which prompted Chief Paul to offer Frank a short but vital lesson in the local blame game.

The most potent complaints came from the second homeowners, the summer people, the folks the locals called "New Yorkers," even though many came from elsewhere, like New Jersey, Connecticut, even Boston, the West Coast some of them, but enough of them Jews to justify the "New Yorker" tag, the most polite way some of the more anti-Semitic locals used to avoid bringing religion into the conversation.

It didn't help their cause that some "New Yorkers" were convinced that the more you complained, the more likely it was that you'd get results.

Ripton locals knew who to call and when to call them whenever anything important went wrong: the Chief with legitimate police problems; the Tree Warden, when lightning brought down a tall pine on the Worthington Road; but the summer folk would complain to any and every town official they could corral no matter the problem. Conservation Commission and Planning Board members, the Building Inspector, and even those who served on the Zoning Board of Appeals would get an earful at the post office. And if they missed running into any of them picking up the mail, they wouldn't hesitate to call them at home, and as late as ten or eleven at night. Unfortunately, many city folk had no clue, or seemed to care, that the locals weren't out clubbing and went to bed three hours earlier than they did because they were routinely up at dawn.

So far as he knew, Chief Paul told Frank, nothing of any great consequence had been stolen yet. But that, and this was something he had never encountered before, there were reports that one family's toaster oven was now working perfectly when it wouldn't even turn on last month. That someone else's refrigerator made less noise than it ever did. That all of a sudden a garage door on Big Oak Road seem to glide open with ease. But clearly many people were severely spooked.

Frank was a bit surprised to discover that many of the second-homeowners never seemed to realize how they might have made themselves targets by building monstrously large houses, atop mountains and at angles no sane local would reasonably attempt, or in the midst of what was once fertile and productive farmland. Some of these mountain manors required driveways that cost more than the homes of the contractors who labored to construct them. Then local carpenters and housepainters and landscapers would watch in awe as the New Yorkers packed their odd and overbuilt mansions to the gills with the best of anything and everything that money could buy.

But at the first sign of trouble, most of them were horrified to discover that Ripton employed only two men, a mere forty hours each a week, to handle police problems occurring across great distances. That even with some auxiliary part-time help, Ripton was in no position to provide the round-the-clock protection they imagined they deserved for their precious property.

Frank began by checking out three properties. First up was the Zuckerman place on Pine Needle Road. He drove down the long driveway to a house almost entirely hidden behind a stand of large trees. Bettina Davis was outside waiting for him.

"Good morning, Officer. Thanks for coming. I tried to convince my husband, Arthur, not to call but he's a stickler for what he calls doing the right thing. We care-take the place for the Zuckermans and the idea that someone has been to the house after we've gone home drives Arthur nuts.

"I tried to calm him down and get him to church, yesterday the same as the last month of Sundays but you know how that goes … it's too early or too late or there's football or he's got chores he can't put aside. But I take the Christian view." She paused a second: "I hope you're not offended or Jewish or a Muslim or one of those weird religions, the Scientists or whatever." Continuing on without waiting for Frank to reply:

"I reminded him the house is empty. Heated and cooled the year round but empty almost all the time. Remember 2 Kings 4:8. That a couple shares their house. One thing I know is my Bible and the Bible says: 'Let us make a small roof chamber with walls, and put there for him a bed, a table, a chair, and a lamp, so that whenever he comes to us, he can go in there.' Told him you never know but that could be Jesus stopping for a moment of rest. But Arthur called you anyway.

"Let me tell you whoever this is, even if he isn't Christ, Our Savior, he's definitely a Christian because when we got back from visiting our second boy who lives in Worcester, all of a sudden the very fancy Miele washer and dryer in the Zuckerman's laundry room were working better than they did the day they were delivered. Mrs. Zuckerman has me clean the sheets and wash the drapes every other week for no other reason except that she can. Not that she's here to use them. Anyway, I must have asked Arthur to fix the dryer a dozen times. Don't tell Arthur I said this, but if the visitor had left us a bill, I would gladly have paid it."

Frank took a look around, checked all the rooms and the basement. According to Mrs. Davis, nothing was missing. Plus, she said, the toaster was shining brighter than before.

The second property was a quarter mile from the Ripton/New Worthington border. The guest house had clearly began its life as an un-insulated summertime bungalow. Now a young couple, Greg and Donna, were paying six seventy-five a month for rent and a bunch to heat it during the winter months for the privilege of providing a human presence on the property. A bargain the McMurrays insisted. Because all they had to do was check on the Main House once a day and vigorously discourage anyone from coming onto McMurray land. Greg and Donna both had full-time restaurant jobs, she serving at BurgerTown and he washing dishes at Leo's. They were gone from three each afternoon to midnight and beyond, extending their day an hour or two later transitioning from on to off at one of several local bars.

Frank could see the accumulated effects of some righteous pot-smoking in their eyes but still believed them when they swore they were sure someone had been in the Main House several times over the past few weeks when they weren't. Offering up as evidence the several compilations they kept finding in the McMurray CD player, music neither of them remembered liking and discs neither remembered burning.

Greg was adamant: "Dude, everyone who knows me knows I hate Maroon 5! I mean I won't deny I smoke a decent amount of weed, no dealing, ever, never, but I do partake. But believe me I'm never going to go for Maroon 5. That falsetto shit." Donna was nodding. "Really, it's heavy metal this and more heavy metal.

Tattoos, Black Sabbath and even more dark with Death and Anthrax. I can't even get him to dance. I played "Pharrell's 'Happy' … everybody bops to 'Happy,' right? He just glowers at me. Even if I offer him … whoops, I don't need to tell the cops that, do I?"

"No, not really," Frank offered. "That's pretty compelling evidence. Mind if I take this CD?"

Donna couldn't help herself. "Really? Because I've kinda gotten used to it. He won't let me play it at home because there's a couple of Maroon 5 cuts but there's stuff I never knew about like that Leonard Cohen guy and this Nina Simone chick. It's got the weirdest combinations. Like some different people put it together. You know I listen to it every day as I drive. I might speed a bit because of it, especially with Taylor Swift … Can you believe I've never been to the city but when that 'Welcome to New York' comes on my foot hits the gas. She says 'the lights are so bright but they never blind me' and man I just love that. It's like the city is waiting for me. Not much chance Greg is going to take me unless it's to see Behemoth … But hey saying I might drive too fast on 23 isn't the same as you catching me as I do it, right?"

"Right, not yet, at least. But you never know with this Supreme Court."

Donna smiled but Greg looked puzzled.

"Speed kills, Greg. So you probably want to tell Donna to slow down. As for the CD, why don't you guys hold onto it. I have a feeling if we find anybody's fingerprints on it at this point, they'll be Donna's."

Donna leaned over and gave him a big hug. "You're the nicest cop I ever met." She looked over to Greg, waiting for him to say something.

He finally saw her glaring at him, then added:

"Yeah, thanks, Dude!"

As he made his way back to the car, Frank smiled, telling himself he wished he could share this one with Charley T, his Training Officer back in NYC. He drove past Tremblay's old dairy farm to check out Complainant #3. Chief Paul had told him that a couple of decades ago, the Tremblays had responded to the falling price for milk and the exhausting hours of dairy-farming with a new plan.

They quickly learned that selling their farmland was a lot more profitable than farming it, then kept forty acres and replaced their cows with Christmas trees, and tapped their many maples for syrup. They managed to survive, but you could still see the disappointment in the eyes of both Tremblays, Joe Senior and Junior. Because they had sold off a significant section of the land to Milton Krause, land where five generations of Tremblays before them had had their furthermost pastures.

Where the town road met Milton Krause's new driveway, he built a three-car garage for his-and-hers BMWs and one of their Range Rovers. So for the very short time they used the place, they'd have the Range Rover for trips up and down their dirt driveway, then switch to their BMW convertibles for trips into town. At the very end of his three-quarter mile driveway, Milton Krause had immediately marked the land as his with a ten and a half million-dollar compound on land where once Tremblay cows happily munched.

Built hardly seemed an adequate way to describe what Krause had wrought, but out back of his already out-of-scale house, he had constructed his own private indoor sports complex. With an Olympic-sized heated swimming pool sitting beside an indoor racquetball court with its own juice bar.

Milton Krause was one of those city guys you heard about all the time. According to the Wall Street Journal article Frank had read last night, he had made his fortune by trading financial instruments. While Frank knew folks in the city who sold guitars and mandolins and fiddles made of wood, he knew absolutely nothing about these kinds of billion dollar deals.

According to the Journal, Krause was the penultimate hands-on dealmaker, very, very good when it came to even the smallest detail of "wealth acquisition." It appeared he brought those micro-management skills with him when he left the office, because somehow on his last weekend here in Ripton, with all the multi-million dollar things on his mind, he noticed that someone had added additional TV shows to his digital video recorder's Record This list.

Which prompted his annoyed phone messages to Chief Paul, and then when the Chief hadn't gotten back within ten minutes, his calls to two of the three Selectboard members who did answer. Which is why Frank was talking to Derek Ford through a little metal box at Krause's gate.

While Krause was back on Wall Street making money, it fell to

Derek Ford, Krause's part-time local handyman, snow-plower, and lawn-mower extraordinaire, to oversee and protect his kingdom. It was Derek Ford who accompanied Frank on his time-consuming room-by-room check of the estate. It turned out that Krause was talking about the digital video recorder in the dressing room by the pool, not the digital video recorder in the living room, or den, or the home entertainment center, or in any of the seven bedrooms with wide-screen TVs. Krause had left a note: not only was he recording "Luther," a show he had never heard of, but someone had left five dollars and ordered "Terminator: Salvation" on Pay Per View.

Frank thought about telling Krause that he had recently seen "Luther" and the intruder might be on to something. Though said intruder quickly lost some credit for wasting five bucks on the newest "Terminator," which seemed only to get worse with the years. Luckily, he kept these thoughts to himself, slowly beginning to appreciate that any or every random remark might make its small town way back to the Selectboard, the Tree Warden, maybe even to the Animal Control Officer over coffee at the General Store. Considering how freaked they were by these break-ins, they just might not fully appreciate the healing powers of irony. So he chose to keep his inner TV critic in check.

Turns out Krause had a fairly sophisticated alarm system for his athletic center, so either someone hadn't turned the system back on after a particularly grueling game of racquetball, or this burglar knew his alarms. Frank still wasn't sure thief was the right way to describe this guy. Because the weird thing was that nothing was missing from the Krause estate. It was a perplexing combination: the ability to get into well-guarded spaces full of all kinds of the most expensive things, coupled with the self-discipline, ethics or just plain disinterestedness to walk away empty-handed.

In all his city years he hadn't ever come across a break-in artist who made things better. Maybe Bettina Davis was on to something: maybe this was Christ or a repentant repairperson seeking redemption for a lifetime's worth of inflated invoices?

He/she was probably using booties and gloves, maybe sweeping away tire tracks. Unless he was in a state or national database, fingerprints wouldn't help all that much. It was just as likely that he didn't even have a record. And for the moment Frank was pretty sure he didn't quite get what was happening here.

EIGHT

Ernie knew no matter what he told the others, he was going to keep on drinking. He had been drinking for years. Some alcoholics spoke about filling a hole. Ernie had filled that hole a thousand times. Because he always preferred an alcohol-induced calm to the jagged edges of what some lying dog teetotaler might call real life.

It was getting hard these days to find anyone to listen to the life story he had told a hundred times already. That his hard times and love of alcohol all began with his accident, the thirty-foot fall from the roof at the paper mill. But everyone who knew Ernie could remember him in high school downing a six-pack on a Saturday night without a sweat. So, yes, maybe the fall took him to the hard stuff but he certainly had a head start.

Thanks to his many millions of alcohol-soaked neurons, Ernie never seemed to appreciate that he was most often operating at reduced capacity. He must have inherited the ability to blessedly misperceive from his father, Daniel.

Perhaps because he wasn't particularly smart or talented, Ernie early on learned to use bluster to the max. To bully. He was one of those stocky, fire-plug kind of guys. No more than five feet nine inches tall, he was deceptively strong despite the impressive belly that folded over his belt.

He had a deep-seated mean streak, and an uncanny ability to smell out people who were weaker than he was. With not the slightest glimmer of a conscience to slow him down. That his three sons were already all taller than him was an annoying mystery and perpetual challenge to him. That Doris' son, Tyler, was not only taller but way smarter was an unforgiveable insult.

To this day nobody has the foggiest idea how Ernie's father, Daniel, won the heart of Josie Pennington, the only, extremely spoiled daughter of the family who owned the Pennington Mill. Old Man Pennington, whose wife had died early, leaving him unprepared to raise a daughter, tried time after time to wrench his clueless Josie from the grip of Daniel. All of which sadly served to strengthen her resolve to marry him. Then, in a graceful surrender, he agreed to give Daniel a job doing odd carpentry jobs around the mill, jobs he did with varying degrees of all too obvious incompetency. Old Man Pennington comforted himself with the notion that this great waste of time and money was nonetheless worth it because it managed, at least, to keep his daughter within sight.

Another man might have been grateful for a decently-paid lifetime job without pressure, but Daniel was even more dissatisfied. Why was the Old Man making him do shit work? What about a desk job? Or, even better, why not make him a manager?

Daniel was always angry and his wife endured several years one more miserable than the one before. With her unplanned pregnancy and the unfortunate birth of their colicky, chronically complaining son, Josie began to feel that she had made a dreadful mistake. Luckily, she had kept a separate bank account from Daniel, magically replenished each month from Josie's fairly substantial trust fund. Her solution was frequent trips to Europe and large quantities of gin, which seemed to work wonders for her, if not her son.

Over time, it became ever more difficult to pretend that the men in her life weren't an unrelenting, bitter disappointment. Her father was devoted to a mill and its machinery. Daniel was a brute and Ernest, well Ernest, however much she wished it, would never possess the grace and skill and intelligence to remain an Ernest. To adequately accompany her to the museums, concert halls, or the fancy summertime parties favored by the Berkshire's best.

It was all too easy to see his heartbreakingly inevitable devolution into just another completely mediocre Ernie. The lowest of common denominators.

Old Man Pennington transcended his growing distaste for his son-in-law and great disappointment in his daughter and, to his credit, tried to see the best in his only grandchild. Especially after Josie died in a traffic accident in Vienna.

Having spent his life getting the most he could from his workers, Old Man Pennington was shrewd enough not to penalize Ernie for his limitations.

Unfortunately, Ernie, a mere fifteen years after his birth, and during a disastrous attempt at high school, was charged with the attempted assault and battery of his Junior Class President. The Old Man managed to disappear the charge with a healthy contribution to the family. In return, Ernie reluctantly joined his father working maintenance at the mill, a second generation indentured servant.

He hadn't been working there more than a month when his life changed forever. Daniel had done more than his fair share of drinking lunch at The Back Door, which made him even more surly and even more careless than usual. Roofing, under the best of conditions, can be tricky, especially on a steep roof. They were working together on the same section, son just a row of shingles below father, working without harnesses because Daniel was sure they would just slow them down. When Daniel unexpectedly shifted backward, his leather boot heel coming down with all its weight on the fingers of Ernie's right hand.

Ernie screamed, then cursed, and couldn't swear whether what happened next was an accident or deliberate. First, his father's foot came off his hand, and he could remember the brief moment of relief. But then almost immediately after, rather than retracting and carefully raising his foot up toward the roofline, his father snapped his boot up and into Ernie's head, knocking him backwards. He tried desperately to grab hold of the roof but was completely off-balance, reaching out in vain to break his fall. After falling close to thirty feet, he landed on his back, and didn't come to until a few days later.

While it was considered a small miracle that he lived, Ernie was more focused on the fact that his legs and back now hurt like hell. Almost immediately, Daniel launched a series of lawsuits on behalf of his minor son, against anybody and everybody, including his father-in-law. All were quickly settled out of court and Daniel was glad to sign a confidentiality agreement.

In what was widely regarded as the hand of fate, Daniel found himself just a short year later falling backwards on the river side of the very same roof, plummeting to his death. And Kenny, Ernie's replacement and Daniel's new assistant, told everybody who asked that Daniel had just stood up and yelled something, swatting at something Kenny couldn't see, swaying just like he swayed so many times before. But this time he lost his balance and never regained it. Probably yelling at him, Kenny speculated, complaining that his shingling was veering off-line once again. But Kenny was listening to Imus on his little radio and couldn't really hear what Daniel was saying.

By the time the ambulance squad pulled his lifeless body from the water, the poisonous brown recluse spider Ernie had placed in his father's flannel shirt, having admirably performed its assignment, had most likely drowned on its way downstream.

Ernie had disability and healthcare for life and now a large amount of money stashed away, money that once his grandfather and the family lawyer died absolutely nobody else knew about.

Cynthia, one of Ernie's nurse's aides, was the first of his many women, the mother of his sons. Raised by a revolving door of foster parents, she yearned for a real family. But, as she liked to tell her girlfriends, Ernie was a hell of a lot nicer when he was under the influence of heavy-duty painkillers. Funny, even, and sometimes sweet.

Ernie enthusiastically pursued her after he got out of the hospital. For the first few months, the Vicodin helped to maintain the illusion he was a nice guy. Her birthday was three days after his, and they married as soon as they both turned eighteen. They had three boys in record time. But whatever charm he had managed to manifest while helpless, then sustain during his brief pursuit, seemed to completely vanish once he had her.

Those early years were for Cynthia all about diapers and the slow unraveling of her dreams. Her chosen family was no better than the state-sanctioned families of her childhood, probably worse as she began to realize, in much the same manner as Ernie's mom, that she disliked her own kids just a little less than she despised Ernie.

As much as she wanted to embrace their specialness, to see their Hallmark halos, they appeared as nothing more than shit-filled, constantly crying variations of Ernie. No amount of wishing otherwise could keep her from acknowledging that she had stumbled and fallen into a life that looked a lot like death.

Tragically, Ernie didn't like the kids any more than she did. Early on they were still too small for him to hit. He was at least conscious enough to know how easily, with a few extra drinks, he might kill one of them. With but one thoughtless inebriated shot to the head of one of the little ones, he might easily find himself relocated behind bars for an awfully long time. So he strategically chose his targets: Bill, the eldest was soon sturdy enough to smack with impunity, and he could and would repeatedly let loose on Cynthia. Because, of course, they were both a predictable recurring disappointment, and a constant provocation.

Looking back, it all came down to his fall. If he hadn't fell, or rather hadn't been kicked, there wouldn't have been the hospital and there wouldn't have been the morphine which made him stupid enough to think he needed Cynthia, and there wouldn't have been the Vicodin which made him make love to her without thinking about the consequences. Because if he hadn't been knocked off that roof, he wouldn't have these three lousy kids.

It took a good half hour that fateful morning for the sound of the crying kids to penetrate the haze of his hangover, stumbling to the kitchen for coffee. Her note was all he found: "Keep everything. I mean everything. I'm out of here." Later he learned that she had hit the road with an anesthesiologist. He and the boys never heard another word from her. Gone like Josie. Mother, then wife.

But Ernie quickly learned there was a substantial pool of women who frequented local bars and whose idea of failure was to have to live alone. Willing to believe that any man was better than none. He counted on them, after a short seduction and a bit more than a month's best behavior, to help raise his boys. They might last as long as several months or even a year or two before they realized that living alone was safer and saner than the painful purgatory of a life with Ernie and his little Ernies. Working harder than ever before, because Ernie, for all the dough he had squirreled away, hated to part with any of it.

Now Doris Deakins, another nurse, a new caretaker, was beginning her second year. While Doris came with a inconvenient son of her own, she sealed the deal with a house big enough for all the Ernies. By this time, it was difficult for those around him to know whether or not Ernie still experienced any real back pain. He had made quite the viable life out of his fall, having so quickly learned to leverage his presumed pain into an excuse which allowed him to avoid doing pretty much anything anyone ever asked of him.

And in the immediate aftermath of the Cynthia fiasco, he had weaned himself from the pills, determined never to be so stoned he'd father another kid. Somehow he was convinced that he was much more capable and cagey under the influence of alcohol than narcotics.

NINE

Tyler, Doris' eighteen year old son, still lived at home. Almost six feet tall but very thin, almost giraffe-like, Tyler was pale, freckled, and socially awkward. He was dreadful at sports and hated the rigid routine of school, his mind and imagination so often out the window to the trees and clouds. His teachers, one after the other, soon found themselves frustrated and annoyed, wanting to shake some sense into him. So he had left Brett High in his junior year.

But he was very good with machines and understood every kind of gizmo. He could figure out what made them tick, and when necessary figure out the best way to stop their ticking. So good at it that he could often make money fixing broken things for the neighbors.

Probably because his own house was never empty and rarely safe, Tyler was always in search of peace and quiet. Between his mom and her boyfriend Ernie, and Ernie's three kids, the house was constantly packed and noisy.

Tyler had learned that if he needed to feel safe, or wanted silence and some space, he would have to find it elsewhere. Not long after he came to this conclusion, his buddy Leonard explained how easy it was to break into other people's empty houses. Because most houses didn't have alarms; and many of those that did, had the kind of cheap alarms you could easily disable.

"House-borrowing" was what Leonard called it. Then gave Tyler a quick lesson in getting past a security system. Laughing mostly to himself: "Everybody calls me 'homeless,' but I've had a hundred homes without a single mortgage." Tyler was incredibly lucky to have met Leonard, his first ever kindred spirit, because Leonard lived in California, moving with the weather from northern California south, but was only here after hitchhiking across the country to what he called "the godforsaken cold" just to say goodbye to his favorite sister, Simone, who was living, actually dying, in his Aunt Ruth's house in Brett.

Tyler had seen Leonard sitting on the bench by the library looking so sad and lonely, then went and brought him a coffee and a grilled corn muffin from Dom's. Which instantly made Tyler Leonard's only east coast friend beside family, and they saw each other many times over the long and painful month it took Simone to die.

Leonard shared his story about living on the street and doing odd jobs and the occasional breaks he took in empty houses. Like Tyler, finding and fixing up what other people mistook for junk. About how exhausted he was from fighting the same Vietnam War he had fought in the nineteen-sixties night after night after night. The explosions, the bowel-clenching fear, the helicopters, the broken bodies, the napalm and the god-awful never ending shootings, so many lost friends and strangers.

Then one day, Leonard was gone. Tyler knew how much Leonard hated goodbyes and missed him very much. But it helped to see him in his daydreams walking in the sunshine along that place Leonard loved, that he called the Venice Beach.

Tyler had told Leonard that home hadn't ever really felt like home. At first it was his father's house, father by blood, who hit him, and hit him some more. A very young boy at the time, Tyler liked to think it was some wandering angel who looked down at just the right moment and noticed enough wrong-doing to know that something must be done, an angel brave enough to magically disappear first father.

But very quickly he required more angels, angels who sadly were busy elsewhere, because it didn't take long for the phony fathers to arrive, that revolving door of angry men his mother seemed to try on like new shoes. Then the most recent, the worst of all, this Ernie arrived. A replacement father so piss-poor he could conjure up just enough energy to smack Doris and hit him, but never enough initiative to go to work. Yet, for some reason unfathomable to Tyler, Ernie seemed like he was here to stay for ever and ever. Somehow appropriating the house for himself and for his kids.

Sometimes, Tyler could see nothing but the crimped and furious red faces of these men, feel nothing other than his body constricting, remembering their smacks, each with his own slightly unique preference for imparting pain. Thinking maybe each of us was given only one angel intervention a lifetime.

Perhaps it was just because so much time had passed, or that he had suffered such a grab bag of substitutions, but he could barely imagine first father anymore. Each time he tried, the blurred memories slowly transformed themselves into Ernie. It was a particularly poignant failure because his mother, all too often after an especially bad spell with Ernie, would inevitably and plaintively complain to him that if she really thought about it, things had been a whole lot better with his real dad. Tyler, with nothing useful to add, stayed silent, having clearly done what was required to effectively obliterate those earliest years.

It didn't help that Ernie's three kids were insatiably mean to him. Bill, Bob, and Buck: twenty-one, nineteen, and almost eighteen. Well mostly Bill and Buck, oldest and youngest. For reasons that escaped Tyler, they walked around desperately imagining they were better than everyone else, especially him. Blond, chunky kids, almost as tall as Tyler, but stronger and much better looking than their dad; from the mother, he imagined. But like their father, they mostly wandered around aimlessly, not terribly engaged by anything, always restless and one small step from a potentially explosive boredom. Tyler figured it was no wonder Ernie's first wife left because she probably never got a moment of peace.

One day, Ernie found Tyler in the dilapidated shed in the back of the property, working by the light of a single flashlight on a Dell laptop computer. Tyler, with several small screwdrivers, a plastic cup with tiny screws, was carefully checking the motherboard. There on the unfinished plywood floor, sitting surrounded by damaged DVD players, some ailing early iPods, and a few cameras that could still point but wouldn't shoot.

Before Tyler knew what was happening, Ernie grabbed him, lifting him off his feet and up, wrenching him left and then right, his mad twisted face only inches away, reeking of alcohol, screaming, demanding to know where he had gotten this stuff.

Traumatized, of course, it was next to impossible for Tyler to think rationally about any of this, let alone manage in the moment a clear answer. So with every added shake, he felt himself shutting down.

When Ernie got tired enough to put him down, Tyler thought that maybe the toaster oven in the far corner belonged to Mrs. Avery living a couple of blocks away. He often fixed things for her and she'd always give him a few bucks for his efforts. But really, right now, he wasn't sure about much of anything. Then Ernie clobbered him one more time, and Tyler crumbled to the floor. Ernie stepped over him, and stormed out.

Two weeks later, Ernie found Tyler alone in the basement at one in the morning, using one of Ernie's hardly used pliers to fix a broken clock radio he had borrowed from a summer home on Bartlett Drive. Enraged, thinking who the hell did this kid think he was, Mr. Fixit? Using his tools, can you believe it? So Ernie slapped him across the face, then thinking once wasn't enough, and about to try it a second time, suddenly felt a knife at his neck.

The knife remained pressed against his throat until Ernie finally realized he would be wise to offer an apology, however insincere. But, as soon as he was free, he went scurrying upstairs, yelling incoherently, shaking, waking Doris, then the boys with his screams and threatening to call the cops.

At eleven o'clock the next day, Tyler found himself in the backseat of Ernie's car, headed across the border to New York State, to an odd, most empty office complex in a small town off Route 23, and then upstairs to a sad and seedy office.

All the while Ernie was leaking fury and his mom was oozing worry. In keeping with the decor, Dr. Alvin Davis Jr. no longer cared to shave. If he once had a receptionist or nurse, they seemed long gone. Ernie and Doris were clearly anxious to get started but Dr. Davis seemed surprised to be starting his day with three people he clearly didn't know. It was only after Ernie reminded him about the knife to his neck and his early morning telephone call and the emergency appointment he made, that Dr. Davis slowly began to appreciate that he had a new patient. At which point he turned his attention to Tyler and asked why he had threatened Ernie with his knife.

Tyler thought it more than just a little bit weird that he and this odd doctor and his mom and Ernie were all crowded together in this too small, stuffy and messy room. But it was a pretty simple question. So he told them all that Ernie had smacked him, and, in fact, the Ernies picked on him all the time, and that it seemed like they all hated him. While he had absolutely no memory of the knife or threatening Ernie with it, at least Ernie hadn't hit him today. But then Dr. Davis began to shake his head, and Ernie was turning red and it seemed like his answer hadn't helped at all. His mom seemed more worried than before.

Then they asked him to leave the room. They all spent a few more minutes talking. When they came out, the doctor took a hundred bucks in cash from Ernie, and put a sympathetic hand on his mom's shoulder. Trying to summon up what used to be his professional voice, he declared that Tyler was, in his opinion, most likely a paranoid-schizophrenic. Handing several prescriptions to Doris, he said that he thought the pills would help.

Even though his mom was a nurse and by no means dumb, Tyler had discovered a long time ago, that whenever she was around men, and almost always to his detriment, she seemed to turn her brain off.

Which is why on the drive back, he wasn't surprised that all of a sudden she bombarded him with a whole bunch of questions. Do you hear voices? Do you think people are out to get you? Do you think you can fly? Are you angry all the time? He said "no" to all of them, but he was lying about the first, second, and fourth questions. As for the third, he was pretty sure he couldn't fly. Or at least hadn't been able to up until now. He heard several voices and they and him didn't just think, but pretty much knew that Ernie and the little Ernies were definitely out to get him.

So how could you not be angry when everywhere you turned there was someone, all the time, trying to smack you? Their last stop was the pharmacy for the pills which, he soon discovered, made him feel like he had a heavy iron band pressing in on his brain, weighing him down.

Then, later that day, Doris and Ernie got into a screaming fight about whether it was Doris' fault that he was so messed up.

"What about your brother who ended up in the loony bin? Claiming he heard voices. If that's not crazy, I don't know what is," Ernie screamed. "That stuff is in the blood." An uncle Tyler had never, ever heard about before. Then because Ernie was getting more mad by the minute, Tyler quickly slipped out the back door.

TEN

It was Ronald, the twelve-year old with the high voice, who reminded him how much better they all felt anywhere, everywhere other than home. In the houses not only were they safer but also doing something good. Which is what Leonard had said about the houses: not fair that they were abandoned. Houses were meant to be lived in, cared for, talked to. That all of God's people, especially Tyler, and the rest of them, too, deserved a nice place where they could make a little noise or maybe take a nap.

Then the very smart lady, Elizabeth, started to explain about the economy and people losing their jobs and the sub-prime problem and the over-valued properties and ordinary people no longer having enough to pay their monthly mortgages. Which the others didn't quite understand but she went on about those people having to sell their houses or sometimes the bank would take them and even leave them empty until they could find new buyers. Which is why, in addition to the empty summer and second homes, there were all these other houses for them to try.

You could head out in any direction these days and you'd quickly see For Sale signs. Or, even better, you could just follow the folks who worked for Barntown Realty in Brett. There was that short lady with the too-bright blond hair who was always smiling and laughing and drove the gray Mercedes and the taller lady who wasn't as happy, who people said was having husband problems, with her new Volvo station wagon, and the two of them were sooner or later out showing the latest and best empty houses.

Then there were those realtors in Barrington, Tyler's favorites, because while waiting for them there was that homemade ice cream at SoCo. Which wasn't always easy because they each had different favorite flavors. Most of the time, Tyler was able to get out of there with a cup of one scoop of coffee, another of black raspberry, all covered with some homemade hot fudge. But sometimes he'd find himself with vanilla which made no sense at all, kind of a waste of the whole ice cream experience.

Thanks to Red, his really old but reliable Tercel, which he bought with the money he made fixing the washers and dryers at the Wash N Wait, he had spent a little bit of time in thirty different houses the past year. Sometimes, he'd just rest for a bit, loving the fact that Ernie and the little Ernies were nowhere to be seen. But with the houses he most appreciated, he'd usually take home a broken appliance, fix it, then bring it back the next time he was there. Keeping track of the different items and the parts they needed helped to steady his mind. Plus, it was nice to know he was giving something back, a fair trade. Leonard would like that.

It quickly became obvious that in these strange houses Tyler found a peace and quiet far more effective than his pills. So after the first week, he opted out. Doris monitored him for awhile but it wasn't hard to slip a pill or two beneath the tongue and pretend to swallow. Then she got bored and Tyler started to flush them down the toilet.

He felt less anxious and it always felt safer without any of the Ernies around. Problem was sometimes the voices inside grew very loud.

It was Elizabeth who used the internet in the Simpson house to do some research. The Simpsons, who lived in Newton, Massachusetts nine-tenths of their time, were both highly-successful corporate attorneys in Boston. They had a really fast PC in their beautiful wood-paneled office off the living room with a snazzy new HP printer and office quality copier.

Elizabeth, who was convinced Dr. Davis was a quack, was more than ready to prove it. Probably a family physician, she figured, and unsuccessful at that. Certainly no psychiatrist. Spending almost no time alone examining Tyler. So how likely was it that he had correctly identified the problem or provided a proper treatment plan.

Yes, diagnosis was always tricky, she was quite willing to concede, but so far as she knew there was precious little evidence to suggest that Tyler was paranoid. As for herself, she certainly wasn't delusional. Or thought that anyone other than real-life bullies like Ernie and his testosterone-fueled idiot sons were out to get them. Not the government or agents of Hydra. She certainly didn't want or need a tin foil hat to ward off evil, or interplanetary probe rays. While she couldn't vouch for who, if anyone, the others were worried about, she had her doubts Dr. Davis knew what he was talking about.

The fact is, it was far more likely that Tyler was suffering from what used to be called Multiple Personality Disorder. Which they now called Dissociative Identity Disorder.

She still had that used copy of "Diagnostic and Statistical Manual of Mental Disorders, Fourth Edition" she bought at last summer's used book sale at the Brett Library. Where she found this description on page 519:

"Dissociative Identity Disorder (formerly Multiple Personality Disorder) is characterized by the presence of two or more distinct identities or personality states that recurrently take control of the individual's behavior accompanied by an inability to recall important personal information that is too extensive to be explained by ordinary forgetfulness ... Each personality state may be experienced as if it has a distinct personal history, self-image, and identity, including a separate name. Usually there is a primary identity that carries the individual's given name and is passive, dependent, guilty, and depressed."

Well, there was no denying that some of this was very upsetting. Because it did seem to her that Tyler was depressed. Guilty, probably. Otherwise things would be different, wouldn't they?

Passive, well that seemed accurate enough to Tyler when she brought it up. "But you try dealing with Ernie and the Ernies," he said more than a little annoyed. "Let's see how well you do." Then, really thinking about it for a while, Tyler had to acknowledge that maybe some of the symptoms made sense.

He wanted to close the book but Elizabeth wasn't done: "Here on page 526," she continued: "Particular identities may emerge in specific circumstances and may differ in reported age and gender, vocabulary, general knowledge, or predominant affect. Alternate identities are experienced as taking control in sequence, one at the expense of the other, and may deny knowledge of another, be critical of one another, or appear to be in open conflict ... There may be loss of memory not only for recurrent periods of time, but also an overall loss of biographical memory for some extended period of childhood, adolescence, or even adulthood.'"

A bit dogmatic, she thought, and far too certain about how things worked for them. Because, in her experience, there were many gray areas. Sometimes they saw or heard or knew each other; other times not. Remembering; forgetting. It pretty much defied any simple summary. But Elizabeth certainly knew the absolutely disconcerting feeling of looking into a mirror and seeing someone completely different looking back. No matter how many times it happened it was always a shock to the system. And she definitely had large and troubling gaps in her memory. As if she was living but a fourth or fifth of a whole life.

Sometimes she was just about to go somewhere, had it all planned out, the best way to get there, what she was going to do when she got there, like the trip she wanted to make last month to the Sol LeWitt exhibition in North Adams, and poof they'd be playing miniature golf because Ronald had taken over. It was sometimes exhausting not doing what she really wanted to do.

Not to mention how bizarre it was to hear Tyler go on and on about screws and wires and transistors and tripping over all these odd-looking and broken machines. Or putting up with that pompous, pontificating Abigail, who without warning could go off on Tyler's complete lack of design sense. Insisting just the other day that if he was going to be bringing things home, couldn't he at least score some decorative art, a decent painting, a tasteful accessory or two, anything besides these relentlessly ugly clock radios and wounded VCRs.

Then Elizabeth was gone and Tyler had but brief moments to enjoy the re-emerging peace and quiet before plunging back into remembering, knowing with absolute certainty that whatever the hell condition it was that they said he had, the doctor or Elizabeth, none of it changed the fact that every day he had to hear his mom and Ernie constantly arguing about bills. The screams, the shouts. With her wanting him to work more, and Ernie yelling about his lower back and his disability payments, which is always why it didn't really pay to work, although this disability never seemed to stop him when he'd run after Tyler or the other kids with a belt. The disability payments that never seemed to make their way into his mom's bank account to help with rent or food or the oil bill.

Elizabeth probably heard him thinking, because now she was back with more:

"It's right here, Tyler, on page 527: 'Individuals with Dissociative Identity Disorder frequently report having experienced severe physical and sexual abuse, especially during childhood. Controversy surrounds the accuracy of such reports, because childhood memories may be subject to distortion and some individuals with this disorder are highly hypnotizable and especially vulnerable to suggestive influences. However, reports by individuals with Dissociative Identity Disorder of a past history of sexual or physical abuse are often confirmed by objective evidence

… Individuals with Dissociative Identity Disorder may manifest posttraumatic symptoms (e.g., nightmares, flashbacks, and startle responses) of Posttraumatic Stress Disorder. Self-mutilation and suicidal and aggressive behavior may occur.'"

Tyler was very quiet and Elizabeth waited a minute before continuing: "Nightmares, check. Flashbacks, absolutely. I'm pretty sure Ronald has a pretty heightened startle response, don't you think. One minute he's here and something happens to frighten him and he's gone for hours, even days. I can't speak for you or Amanda or Ronald but I can pretty much guarantee that Tony and his knife fits the bill when it comes to aggressive behavior."

Tyler tried to massage his neck, to stop the headache that was gathering like a storm. "This is all too much," he announced. "I'm going down to the basement to lie in the dark." Because nothing helped so much as the dark, the silence …

The headaches were his private hell. Sometimes so bad even the slightest noise, or any light, would leave him gasping, praying for a permanent end to the pain. There was no standing, no driving, just lying there.

It always helped to remember that when the headache passed, and they always had up to now, there were safe houses waiting.

ELEVEN

There was a reason people kept saying "ignorance is bliss." Probably because, as Penny was learning, it is so very difficult and painful to finally see what you haven't let yourself see before. She was often overcome with a profound sense of embarrassment, which mostly she kept to herself, and shared mainly with Dr. Irving Martin Schulman, her new therapist.

Although Dr. Schulman was quick to point out that most people live a kind of shadow life, Penny was still shaken by her lack of vision. That she could have remained married so long to a man who, in the deepest sense of the word, had "used" her to get back at her father.

Now, even though she liked Frank a lot, she didn't trust herself or her feelings. Or trust Frank, with her heart at least. She certainly didn't want to hurt herself or hurt Frank.

So once a week, they had dinner or a brunch. If anyone could appreciate Penny's hesitancy to commit it was Frank. He, too, didn't trust his instincts when it came to relationships. It was all too easy, when contemplating the future, to see the wreckage that lay behind him: a bad marriage, a gaggle of disappointed lovers.

Even Danger, the adoptee parrot he had inherited from Dr. Silver, seemed to be hedging his bets about Frank's ability to come through in the long term. Frank had spent many an hour trying to get Danger to offer a heartfelt "Good morning, Frank!" but the more he tried, the more Danger would look him straight in the eye and declare with great enthusiasm: "Good morning, Danger!" Then smile, as if all too aware that one morning Frank just might not be there. Convinced Frank hadn't yet earned a more permanent acknowledgment. Because it's not like these humans hadn't passed him around before.

Then Danger all too quickly would change the conversation to what was most important: "Cracker!" Because having resisted all that pressure, he certainly deserved a breakfast treat.

So it wasn't surprising that Frank often wondered whether he really had that much to offer to either of them.

TWELVE

Tom Templeton felt like he was simultaneously playing table tennis at eight different tables with eight other players all sending ping pong balls his way. He had eight properties to show to twenty possible buyers in the next two days. Plus, he and Susie were often interrupted and asked to shepherd the efforts of all their other agents. His office phone, his home phone, and his cell phone never stopped ringing. Then there was always email. On any given day he'd have more than a hundred emails and many dozens of text messages.

So he couldn't say he was surprised when his early morning breakfast at home was unceremoniously interrupted by Arthur Davidson's loud shouts and vociferous complaints that his very favorite white rug was missing from his lakeside home. Reminding him several times over that the last person to show the house was Tom's agent, Alex. So what exactly was he going to do about it? This, of course, was no cheap Martha Stewart K-Mart rug, but a rare, one-of-a-kind handmade Finchley sheepskin, which his decorator, Marco Pizzarelli, yes the five hundred dollar an hour Marco Pizzarelli from New York City, absolutely insisted made the living room come alive. Reminding Tom that he never, ever in a million years would have authorized a mere real estate agent to make decorating choices, let alone remove a handmade Finchley from the premises.

Tom bit his tongue, wanting so much to tell, but not telling Davidson that he just happened to know more about rugs than Davidson would ever know, and that whoever the hell this Finchley was, his rug was a minor abomination. It was, both he and this over-priced and obviously pretentious Pizzarelli should know, an insult to all the sheep who had sadly sacrificed their wool for such an absolutely unworthy endeavor.

Because, even as he struggled to stay silent, he quickly calculated the potential fees Alex and the office would get if they sold the place, versus the now ever so obvious grief they would surely continue to suffer if they kept Davidson as a client. Davidson was asking $875,000 for a property Tom knew wouldn't sell for any more than $725,000. If he was right, and they could talk Davidson down to a reasonable asking price, Alex and GB Properties would split $36,250. He knew Alex could certainly use the money, and so as much as he wanted to hang up, he found himself offering an extended reassurance.

"Mr. Beaumont would never presume to change your house without your permission. We have an iron-clad policy about such matters, and we always leave a property the same exact way we find it. We are here merely to help you sell what we all believe is a special place. Rest assured, Mr. Davidson, I will personally follow up on the matter. Your trust means the world to us, and to me, in particular."

When Tom called a short time later, Alex tried not to laugh at the notion that he or Penny would ever take one of the world's worst-looking rugs along with them to see four more houses.

"Tom, as much as I believe that whoever took the rug was performing a public service, I swear to you it wasn't me. I've got Penny as a witness. There's a sofa at the Perkins property in Brett that I wouldn't mind having, but please reassure Mr. Davidson that we left his house the way it was when we got there."

Another long phone call later and Arthur Davidson still wasn't sure he believed Tom Templeton. Wanting to know how many copies of his keys Tom and his agents had made? Because it certainly wouldn't be hard for one of them to give his key to an accomplice. There was that place on the internet his nephew who hardly ever left the house was always going on about, buying stamps and coins and comic books from God-knows-where and selling them to God-knows-who, Seebuy or something like that, which all the thieves could use to dispose of what they stole. Maybe he'd have his computer guy check to see if someone was trying to sell his Finchley right now. In the meantime, he was definitely going to call the Ripton cops. Maybe they could fingerprint the couch and coffee table.

*   *   *

Chief Paul didn't know one rug from another. Also, because you really couldn't beat the prices, he and Margaret did a lot of their shopping at K-Mart. So he wasn't particularly thrilled to hear Arthur Davidson putting down the place. Margaret had filled their home with lots of Martha Stewart stuff, all of which worked perfectly fine.

Still, he assured Davidson, he'd immediately check into it. Though he couldn't help thinking how unlikely it was that a highly motivated real estate agent would jeopardize a significant commission by swiping a single rug. Still, he'd add the Davidson rug to Frank's list.

So first thing Thursday morning, the Chief called while Frank was feeding himself and Danger. By this time, a stolen rug was business as usual and it hardly fazed Frank. Taking someone's sheepskin and leaving everything else made as much sense as re-programming someone's TiVo or repairing their Mr. Coffee.

Frank lived only several blocks away from the GB Properties office on Grant Street, the closest thing Great Barrington had to a miniature version of Manhattan's Columbus Avenue: a collection of small upscale shops and restaurants two short blocks long. GB Properties had one of the nicest storefronts: its large windows filled with beautiful photographs of their properties, and within, a big oak table, a comfortable array of contemporary couches, and a tasteful marble counter with their large computer screen.

Tom Templeton was tall, thin and fit, with a twinkle in his eye, and the ability to quickly size people up. While he had grown up in the Berkshires, his formative years as a movie producer in LA, while probably hastening the loss of most of his hair, had added a big-city sophistication and masterful ability to negotiate to his small town appreciation of country living: the hills, the fields, and the importance of a handshake deal.

"You know, I'm very fond of Katie, and it's good to finally meet you," he told Frank. "It's just hard to believe that the reason we're finally meeting is that stupid rug. I tried to explain to Mr. Davidson that everything we do here is about trust. We promise to do our very best for our clients. They have a house to sell, and our job is to sell the house in a fair and honest way. Or to find the right house for those hunting for a house. Sometimes that means delivering news our clients may not want to hear: like they are not going to sell their house for $450,000 when their neighbor's house, in better shape, just sold for $375,000. Or that their dream house is rotting from the bottom up and needs a hundred thousand dollars' worth of work.

"I've helped Alex learn real estate. I've worked with him many times over the past two years. It makes no sense at all that he would sabotage a sale that's worth so much more than that ridiculous rug. Not only that he has integrity.

"You know, I've spoken to quite a few brokers who have been dealing with similar incidents. They've kept it quiet and my guess is they've advised their clients to do the same. Reporting these kind of problems to the police could easily backfire. No one wants potential buyers to think they might be buying a property that may not be safe. You've worked in New York and I've spent time in LA. I think we might have a slightly different understanding of what serious crime is than Mr. Davidson and the folks around here. I remember when my father found out I had smoked a joint. It was all my mother could do to keep him from tying me up and dragging me to the police station in Plattsford to turn me in. For my own good, he kept saying. Luckily, I was still stoned and it was more funny than horrifying.

"So keeping these things quiet is probably just some very foolish short-term thinking on the part of these brokers, but it's happening nonetheless. You've probably only heard about a half of the weird things that have been happening in houses around here.

"Since the Davidson house is one of ours, I'd prefer it if we could keep this conversation between us. Mr. Davidson is not the easiest of clients, and he has an inflated sense of the worth of everything he owns, especially, for some inexplicable reason, this dreadful rug. He seems to like it even more now that it's missing … Oh and in case you're concerned, smoking dope is a habit I've long outgrown and I'm not holding.

"Good thing … because I left my rope home, don't have the energy to drag you anywhere, and besides we're in GB not Ripton. Last thing I need is a jurisdictional dispute with my local compatriot cops."

"Anyway, I hope this helps. Alex should be here any moment and I'm sure he'll be glad to fill in whatever I might have missed. You're welcome to wait but I've got to show a house in Lenox in twenty minutes. I'll make you a deal: if you sell any houses before Alex gets here, I'll cut you in."

Frank laughed, "That sounds a lot better than my current deal but I'm pretty sure the only extracurricular activity my Chief will tolerate is fishing or hunting, some variety of proving man's dominance over other life forms, activities which you country folk seem to love. Thanks for the candid conversation, and I just want you to know how much I appreciate what you did for Katie. The house you found for her may have been spoiled a bit by what happened there recently, but it fits her perfectly."

"Well I hope I see you under better circumstances the next time," Tom said as he waved.

Alex met Tom on his way out, so Frank didn't really have a chance to test his inner real estate agent. Frank was immediately reminded of one of the most compelling realities of his new job: the amazing mix of informality and formality you had to bring to it. Hardly ever in the city did you know the victims, the suspects, the witnesses to a crime, and the friends or family of them all. But here in the country you occasionally found yourself prying into the lives of people you knew in other ways. Because it was only last week that he and Penny had gone to dinner with Alex.

Who smiled nervously as he locked the front door then flipped the sign, "Agent Out Showing Property – Back Shortly," so they'd have some privacy. He turned back to Frank. "Well, this is a little different than sharing eggplant parmigiana and garlic bread at Zia Maria's. I assume, since you're investigating a crime, you have some questions for me. Which means I need to tell you some things I would have waited to tell you until we knew each other a heck of a lot longer and a lot better. Things I hope you'll keep to yourself unless and until it becomes official police business."

Frank, a bit surprised, slowly nodded: "OK, that sounds reasonable, Alex. I can do that."

"The only ones who know this are Tom and Susie. I felt I owed them the truth. I've tried in the past to share this with other people and it always seemed to spoil the relationship. So I haven't told Penny yet. I hope you'll understand. I don't feel good about keeping secrets but some secrets …"

He paused, and slowly the story tumbled from him: "I know a bit about being questioned by the police. It hasn't gone particularly well for me. So if things go sideways here I reserve my right to an attorney. I served six years in Nevada for assault … I was convicted of shooting my so-called boyfriend … Supposedly I was jealous. I've given up telling people I didn't do it. I didn't do it and nothing happened the way they said it did. In fact, he's the one who could have killed me if I hadn't pushed the gun away from me. But he was a Congressman's son and I was poor and gay …

"I don't really expect you'll believe me. I'm sure you've heard similar stories from, well, especially with your work in the city, from just about everybody you arrested. The inmates I jokingly called my fraternity brothers at Lovelock certainly didn't believe me when I said it was self-defense. Actually only one person has ever believed me and that's my sister. Then, thank God, Susie believed my sister and luckily for me, Tom believed Susie.

"In any event, I've done and survived my time. I love it here. I'm incredibly grateful to Tom and Susie for giving me another chance, and so even if I had an overwhelming desire to swipe a rug, I wouldn't wish this particular rug on a mangy dog. It certainly isn't worth ruining my life a second time. Even if I was temporarily insane, I would certainly do everything in my power to control the impulse out of respect for Tom and Susie. There's also the fact that, except for some bubble gum I took from a candy store when I was twelve, I've never stolen anything." Then he was silent. The silence lasted a very long minute.

"Well, I appreciate your telling me the truth, Alex, and I certainly understand your reluctance to tell people. I'm sure it frightened the hell out of those you told. Because you look and talk just like them. Or, as my Hungarian Jewish grandmother might have put it, "God forbid a man like you ends up in the slammer." Then, God forbid two times over you should be innocent. Because if an innocent man like you ends up in prison, well then maybe it could happen to any one of the rest of us. I've read enough of the Innocence Project reports about DNA evidence to know that it happens more than any of us in law enforcement want to imagine. And that there are far too many innocent people in prison.

"Anyway, it turns out this isn't the first incident of something going missing in a house around here, especially homes that are for sale or often empty. I'm hoping you'll keep an eye out, both to stay safe, and to let me know if you see anything that seems suspicious about any of the houses you're showing. If you do see something, please get out of there as quickly as possible without scaring your client. And if you could, give me a call as quickly as you can any time at all on my cell phone."

THIRTEEN

It was eight-thirty and very dark outside. Tyler Deakins wasn't exactly sure why he was driving east on Parkside Avenue in Great Barrington except that he felt like he was keeping a promise he couldn't really remember making.

The white rug was folded up in a shopping bag scrunched up behind the driver's seat. Then softly in the back of his brain he began to hear Abigail. Whispering a rather insistent reminder to leave it, not in the living room of the Thompson house, not in that odd den, but where it actually belonged, right besides the bathtub in the upstairs master bathroom.

Thinking as he drove that if it was up to him he wouldn't have wanted the white rug anywhere in any of his houses, which actually weren't really his houses but still ... All of which prompted Abigail to tell him to stop daydreaming and focus on the task at hand. Which he thought was driving but she knew was swapping rugs. Which is why she reminded him again to make sure he brought back with him the thin rug the Thompsons were using in the upstairs hallway. Then when Tyler didn't answer immediately, growing more annoyed at him for not displaying the kind of enthusiastic support she expected for this important project, which was after all a very significant feng shui fair trade. A rare win-win for everyone concerned.

The Thompson house was at the very end of the street with a fairly long driveway. The easiest way in was through the open garage. One day he had found a spare key inside the fuse box. All the guys at Burke's Hardware in Brett knew how he was always fixing things for folks in the neighborhood. Pretty much everybody liked Tyler. And because he so often came in to copy keys, Jerry was glad to show him the best way to make perfect copies.

It didn't take much searching on the internet before he found a really inexpensive used ND 045-110V Key Duplicator from a hardware shop going out of business in Honesdale, Pennsylvania.

Like most people, the Thompsons didn't want to sign a three-year contract with ADT or Brinks and pay that monthly fee. Not that those precautions would have really kept him out but, at least, they made getting in just a bit more involved.

But now that he was in, he wasn't quite sure whether to place the white rug by the sink or alongside the bathtub. He stood there for a while staring at himself in the mirror, hoping Abigail would step in. This was so not his department. But now that he actually needed her, Abigail was nowhere to be found. Probably having left in a snit because he was slow to answer before. Not that she wouldn't have a whole lot to say later about what could very easily turn out to be an aesthetic catastrophe.

Then, all of a sudden, he saw himself still wet getting out of the shower knowing it would feel good to step out onto a soft rug. So the bathtub won.

The next step was a lot easier. No judgment calls, no design decisions. The thin rug – the other half of the trade – was in the hallway. He carefully rolled it up and put it under his arm.

He made it downstairs and was about to head to the back entrance to the garage when he glanced out of the living room windows and saw headlights swing into the driveway. His instincts kicked in and he hit the floor, hoping he hadn't been seen. The car came up a bit further toward the garage.

He lay there waiting to hear the sound of the car door opening but instead watched as the headlights swept across the ceiling, and the car made a U-turn and headed back down to Parkside. The old turnaround in someone else's driveway.

He stayed for a few minutes more, took the new rug and headed home.

FOURTEEN

Katie was wondering whether she had finally managed to successfully deep-breathe herself to an alternate universe. Yes, there was that one night after Frank and Penny had returned from Michigan, the night the three of them together threw the *I Ching*. That had been amazing in itself, but she had always assumed that Frank was just going along with what Penny wanted, so very relieved and grateful that his sister and her client/friend had survived their attempted murder.

But now these many months later, and out of the blue, here was Frank in her living room asking about a case he was working on. Hoping she would help him throw and interpret the coins.

He with his coffee, she with her tea, as he took the three llama coins, paused, then asked aloud: "What is the secret to the break-ins?" The first she had ever heard about any break-ins.

His first toss was a head and two tails, a seven, and a straight line. Katie watched as Frank picked up the pencil, and began to draw his hexagram. The second and third throws were two heads and a tail, eights, and broken lines. The fourth throw was a head and two tails, another seven, and a straight line. The fifth throw was two heads and a tail, an eight, another unbroken line. His sixth and last throw was a head and two tails, another seven, and straight line. No changing lines.

Frank checked the index and quickly discovered that he had thrown "Shih Ho / Biting Through."

"Well, Frankie, someone I saw just threw the exact reading a few weeks ago. Do me a favor and pick out some selections that seem most relevant to you. I'm curious to see what's similar and what's different for each of you."

Frank smiled and began by writing "Notes – *I Ching* Break-ins" in large letters at the top of his yellow pad, then began to read to himself for a bit.

"Whoa ... There's a lot here about dentistry and teeth and lips and biting. I don't remember, but did you have to go to that crazy radical dentist Carl and Theresa sent me to? The guy drove me nuts. One morning he tells me he has to fill a cavity. So he stuffs my mouth full of those little cotton thingies to absorb the blood and saliva. They look and feel like thick white tootsie rolls, and he sticks that suction thing in my mouth. Meanwhile, the phone rings and he goes off into the other room to spend what feels like a half-hour arguing politics while I'm freaking out and choking on my own saliva. Which is my way of saying I'm going to skip all this *I Ching* mouth stuff."

Katie laughed, then reached out to take the book from him. "Maybe this will go faster if I do some of the reading."

They both heard the sound of Rabbit's paws as he made it down the stairs, moving gracefully toward them. Then arching, stretching his back as he settled beside Frank.

"Glad you could join us, Rabbit," he offered as Katie read a little more to herself. Then she asked: "What about this section about the law?"

> Recourse to law and penalties overcomes the disturbances of harmonious social life caused by criminals ...

"Considering all the complaints Chief Paul's been getting, it's fair to say that even though this so-called criminal doesn't seem to be hurting anyone, he's certainly messing with the harmonious social life of our homeowners. They're upset and pissed off. So I'm playing the part of recourse to law in this story."

Katie read some more. "Hmm, well this might help."

> ... a talebearer and traitor who is interfering and blocking the way. To prevent permanent injury, vigorous measures must be taken at once. Deliberate obstruction of this sort does not vanish of its own accord. Judgment and punishment are required to deter or obviate it.

"I'm assuming," Frank began, "the 'talebearer' doesn't refer to those furry critters your half-drunk fluorescent orange rifle-toting guys are looking to shoot at six in the morning."

"Probably not," Katie offered.

"I haven't really told you about what's going on here, but so far we're talking about someone sneaking into empty houses and reprogramming digital video recorders, or fixing clock radios or clothes dryers. The whole thing is weird, and I certainly don't have any idea who's telling or bearing tales at this point."

"Well let's read some more," Katie suggested:

> The hexagram combines Li, clarity, and Chên, excitement. Li is yielding, Chên is hard. Unqualified hardness and excitement would be too violent in meting out punishment, unqualified charity and gentleness would be too weak. The two together create the just measure.

Frank paused for a sip of coffee, then smiled. "Well, that helps. Because the last thing I want to do is go completely 'Chên' here, like bringing in Tactical or Homeland Security with their armored personnel carriers to deal with a missing toaster oven."

Rabbit stood, took a long look at Frank, then offered a husky howl, one two three seconds long. He shook his head then headed to the door. "Well," Katie said as she got up to open the door for him, "clearly Rabbit and I hope you can do this without tanks. Because you may not have noticed but this is the country. I live on a small-town dirt road, and say 'good morning' to my neighbors."

"Noted my dear ..." Looking back down to the text: "But then your *Ching* offers more lightning and thunder, feet and toes, and meat, and some stories that might make more sense to you. And this interesting selection:"

> Punishment is to be carried out by someone who lacks the power and authority to do so. Therefore the culprits do not submit ... and ... by taking up the problem the punisher arouses poisonous hatred against himself, and in this way is put in a somewhat humiliating position.

"This bothers me, Frank. You're supposed to be the recourse to law, it's your territory and your responsibility, but it seems there's someone else, outside the law, punishing people …"

"Well, that's no good." Pausing as he read to himself, then a minute or two later, "then, there's this:

> The case to be decided is indeed not easy but perfectly clear … It is only by remaining conscious of the dangers growing out of the responsibility we have assumed that we can avoid making mistakes.

Frank was quiet, then announced: "Conscious and responsible. I can try that. Of course, I have no idea what your other client made of this advice, but I have a feeling it's going to take some time for me to understand all this. What bothers me the most is exactly what concerns you: the possibility there's someone, or some others, involved in handing out punishment. Oh yeah, and the 'poisonous hatred.' I'm certainly not thrilled about that."

"Well, Frank, to tell you the truth, 'Shih Ho' feels very different this time." Katie reached for a book on the end table. "I'd like to check Carol Anthony's *A Guide to the I Ching*, just to get a very different perspective."

Katie turned to Anthony's commentary. "Interesting … for Anthony, 'Shih Ho' is about finding the deeper truth:

> Forgiveness means that we try to understand how people are motivated to do wrong. It is to understand the power that fear, doubt, and bad habits of mind have over people. It is also to understand that the Creative is capable of penetrating people's hearts and enlightening their minds.

> … The sole purpose of punishment is to restore order, therefore we may punish only until order is restored.

"Well, Katie, getting to the truth here is exactly what I'm struggling with and why I came to you. I don't know what this guy is up to or why he's doing it? What any of these folks are doing. Or the fear or doubt and the bad habits she's talking about. Until I do, and better channel my own creative spirits, this restoring order may not be so easy."

FIFTEEN

Ernie, Bill, Bob, and Buck were all hanging out in the living room when Tyler made it back a little after nine. There were crumpled beer cans and two open pizza boxes with a couple of cold slices of pepperoni scattered about the floor. Ernie had a glazed look in his eyes, a thin layer of alcoholic confusion barely covering the perpetual anger that seethed beneath the surface. Tyler figured that Ernie had started with scotch before adding beer to the menu.

So glad he had completed the mission, dropping the thin throw rug off at the Davidson house before coming home to this mess.

Sometimes the four of them reminded him of a pack of pit bulls. Knowing his mom had probably fled to bingo didn't help, once again leaving him alone with them.

"Where have you been?" Ernie began as he slowly emerged from his groggy universe.

Tyler knew that there was no right answer. Never. No words he had ever found had worked.

"Driving," he tried.

"Driving … where you been driving?"

"Just driving."

Ernie was shaking his head now. "Just driving?"

Bill and Buck, realizing things were about to get interesting, began to snicker. Bob turned away.

"Well I like to drive," Ernie sneered, "but that doesn't mean I do it all the time." Then the questions came rapid-fire: "Where do you drive? How much does it cost? What do you make driving? How much of that money are you giving your mama for rent?"

Tyler felt both adrenaline and Tony stirring within. Tony, who believed in fighting back. Who wouldn't hesitate to use the knife he kept in his right front pocket if Ernie went too far.

"Right now I'm doing some odd jobs for the bicycle shop," Tyler managed. "Fixing bikes. I give Mom as much as I can."

Ernie wasn't happy with the answer but for the moment wasn't sure what to say. He looked to Bob, but Bob was looking away, mainly because he hadn't worked in the six months since Kentucky Fried Chicken left town. Bob feeling momentarily embarrassed that he had never given any of the money he earned to Tyler's mom. Wondering what had happened to his life.

Ernie looked to Bill who began to puff himself up. Bill had studied karate as a kid but then dropped out because Ernie drove him nuts whenever he lost. But Bill had nonetheless convinced himself he still knew the moves. Trying his best to rally his beer-soaked brain to stand up and confront Tyler.

Tyler knew he was running out of time. He could feel Tony feeling around his pocket for the knife. Bill was on his way out of the chair when Tyler pushed past him. He could hear them all yelling as he quickly rushed back out to his car. He was halfway down the driveway when they made it out of the door, screaming.

Tyler could feel Tony getting smaller, his angry chatter fading. He drove through the streets of Brett in a fog. He couldn't ever remember feeling safe; couldn't ever remember feeling he belonged. As a little boy he sometimes cried in his sleep. Even now he could remember his mother lifting him up from his bed to shake him, saying again and again, more loudly every time: "Shut up! Please shut up! You'll wake your father!"

He could still remember the first time he heard Elizabeth, the smart lady. She laughed at his mother. Saying, "she's the one making the most noise. If anyone is going to wake your father, it's her! How stupid is that?" And, even though he was very little, what Elizabeth said had made sense, because all he was doing was crying softly. But his mother would often go nuts, so afraid his father would wake up angry.

Sometimes he would sneak under the bed, hoping they couldn't hear him there, but somehow she'd find him and poke at him with the mop handle to dislodge him. Which really hurt. Then he'd howl and sure enough his father would wake up. Yelling how he worked his ass off for them from midnight to eight at the mill, and the least they could do is let him sleep until ten.

Before he knew it, Tyler was on his way out on Monument Valley Road, then onto Route 23, then to Ripton, careful to keep to the artificially low speed limit of 35. Usually, the local cops only did speed traps on the weekend and special holidays, but you never knew when the State Police might be out at night to meet their quota of speeding tickets. Not sure where he was headed or why until he found himself approaching the Krause property

All these years and tears later, he could still hear his father yelling. Then, after his father left for work and never came back, his mother, whenever anything went wrong, big, small, the slightest problem, would somehow still be blaming him for never letting his father rest.

"Of course," she'd yell, "of course he left us. You never gave the man a moment's peace."

Then the strange men. For a while he kept track of their names, until the time he mistook Matt for Jimmy and got clobbered. After that, he'd just mumble a greeting. Most of them took him for a moron but that was safer.

He never told her about Marvin, the skinny wiry guy who brought Tony to life. Tyler had never met Tony until the day Marvin came into the bathroom when he was on the can, staring at him, until he tried to touch him in a weird way. He was completely freaked out, wanted to yell, "stop," but the word got stuck in his throat. Next thing he knew his knee was driving upward into Marvin's crotch. He somehow stumbled to his feet, lifting his jeans. When he heard Tony, yelling in a deep voice he never knew could come from within: "You motherfucker … Touch me again, I'll kill you." Then, somehow finding the power to kick him hard enough to propel him out the bathroom door. When his mom came home later, asking where Marvin was, he said: "Went to the store for cigarettes." Cigarettes, Tyler assumed, he was still looking for somewhere else.

Then, all of a sudden, Elizabeth was trying to pull him back from the problems of the past to the challenges of the present, offering rapid-fire advice. If he insisted on going back to the Krause house, he better be on guard. Take the long way around, she said firmly, past the driveway and fancy garage, and hike back. Focus on the right now, so we don't all get caught.

Tyler decided to park out of sight in the first of the hard-to-find roundabouts. Wearing the Brink's Security jacket and the black baseball cap, his face now hidden. Luckily, because Elizabeth was right, and since they were last here, Krause had installed a whole bunch more of his small surveillance cameras in the trees.

Moving ever so carefully through the woods when out of nowhere he felt a slight pressure on his right thigh. Trying not to freak out, Tyler looked down to see the husky beside him, muzzle slightly tilted toward him, the dog's two dark eyes staring into his. Then licking his hand until as suddenly as he had appeared, the dog was gone into the night.

Tyler stood there silently for several minutes until he was

breathing normally. Then he continued on.

Krause, it seemed, had made some upgrades to the keypad system to his doors and it took him just a bit longer to make it in.

When he was safely inside, he realized how much he needed to rest and relax. And while Tyler just craved some simple consolation, Krause was providing comfort times a thousand. For he had spared no expense. It wasn't just television. Krause had built his own private and wholly luxurious TV heaven. His digital projection TV was the size of half his mom's house and there were speakers everywhere. Krause must have spent as much on his glorious couches as ordinary people spent buying their homes.

All Tyler wanted, all he needed was a few hours alone, sunk into the long black leather couch, melting into another universe. It didn't matter whether he was watching cops or con men or mad men or ghosts or ghouls, just so long as they were someone else's monsters. Or someone else's mom; someone else's Ernie.

Unfortunately, he couldn't help but notice that Krause hadn't taken any of his advice. No episodes of "Primeval" or "Fringe" or "Stargate Universe" on the digital recorder. All gone from the Season Pass Manager.

Krause didn't know what he was missing. But still, the bunch of boring news programs were heck of a lot better than the Ernies. So Tyler decided to program a new set of shows, to try one more time to make Mr. Krause's life just a tiny bit better. It was the least he could do, considering Krause had lent them the room.

SIXTEEN

Having secured a one-day waiver from Katie's ultra-healthy diet, Frank decided to treat Katie and Penny to a homemade dinner on Saturday night. Every few years he summoned the energy to recreate one of his mother's Italian extravaganzas. He started the red sauce the day before, in the largest pot he had, with oregano, basil, parsley, bay leaves, crushed garlic simmering for the briefest time in olive oil, then adding cans and cans of tomato puree, with some grated parmesan and Romano and a bit more olive oil to sweeten it.

Then he turned to the meatballs: a mixture of ground beef and ground pork and ground veal, some egg and bread crumbs. Browning in olive oil in the large frying pan beside the sweet Italian sausage. For Frank it was the smell of childhood, his mother Theresa moving briskly and with great purpose about the tiny kitchen in the Bronx, wooden spoon in hand, always managing to remember to stir the sauce, move the meatballs, or take a swat at him when he tried snatch a bite before it was ready.

Always reminding him that the secret was the ground veal. Then to keep him busy, having him chop the onions, slice the mushrooms, trusting him with the sharp knife.

Even though you could buy homemade pasta at Guido's, he got Ronzoni lasagna at the Big Y. Though they had changed the packaging, it was still the affordable pasta Theresa had bought all those years ago.

Danger, clearly impressed with his efforts, urged him on: "Good boy … Good boy … Do you want a cracker?"

"Thank you, Danger, I appreciate the vote of confidence, but we both know you exaggerate."

He loved assembling the lasagna: the sauce, then the pasta, more sauce, then meat, and atop it the ricotta and mozzarella and some parmesan, a bit more sauce, then repeating the process, finally brushing the top layer of pasta with more sauce, and some final clunks of cheese. Then into the oven.

He had looked in vain for the crisp and chewy Italian bread of his childhood, but all he could find was some thoroughly inauthentic Wonder Bread like facsimiles, so he opted instead for a French baguette which he turned into garlic bread.

Katie brought an incredible salad she had made with local greens and apricots and avocadoes and pecans and a homemade vinaigrette. Penny brought a blackberry pie from Taft Farms.

After they were stuffed with too much lasagna and salad and dessert, wine and coffee and tea, they moved into the living room and got comfortable. Frank, Danger on his shoulder, looking from Katie to Penny, asked if he could talk about his current case, the case that in so many ways was still a puzzle to him. Katie smiled, then Penny added:

"It would be a great relief to think about someone's else mystery considering how much time we spent on mine."

Frank smiled: "Well, it turns out you're already slightly involved in this one, too."

"What do you mean?"

"You were with Alex the last time anyone saw the white sheepskin rug that went missing from the Davidson house on Pickwick Road."

"You don't mean that scraggly rag-like thing in the house by the lake?"

"Actually, all I've seen is a fuzzy photo of it."

Penny laughed: "So this is a case about a missing rug? Sounds like fun compared to my murderous husband and his psychopath brother."

"You know it's all relative."

Katie shook her head: "Forgive my brother," turning to Penny to explain, "he inherited our father's habit of inflicting bad puns on us."

"Sorry, Sis … Actually, the rug is just the latest incident. There have been a string of break-ins in the area. Some in Ripton, some here in Barrington, in Saintsville, and Brett. Whoever it is takes things of little or no value. Sometimes things disappear for a week or two, then they reappear having been fixed. Sometimes they're replaced with something similar. He or she is very clever, and has managed to completely cover his or her tracks.

"In the city, I dealt with highly professional jewel thieves, and art thieves who meticulously plan and execute their robberies, but also small-time burglars looking for silver, laptops, and cameras they can quickly hock and cash. They're strung-out coke heads or junkies and far from careful, and they can often be unpredictable, unstable, and sometimes dangerous.

"So I'm still adjusting to my new Ripton reality. Unfortunately, this one particular homeowner has somehow got it into his head that Alex took his prized rug. He's been stirring up his neighbors about the break-ins. The Chief and I are feeling the pressure and trying hard to figure this out."

Danger flew to Katie's shoulder, cackling and laughing. "I'm a gecko! … Fifteen minutes … Everybody knows that."

Penny started to laugh, then Katie, as Danger, with a squawk, headed for higher ground on the refrigerator. Frank managed through his laughs: "Well, if you're a gecko maybe you can get me some GEICO job insurance."

Danger, mimicking Frank's laugh then bobbing his head: "Fifteen percent or more … Everybody knows that."

"OK, that settles it," Frank answered. "Too much TV … I thought I left him watching 'Sesame Street.' He probably found the remote."

Danger tried one last time to convince everyone: "GEICO. I'm a Gecko!"

Frank was shaking his head, aware he'd never win this one. As Danger offered one last Frank laugh.

"Uh, so where was I before my parrot tried to sell me car insurance?"

Frank got up and retrieved his copy of the *I Ching* from the end table: "Right … So Katie helped me throw the coins. I asked the *I Ching*: 'What's the secret to the break-ins' … So I've been trying to wrap my head around 'Shih Ho / Biting Through' and how it relates to my question."

Penny looked from Frank to Katie, then reached for the book. "That sounds familiar. Wait a second, Katie, 'Shih Ho,' wasn't that the hexagram I got when I asked about my new life? The whole thing about teeth and obstruction and justice?"

Frank started to laugh, then looked at his sister. "You mean your other client was Penny?"

Katie smiled. "*I Ching* client confidentiality, remember?"

"I remember … But it is kind of spooky we got the same hexagram. Actually, Penny, 'Shih Ho' probably fits better with your story: the criminals, the traitor, your husband and his brother, and the whole issue of punishment."

Katie waited a while longer before she began: "Frank, you've told us how these crimes don't make sense in the way you're used to. Maybe the secret is right before you, only it's presenting itself differently. Reminds me of your chameleon. Do you remember when you convinced Carl and Theresa to get you a chameleon, and then a week later you lost it in the living room? It was always changing colors, blending in. Sort of brown sitting on the wood floor, then green sitting next to some of Theresa's plants. I get the sense there's an explanation for this person's behavior that may have revealed itself to you, but you're just not seeing it yet."

"Luigi, his name was Luigi. You mean like what that Carol lady, with the other *I Ching* book, said about looking deeper, for the motivation behind things. The bad habits of the mind. The fear, and doubt. Figuring out why people do wrong."

Frank found the protruding bookmark in the *I Ching*. "There's something here that makes a lot of sense to me:

> Clarity prevails when mild and severe penalties are
> clearly differentiated, according to the nature of
> the crimes.

Penny nodded: "Let's try working backwards as Katie is suggesting. You know who this person isn't: he's not a brilliant jewel thief, or a violent burglar, so by studying the nature of these crimes you might be able to figure out who's actually committing them."

Everyone was quiet until Danger, looking down at them from atop his cage, announced in his best gecko voice: "Fifteen minutes." Then he began to laugh another perfect Frank laugh and soon they all were all laughing with him.

SEVENTEEN

Ernie and the little Ernies tried very hard to wait up for Tyler but they all had had much too much to drink and were pretty useless by midnight. They never heard him come in at three that morning after television at Krause's. Or leave at seven to go work on two broken washers and a dryer at the Wash N Wait. They did manage to make it up by eleven, all extremely messed up. Then because Doris was at work in Connecticut at the hospital, very quickly pissed that they would have to make their own coffee.

So they found themselves sitting at the kitchen table, three different boxes of dry cereal open, a half gallon of milk mostly gone.

"Who the hell does that little prick think he is?" Ernie managed through his Cheerios, milk dripping down his jaw. "He comes and goes like he owns the place. Sneaks around and won't say where he's going. Or what he's doing. Using my tools when I'm not looking. Thinking that just because he's his mom's only kid he's better than my boys."

Bill was too hung over to speak. It was hard enough guiding the spoon to his mouth without spilling everything. Bob was waiting for Bill to say something since he was the oldest. Buck was getting scared. He knew his dad hated it when they didn't all immediately agree with him. He kept looking from one brother to the other but they were both mute. Shit, he thought, just too much silence. Their dad could go ballistic any minute now. He very reluctantly offered a "Damn straight, Dad."

Ernie had been waiting for Bill to say something. He was just about to reach out and smack Buck, the closest to him, when he realized that this one was actually agreeing with him.

"About time … You're fucking-A right, Bill!"

"I'm Buck!"

"Whatever …"

Both Bill and Bob looked up, realizing they had blown it. That Buck had beaten them to it, wondering how they'd pay for this mistake.

Ernie glowered at his two oldest boys: "Glad you could finally join us. So what exactly are we gonna do about Tyler?"

Buck figured he had done as much as he could, leaving it to the

71

others.

Bob was hoping Bill would step up.

But Bill was trying to figure out the right answer.

Ernie slammed his spoon down. "You deaf? I said, what are we gonna do about it?"

"Teach him a lesson," Bill offered a bit tentatively.

"Yeah, let's teach him a lesson," Bob added loudly, thinking it might help if they all agreed, then looked over to Buck to silently urge him to chime in.

"Yeah," Buck tried, "teach him a fucking-A lesson!"

Ernie swiveled his head in Buck's direction: "You making fun of your dad, boy?"

"No … no, Dad … I just mean you're right: let's teach him a fucking lesson."

"Yeah, OK … Good idea, Buck." Turning back to Bill and Bob: "Why didn't you jokers come up with that?"

Bill bristled. "Whaddya mean, Dad? That was my idea!" Looking pissed at Buck now.

Ernie smiled. "So what's the big idea, Bill? What kind of lesson?"

Bill all of a sudden knew that he had somehow trapped himself. Just like the way his dad always got him when he was a kid and they played tic-tac-toe or checkers. He'd think maybe he had a chance and then, all of a sudden, his dad would take his checker and jump over one, two, three of his checkers, laughing all the while. Now Bill was desperately trying to find a way out while he thought some more.

"Show him who's the boss …" he suggested.

Bob and Buck were both waiting to see whether the answer would be enough. Ernie took a sip of coffee. Then a bite of English muffin. He could feel his beer-induced headache throbbing in the background. Usually coffee helped. He took another sip. He was losing interest in this game. He wanted the house to himself.

"OK, we'll show him who's boss … But I want you all together on this. I'm gonna let Bill drive my car, but you all better bring it back cleaner than it was, you get that. No Big Mac wrappers this time. No soda or beer cans. No smoking dope. When you're done I want to know everything about the little prick! Where exactly is he going and what is he doing there? Then we make a real plan!"

EIGHTEEN

The washers and dryers at the Wash N Wait never got a break. From seven in the morning until ten at night, they were filled to the brim, spinning and banging and clanging. It got worse as the economy tumbled and more and more people decided to hold off buying their own machines for the privilege of stuffing quarters into the machines at Wash N Wait.

It took Tyler most of Thursday to get three washers back on line, checking and rechecking to make sure they were working right. Occasionally, he'd look out the window across the street to the three Ernies trying to look inconspicuous in Ernie's car. Every hour or so one of them would wander out looking for more snacks. It was like watching the world's worst stakeout.

He had five twenties in his pocket for the day's work and access to the back room's extensive if eccentric collection of lost and left clothes to choose from. He picked the slightly faded New York Yankees cap and a blue pea coat and waited for old Mrs. Rodriquez to finish folding her clothes. He offered to carry her laundry basket and the two of them hobbled out together while the Ernies argued about who had gotten more French fries. He carried her laundry to her second floor apartment, refused the quarter tip she offered, and instead pressed a twenty into her hand.

The Ernies were all focused on Wash N Wait, so it wasn't hard to make it from Mrs. Rodriquez's apartment back to his car without being seen. As Tyler got his car keys, Tony, out of nowhere announced that as he far as he was concerned, bullies were fucking scum, and the only smart thing to do was walk right up to them and spit in their faces. Elizabeth quickly interceded, thanking Tony for his initiative, but assuring him that for the moment that really wasn't necessary. Right now, the best thing they could do was ignore them. Just take a look, she insisted: they clearly had inherited Ernie's stupid gene.

Tyler started Red, looked both ways and decided to risk an illegal U-turn rather than drive right by them. Bill, who was leaning on Ernie's hood wolfing down his fries, heard the squeal of Tyler's tires then looked up to see the red Tercel accelerating down Route 20. By the time Bill screamed at Bob and Buck and got them all settled and ready to go, Tyler's car was out of sight.

Tyler was driving a bit too fast until Elizabeth took over. "I suggest we slow down. Let's turn down the next street and wait a few minutes. They're probably a bit frantic because we lost them. They're probably trying to figure out what to tell Ernie. I say we go somewhere they won't expect us to go."

Tony piped in: "Let's go home for a bit, look Ernie straight in the eye, smile, then get a sandwich and take off before the morons make it back. That's sure to shake things up. Ernie will go nuts on the little Ernies. Then we can find a nice place for the night."

Abigail had an idea: "After we eat, how about we check out that new house the folks from O'Reilly Realty are showing. The one just before the Ripton/Otis line? I'm dying to get a look at the interior."

Tyler lost the vote. If it were up to him, he would never ever see Ernie again. Or the Ernies. Why couldn't they all just split and disappear like his dad did?

Just as Tony predicted, Ernie's car was nowhere to be seen in the driveway. The little Ernies were probably still driving around, searching everywhere for him and Red. He could see Ernie peeking from behind the curtain out to the driveway. Tyler took a deep breath, closed the car door behind him, and tried to walk as confidently as he could to the door. Ernie tried to move back from the window but Tyler caught him trying to straighten the curtain.

"Uh … hi Tyler … uh …" Ernie tried to be civil, thinking what he really wanted to do was to haul off and deck the little snot. Wondering why Tyler was here while his boys weren't? Trying to remember the details of his Tyler plan. Thinking he really needed a drink.

As he stood there in the kitchen Ernie couldn't help but remember the time when he heard that strange and scary deep voice coming from Tyler, and without knowing how it happened so fast, feeling that sharp knife against his neck. Wanting, from that moment on, to make Tyler pay. But realizing that if he wasn't extra careful that same thing might happen all over again. Which probably why he wanted the boys around.

So he decided to play it cool: "Hey, you haven't seen the boys have you? They said they had some errands to run. Gave them my car … Probably a mistake …"

Tyler, not sure what to say, hesitated until he heard Elizabeth whispering in his ear, and he found himself repeating word for word: "I think I saw them when I was working at the Wash N Wait. Hanging out across the street. Maybe they were just taking a break from their errands. But they certainly seemed to be enjoying their burgers and their fries, lots of fries …"

Tyler sort of tailed off … and smiled at Ernie, not sure if that was all Elizabeth wanted to say. Then he heard her laugh, and she began again. Which he offered Ernie:

"I tried to wave to them but by then they were really into eating … If I see them later, I'll let them know you've been asking about them …"

Tyler walked past him still smiling and, though he didn't look back, he could feel Ernie radiating hate.

He quickly changed out of his work clothes. He still had eighty dollars left and all that talk of burgers and fries had made him hungry. He decided to stop at Dom's, and then figure out where to spend the evening.

He was out the driveway and heading down the street just as the Ernies headed toward the house. He couldn't help himself and waved as they drove past each other.

NINETEEN

Milton Krause called the office and left Chief Paul a message. Then called the Chief's cell phone, a number supposedly only known by Frank and the Chief's wife, Alice.

Small town politics were the worst politics of all, and in the Chief's lifetime the town had changed to the point where the summer folks, the rich weekenders, and the recent transplants from the city exercised more and more influence over the Selectboard. So it was one of the most painful realities of the job these days that the Chief couldn't just tell Krause to go to hell. In fact, what would have been unimaginable even two decades ago had come to pass: two of the three Selectboard members were now retired New Yorkers. And they wouldn't know how to milk a cow if their lives depended on it.

For some reason, Krause, while flying first class from Kennedy to Heathrow, thought it necessary to call him at home on a Sunday night not to report a murder or a car crash but to tell him that he had had a bad feeling about his Ripton house. Chief Paul, who just wanted to treasure these the final hours of his day of rest, feet up in his favorite recliner, watching the seventh inning of the Red Sox game, was thinking but didn't say: "I don't really need to hear about any of this right now, do I?" But Krause, absolutely oblivious to what was going on with the Chief, went on to explain that, prompted by this feeling of dread, he had sent Derek Ford, his handyman, over to the house earlier in the day.

Chief Paul must have zoned out for a few seconds as Dustin Pedroia stole second base, but was wrenched back as Krause transitioned from explanation to recrimination, raising his voice more than a few decibels to insist with great vehemence that this thief had the unmitigated gall to come back and not only watch his TV, but once again re-program his TiVo.

So he was calling to tell the Chief in no uncertain terms that this had gone on long enough. Because while God and everyone else he knows and works with will confirm that he's a patient man, nevertheless … which got the Chief thinking, as the remainder of his precious night off was circling down the drain, in what strange and distant universe was this a patient man?

Then Krause was telling him he'd be spending a few days in

London before he was on to Geneva, but would be back in New York in ten days and he'd call for a report. Sure that the Chief would make certain that by then the thief would be in jail. A threat far more than an expression of confidence. Then abruptly hanging up. Somehow the inning was over without the Chief knowing how the Sox had scored a run.

Alice didn't like him to curse in the house so he was trying to hide his annoyance. But before he had a chance to calm down and return to the game, the phone rang and then rang again and he heard in rapid fire from all three members of the Selectboard and a particularly enthusiastic member of the Cemetery Commission. Each in his or her own way compelled to express great concern that such a distinguished member of the community was being so unforgivably harassed. Someone who, the Chief might have forgotten, they expected to generously contribute to the construction of the proposed new Ripton Community Center.

Abandoning any hope of enjoying the rest of the game, the Chief reluctantly began to dial. Shaking his head while he apologized for calling Frank so late. To give him an update, but probably more to share the pain, imagining for just a moment that just maybe, now that he had someone as competent as Frank on board, he could take that retirement that Alice was always going on about. To join her sister in North Carolina. So he went to sleep pretending he knew how to play golf. Which is what his brother-in-law did every other day in Carolina.

Frank wasn't sure why but sometime during the night he got the idea that Rabbit could help. A year ago he would have laughed at the suggestion but Rabbit had saved his sister's life. Since then he had come to believe that Rabbit saw and smelled and knew things most people missed. So the next morning he stopped off at Katie's to pick Rabbit up before he met Derek Ford at the Krause property.

Ford had grown up with dogs and like many a country folk was used to dogs going everywhere their humans went. He hardly noticed Rabbit, who was quickly out of the car and off exploring.

While Ford had learned out of necessity how to roll with Krause's punches, the blows were taking a toll. Born and bred in Ripton like his father and grandfather before him, Ford had adapted to the changing reality of country living. Once his family had been fiercely independent small farmers, with pigs and chickens and a few cattle, now he and his brother paid their bills mowing lawns, plowing snow, cutting and selling firewood, fixing doors and windows, and checking on the health of the humungous houses of the wealthy weekenders who had swiftly bought up their birthright, the modest homes of their forefathers. Purchasing, then transforming what was fertile, working land to real estate.

Rabbit was taken with the smells, traveling deep into the woods, padding along several intersecting pathways to get from there to several heres. The main scent something new, a patchwork of slightly different odors, an intricate weave of alike but not quite. Which he followed to a roundabout where once a car sat.

Meanwhile inside, Derek talked while he walked Frank over to the video surveillance room: "Mr. Krause has me checking the house every day now, mostly his big screen TVs and these digital video recorders he has all over the place. I think that's what bothers him the most. Someone playing with his toys. Questioning his taste and way of doing things.

"He's yelling at me enough as it is, even though I have nothing to do with this, and now he's pissed about every measly bill I send him. If I'm not here checking the place, he's pissed and then when I come he's pissed, like I'm somehow ripping him off by doing exactly what he asks me to do. As if my time doesn't really count."

Frank couldn't help but remember Carl's many talks about owners and workers and surplus value and how the rich lived off the labor of the poor.

"Anyway," Derek continued, "I didn't want to make it worse by telling him what I found. So I hope we can keep this to ourselves for the moment."

Sitting down at the computer, and motioning to Frank to sit beside him. There were a dozen small video monitors showing live feeds from cameras inside and out. There on Camera 5 was Rabbit taking his time smelling one tree then another.

It took a moment for Derek to access the recorded footage from the latest camera he had rigged in the woods out back. Frank watched as Derek doubled-clicked on a video file he had named "Intruder."

The recording offered a wide view of the area leading to the rear entrance to the sports complex. They watched as a solitary figure emerged from the blackness behind the camera into the pale light. He or she had a baseball cap covering the head, was walking slowly yet purposefully, without the slightest sense he or she shouldn't be here. As he or she got closer they could make out the Brinks' insignia on the jacket. Derek started to laugh. "Sorry, but you've got to hand it to the guy. He's got a sense of humor."

He managed to block a clear view of the security pad, and a minute later they watched the door open and close behind him. "He usually knows where my cameras are, but I caught him by switching locations and adding a few more. I'll skip him walking through the main house on his way to Krause's home theater. He pulled his cap down even lower so you can't even see a face.

"I'm only guessing, but I think it's a guy. Skinny and tall. I'm betting he can't weigh more than 160 at the most. Anyway, here's the second thing I didn't share with Mr. Krause, 'cause I knew it would just completely drive him up the wall. The guy left a note."

Then Derek pulled out a baggie. "The wife and I like to watch 'C.S.I.' The original 'Crime Scene Investigation' that takes place in Vegas." Handing the baggie over to Frank: "Just in case you want to check for fingerprints."

Frank unzipped the bag, and pulled the paper out with his fingers. "Thanks, Derek, but this guy is at least a step ahead of us. He's wearing gloves or keeps his hands in his pockets when he knows he's on camera. With baggies over his shoes. I'll bet he's been watching 'C.S.I.' too. But let's see what he says:

"Dear Sir or Madam. We've tried again to find some new shows for you. We hope you enjoy them. We know we will. Thank you very much."

"Knowing Mr. Krause, he is going to go ballistic when he sees this," Derek offered. "Take it as a challenge. Which is why I wanted to show you and see what you say about it. Personally, I think the guy means it when he says he hopes Mr. Krause likes these shows."

"You're probably right on both counts. Mr. Krause will want to fight back. But maybe he should, considering this guy continues to invade his property. Though, I'm not sure what he can actually do short of hiring guards 24 hours a day. You've got a life, and I'm dealing with other issues. So far we're lucky that the only thing this guy seems to want to do is to hang out and watch a little TV. If this were New York City he probably would have come with some moving vans and taken everything that wasn't nailed down.

"As for the note, it's from a standard 8½ by 11 notepad. I use them all the time, and he or she probably used the left hand to write these block letters with a Sharpie. It's pretty interesting, don't you think, that he wrote 'we.' Have you ever seen more than one person on the surveillance tapes?"

"Nope … just the one. But he almost always dresses differently. I have to recycle the footage because it takes up a lot of space on the hard drives but when I first saw the Brinks' jacket, I had the strong feeling that I may have missed some earlier break-ins. Like a little while ago there was a guy with a jacket on, 'Associated Lawn Services.' At the time I just assumed Mr. Krause had hired someone new for the day because friends of his were unexpectedly going to be using the house for the weekend. Then someone with a Verizon cap a few weeks ago. The guy's probably been swiping uniforms. Damn, I bet I missed him a couple of other times."

"Uniforms … That's pretty good, Derek. Second hand stores? Goodwill? Dry cleaners? Did you ever see anything about uniforms on 'C.S.I?' Maybe he did, too."

"No, but I'm sure I missed some episodes …"

Frank, holding up the note: "I think your instincts are right, there's no reason Mr. Krause needs to concern himself with the note right now. Meanwhile, I need to get a fix on this guy and what might be motivating him, so how about we take a look at the shows he thinks Mr. Krause should be watching these days? Maybe we'll learn something useful."

Derek took him to Krause's favorite TV room. The remote control was more like a mini-computer than any remote Frank had ever seen. So it took five minutes of trial and error for Krause's Season Pass Manager to appear on a screen as wide as Frank's living room. Mr. Krause was now reluctantly recording: "The Mentalist," "Stargate Universe," "PBS Newshour," "Antiques Roadshow, U.K." "How Clean is Your House," "The Bachelor," "Days of Our Lives," "So You Think You Can Dance," "America's Top Model," "The Good Wife," and "Monday Night Football."

Frank was shaking his head: "What a strange collection of shows."

"Don't know if you know this but 'The Mentalist' is about a former phony psychic whose wife was murdered, and now he works with the police in California. Everything is always different than it seems. He's always playing tricks, and creating these elaborate cons to catch the bad guys. My wife and I love it. Even though I haven't seen any more than one intruder, if this was 'The Mentalist,' there'd be some kind of switch. Like maybe the first break-in guy was one person, but the Brinks guy was a second, the lawn mower guy a third, and our Verizon repair person a fourth. Maybe a small crew, because this is like an entire family's worth of shows. You've got your football, your news, your romance and women's shows, your fix-it and doodads shows, and then the science-fiction stuff. Maybe some of them are ladies and some are guys?"

"Well, Derek, that's probably a lot easier to pull off on a TV show than to coordinate in real life. With special effects, and stunt doubles and look-alike actors."

"Or maybe there's some kind of break-in contest among local thieves."

"Thanks, Derek, I'll keep your theories in mind. But for now, I think I'm going to have a hard enough time catching a single burglar."

TWENTY

For the first time in his life, Tyler hadn't come home at night. Which, it turns out, was just as well. Because Ernie was still pissed that he had to watch Tyler prance in, grab a sandwich then prance out like he owned the place. The Ernies, too, who had to absorb Ernie's rage for losing him in Brett, were all up late, waiting and ready to make Tyler pay for what they suffered, their anger multiplying like cancer cells as the hour hand trudged its way around the clock.

So rather than go to bed at eleven, at twelve, or at one in the morning, Ernie had sat at the kitchen table, waiting like a cat to pounce on the mouse that never came. Then finally, without knowing when, fell asleep in his chair.

Doris, looking to make some extra money, had doubled up, following her day shift at the hospital with the night shift at the nursing home. So she came home completely exhausted at eight in the morning with absolutely no idea that Tyler hadn't made it back that night. She had learned the hard way that Ernie didn't do well without at least eight or nine hours of uninterrupted sleep, and determined not to repeat her many past mistakes, managed to tiptoe past him in the kitchen, his snores like loud foghorns. Then gratefully tumbled into bed, safe for the moment at least.

TWENTY-ONE

Tyler woke a little after eight that morning scrunched halfway over the gearshift in his car, shoulder and neck aching, more tired than rested, with hardly any idea of where he was. The floor in front of the passenger's seat was littered with the crumpled packaging of two large Whoppers with Cheese and a supersized soda. But it wasn't until several minutes later, as he drove down the driveway and saw the GB Properties sign that vague memories began to surface of a time last evening when Abigail had prevailed, and they drove to Ripton.

Now, unfortunately, it was much too bright out. Looking even more vigilantly than usual to the left then right because, as Leonard often reminded him, it just wasn't a good idea to leave a property when anyone and everyone could see you.

He was very hungry and thirsty and desperately needed coffee. As he turned right onto Route 23, he remembered just enough about yesterday's stakeout at the Wash N Wait to realize he was probably better off going to Great Barrington to grab something at The Donut House rather than heading home.

Which is when he saw the dog walking slowly by the side of the road. Turning toward him. Looking right at him. Like one of those bright Star Wars light saber beams piercing right through him. Slowing down without thinking, the dog nodding, smiling. One of those ice and snow dogs. A husky, Elizabeth reminded them.

Tyler pulled over, opened the passenger door and without a moment's hesitation Rabbit jumped in. Tyler checked the dog tag: Rabbit c/o Katie Greenberg, Box 146, Long Pine Road, Ripton, MA. Easy enough to drop him close to home.

TWENTY-TWO

After several months of phone calls and a flurry of email exchanges, Alex met Dr. Rosen and his wife Gloria for the first time. They had driven up from Montclair, New Jersey the night before, and were staying in the Ripton vacation home of one of Dr. Rosen's colleagues. Alex had sent them photos and fact sheets, and together they had selected a bunch of properties to look at over the weekend. On Saturday, they had seen several places in Great Barrington and one they really liked off of Bixby Hill Road in Mount Washington.

Even though it was only a twenty-minute drive from busy Great Barrington, it was up the mountain then a half-mile down a dirt road. The house sat beside the state forest, seemingly tucked far from the rest of the world. There were no cars to see or traffic to hear and most of the windows faced the forest. The large living room had exposed beams and wide plank floors. An oversized corduroy couch faced the beautiful hand-made stone fireplace. There was a small study, an adjoining bathroom, and a kitchen that artfully combined surprisingly modern appliances with a comforting rustic feel.

Upstairs, there were master and guest bedrooms and a newly renovated bathroom with a Jacuzzi tub.

The two-car garage had been designed to match the house, and the owners had put great care into the four acres of land that came with the house: there was a large vegetable garden, a beautifully contoured rock garden and the well-managed small forest. The Rosens were clearly taken by the place, but Alex had learned many times how quickly people's minds could change.

So, even though he always tried to match and encourage his clients' enthusiasm, he reminded himself not to get carried away by the moment. All it took was for Gloria Rosen to see another house with completely different charms. Or a brief conversation between them about their pre-existing financial commitments.

As they drove down off the mountain, he could see Gloria looking out the window at the dense forest to her left and the distant hills to her right, and in her eyes the very first hints of concern that the property might be just a bit too "country." A moment later, Gloria asked the question so many of Alex's clients sooner or later found themselves asking: "What do you do around here when it's not summer?" Imagining how boring it must be once all the most interesting people had returned to their cities.

He had learned that the most strategic response was a sweet and understanding smile. Followed immediately by one of the more enjoyable parts of his job, sharing his very real enthusiasm for the Berkshires. Because in truth Alex still felt so blessed to have landed here. While there were none of the drop-dead gorgeous views he had become accustomed to while driving to and from Vegas, the magnificent canyons, the incandescent high-definition skies of Santa Fe or Taos or the incomprehensible scale of the Rockies, there was a soft and comforting beauty to these smaller hills. Though the views were of dozens of miles, not hundreds, a Berkshire sunset could still melt his heart.

Alex was most impassioned when he spoke of the great combination of small-town living and urban culture: the independent films you could see at The Triplex in Barrington, at The Little Cinema in Plattsford, or Images in Williamstown. There was world-class art at both the Williams College and Clark Museums in Williamstown, or contemporary art and sculpture to see at the trend-setting renovated mills of MASS MoCA in nearby North Adams. Summers brought the Boston Symphony Orchestra to Lenox, and dance companies from around the world to Jacob's Pillow in Becket. There was theater galore throughout the county. There was a reason, Alex told all he talked to, why Nathaniel Hawthorne and Herman Melville and Edith Wharton had come here to live and work.

That seemed to resonate with the Rosens. Who, even though their friends had already made the summer/weekender jump, were still a bit worried they might be stuck up here with nothing to do.

Now they were headed to a couple of places in Ripton. The Stoughton house was new to the market. A property he thought Penny might also be interested in if it turned out the Rosens weren't. Olivia Stoughton had made it to ninety-four, outliving all of her Ripton friends. Never married, she had long ago willed her properties to a variety of local charities, all thrilled at the prospect of a quick sale and a timely infusion of cash during these difficult times for non-profits. Everyone except the yet-to-be found potential buyer was hoping the house would sell as high as possible.

Alex had met Olivia at one of Tom's wonderful summer parties. Even in her nineties, and though she knew she was dying, Olivia was filled with youthful enthusiasm. She had a wicked sense of humor, though one could often miss it, it was so subtle, even surgical. Her eyes twinkled and she had gotten used to the several second delayed effect her words often had. Because it sometimes took a while for the person on the other side of the conversation to realize, if they ever did, that she was being what her generation called "arch," or what the young, with a less sophisticated idea of satire called "sarcastic." Those who did appreciate what was happening, would often offer an overdue smile, trying to catch up.

Olivia liked Alex immediately. Who, quite unexpectedly, after just a few short minutes found himself sharing his story with Olivia. The very next day she told Tom that she wanted Alex to handle the sale of her house, because Alex not only understood irony, he had lived it.

It was hard to imagine the house without Olivia. Everything within seemed imbued with her spirit; and almost everything except the most basic acknowledgments to contemporary living, like phone and plumbing, were older than she was. The handcrafted wood furniture had aged as she had, polished by time.

Alex had vivid memories of the last time he had seen Olivia. She had asked him to lunch. She had made a salad, and all the ingredients except for the roasted pecans and several cheeses had come from her garden. "I do love my cheeses," she said.

As they ate, Olivia talked about her years in finance in New York, then having started late, the thirty years of painting she had done up here, and the storage space she had created for her work in the basement. A space no one had seen except the local carpenters she had sworn to secrecy for the art she had never shared with anyone. Her unknown children, she called them. Almost embarrassed to admit to Alex how fond she was of them. Not knowing if anyone else would care, but emphasizing the great pleasure painting had brought her all those years.

Then wishing that Alex might find something similar in his own life. She seemed able to see Alex as no one else had. Never doubting his present worth, while believing even more in his potential. Talking directly to his better self, urging him to use the coming years to become his best.

Then she informed Alex that she had told Tom that she wanted him, and only him, to handle the sale of the house. Then gave him the key to the basement storage room, saying "I'm hoping when the time comes, Alex, you'll figure out whether this is worth anything to anybody else."

Suddenly, as Alex parked, he found himself wondering whether the Rosens really deserved Olivia's house. He had never before felt this way, but then he had never been so connected to or felt so protective of any other Berkshire property.

The path to the front door meandered beneath a canopy of tall trees. Alex loved the sense that you were sheltered on your way home. Olivia had called it her cathedral of pine. A similarly wooded path led down to the lake. He was mildly relieved to hear Gloria Rosen complaining about how dark it was. But shuddered a bit when he heard Dr. Rosen tell her they could always cut the trees down.

The front door to the house had a still-working, old-fashioned, hand-turn doorbell. The foyer had beautifully hand-carved wooden pegs for coats on the right side, and a hall tree with a small drawer, mirror, and umbrella stand on the other.

"I was about to say that the house is filled with antiques," Alex began, "but to the previous owner, these were just the things she had known as a child in her grandparents' house. Everything is the way it was."

Gloria Rosen, who led the way, stopped dead before the living room: "You must be kidding!"

Alex couldn't keep his "Oh, my God" from slipping out. The entire living room had been re-arranged, and Olivia's sofa and fainting couch had all been covered with large swaths of brand new polyester fabric: deep purple and shocking pink. Olivia's simple, but tasteful arrangement, the four comfortable armchairs surrounding her beautiful oak coffee table, had been completely undone. Someone had moved everything against the far wall. The chairs were covered with lime green fabric.

All the art had been moved from the walls to the floor and there were a pair of drop-clothes covering a large portion of the floor. There were several cans of paint: two gallons of Glidden Marigold Petal, a bright orange, and two of Glidden Cool Cobalt, a blue. Luckily, they hadn't been opened.

Alex smiled weakly at the Rosens, and quickly offered an apology. "There must be some mistake. The painters must have come to the wrong address. Why don't you go out to the car and we'll head on to the next place. I just need to call the office and clear this up."

As the Rosens made their way out, Alex dialed the Ripton Police Department. He got the machine and quickly but calmly reported that the Stoughton place had been broken into and someone was getting ready to paint it. Emphasizing that Olivia Stoughton had expressly asked him to supervise the sale of the house, and there were, and are, absolutely no plans to paint it.

Luckily for Chief Paul, the frantic calls had started at eight in the morning, not six. Jimmy Welles said his shed had been broken into sometime last night and he was missing several painters' drop clothes, and some of his best brushes. He was due at nine at the new contemporary, the house right after Billy Beck's on the left side of Fairview Road. Now he would have to replace everything before he could even start the job. Could he drop a list off and make an official complaint so he could at least put in a claim with his insurance company?

Rebecca Brackett had called a few minutes later to say that the four cans of paint they were going to use to paint some of the floats for this year's I Love Ripton Day had gone missing from the Church basement.

Then when he heard Alex's message, the Chief quickly called Frank to have him meet him right away at the Stoughton place.

TWENTY-THREE

The first coffee at The Donut House and the accompanying blueberry muffin, a potent swirl of sugar and caffeine, had managed to rouse Abigail, the young and enthusiastic interior decorator. Who felt it necessary to explain once more that she really hadn't properly planned things out. That making do with the materials she was able to scrounge up only at the very last minute last night, well it's fair to say that just didn't cut it when it came to feng shui best practices.

Another sip of coffee, then quickly shifting from half-hearted apology to insisting that in the future she would require a whole lot more time if they actually expected her to do some quality re-decorating. Reminding them all that some of these homes needed major help. Thankfully she had stumbled upon paint colors that were bold and could add some spark to that dark and dim mausoleum. Because you had to start somewhere.

Abigail was the first to acknowledge that she was entirely self-taught. She had learned about feng shui late one night on a laptop that Tyler was fixing for Eli, a young community college student who worked part time at Fin, Fur, and Fly, the local pet shop. The point, Abigail quickly discovered, was to create balance and harmony, and to do that it was especially important to arrange your living space in such a way as to ensure energy flowed in the most positive ways. Because with all the disorder in the universe, everyone could and should do her part. She didn't remember everything she read but there was something about how feng, which was pronounced fen, was the wind, and the water was shui, sounding like schway. So where we put our furniture and where we slept and where we ate determined how the energy circulated.

While nobody had said anything specific, she could sense that everyone was a bit uneasy this morning. So she tried again. It was pretty obvious that the feng shui in that Ripton house was completely messed up. She felt death there. Maybe in the past the life force of the owners could counteract all that dark wood. But now it was pretty obvious some bright color and new energy was needed.

It was too bad, she admitted, that the house didn't have the internet and she hadn't had the chance to access the online feng shui color wheel. It had a whole lot of important information about color. Like blues and greens and purples and whites were either wood or earth or fire or wind, and they promoted different feelings.

Purple stimulated wealth and prosperity. Red was fire and helped with fame and your reputation. Pink promoted love and receptivity and relationships. Which is where she got the idea to redecorate the chairs with new fabric. To shake things up.

That orange, the best she could come up with under the circumstances, well maybe with the benefit of some caffeine, it's fair to say it wasn't perfect. She was hoping for something like a feng shui sun. Together with that cobalt blue, sort of like the ocean, which is where most life comes from. Because the trick is to get the colors working together just right.

Obviously, she needed more time. She had barely gotten the fabric over the furniture and the drop clothes over the table and book cases. But then, before she knew it, it was daylight with Elizabeth freaking out, telling everybody it was time to get out of there. Pledging she would work more efficiently next time. And to avoid misunderstandings, have the client sign off on the changes.

Speaking of which, now that she thought about it, she couldn't remember meeting the client. Or giving an estimate. Or signing an agreement, and getting a deposit. All the things she had read a well-prepared professional feng shui consultant needed to do. Of course, she hardly got enough time on the computer as it was, let alone have the opportunity to create and print out a contract. Hopefully, Elizabeth had taken care of all that, because knowing Tyler, it was highly unlikely he had remembered.

To be honest, so much of the long night was a blur. As the sugar from the second blueberry muffin hit the bloodstream, she reached for Tyler's cafe latte. Re-energized, she turned the paper placemat over and started to draw a couple of couches and some chairs.

When all of a sudden, one little Ernie sat down in the booth beside her, and two other Ernies across from her. Laughing.

"Art class, huh?" Bill sneered. "Missing high school?"

Buck, trying to match his brother, grabbed the pen and started to draw a tic tac toe game over the sketch.

Abigail looked from one to the other then to Bob who hadn't said anything yet and then told herself with great conviction:

"There's just no place for violence in interior design" and quickly melted away.

Tyler was very tired. He wasn't sure why the Ernies were here at The Donut House. Buck seemed to be furiously scribbling one game of tic tac toe after another while Bill was smirking with all the energy he could muster. Only Bob appeared embarrassed by their behavior.

Tyler was hoping that somehow he was day-dreaming, and that if he closed his eyes they'd go away. Because it didn't make sense they were all at The Donut House this early in the morning and not his mom's house.

But they were still there when he opened his eyes. Then Bill pushed him further into the farthest end of the booth. While Buck having beaten his invisible opponent was now furiously erasing any trace of what had been drawn before.

"So brother Tyler, well actually half-brother Tyler, not really brother Tyler," said Bill as he took the placemat from Buck and held it up, "What is this? What are you doing?"

Tyler watched as Bill's face, his brow marked by creases, looked down at the scribbled mess, unable to make any sense of it.

Tyler, too, wasn't really sure what it was at this point. "Beats me," he said.

Bill looked at Buck, then paused for a second and looked to Bob. "I don't think Dad is gonna be happy with a 'beats me,' is he Bob?"

Bob was hoping this didn't get too complicated, the way it sometimes did when in their dad's absence, Bill pretended to be smarter than he was. Asking questions like his dad did, as if he knew the answers, but like now, not really even understanding the question.

"Happy?" Bob repeated, knowing that nothing made his dad happy. Instead, pretty much everything made him unhappy. So what was the right answer to this dumb question? Maybe he'd try something new just for the hell of it, like repeating back what Bill had said: "Dad … I don't think Dad is gonna be happy with 'beats me.'"

"Right you are, Bob," as Bill smiled, then couldn't help but take it further. "Not happy, Tyler. Absolutely not happy. You know what our dad does with his belt when he's not happy."

Buck couldn't hide his involuntary shiver. As he started to rub his right shoulder, the most recent of the many landing places for Ernie's wide black leather belt.

Bill was sure he was on a roll: "Dad wants us to find out what you're up to, Tyler, and where you disappear to all the time."

Buck could still feel the belt, a strong reason he needed to get in on this action and earn a little credit for initiative. When Bill inevitably reported back to Ernie. So adding loudly, "and the money, Tyler!"

"The money?" Tyler asked, trying to remember what he had done with those Wash 'N Wait twenties?

"Dad wants his share of the money," Buck said. "Says you got to be making a bunch doing whatever it is you're doing. Sneaking around, stealing money from wherever it is you go. It's only fair what with Dad being your new dad in a way."

"Which makes us your brothers," Bill added. "So we should get some money too."

Tyler was trying to remember whether he had paid Natalie for the coffee and donuts. "Hey, Natalie, how much do I owe you?" he called out to her as she was putting a couple of frosteds into a to-go bag. She looked up: "You're cool, Tyler. You paid an hour ago."

"I gave Natalie my money," he told Bill. "I usually get a couple of blueberries. Maybe next time, if I see you here, I'll get you each a muffin."

Buck looked up. "Forget the muffin. I'd rather have a donut." Pointing to the display case, "Chocolate inside and out."

Bill wanted to smack Buck for letting Tyler off the hook. "Hold on. Dad isn't interested in donuts. He wants to know what's up." Then pointing down to the scribbled upon placemat.

All of a sudden Bob had an idea. "You were making a map, weren't you? Where you were going to steal something, right?"

But Buck was still dreaming about that chocolate donut and felt he ought to defend himself. "You know, Bill, I don't see you ever buying us any donuts."

Whatever patience Bill had marshaled was gone. His hand flew across the small space of the table to smack Buck across the face. Buck was stunned and tried as hard as he could not to break out in tears. Natalie who couldn't help but hear the loud whack, headed to the booth while yelling. "Out Bill! You've got exactly ten seconds to get the hell out of here before I call the cops. No way you're doing this on my shift," adrenaline surging, puffing herself

far larger than her five foot four frame.

Bill slowly began to regroup, leaning in toward Tyler. "We'll talk soon," then moving out of the booth. "Let's go Bob, we're outta here. Buck, get your ass in gear."

Tyler looked down at the placemat and while not quite sure why, slowly folded it and put it in his pocket.

TWENTY-FOUR

Danger took a moment from his muttering and impatient back and forth pacing to look down from his perch at Frank. It was pretty obvious his human was off. As was he, for while Danger enjoyed the constant noise that spilled from the big TV during the long day, he wasn't particularly happy about being left alone so much.

Frank, too, had been pacing. Because for the first time he felt that this break-in thing might be spinning out of control. The paint cans, the drop clothes, the odd and inappropriate fabric, well there was a crazed, manic feel to it all. It was one thing to playfully re-program a digital video recorder, but it was another matter altogether to seriously mess up someone else's house. This seemed completely over the top.

So he was trying to distract himself with chopping some fruit and broccoli for Danger, then refilling his water dish. While Danger moved down to hang impatiently on his little door, poised and ready to fly to freedom.

Frank had learned from Danger how important it was to spend some quality flock time together, eating and drinking, dedicating at least some time each day to check in with each other. So Frank made himself a turkey and Swiss on rye with mayo and put their meals on a couple of paper plates, then opened Danger's door so Danger could join him.

"Good boy," Danger offered. "Good boy ... I'm a gecko."

Frank shook his head: "Really, enough with the gecko!"

Danger was out and onto the kitchen table in a flash and quickly had half a grape in his beak. There was more to say but any answer would have to wait, because as soon as he was finished with the grape, there was a blueberry with his name on it.

"Geckos are lizards, Danger. Your favorite gecko, that little green GEICO gecko isn't even real. He just exists to sell you car insurance. In case you've forgotten, you're a Quaker parrot and you don't even drive. You fly. At least a little bit."

It was clear the blueberry might have to wait. Danger looked up to Frank and tried to speak a little slower, thinking that might help: "I'm a gecko ... I'm a gecko ... I'm a gecko." Three times the charm. Adding a Frank laugh, and only then, finished with his lesson, did he reach down for the blueberry.

"Well, two can play the same game, Danger: 'Fifteen minutes can save you fifteen per cent or more.' How's that?"

Danger finished his blueberry, then looked left, then right, and suddenly let loose another pitch perfect Frank laugh. He flew back to the top of his cage and looking down at Frank, cackled and declared: "Everybody knows that."

At which point Frank couldn't help himself, and uncontrolled laughter bubbled up and out.

Which earned a second "Everybody knows that. "

Frank laughed and laughed some more until Danger nodded, flew back to the table, and they laughed together.

"Yes, Danger, everybody knows that."

It took a while but the laughs slowed and Frank got up from the table to find a treat for Danger.

His sandwich supper done, Frank found himself thinking about the Stoughton house. It was hard to square what happened there with the methodical, exceedingly careful actions of the previous break-ins. This was chaotic and undisciplined vandalism, verging on the violent. Like trying to wrench a house from a century ago into the new millennium without subtlety or care.

This was also the second time that something had happened to a house that Alex was connected to. In this case, more than just connected. This house was now his responsibility. Did any of this have something to do with Alex, and if so, what?

Danger, having finished his food, slowly walked up to Frank: "Chase … So you can."

TWENTY-FIVE

The Ripton Police Department operated out of a single modest room on the second floor of Town Hall. There were two desks, each with a chair, a phone and a couple of lamps and old-fashioned leather desk pads, two filing cabinets, a town map on the wall, and four wooden chairs for people who came to see them. Like every other small town in the Southern Berkshires without jails of their own, when the occasion called for it, they'd transport the problematic offender to the lockup in Great Barrington.

Alex spent about a half-hour telling both Frank and Chief Paul that he had last been to the house four days before just to do some vacuuming, and to make sure everything looked good. Because beside the Rosens, he had another interested client, plus there were two other independent brokers who also had clients who wanted to see the place. Reiterating that when he left Olivia Stoughton's everything was in perfect order.

Alex was completely stunned, not to mention totally embarrassed, that the Rosens were witnesses to the chaos. He insisted that he had never, ever authorized anyone to do any work on the place. That if he had, he would surely have hired professionals. Whoever these people were, they seemed not to have a clue about the house, its furniture, its aesthetics, and its history. Thankfully, he had gotten there in time, because they probably would have ruined the entire house.

TWENTY-SIX

Tony was just plain pissed off: "Man, I keep having to say this. There's no way they're going to respect you if you continue to put up with their shit. I say take your chances and pop the sonofabitch. One good shot to Bill's nose and the little Ernies fold. Remember how he punked out of his martial arts class?

"I know you're thinking there are three of them, and they're bigger and stronger, but what the fuck. You want them telling you where you can go and what you can do? Like The Donut House. That's your territory, man! Your place for coffee and muffins. Everybody there knows you. Natalie knows you. Remember the time their dishwasher was on the fritz, and they were all freaking out, and you went behind the counter and had it fixed before Natalie even got the plumber on the phone.

"You don't stick up for yourself, it's over. Otherwise, put me on the case. I know I promised to stay out of sight ever since the knife but you just give me the word and I'll show them what's up." The threat hung in the air. No one else said a word.

TWENTY-SEVEN

Ernie cut himself shaving. All because, boom, with no warning, Tyler popped into his head. The little prick was haunting him.

Which all began that time Tyler pulled the knife on him. Surprising the shit out of him. Changing everything. Now never knowing if or when it might happen again.

Discipline. That was what he had tried to teach his kids. It was all about the discipline. Listening to your father. Tyler had no discipline and no sense of respect, and Ernie knew how easily his lousy attitude could spread and infect his own boys. Of course, it was all her fault. Doris. Spoiled the kid rotten. It was pretty obvious he wasn't taking those pills they got from the head doctor. But she hardly noticed. Or cared that Tyler used his tools. Or cared about all the electronics he had in the shed.

Who knew where he was ripping all that stuff from? Plus if this stuff was what he was willing to leave out in the open, what had he done with the really good stuff?

Ernie reminded himself that he had given the kid several breaks along the way. But nothing had come of it. Then the knife to his throat. Could easily have killed him. Fact is, Tyler was dangerous and he'd be completely justified if he got rid of him.

With Doris here, it's not like Tyler was ever going to leave town. Even when he was drinking peacefully at The Back Door, somehow Tyler would pop into his head, and with it the worst bad mood ever.

It might have been different if Tyler invited him and his boys to help out with his … well whatever this hustle was. Then, maybe, there'd be no need to …

TWENTY-EIGHT

Doris was sick and tired of turning patients over, of taking temperatures, checking blood pressure, and wiping drool from the chins of the stroke victims at the nursing home. Then coming home completely exhausted to a living room filled with empty beer bottles and greasy pizza boxes and pizza crust left everywhere. The cigarette butts stubbed out on her plates.

So pissed she made the mistake of telling Ernie that if he wasn't going to work, well the least he could do was to get off his ass and clean the place once in a while.

For someone with more than half a dozen beers in him and God knows how many shots, Ernie was surprising fast. Before she knew it, he was up off the couch, the beer bottle in his right hand crashing across her cheek. Barely able to maintain her footing, swaying woozily back and forth, it was only until she watched the blood splattering against the floor that she realized how badly hurt she was. Luckily, Ernie was all about congratulating himself for showing her who was boss, so she was able to grab her purse, a washcloth, and stumble outside and back to her car before he realized she was gone. Still trembling, she drove to the emergency room with one hand, the other hand pressing as hard as she could to stop the bleeding.

Doris, of course, knew the routine. She told the admitting nurse she was trying to make an apple pie from scratch when she cut herself with the paring knife. Which, based on her experience, she knew sounded just plausible enough to keep the police out of it. The last thing she wanted was the cops going after Ernie or those busybody social workers coming around.

Because somehow whenever someone with a badge or authority came to the house, Ernie summoned every ounce of intelligence he had neglected over the years to actually make himself utterly believable. Sensible and sober though his cells were bathed in booze. Showing Academy Award-winning sensitivity and concern. Even loving. So Doris quickly surrendered. Then, once again, there was the Ernie she had fallen in love with, the Ernie she could grow old with. The Ernie who could actually say he was sorry.

She had done such a good job stopping the bleeding, she was able to wait there patiently for the hour it took to get to see the doctor and get the stitches she needed. Convinced that when she got back home, things would have quieted down and life with Ernie would be tolerable again.

TWENTY-NINE

"What am I missing?" Frank asked as he threw the coins. Two heads and a tail, an eight. Two tails and a head, a seven. Another two heads and a tail, an eight. Three tails, a six, and a changing line. A second three tails, another six. Then, three heads, his third consecutive changing line, a nine."

He watched as Katie finished drawing the two hexagrams, then turned the yellow pad so that he could see what she had drawn:

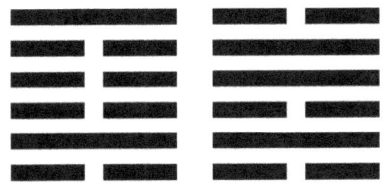

He found the first hexagram, "Mêng," then bookmarked the second, "K'un." He began reading:

Mêng / Youthful Folly

In this hexagram we are reminded of youth and folly in two different ways …

Stopping in perplexity on the brink of a dangerous abyss is a symbol of the folly of youth …

Frank paused, "I'm certainly more guilty of folly than youth at this point in my life. This passage suggests that my perpetrator/perpetrators are also confused. Young and possibly even more foolish than me, and in danger. Which matches my feeling that things might easily spin out of control."

"Well," Katie offered, "let's see what else the *I Ching* suggests:

… the two trigrams also show the way of overcoming the follies of youth. Water is something that of necessity flows on.

When the spring gushes forth, it does not know at first where it will go. But its steady flow fills up the deep place blocking its progress, and success is attained.

Frank laughed: "Yet another benefit of country living: water from gushing springs instead of faucets. I'm glad to hear about my eventual success but I'd like to know how to make that happen."

Katie smiled and jumped ahead:

YOUTHFUL FOLLY has success.
It is not I who seek the young fool;
The young fool seeks me.

"Uh oh," Frank offered, "I must not have gotten the *I Ching* memo because I've been driving around dealing with what he's been up to. That's me seeking him, and until this mess he made at the Stoughton place, thinking he was quite clever."

"Well, there's more, Frank:

In the time of youth, folly is not an evil. One may succeed in spite of it, provided one finds an experienced teacher and has the right attitude toward him. This means, first of all, that the youth himself must be conscious of his lack of experience and must seek out the teacher. Without this modesty and this interest there is no guarantee that he has the necessary receptivity ... This is the reason why the teacher must wait to be sought out instead of offering himself.

"Frank, like most young people he or she might be in over his head and looking for a better way to do things, even if he doesn't fully know it yet. So the cleverness you saw early on might be something very different than evil. Which is perhaps why the *I Ching* is imagining its own version of a Big Brother program. With you as that kind of a teacher. Maybe if you offer the opportunity, and he chooses to take it, you can help transform, and build upon that cleverness. To help make sure that along the way he learns something important about life."

"Right now I'm more a policeman than a teacher. So I do hope he's looking for me, and that he finds me sooner than later."

"Well, if I'm remembering 'Mêng' correctly," turning the pages, "there's some advice that specifically relates to that."

> Law is the beginning of education. Youth in its inexperience is inclined at first to take everything carelessly and playfully. It must be shown the seriousness of life. A certain measure of taking oneself in hand, brought about by strict discipline, is a good thing.

"Suggesting you bring both law and learning to bear. Trying as best you can to distinguish between carelessness and criminality:

> To bear with fools in kindliness brings good fortune …

> The son is capable of taking charge of the household.

"And, not surprisingly, the longer explanation:

> These lines picture a man who has … the inner superiority and strength that enable him to tolerate with kindliness the shortcomings of human folly. The same attitude is owed to women as the weaker sex.

"As always, I remind myself that this was written a very long time ago by men, and so I take this 'weaker sex' stuff with as many grains of salt as I can gather …"

> One must understand them and give them recognition in a spirit of chivalrous consideration. Only this combination of inner strength with outer reserve enables one to take on the responsibility of directing a larger social body with real success.

"Now if you were asking about your relationship with Penny I would emphasize understanding and chivalry." Adding with a smile: "But I'm pretty sure you weren't, so … "

"Thanks, dear. Maybe next time. For the moment, I'm still focused on this young fool. And now with the help of 'Mêng' trying to better accept the shortcomings of human folly I'm encountering these days."

"Well, let's focus on this foolishness, Frank:

> For youthful folly it is the most hopeless thing to entangle itself in empty imaginings. The more obstinately it clings to such unreal fantasies, the more certainly will humiliation overtake it …

"In which case, dear brother, this approaching 'humiliation' might explain these dark thoughts of yours."

> Often the teacher, when confronted with such entangled folly, has no other course but to leave the fool to himself for a time, not sparing him the humiliation that results. This is frequently the only means of rescue.

A convenient way of turning his inability to find this guy into something positive, Frank thought. Let the fool contemplate his failure to remake the Stoughton home. Smiling, as he imagined explaining to the Chief how leaving the trespasser to his own devices would succeed in the end. Imagining the Chief telling the Selectboard that "often a Police Chief has no other course but to leave the fool to himself for a time …" Then, just as quickly wondering if his old precinct in the city would take him back?

When luckily Katie short-circuited his increasingly confused musings. "There's still more about your law and order business:

> In punishing folly
> It does not further one
> To commit transgressions …
> The only thing that furthers
> Is to prevent transgressions.

Sometimes an incorrigible fool must be punished ... But the penalty should not be imposed in anger; it must be restricted to an objective guarding against unjustified excesses.

Punishment is never an end in itself but serves merely to restore order ...

Governmental interference should always be merely preventive and should have as its sole aim the establishment of public security and peace.

Frank's sigh slipped out without warning. Thinking that at least the *I Ching* had caught their fool. Then the question became about the most appropriate punishment ... And could he make that happen? Locating, stopping his own inexperienced youth? Delivering a victory even if delayed? Would he see the Chief smiling and the Selectboard satisfied? Would he still have his job?

Katie put the *I Ching* down, and paused long enough to wait for Frank to return from what she knew was his own private daydream-land.

"You know, Frank, despite the eventual success of 'Mêng', let me remind you that you asked 'What am I missing?' Well, the *I Ching* suggests that on behalf of the government of Ripton, Massachusetts you're dealing with a youthful offender who may be moving toward even greater problems. If I remember correctly, not only can 'folly' be a lack of good sense, but in older days, the word was used to describe tragically foolish actions. From the French, there's *'folie,'* madness, a derivation of mad or *'fou.'*

"So there's a warning here, and maybe I'm emphasizing it because it took me much too long to fully appreciate the danger Penny was facing, but the *I Ching* uses the word 'incorrigible.' So beyond the standard teenage stupidity, there might be something more ingrained and deeply rooted and more difficult to control ...

"I don't know why but all of a sudden I flashed on Herb the artist and his wife, Cynthia, those friends of Carl and Theresa who lived in Greenwich Village. I seem to remember that Cynthia had gone with Carl one time to Nicaragua to help out right after the Sandinistas won, when things were very hopeful. Anyway they adopted this little boy. Do you remember Barry? He was closer to my age than yours. I was always frightened when I was around Barry. I tried to talk to Theresa about it but she just thought I was being my usual oversensitive self. But even as a kid, I could tell there was something deeply wrong with him. Like his wiring was off. There was this great anger inside him, an unpredictable rage.

"Not to completely lose you all over again, Frank, but some people can see the subtle auras we project, the human energy field that radiates out from people, sort of like their own private rainbow. I'm not able to see those colors in the way they say they can, but for me, it's more like a hypersensitivity to what is going on inside of people, and how they are feeling. But if you pay close attention to the way they look at you, how they act in the world, then you start to see more than one layer to them.

"Sorry if I'm taking the long way around here, but I remember not being surprised at all when at seventeen Barry murdered their next door neighbor. Carl and Theresa seemed so terribly shocked, but to me it was as if they had never really seen the real Barry."

"So you're suggesting I might be dealing with someone who's more than just foolish but seriously ill, dangerously ill?"

"I don't know, but what I learned working with Penny is that there are many things at work that you just can't, you just don't see at first. People you might not be seeing clearly, or who for the moment are lurking, just out of sight. So, yes, I'm suggesting it's worth preparing yourself for that.

"Then to confuse matters even more, what you're seeing could be what it seems, the kind of chaotic youthful folly that is just plain annoying, maybe even mildly criminal, but not anywhere near the homicidal madness of Donnie and Petey Kean."

"Unfortunately, Katie, in my experience there's always a fine line here. People who live their annoying, pain-in-the-ass, basically everyday unremarkable neurotic lives can sometimes snap, and all of a sudden, you're dealing with the consequences of an uncontrollable, sometimes lethal burst of violence."

Frank realized how tight his neck and shoulders had become. He took a series of deep breaths, closed his eyes for a second, and tried to let some of the tension slip away.

When he opened his eyes again, he smiled at Katie: "I'm thinking it's time for those apricot ginger scones I brought from Fuel." He offered Katie a scone and took one for himself.

Katie got up and went to fix herself some tea. When Katie

settled herself, she looked over to Frank and asked, "OK, big brother. What do you think? Are we ready for the second hexagram?"

Frank found the next passage and began to read aloud:

K'un/Oppression (Exhaustion)

... everywhere superior men are oppressed and held in restraint by inferior men ...

Times of adversity ... can lead to success if they befall the right man ...

He who lets his spirit be broken by exhaustion certainly has no success. But if adversity only bends a man, it creates in him a power to react that is bound in time to manifest itself. No inferior man is capable of this. Only the great man brings about good fortune and remains blameless.

When adversity befalls a man, it is important above all things to be strong and to overcome the trouble inwardly. If he is weak, the trouble overwhelms him.

The *I Ching* reminding him there was adversity and trouble everywhere. Mr. Krause's kind of trouble. Now his trouble. Perhaps the broken spirit of his youthful fool. Impatient now, Frank skipped ahead to the final passage:

A man is oppressed by bonds that can easily be broken. The distress is drawing to an end. But he is still irresolute; he is still influenced by the previous condition and fears that he may have cause for regret if he makes a move. But as soon as he grasps the situation, changes his mental attitude, and makes a firm decision, he masters the oppression.

"Well Frank," Katie added, "let's imagine that our youthful

offender is in the midst of a difficult struggle. Oppressed. Distressed. Afraid. Perhaps that is the part of the story we haven't seen yet, don't know ... So let's hope that he or she finds a way out. Soon."

Frank was silent, then reached for another scone.

THIRTY

Until recently, Ernie's favorite, The Back Door, was your ordinary small town seedy bar, located a half block off the main drag in Brett, where the drinking began at eleven in the morning and continued on until closing at one or two or two-thirty the next morning, depending on whether the cops stopped by that night or not. But lately, with the passing of Old Man McIntyre and the intervention of his only daughter, Margaret, The Back Door had hired an Iraq War vet who actually had some restaurant experience, and a bunch of ideas about bringing in some new blood.

He began with a pool tournament, some Texas Hold'em charity poker games, got satellite TV and put in some new flat screens, with the premium baseball, hockey, football and basketball packages, and then started to book some rock and roll bands.

For Ernie, the changes were a royal pain. "Just another way to fuck me up," he told whoever was sitting next to him. So his way to fight back was to come early enough in the day to sit at the bar, slug whiskey, and sulk away as much of the day as he could before the new and younger crowd arrived and their organized activities began. But he hated that this wasn't his bar anymore.

It was at The Back Door that Ernie heard about the break-ins. Jack was the first shift bartender. His brother-in-law Pete was an auxiliary cop in Brett and so Jack was telling Ernie, well actually, the truth was he was really talking to the guy next to Ernie, saying that all the police departments in the South Berkshires were on alert now because someone was sneaking into empty houses and swiping things, appliances, even switching some furniture around. That no one so far had figured out who was behind it.

Ernie remembered the times he had seen Tyler sneaking around the shed, with all that stuff he had stashed. He was about to say something to Jack but then, even through the alcoholic haze that swirled about his pickled brain, he realized there just might be something in this for him. Because now his suspicions were based on something pretty close to official. The little prick was clearly holding out on him big time. Stealing things and using his tools and the shed to make a bundle.

Ernie was thinking about all those swanky houses around here, packed full of expensive stuff, diamonds probably, cash, and the best electronic gizmos. The kid had to be squirreling all this stuff somewhere and hiding the dough.

It took some major discipline to pry himself off the stool. But energized by the thought of everything he'd soon take from Tyler, he dug out a twenty for his last shots, and somehow found his car keys.

Ernie opened all four windows. That always helped when he drove back from the bar. Under the influence, they called it. He had only been caught twice but the third time and your license was gone and so it was important not to get caught again. So he tried really hard this time not to drive too fast or veer into the other lane too many times. Every once in a while it helped to give himself a sharp smack to keep from falling asleep.

Of course, thinking about how pissed he was at Tyler worked too. Then about Doris, who had never disciplined the kid in the first place. Doris feeling sorry for him just because his dad left, when the reason his dad left was probably because she spoiled the brat to begin with. If the kid had only come to him in the first place and let him in on the scam.

The first thing he did when he got back home was splash cold water all over his face. To get ready for the treasure hunt. Tyler was obviously a pretty good sneak but there weren't too many places he could hide things around here.

The boys were lounging on the living room couch arguing over the PlayStation again. Ernie grabbed Bill's ear and yanked him up. The effort almost sent Ernie flying but somehow his right foot managed to stabilize, and though he wobbled, he didn't fall over. Bob and Buck took the opportunity to slide over and gain control of the video game.

"Time for you bums to help," he growled. "I heard down at The Back Door that someone has been ripping off houses around here. I'm betting it's that weasel Tyler. So he's got to be hiding the stuff somewhere around here."

All of a sudden Ernie started to smile, then chuckle. He could see himself counting the cash.

"Just one of him. We're Ernie times four ... Now, what I'm thinking is that Bob and I should check out the shed. Bill, hey I'm talking about you, Bill. Stop rubbing that ear already and stop moping. You think it hurts now ... I'll show you what hurts! I want you and Buck to take apart Tyler's room inch by inch. Don't quit until you find something worthwhile. And don't even think about keeping any of the loot for yourself. Whatever it is: cash, jewelry, you better hand it over. Then I'll divide it."

As Ernie reached to grab the PlayStation controls from Buck, Bob immediately dropped his controller to the couch. Time had run out and the main thing now was to avoid any attempt Ernie might make at their ears.

Ernie waited till they stood up then grabbed Bob by the arm. As he moved him to the door, he looked back at Bill and Buck to yell: "Now! Start looking now!"

Ernie had promised Doris he'd fix the shed a couple of years ago but just hadn't gotten to it. At this point, it probably made more sense to tear it down. The roof was sagging and there were small holes in several sections. Ernie yanked the door open to the one big dilapidated room filled with piles and piles of stuff.

"Go back inside and get us some of those big black plastic garbage bags. We'll keep the good stuff and toss the rest."

Bob was glad to escape for even the very short amount of time it would take to get the bags. Because these were the most scary times. When Ernie had that crazed look in his eyes, the look he got when he was expecting some great big payday. When he was convinced he would win.

Like when Ernie, after an afternoon spent drinking himself half dead, head on the bar at The Back Door, had drunkenly daydreamed winning a million bucks in the lottery, even imagining the celebratory drive to Springfield to pick up his check. Then when he finally realized it hadn't happened convincing himself it was just about to. Somehow managing to get himself to the liquor store and back home clutching two hundred dollars worth of five-dollar lottery scratch tickets and some more Jack Daniels. But with each losing ticket, the curses grew louder. Until that last ticket, the dream defeated, and Ernie just had to throw his empty bottle of Jack through the living room window.

Or demanding to play basketball with Buck down by the skateboard park. Buck was smart enough to know this was a tricky proposition, but not smart enough to know what to do about it.

First, Buck decided to lose but Ernie screamed he wasn't playing hard enough. So Buck upped his game. You could see Ernie getting closer and closer to exploding as Buck started to win. Turning basketball into street fighting, an elbow into Buck's kidney, a knee to his groin. Until Buck, on the verge of tears, walked off the court. So Ernie called him a pussy, and threw the ball with everything he had into the back of Buck's head.

So they had learned it was the person closest to Ernie who would pay the worst price. As much as it would piss his dad off to waste time finding the garbage bags, at least Bob knew he was safe for those precious moments.

Meanwhile, Ernie was grabbing and throwing things out from the shed onto the grass. He was still woozy, slowly making the transition from The Back Door to home, from drunk to hung-over, a massive headache beginning to form behind his eyes, not quite sure what was junk and what might be worth something.

"Bob," he screamed. "Where the fuck are my bags? I need bags, Bob. Don't make me come in and get them!"

Whereupon Bob, the box of bags in his hand, had a brainstorm. He moved quickly to Tyler's room, where Bill and Buck were sitting on Tyler's bed, smoking a joint, a box of chocolate chip cookies between them, giggling as they checked out one of Tyler's weird hand-drawn maps, with little roads and little boxes of different colors that were probably houses. A few with little x's beside them.

Bob tapped Buck on the shoulder: "Dad has a job for you. He wants you to bring these bags and help figure out what's what in the shed. He called me a moron. Said you're the smartest of the three. Congratulations!" Helping him up and slowly urging him out the door.

Bob sat down and took the joint from Bill. He started to relax.

Buck moved slowly, watching as Ernie tossed stuff out of the shed like a maniac, taking a circuitous path, trying his best to make sure he wouldn't get beaned by a flying toaster. By the time he reached the shed, he had opened the box of bags, thinking the easier he made this, the less chance his dad would go psycho on him. He carefully pulled out a single black bag. Ernie was leaning into the shed, his left arm in and rooting around for something to grab. Buck eased the bag to Ernie's free right hand.

"Here's the bag, dad."

"Took you long enough, Bob." Throwing the bag to the ground. "But I'm tossing. You're bagging."

"Buck, dad. Bob's helping Bill."

"Bob, Buck, Bill. Who gives a fuck. Take all that shit I've

already thrown out and start putting it in the bag. Make one last check to see if I missed anything. Like diamonds, pearls, anything shiny, and no pocketing any of the cash, even dimes and quarters, especially quarters. I can use them for tips."

Back inside the house, the joint finished, Bob began to get paranoid, imagining Ernie busting in, seeing that they hadn't done jack shit in Tyler's room. Then feeling better because at least he had the map.

Bill saw Bob's slight smile as he took Tyler's drawing and began to fold it up. Just as he was about to put it in his shirt pocket, Bill reached out to grab it: "I'll keep this. Just in case it's important."

Bob wondered whether Bill was stoned enough so that he might actually be able to take him this time, but realized he was much too stoned himself. He could easily get his ass kicked.

Instead, he rolled off the bed to check whether Tyler had stashed anything underneath. Anything he could use for his father's inevitable show and tell. When rummaging through some Big Mac wrappers and empty French fries containers, he felt a bunch of books and magazines.

"He's got some books under here," Bob announced, pushing them out from beneath the bed. But Bill was focused on checking Tyler's clothes in the closet, growing more frustrated with every additional empty pocket. When in one of Tyler's worn plaid shirts, he found a crumpled twenty. He slowly shifted so that Bob couldn't see him slip the bill into his right pants pocket.

"Great work, Bob, let me finish with the shirts. Why don't you check the books and I'll join you in a minute or two," imagining his new found twenty turning into a bacon cheeseburger and hot fudge sundae.

Bob started with "Berkshire Maps," Tyler's collection of maps of every town in the county. There were three different issues of Berkshire Homebuyer's Guide. A bunch of used books: *The Idiot's Guide to Computer Repair*, *Feng Shui Decorating on $10 a Day*, *The Art of War* by some guy named Sun Tsu, and *The Merry Adventures of Robin Hood*, by Howard Pyle. Bob quickly flipped through them looking for any cash Tyler might have stashed.

Then he took a second look at *Robin Hood*, deciding to slip it back beneath the bed for later, thinking he could always pretend he had missed it.

Bill continued to check Tyler's odd collection of clothes. Many still had those little colored tags from the dry cleaners. Weird styles and wild colors that somehow just pissed Bill off. Throwing clothes out of the closet and onto the floor. Shirts on hangers still covered by plastic, light-weight jackets with all kinds of patches: "Reid & Sons Laundry and Dry Cleaning," "Compton's Satellite TV," "Brett Lawn Services," "Brinks Home Security," "Terminix," "Kelly Electric," and "Verizon." Thinking that these at least were cool, kind of like bowling shirts or his Red Sox jacket. So he kept them on the pole and yelled over to his brother:

"Bob, put those books down and get your ass over here. There's a whole bundle of clothes down here on the floor in the closet. I want you to check them in case I missed something."

Bill was flinging them out one by one as he moved from the center of the mess to the right hand corner. When suddenly, touching wood and metal, he thought maybe he had found a box of cash. Then he heard the click, and the metal bar snapped with surprising force across his fingers. Bill screamed as he yanked his mousetrapped hand from the closet, cursing and yelling for Bob to help.

Meanwhile, outside, an increasingly annoyed Ernie was haphazardly tossing items out the open door of the shed while Buck did his best to catch the smaller items like the occasional dirty wrench, the flashlights, and old toasters, while dodging the items that might seriously maim him, like the three manual typewriters Ernie flung at him, one after the other.

Then Buck heard the scream as Ernie's left hand found another mousetrap, and with the shock of the snap, jerking up uncontrollably, smashing his head against a rafter. Buck looked in just as Ernie lost his balance and came crashing to the floor. When just a millisecond later an old microwave teetered and fell from Tyler's jury-rigged shelf onto Ernie's right leg. Buck couldn't help but think for the first time in a very long time that just maybe there was a God. Then he took a long, deep breath, yelled out to Bill and Bob, and reluctantly went to help his dad.

Ernie lay there, watching as several mice scrambled over him, yelling: "My fucking leg," wanting but unable to kill the mice, who were moving much too fast, dreaming of grabbing Tyler by the neck, whose fault this whole thing was. Instead, he settled for grabbing Buck's arm as soon as he got within reach. "Get this fucking thing off my leg."

Buck, whose right arm was still tightly gripped by Ernie, tried to lift the microwave with his left hand. But that just moved it closer to Ernie's kneecap, prompting another scream and a new round of cursing. Without thinking Ernie moved his hand from Buck's arm and tried to smack him in the head. But Buck successfully ducked, then managed to get both his hands under the microwave and lift it off his dad. "About fucking time," Ernie managed, then started to moan.

Bill and Bob finally made it to the shed and managed to help their dad up and out and into the backseat of the car. But that didn't stop the constant barrage of Ernie's moans and curses, as Bill and Buck settled into the front seat. Yelling out the rear window: "Bob, you make fucking sure that while I'm in the emergency room you go through that crap in the shed. Put aside anything that might bring us dough, and keep your greedy hands off the cash!"

Bob waited and watched as the car pulled away. Then moved quickly to Tyler's room, reaching beneath the bed to gather *Robin Hood*, and taking it to the room he and Buck shared. At least he had the upper bunk. Stuffing the book in the extra pillow he hardly ever used.

Then Bob went back outside. For the first time in a very long time, he was alone. Hard to remember but it seemed as if the last time he was absolutely all by himself was high school just after Bill dropped out. Unfortunately, Bill flunked just about everything he took in his school career, and had been left back early in the game. So from the fourth grade on, Bob had to share his classes with his older brother. And Bill's inappropriate hostility to both teachers and fellow students alike couldn't help but continually spill over onto him.

Left to his own devices, Bob probably would have done well in school. Several teachers had praised his writing and his storytelling. But Ernie took advantage of Bill's expulsion to pressure Bob and Buck to leave school as well, thinking of the cheap labor they represented and all the school supplies and decent school clothes he wouldn't have to spring for. Finding ever more clever ways to satisfy the School District by describing their obligatory chores as home schooling.

The inside of the shed, and now thanks to Ernie, the outside as well was a complete mess. Buck, obviously overwhelmed by all the stuff Ernie had thrown at him, hadn't bagged any of it. So Bob decided to start with everything that had already made its way outdoors.

There were several old typewriters, manuals and electrics, that somehow hadn't been completely trashed. The glass door to one toaster oven had been smashed, and another toaster had lost its up and down lever. The three VCRs had been scratched real bad when they crash-landed and he had no idea whether they would ever record again.

So he began to pile them neatly up against the shed, with a begrudging but growing sense of appreciation for Tyler's willingness to tackle such a wide variety of mechanical challenges. For the tiniest of moments, he wondered if he and Tyler could have been friends in other circumstances. But the image of the taunting, and the torture that would come of it ever so quickly overtook the daydream, and he returned to the task.

Once he had stacked everything on the outside, he decided to turn his attention to the inside. The first thing he removed was the large microwave. It was surprisingly heavy and he could see bloodstains on the corner where it had smashed his dad's leg. No wonder his dad was headed to the hospital. This sucker could cause some serious damage. If only it had hit him in the head.

There were a couple of old Power Mac's, the gray towers, some PCs, and three monitors. Tyler had a big box filled with computer hard drives and motherboards, a coffee can filled with memory chips. With some large rubber bands, Tyler had adapted a silverware tray to secure a bunch of pliers and odd-shaped spindly screwdrivers. There was another coffee can filled with a variety of magnifying glasses. And, beneath it, a series of service manuals from several computer companies.

Once he managed to haul out a deceptively heavy old-fashioned sewing machine with foot pedal, and dismantle a wall of small televisions, Bob could see some sense to what had seemed complete chaos. There was a slender pathway to the rear of the shed leading to a work table, chair and lamp. On an easel were a couple of old posters Tyler had found from the sixties, several black runners standing on a podium with their fists raised. With the words "Power To The People" in bold type. Plus a multi-colored psychedelic poster for a Jefferson Airplane concert at The Fillmore West.

Bob could see that Tyler had covered a long extension cord with a throw rug. He followed it to a crack in the far wall. Then when he went back out and around, he saw how Tyler had carefully buried then slipped it under Mr. Murphy's fence. Tapping into one of the Murphy's outdoor outlets by the garage they hardly used. Guessing Tyler was also sharing their wireless network. Smiling as he went back inside, appreciating even more Tyler's idea of people power.

Hidden beneath the work table, he found another small dense machine. He struggled to lift it onto the table. It had to weigh more than thirty pounds. The ND 045-110V Manual Key Duplicator.

Bob took a look at his watch. It was four twenty-five. Somehow they had been gone two glorious and peaceful hours. Two hours that were actually interesting. When he hadn't had to flinch, and wasn't waiting for something to come flying at his head.

He really liked Tyler's hiding place. He wished he had one. The dirt didn't matter. The mess didn't matter. It was a tiny corner of the world where you could think and work, maybe write and breathe easy.

He seemed to have made a decision. He returned the ND 045 to its nook below the table. He slowly and carefully rebuilt the TV wall and as best he could recreated the jumble of equipment that had effectively shielded Tyler's inner sanctuary.

Bob went back outside and spent the next hour bagging what was broken and returning what wasn't. When he was done and the sweat was slowly trickling down his face, he went back to the house. As he washed, he could see in the mirror that his eyes were alive and wide and that he was smiling.

When they came home, which they unfortunately would, he would simply explain that he went through everything and that it was just a bunch of junk. Which is why he left the mess for Tyler to deal with. If Tyler had diamonds or pearls and coins and cash, they were someplace else.

THIRTY-ONE

Tyler made it home about three in the morning. He could see some blood-stained bandages in the garbage, and immediately went to check on his mom. He took a peek at them in bed, his mother and Ernie taking turns to snore, both looking the worse for wear. His mom's face was a patchwork of bruises. He knew what that meant. When he headed for the bathroom, he could see his room had been trashed.

It was all he could do to squelch Tony's desire to go after Ernie right then and there. Then almost immediately, the chaos, all the voices at full blast, with completely different ideas about what to do and where to go. He quickly found the newly prescribed painkillers in the bathroom cabinet. He took a couple of Percocet from his mom and a couple of OxyContin from Ernie.

There was no denying the headaches were getting worse. Not that they were ever not bad, but lately they were close to crippling.

He couldn't remember a time when he hadn't had them. When he was twelve he had a job after school carrying groceries out from the store to the parking lot, and he could remember sometimes carrying the bags while almost on the verge of blacking out. It was as if his entire head from temple to temple was caught in a vice. There was a throbbing pain behind his eyes, and his neck and shoulder muscles would contract, turning his upper back into hard steel.

He was smart enough to get out of the house. Then found himself in the driveway behind the wheel. There were always bottles of Excedrin PM and Tylenol and aspirin in the glove department. A spare can of Pepsi. But today the stars took pity on him and offered up a spare Axert, probably the most effective of the very expensive migraine prescription drugs he always searched for in the medicine cabinets of the houses he was caretaking. There was Imitrex, and Zomig, or sing hallelujah, Axert. The greatest gift, so he was always careful not to take more than he needed.

By quickly downing the pill, and getting the hell away from home, he might be able to shut everyone up. And make it to one of his houses before the drug made driving too dangerous.

*   *   *

The next morning, as the sun sliced through the windshield, Elizabeth made the transition from a drug-induced sleep to yawning then coherent enough to begin explaining once again how important it was to develop a long-range plan. Living hand to mouth, waking up in the car, well this was risky behavior and a clear indication of self-destructive, short-term thinking. Luckily her lecture was cut short by the sound of a car turning in from Route 23. Tyler ducked down just as Alex and Penny drove past the secluded driveway of the Pierce house on their way to the Stoughton house.

The cleaning company had gone through the entire house. Everything was back in place and looked great. As crazy as the whole experience had been, in a weird way Alex was relieved. Because the Rosens might very well have bought the place. If only to change it all.

These days more and more of their clients, many with seemingly unlimited funds, were buying then tearing down what they didn't like, including perfectly fine hundred-year-old properties and small forests, then spending enormous amounts of money to build idiosyncratic mansions in their own image.

Now that the Rosens were on to other properties, Alex was thinking that given Olivia's great attention to detail and her exquisite grace, this just might be Penny's dream house. More and more he could see her slipping without effort into Olivia's world: a world so aesthetically pleasing and without any of the pretension Penny wanted to avoid.

Alex loved its gentle access to the water. The path that so effortlessly blended with the surrounding woods you could easily miss it from across the lake. Unlike so many of the other lake properties, it was without the accompanying showy boathouse, but had instead a half-century-old beautifully handcrafted raft connected by a simple but sturdy ten foot ramp that the Grayson boys – Olivia had referred to them as boys well into their fifties – would haul to shore every autumn before the ice came, then restore late the next spring.

Tyler watched as they pulled into the Stoughton place. He wasn't sure why but he felt bad: he had the vague sense that a line had been crossed here, and that for the first time in his house borrowing he might unknowingly have violated the code he had set for himself. His version of Robin Hood: these houses were safe places. His Sherwood Forest. That in return for a place to stay, he would find a way to repay the favor and leave it better than he found it. A fixed clock radio, a toaster repaired. But when he looked out at the Stoughton's driveway, his face grew hot. He tried hard to recall exactly what might have happened, but all he saw looking back was darkness. No one else seemed anxious to help him out.

Penny loved the path leading to the house, how the trees formed a larger more natural version of a man-made arbor. As they walked toward the house, Penny felt as if she was leaving the contemporary world behind. The smell of pine, the bright light fading to shade.

As Alex opened the door to the vestibule, and Penny saw the simple but artful wood pegs, she thought maybe this is what I need most: a kind of time-travel, a return to something older and more reliable. She remembered how Alex had talked about Olivia's paintings, and she could see art in just about everything around her. The time-weathered wooden kitchen cabinets and counters, the extra large roman numeral clock Olivia had rescued from an abandoned railroad station waiting room in northwestern Connecticut, the wide-board wooden floors. All of which reminded Penny of the comfort of her family's lake house in Little Pointe. While blessedly lacking any of its treacherous emotional baggage.

Penny moved into the living room, to see it as Olivia had left it, the beautifully tasteful couch and sofa, the built-in bookcases lovingly filled with leather-bound books, the windows looking out at the trees and the sliver of lake peeking out in the distance, while the birds offered a stereophonic backdrop, home and nature seamlessly matched. Thankfully, Olivia had resisted the modern day temptation to convert her wide stone fireplace to a gas-burning faux wood facsimile. Penny imagined many a warm night watching real logs burn.

Because Olivia loved to grow and cook as much local food as she could, she had integrated her six-burner Garland professional stove into her large traditional kitchen. Penny absolutely loved the little eating nook that Olivia had created off the kitchen for the overwhelming majority of times she hadn't wanted to use her more formal dining room.

Both the downstairs and upstairs bathrooms had large, long

claw-foot bathtubs. There was a study downstairs with a beautiful roll-top desk and comfortable reading chair. Penny could see herself, legs curled up beneath her, reading for hours on end.

As Penny checked the three upstairs bedrooms, Alex wondered if he had fallen under some spell of wishful thinking, a mirage of his own making. Alex was glad to help his clients find a house that worked. But he had never felt anything so deeply satisfying as the feeling that was growing within. He could imagine Olivia smiling, and could easily imagine Penny at home here.

Penny, too, was smiling. She asked Alex if she could see Olivia's artwork. Together they went downstairs to the basement. Despite her seeming disregard for recognition, Olivia had clearly cared for her creations. She had built beautiful cabinets and racks for the work.

Penny carefully looked through the drawings, then paintings. Olivia used simple, direct strokes to create extraordinarily vibrant landscapes: the lake at dawn, at dusk, from many different vantage points. Penny, who had spent some of the happiest hours of her life in her own gardens, was thrilled to see how Olivia had brought to life her Ripton flowers and vegetables, captured with courageous colors: shades of yellows and reds and blues and purples that Penny felt she was seeing for the first time.

Alex watched as Penny carefully looked from one painting to another, her quiet excitement visible, eyes sparkling, head nodding ever so slightly.

Penny closed the cabinet, then looked up at Alex: "I'm going to head outside for a bit to look around the front of the house again, then take a walk down to the lake. I just need to think a bit. I'll be back in about ten minutes."

Alex watched as Penny headed up the stairs and made sure everything was back where it belonged in the basement.

*　　　　　*　　　　　*

Tyler could feel something shifting for him and for the house. He saw the lady walking around the front yard. He remembered seeing her before, but this time, she seemed to be here in a strong way, belonging here. He could sense that this house was no longer available.

Then for a brief moment he could see Abigail moving things

about in the living room, the odd colored fabric. So very embarrassed by that quick bright flash of memory, the knowledge that he hadn't done right by this house. It lessened the shame only a little knowing the lady would do a good job here, and help to make things better again.

*   *   *

Somewhere at the edge of consciousness Penny heard a car starting. She looked up to see an old red car turn from a driveway up the road and head off. Then returned to thinking about Olivia's house.

She had heard of people spending years looking for a house. Now, all of a sudden, she could see herself in the kitchen making breakfast – she had almost said for Frank – and kneeling in the garden, her hands planting. She saw Olivia's paintings freed from the basement, alive and proudly displayed on the walls.

As she walked slowly through the trees toward the lake, she could see the sun sparkling diamond-like upon the small patch of blue green water. Even though Olivia owned twenty acres, she had only used the smallest portion of it, leaving the woods as woods. And because of that, you couldn't feel the neighbors.

With every passing minute, she was more and more willing to acknowledge that she would indeed be living here, overcome with a deep sense of appreciation for what Olivia had and hadn't done. After the great trauma of last year, she was so very glad to be alone standing now before this small world of water, water that looked and felt as it might have a hundred years before. This water she would soon be sharing her life with. Slowly the tears trickled down her cheeks.

THIRTY-TWO

Bob snuck into their bedroom at about two in the morning, silently going through Ernie's pockets, his wallet, and Doris' purse. Managing to get away with a twenty and a ten and two singles, thinking they probably wouldn't miss thirty bucks.

Doris was up by six-thirty. Glad to be heading for an extra morning nursing shift in Connecticut, and on her way to McDonald's for breakfast-to-go as Ernie and the kids slept on.

It had been days since Doris had seen Tyler long enough to talk to. Not that she was ever any good at talking to him; or for that matter any good at being a mom, certainly not his mom. Or to Ernie's kids, who, if truth be told, she didn't even like, except maybe Bob a bit of the time. Bob only because she could sometimes see just a tiny glimpse of kindness in him, just an occasional hint that he saw her as a human being. Or maybe she was confused and it was simply pity. Even so, anything was better than the vacant coldness of the other two.

In Tyler's eyes, she just saw pain and sadness, his endless vulnerability. Like one of those old home movies, the flickering image of her little boy trying his very best to understand why his dad was always so angry at him, trying to figure out how to please him, looking for even the smallest scraps of love.

The way he looked at her. Maybe she had imagined this, but he seemed most of the time to be needing her, his little boy big brown eyes silently begging her to help.

Which she never did. Which her own mother never did for her. Which maybe she never learned to do. Instead, forcing herself to become a nurse, even though she hated hospitals and hated doctors. Maybe as penance, the penance she had heard about in church, because her mother always dragged her to church. So, once a week, she heard about a world that never really existed anywhere else for her. About a Jesus who, it was said, loved her, and was there to protect her, and maybe he did for those two hours on Sunday mornings, but never ever, as far as she could tell, at any other time in her life.

It always hurt to think about all this, which is why she always tried to push these thoughts down as deep as she could. At the hospital, she had an exhausting battle to make herself stay, as Jesus might have stayed, with the sick, with the wounded, with the helpless. Knowing it was so much easier to help because she didn't really know them. No blood connection. A responsibility that began and ended with her shift.

As she finished her Egg McMuffin, she could see Tyler's room in her head. Something must be happening with him, something more disturbing than his usual always off behavior. His room looked as if a hurricane or tornado had passed through, one of those major storms that could pick things up and toss them about like twigs.

But then she realized, like she had always realized in the past, that she didn't know what she could do, after all these years, to make it right. Because, really, how could it ever be right. For Tyler; for her. Because it had never been right. She didn't even know what right looked like. At least she had Ernie; at least she wasn't all alone in the universe. Which was what her mother had promised would be her lot in life: all alone for ever and ever.

She had five minutes to park, clock in, and begin her shift.

*   *   *

Bob had gotten up before his dad and brothers, scrawled out a note, and put the cash under the sugar bowl. Then he headed back to bed and waited till Bill and Buck and Ernie woke up. He dressed and washed and came into the kitchen as they were fighting over the cereal boxes.

Ernie looked up, then pointing to the note commanded: "Read this to your brothers, Bob!"

Bob picked up the note and read out loud: "Dad. Went through the shed when you went to the hospital and checked Tyler's room. Checked it twice. Found this in different places. Bob."

Ernie reached out to move the sugar bowl and quickly pocketed the cash. He nodded in Bob's direction, offered what seemed like a grunt of affirmation, then turned his attention to his cereal.

If Bob thought the money would do the trick and defuse his dad, he was wrong. Because Ernie was beginning to sense that things were slipping away from him. Usually, after a beat down, Doris was looking for some love and reassurance. But the other night she just lay there, her back to him, and he could feel the resistance radiating from her. Unfortunately he was still so sore from the microwave attack, he didn't have the energy to teach her a lesson.

Plus, there was Tyler. He knew wherever he was Tyler was laughing at him. If he didn't do something about it, it would spread to his own kids. So, in his mind, this little bit of cash that Bob found was only just the beginning. Like interest he was due. Now it was time to take control of the situation.

*   *   *

Tyler was getting used to not knowing where he was in the morning, the soreness from sleeping upright in the driver's seat or scrunched in the backseat. Trying to figure out exactly which back road he had made it to before surrendering to sleep. This time he realized he had driven to another dirt road on the Tremblay farm.

Had he spent time last night watching TV at the Krause house? If he had, he couldn't remember. Which was too bad, because he would have enjoyed some TV time.

It took a while to fire up the brain. In the meantime, Elizabeth was going on about how things were falling apart. Beginning with what had happened at the Lake Garfield house and the mess Abigail had made, then how Ernie and the little Ernies were getting ever closer to the edge, and how Tony wasn't about to let them get away with any more stuff, then how everybody had a different idea about what to do and how to do it. Mostly Elizabeth was saying that it just wasn't enough to go from day to day without having a plan. How now was the time for Tyler to figure some things out.

So she wasn't going to stop talking until he agreed to go to the library in Brett. She had a list of books to check out, then reviewed how to use the computer for inter-library loans, and reminded him about his library card, the card she insisted he get last year. So he made a deal with her, first some breakfast at Dom's, then to the library. And finally some silence.

*   *   *

Deb Spencer didn't have to ask Tyler what he wanted. Joe Montano had told her he had gotten the same thing at Dom's since he was five: two eggs over medium, well-done bacon, French fries instead of home fries, and rye toast. A glass of water, a small orange juice, and now coffee with a lot of room for milk. If he could, he always sat at the smallest table right by the door to the bathroom, the furthest table from the front door, in the seat facing toward the door. Most people avoided the table because it was a bit claustrophobic but it seemed to calm Tyler down.

A lot of people were uncomfortable around Tyler: sitting there, sometimes making facial gestures, seemingly arguing with himself, or the long dark silences and blank stares. But Deb had always known that Tyler liked her, and for some reason she trusted him. A feeling that was only strengthened by sharing the recent difficult journey Penny had taken to get the better of her amnesia.

As she poured his coffee, Deb thought that Tyler might benefit from seeing Katie.

*   *   *

Frank was surprised to see a number he didn't recognize appear on his iPhone screen. He had only given out this number to the Chief, to Katie, and Penny.

He gave in to curiosity and decided to answer with a curt "Yes?"

"This is Milton Krause and I have about had it with you folks. I just happened to call my man up there and he tells me they broke in again. I heard you used to be a hotshot cop in the city, so I figure you've got to know more than those hicks in Ripton. Believe me, I gave your Chief enough time. I'm a patient man, but I've run out of patience. You understand me, don't you, Detective?"

Frank was doing his best to summon the spirit of his sometime therapist, Dr. Silver, to call forth forbearance, to better embody understanding and channel some extra empathy, when mostly what he wanted to do was tell this arrogant asshole to go fuck himself.

"Mr. Krause, I understand you have good reason to be upset. But this is my private line and I'd appreciate it if in the future you called the Ripton Department. We are always glad to hear from residents."

"Detective, I run businesses worth close to five hundred million bucks. If I wanted to waste my very valuable time I would have called the Department and gotten the answering machine. Do you know how people like me get to be as rich and powerful as we are, Detective? It's because we care about every penny, every little

126

detail, and what every single employee is or isn't doing."

Frank jumped in: "With all due respect, sir, Chief Paul is a very competent policeman and we are both working very hard to solve these crimes. You, probably better than most, must realize that in the city, a thief with this kind of competence would have cleaned out your entire house. So we've been more than fortunate that …"

Krause interrupted: "Listen, the house in Ripton is only one of six houses I have. But do I care that some creep is watching my TV when I'm not even there? Damn right I care! Why? Because it's my house! My property! Because he's invading my space. So I'm calling to tell you that if you don't catch this prick, I might just suggest to the Selectboard that they hire someone who can actually catch criminals. Hell, I might even contribute to his salary. In the meantime I've hired Apex." With that, he was gone.

$$* \qquad * \qquad *$$

After some deep breathing, and deciding not to drive down to the city to find Krause, Frank called the Chief to let him know that he was following up on Mr. Krause's latest complaint and was on his way to meet Derek Ford again.

You didn't have to be a great detective to see that Ford was fit to be tied. It took him less than ten seconds to start venting: "Can you believe that guy: after he spoke to you, he called my house. Yelling at my wife, telling her how incompetent I was and that I was hardly worth the money he was paying me. She's got breast cancer and had surgery a month ago and now I take her to chemo. She's always listening to these relaxation tapes to calm down. The last thing she needs is to hear Krause say I might lose this job.

"All because his nephew Carter had come up and saw some new TV shows were programmed. The lazy little shit sometimes comes on weekends to pick up the local girls, showing off his uncle's big screen TV and the hot tub and swimming pool … I don't trust him and he knows it. Carter probably told him I'm involved somehow because Krause said he's hired someone to check on me and the property."

"I'm very sorry about your wife, Derek, and sorry you have to go through this," Frank offered, knowing that any words of concern didn't quite cut it.

"Luckily," Derek continued, "I walked in and got the phone

away from my wife. Last thing he told me was the clock was ticking, and hung up before I could ask him for any details."

"Well, the kind and considerate Mr. Krause mentioned Apex Security just before he suggested he might just have me fired as well."

Whatever the thief or thieves had done, they had certainly done a great job of cleaning up the entertainment center. Which made the large note sitting in the middle of the coffee table that much more noticeable:

"Dear Mr. Krause:

You have erased all of the new programming, so it is obvious that we have very different tastes when it comes to television. Please believe that we only intended to offer you something new and exciting and something you might enjoy. Please accept our apologies. We intend to make sure this is made right. Thank you for your hospitality."

Frank was quiet, as he read the note a second time to himself. "Krause never mentioned a note," Derek said. "So he must have written this after Carter left."

"You know Derek, maybe it was written by a woman. It's got the flourishy loops and cute little circles dotting the letter 'i' that all the girls at my school used when they wrote, just another confusing thing about all this. Like the 'we' instead of 'me.' But still the video surveillance you showed me makes me think we're dealing with a single intruder."

"And when he talks about making things right, well he'll probably be back … But maybe that's Apex's problem." Derek's voice trailed off and he took a final look around the room.

*   *   *

Chief Paul told Frank that for thirty years he had played softball with Derek Ford every Sunday at the Ripton field until he could no longer bend down quick enough to stop a ground ball. That Derek worked hard.

"Several times over the past two years I stopped that kid Carter going sixty in the thirty straightaway on Route 23. He's as arrogant as he is young and stupid and rich. I'm sorry, Frank. But this is the reality of small-town policing. I have the feeling this is going to get worse before it gets better. For Derek and for us."

THIRTY-THREE

Katie could certainly get used to brother Frank making breakfast: the smoked salmon, the onion and garlic bagels, the cream cheese and scallions. A delicious meal and some almost tolerable tea, and now Frank clearing the table, Katie smiling as he moved about his modest kitchen with faint wisps of father Carl trailing behind. It was Carl who whenever something unanticipated was happening would offer a wistful sigh followed by his "who would've thunk?" His small and unusually modest acknowledgment that the universe had once again taken him by surprise.

Rabbit was still reconnoitering, this the first time he had been to Frank's place, sniffing this and that, then summoned to the den by the call: "Danger, Good bird ... Good boy ... Good morning ... " Then a moment later sounding suspiciously like Julianna Margulies, who Danger encountered once a week on TV as Alicia Florrick of "The Good Wife," and much more often as the friendly voice-over bank saleswoman: "Chase: so you can ... so you can ... so you can." With his added echo effect, then his best Frank laugh, with Rabbit offering an accompanying husky howl.

In the kitchen Frank and Katie smiled together at the collective sounds of their far-more-than-pets. Frank gathered his copy of the *I Ching* and a yellow pad and pen, as if this was now the most natural of activities. Picking up the three coins from the kitchen table, anxious to get to it. Prompting her own silent "who would've thunk?," not wanting to jinx Frank's growing willingness to trust the Oracle.

"Last time it was about what I was missing. This time I want to ask the question in a more direct way: "What can you tell me about the thief?"

Frank gently shook the coins in his cupped hands. His first throw was three heads, a nine, and a changing line. He drew the straight line on the bottom of the first hexagram, and a broken line for the last line of the second. His next throw was three tails, a six, a broken line, and another changing line. He paused and silently repeated the question to himself, then threw three more tails, a six, and his third changing line. He made a broken line for the first hexagram and a straight line for the second. His fourth throw was three heads, his fourth consecutive changing line.

He shook the coins once more, Katie wondering if he'd throw yet another changing line but his fifth toss was two heads and a tail, an eight, and a broken line. Then the last toss, two tails and a head, a seven and a straight line.

When he was done, he had these two hexagrams:

Frank, after a quick look through the index, found he had thrown "Shih Ho" and "Ku." He handed the book to Katie, and gathered pad and pen.

"Maybe it's the coins," Katie offered "or maybe it's me, but it seems there's a message that just isn't getting through, because here comes 'Shih Ho' again. With a new second hexagram to help us."

"Right," Frank was remembering, "the stuff about biting through what blocks us … Well, considering my last day or two, it's pretty obvious I'm blocked and have to do a better job."

Katie skipped ahead. "Remember, there's this to look forward to.

THE JUDGMENT
BITING THROUGH has success.
It is favorable to let justice be administered.

"Yesterday, Katie, was the worst, having to deal with this incredibly entitled homeowner who's furious about these break-ins. Trying my best to be patient, because there is something going on here that I just don't get … First, breaking and entering but not really stealing anything. Then, if it's even the same person, one person or many, all of a sudden, for no apparent reason trying to completely trash another place.

"And now for the first time expressing some remorse. Not for breaking in but sincerely surprised and sorry that the aforementioned furious homeowner didn't appreciate the television shows they programmed for him. Never acknowledging doing wrong. So until I understand what these crimes really are, and why they're happening, it's hard to know what justice looks like."

"Remember, 'Shih Ho' also says this about dispensing justice:

> It is of moment that the man who makes the decisions … is gentle by nature, while he commands respect by his conduct in his position.
>
> … The laws specify the penalties. Clarity prevails when mild and severe penalties are clearly differentiated, according to the nature of the crimes. This is symbolized by the clarity of lightning. The law is strengthened by a just application of penalties. This is symbolized by the terror of thunder. This clarity and severity have the effect of instilling respect; it is not that the penalties are ends in themselves …

"So I better get this right. Because while some of these homeowners are clearly rooting for severity and the thunder, I could really use some clear light and some lightning."

"Yes, I think so, Frank. But then there's this to look out for:

> It is easy to discriminate between right and wrong in this case … But one encounters a hardened sinner, and aroused by anger, one goes a little too far.

"Perfect! So somewhere, somehow I'm going to find myself an angry, hardened sinner. Maybe someone besides my annoyed homeowner. Which could explain how some fairly harmless pranks transformed themselves into the kind of manic destruction we found at the Stoughton house. Unless the *Ching* is really talking about me and what I'm about to become if I don't figure this out."

Katie couldn't help but laugh. "Angry maybe, but I don't think I've ever seen you do hardened. So, for the time being, let's assume 'Shih Ho' has someone else in mind. Plus, there's this hint:

> The matter at issue is an old one …

"That whatever's going on likely has its roots in things that happened before you got here ... Still, Frank, I have to admit considering my recent history with Penny, I'm worried that this sinner is someone to reckon with ... These days I tend to take *I Ching* warnings much more seriously than I ever did, and it appears he's bringing some significant trouble with him:

> ... this line refers to a man who is incorrigible ... that is to say, he is deaf to warnings. This obstinacy leads to misfortune.

"Well, Katie, I certainly didn't get the feeling that the note I read was written by an incorrigible, obstinate man. But I could be wrong. Maybe there's bad blood and some unhappy history between our intruder and these homeowners? A local contractor, some guy who mowed lawns or plowed driveways, a carpenter or plumber who felt cheated. A lot of folks to check ... So let's see what the second hexagram says:

Ku / Work on What Has Been Spoiled

> The Chinese character *ku* represents a bowl in whose contents worms are breeding. This means decay ... the conditions embody a demand for removal of the cause ...

> What has been spoiled through man's fault can be made good again through man's work. It is not immutable fate ... that has caused the state of corruption, but rather the abuse of human freedom. Work toward improving conditions promises well, because it accords with the possibilities of the time.

> We must first know the cause of corruption before we can do away with them; hence it is necessary to be cautious ...

"Worms, just another reminder that I've left concrete for the country. You can go a lifetime on the West Side of Manhattan without bumping into a worm, at least a non-human one ...

Anyway, as you pointed out, it certainly seems that this problem and this corruption isn't new.

"Plus it's a bit hard for me to believe that so many homeowners spread across such a distance would have dealt with the same person …"

"Well, Frank, here's more from 'Ku':

> Setting right what has been spoiled by the father
> …

> It is as if the son were compensating for the decay his father allowed to creep in …

"And it's not just the dad but the mom as well:

> Setting right what has been spoiled by the mother
> …

> In setting right in such a case, a certain gentle consideration is called for. In order not to wound, one should not attempt to proceed too drastically.

Frank sat there quietly trying to process this. Even though these were serious trespasses and continuing violations of private property and personal privacy, there was something so very not city, and something so very country about this.

And while he wouldn't share these thoughts with the Chief and certainly not the Selectboard, there was something naive and innocent, even sweet about the intruder's attempts to try and please Krause … So maybe this was what used to be called "juvenile delinquency." Which was probably why the *I Ching* was prompting him to consider the influence of the mother and father in all this.

"There's some more about the father," Katie added:

> Tolerating what has been spoiled by the father. In continuing one sees humiliation …

Katie looked up. "You know I can't help but think about Penny and all the work we did to penetrate her not-knowing. In the end it all came down to how terribly twisted her family, and her husband's family, had become … Here, too, we're told how much has been spoiled between the parents and the son."

"Well, Katie dear, we all want so much to be loved and cared for by the adults we're most dependent on. I remember my first partner telling me that when it came to crime, and especially when it came to murder, to first look closest to home. I argued but it didn't take long before I was dealing with the most gruesome family murders … "

"Frank, this is way too depressing for breakfast … Thankfully, just in the nick of time, 'Ku' offers a possible breakthrough:

Setting right what has been spoiled by the father. One meets with praise.

An individual is confronted with corruption originating from neglect in former times. He lacks the power to ward it off alone, but with able helpers, he can at least bring about a thorough reform, if he cannot create a new beginning, and this also is praiseworthy.

"So Katie, we've got past neglect and limited resources, and a great 'Ku' suggestion. How about we try this: 'Under the powers vested in me by the Commonwealth of Massachusetts and with the received wisdom of several very old Chinese wizards, I, Frank Falco, Assistant Police Chief of the Town of Ripton, do hereby invest in you, Katie Greenberg, the powers of 'Able Helper,' and charge you with helping me to bring about a thorough reform in the behavior of those engaged in a series of break-ins in and around Ripton and nearby villages … So please place your hand upon the *I Ching* and repeat after me: 'Absolutely!'"

Katie put her hand on the book, smiled and said: "Absolutely several times over!"

"Good," Frank offered. "So what do think, Able Helper?"

"Well, I'm not sure you know this but in college I thought about becoming a psychology major. I was especially interested in family therapy, probably because our family was nuts. Anyway, there was this guy I studied, Salvador Minuchin, and one of the things he said is that every troubled family designates one family member as the problem person, and everyone else sort of believes that if they could only fix … well, for the moment, let's just say brother Frank. 'If only Frank would spend more time with us; or if only Frank wasn't so stubborn and disagreeable and rebellious, well, family life would be so much easier.' It's actually very political in a way because family interactions are marked by a series of changing power relationships. In Minuchin's theory, Frank would be 'the identified patient.'

"So I was reading all this and I got the bright idea to suggest to Theresa that we all should go to family therapy. Of course, I was delusional, because at the time I was the only one of us even remotely interested in therapy.

"Which is just a long way around to suggesting that this reading reminds me of problematic family dynamics. There's 'what has been spoiled by the mother' and 'what has been spoiled by the father' and it doesn't take a rocket scientist to imagine how those failures can affect and live on in the son or the daughter.

"This may be simplistic, but the *I Ching* teaching here is about the results of neglect. We've already been alerted to 'youthful folly' and told he or she is looking for you. Which might be a poetic way of saying he or she needs guidance, an alternate or an alternative father figure. So maybe you are being asked to look not only at the present-day reality of break-ins and missing property, but the past actions that brought you and the thief to this moment.

"While I am enormously flattered, Frank, that you've deputized me, the reading speaks of 'able helpers,' not just a single helper. Lastly, let me remind you that you asked 'What can you tell me about the thief?' So perhaps, even more than you, it's really your thief who needs the most help and requires those 'able helpers? Just maybe he's found one of them.'"

THIRTY-FOUR

Penny purchased Olivia's house for eight hundred seventy-five thousand dollars, the full asking price, then told Alex she'd like to find an additional place in Ripton that might serve as a modest exhibition space for Olivia's drawings and paintings. Alex was thrilled, not only because Olivia's desire to help out local non-profits would happen so much sooner than later, but because Penny had chosen to be the guardian and advocate for Olivia's artwork.

Penny remembered the day at Katie's when she threw the "Shih Ho" hexagram, thinking now that finding her new home might be the clearest evidence that she had successfully persevered. Proud but sad that she never got the chance to meet Olivia, yet thrilled she would be surrounded by what Olivia had brought to life.

So it was time to celebrate. First, survival: that in spite of the best efforts of her husband, Peter, and his brother, Donnie, she was still here, walking and talking and breathing. Then, transformation: a new start and new home and new friends.

When she thought of celebrating, she found herself thinking first about Frank. Remembering the day she met him at Katie's, still suffering from amnesia, when she threw the hexagram "Ching / The Well." When she first encountered "the able man," somehow sure the *I Ching* was talking about Frank, this strange policeman she had never seen before:

> He is like a purified well whose water is drinkable.
> But no use is made of him. This is the sorrow of
> those who know him ...

She had never before experienced getting to know someone in the midst of crisis, when she was so vulnerable, the stakes so very high. Even though she could only barely appreciate at the time that he was still recovering from the loss of love, of confidence, and recuperating from the tragic shooting of a young man, he had made himself immediately available to her.

When in the most severe example of irony imaginable, she, like Frank, so unexpectedly found herself killing a man in self-defense. Then watching Katie's boyfriend die at the hands of the brother-in-law she never knew, feeling in so many ways responsible for his death. So touched that Frank was there to take her back to Little Pointe, helping her transition from a life of deception to one of hope. And while they had never talked about coming to the Berkshires, here they both were because of Katie.

From his own so very painful journey, Frank had learned about taking time, of the often odd and indirect route you needed to travel to become whole again. Although he had resisted initially, with the help of first his therapist then Danger, his wary bird, he had learned about the small steps you took to rebuild trust, to slowly rediscover self-awareness and self-confidence. About perseverance.

But on this night, Penny had come to a new awareness: Frank was just a bit too patient, too overly concerned with what could go wrong with them. He might well defer to her for another decade. So she headed for Domaney's and picked up a really good Merlot and a Malbec and a lever action corkscrew, guessing that Frank didn't even have one.

She knew from the time he helped her back in Michigan, and the times they spent with José and Juan, that he preferred beer to wine, so she got him a six-pack of Corona.

Frank was lying on his back in his underwear, Danger on his knee, doing his stomach crunches and watching baseball. It took him a minute to realize the knocking he heard was his front door, not the TV sound of an over-excited fan banging on the roof of the Red Sox dugout. He yelled, "just a minute," and got up to put on his jeans and then quickly moved Danger away from the door and back into his cage. Always concerned that in a moment of exploratory exuberance, Danger would find himself flying out from any opening into the beyond, without any idea of where he was or how to get back home.

Frank's first thought was there was a problem, the Chief, or one of the local Barrington cops, but opened the door to Penny, arms full.

In that moment, as she saw the shock in his eyes, Penny thought oh my God, this was dumb, so incredibly dumb. But she watched as Frank's wariness turned to a smile. As he quickly reached out to take the wine and beer from her and ushered her in.

"I'm a mess," and gesturing with his head, "and my apartment, too. But please come in. There must be some space on the couch.

Danger and I took the evening off: a no cleaning night. One of our favorite nights of the week."

Frank opened the bottle of Merlot, searched in vain for a proper glass and settled for a clean coffee mug, then opened a Corona for himself. He gave Penny the wine with a brief, "sorry," put his beer on the coffee table then quickly rolled up his exercise mat. Then sat beside her on the couch, raising his bottle as she raised her mug.

"I heard about your new house, Penny. So here's to you. Great work," then clinking her mug with his bottle.

"Thank you, Frank." Then she drank her wine as if it were water.

Frank laughed, got up again, and went to bring the bottle back to refill her glass.

Penny talked about the house, about Olivia, about Olivia's art, about the path down to the water. She talked and drank. Then Frank talked about the case, about his latest *I Ching* reading, then about how silly he had thought the whole thing was, that very first time with the coins and the dead Chinese prophets, and now, well how amazing it was that he had come to appreciate the process.

She had had two lovers before she had met Peter, and had been faithful throughout her marriage, so she was operating on very old instincts here. But as she finished her third coffee mug of Merlot, she looked up at him and said: "Shut up, Frank, let's go to bed." Then both hands in his, guided him off the couch and toward the bedroom.

*   *   *

The first "good morning" Penny heard came from Danger, not Frank, who was not even in the apartment any more. At least, she remembered a goodbye kiss, or at least she had dreamt of one, and a sweet note with many "sorrys."

Then hoping he was not one of those disappearing men her single girlfriends had spoken about so often back in Little Pointe. The guys who would disappear after either the first night or first week or first month as sex slowly began to evolve into relationship. With an explanation like, "it's just not working for me," or "we both know this isn't going anywhere," and who, if pressed for additional info, would get that deer-in-the-headlights look or worse begin to act like, as expected, they were already being nagged.

In those days, with her supreme belief in the solidity of her marriage to Peter, she had been the oft-chosen sympathetic listener, who though she rarely admitted it, never really understood why her women friends had even trusted those lame guys in the first place. If only they had found a Peter. Just goes to show you, she thought.

In spite of her many attempts to caution herself, and her determination to act as casually as she could, she had opened herself up to Frank these past months. She wondered now if she had ever done casual well. How else to explain how quickly and easily she fell into Peter, under his spell actually, and how she had remained there for so long. Her mother had always been cold: the home she insisted Penny and Peter accept as a wedding present was in many ways a monument to the frigid. Cold marble. Large open mostly lifeless spaces. While her father, who though he steadfastly proclaimed his limitless devotion to her, was most times not there, and so often unreliable.

So just maybe she had pined for love, was waiting expectantly for it, yearning for it on a cellular if not conscious level. And quite possibly she was still without the ability to tell the difference between the very complicated real thing and the twinkly Hollywood-induced illusion.

THIRTY-FIVE

Elizabeth had made him promise that he would read the books they had gotten from the Brett Library. While he much preferred fantasy to truth, Tyler nevertheless knew that a promise to Elizabeth was a promise best keeping.

He started with Deborah Haddock's "The Dissociative Identity Disorder Sourcebook," which with its big words unfortunately reminded him of school. It was a bit scary but Tyler knew that if he stuck with it, like his previous challenges with computers and carpentry, he might be able to figure it out.

It seemed this DID thing was about how some people coped with something really bad that had happened. Like the brain trying to figure out a way to survive terrible things. Sometimes creating several different personalities. So that whatever this terrible thing that was happening was maybe happening to someone else. But what made it even more complicated was that a lot of the time the person himself or herself wasn't even aware that this was going on. Not remembering, especially the bad things, but also spacing out a lot on the everyday things. Especially if and when any of the other personalities had taken over.

Everyone, all through his growing up, talked about the times he just didn't seem to be there. So he certainly could imagine the forgetting part of the DID. If he actually had it, which he was still pretty sure he didn't. But the forgetting seemed to be getting worse for him. Like the last week or so, waking up in the car on back roads, with no real memory of having gotten there, let alone what might have happened during the time he was there. Or what kinds of feng shui stuff Abigail might have done when he wasn't looking.

The Haddock lady talked about the amygdala, this small part of the brain which tries to deal with experiences that might be threatening. Sometimes the brain just doesn't do a good job of processing the information, of developing what she called a healthy "sense of self."

Reasonable, considering his mom and dad and what went on with them, and now Ernie and the Ernies, who all seemed pretty nuts to him.

Other parts of the brain, she explained, try their best to keep this tough and painful stuff under control. But the mind can get overwhelmed, like when the person is being seriously mistreated, or when they're too tired or like maybe having nightmares, or drinking too much or taking drugs, which a lot of kids he knew from high school did. Or like with that Post Traumatic Stress, the PTSD thing they talk about now on TV wherever some Iraq War vet blew away his wife or mother-in-law or other folks he worked with.

Tyler knew Eric Davis, Junior, the older brother of Sam Davis, a kid he went to school with. Their dad, Eric Davis, Senior, had been a marine in Vietnam and Eric, Junior – a lot of folks called him EJ – well he couldn't wait to get to Iraq. He came home from Basic in his uniform, all buffed up, scary big, and partying and drinking. But when he came home for good after a year of combat, he was off. Real spooky quiet. Like he wasn't quite there with you. Like maybe he was haunted. Back home but not really back. Probably as much still over there as here. One night EJ told him about a Humvee that he and some of his squad was on that hit something he said was an IED, and then next thing he knew there was blood everywhere and screaming and two buddies died and one lost his leg. But that was the first and last time EJ ever mentioned the war to him.

Tyler would hear how every once in a while, EJ would get completely pissed at someone for maybe saying the wrong thing. A little dispute becoming much bigger for him, like him thinking this guy was threatening his life. Especially if he had spent too much time at one of the bars in Brett. Then they'd have to keep EJ from taking the guy out. Someone told him that was the PTSD coming out.

Pretty depressing. He was thinking maybe Elizabeth having him learn about DID was her way of wanting him to say something to EJ or maybe help him in some way. Maybe EJ's computer needed some work or his new smartphone was on the fritz.

He knew Elizabeth wanted him to read the entire book so he promised he'd get back to it later in the day.

*   *   *

One of the first things Ernie had done was convince Doris that she really didn't understand the way money worked. That if you didn't have debt, you didn't have good credit, and you needed credit just in case. For emergencies, or to get equity loans. In fact,

Doris didn't know much about money, although she did work her ass off and despite her bum of a first husband didn't owe anyone a cent.

It didn't take too long before Doris put Ernie's name on her checking account and he had applied for three or four credit cards which he often used, he said, for household expenses. It was one of these VISA cards he used to rent the car for "Operation Tyler."

The plan was to have Bill drive his car, and he'd drive the rental. With two cars, they'd be able to use the map Tyler had made with all the x's, cover twice the ground, and track him down. Finally figure out his angle, find the stolen loot, and teach him a lesson.

Bob and Buck jumped into the car with Bill, hoping they could avoid driving with their dad, but Ernie stuck his arm through the open rear window and grabbed a chunk of Bob's coat. "You're with me!" forcing Bob out and providing Buck with a moment of joy.

Ernie and Bill had divided the addresses, agreeing to call each other every hour to report on their progress. Ernie handed Bob the map, making him the navigator.

But it wasn't easy figuring out Tyler's code: there were red x's and green x's and blue x's. The first red x they hit was on Main Street in Brett, and it was hard to tell whether it was for Señor Guacamole, the bright, brand new Mexican restaurant, Tony's Barber Shop, or Green Valley Realty. So Ernie sent him out to reconnoiter. Bob took all the time he could, saying hi to Tony and with a quick look in, checking out what some of Guacamole's customers were eating, then sauntering back to the car to report that the beef burritos looked really good but Tyler was nowhere to be found. So maybe red was for "realty?"

Then onto the first green x. Twenty minutes later, after a few wrong turns and a cascade of curses, Bob led them to a long abandoned dirt road with a half-burned barn. Which obviously didn't make Ernie happy because it prompted a sharp slap to the back of Bob's head. If only, Bob was thinking, he had made it to the front seat of the rental car before Buck had.

The first blue x was located off of Stone Valley Road, and if Bob had picked the right driveway, up an almost impassable driveway. Bob kept asking Ernie whether or not they were trespassing, and if they could get in trouble, or what they would say if someone were home. Hoping he could persuade his dad to bag

142

this crazy hunt, silently praying that Ernie would soon need a drink more than he wanted to catch Tyler. So he could steer him to The Back Door where he belonged, and where he couldn't torture them.

Instead, they managed to make it to the top, where they found a large log cabin, seemingly empty, with no evidence that Tyler was nearby. Not convinced, Ernie insisted they walk their way around the property.

Already pissed at Bob for his obvious lack of enthusiasm, Ernie called Bill, looking for good news. Before Ernie even got his answer, he could hear Bill and Buck arguing, Buck yelling to remind Bill that he had failed his written test, and didn't even have his driver's license yet, so how the hell was he supposed to know the best way to Greenway Drive in Hartsdale. With Bill screaming back, "because that's your job as navigator! And my job is to drive."

Bob could see that Ernie was about to lose it, and he leaned in close enough to the phone to yell: "Did you find Tyler?" Thinking he was helping out, but clearly misjudging his contribution, as the back of Ernie's hand smacked him across the ear. He couldn't help but scream, which earned him another smack.

The sound of the smacks seemed to work wonders and the chaos on the other end of the phone was immediately replaced by silence. "No sight of him yet," Bill offered quickly. "But we had some problems navigating and only went to one place." Then Bill tried to change the subject away from their obvious failure. "I was reminding Buck about all those uniforms we found in the closet: remember I showed you, Dad, from Brett Lawn and Apex and Kelly's and Brinks? Anyway, he could be in a disguise so we're also looking for any kind of suspicious-looking repairman."

"Good work, Bill. You make sure Buck keeps an eye out, and I'll see if I can get Bob here to do his job for a change," hanging up.

His ear still stinging, Bob tried to keep himself from reacting, summoning every ounce of submission he could call upon, as he quietly walked back to the car.

Ernie was feeling better, believing Bob was ready now to buckle down, and glad that Bill was taking some initiative. Somehow he had forgotten about the uniforms. Tyler could easily be in camouflage.

Unfortunately, with his bad back Ernie had never had the opportunity to serve but he had always known he would have made a great soldier. An officer. A leader of men. And he was even more aware now that he had to go about this effort as if this was a military engagement. Wondering, just maybe, if it was possible he had underestimated the enemy.

*　　　　*　　　　*

Alice Parker had been admitted shortly after Doris began her shift. She had been beaten so severely they were worried she might not make it. Somehow she had had just enough energy and presence of mind to grab her son, and make it to the emergency room before she collapsed.

It was hard to see the five year old sitting there all alone in the waiting room, rocking back and forth, eyes closed tight, without thinking about her Tyler. It was hard to see the bruised and battered woman without thinking of herself.

She made a point of bringing the little boy some juice from the cafeteria but he looked at her blankly and continued to rock.

Luckily, they had been able to stabilize Alice after four hours in the operating room, and despite her broken ribs, broken right arm, and broken jaw, she would live.

When Doris came back to the boy to tell him that her mother was very sick, but would get better, he looked at her for a brief moment, then quickly closed his eyes again.

The social worker from Family Services picked him up an hour later. He hadn't said a word to anyone.

*　　　　*　　　　*

Ernie stopped at DeMarco's Package for a bottle of Jack Daniels then gave the car keys to Bob with a stern warning: not even a scratch. A couple of swigs later, he was feeling just a little bit better. There was always a battle to be won: making sure there was enough liquor in the blood to smooth things out. Too much and the anger would rise; too little and he would remember how his life had turned to shit.

*　　　　*　　　　*

Tyler couldn't remember the last time he had dinner alone with his mother. But she had made it impossible to say no. Every excuse he offered up, she countered. So he sat across from her in a booth at Harry's Bun and Burger.

The first few minutes were very confusing. She kept saying how sorry she was: talking about the time his father had left him at the playground when he was two and a half, and how she found him alone at the swing-set at nine that night; the time a few months later when his father had nailed a two by four to the door jambs locking Tyler into the bathroom; and the time he was three and a neighbor had found him crying in the backyard all by himself chained to the swing set, his left arm broken. The neighbor had driven him to the hospital and she got a call from a nurse she knew at the emergency room. Tyler wasn't really sure what she was talking about because he had absolutely no memory of those moments.

Then she started crying which made him very nervous. He reached out to pat her arm and told her not to worry, that everything was fine. Which helped to stop the tears. Hoping real hard that the waitress or other customers wouldn't say anything.

Then she started to talk about Ernie and the little Ernies and how she knew it wasn't fair to him, and that she wished she had the strength to leave, but wasn't sure she did. Then about the time Ernie did this and Ernie did that, and Bill and Bob and Buck too, and how bad she felt, and he could see the tears beginning to form all over again, and he just really wanted to finish his cheeseburger and fries and get the hell out of there.

Until slowly she began to calm down, focusing her attention on her tuna salad sandwich. When after ten minutes of quiet eating, she smiled, telling Tyler how much better she felt and how they needed to do this more often.

*　　　　*　　　　*

For Elizabeth, this was teachable moment time. Because if ever there was a perfect example of "dissociation" this was it. She had watched Tyler and his mom all during dinner, watching as he gradually shut himself down. So as Tyler pulled out of the parking lot, she decided to raise the issue one more time.

It was never easy trying to do complicated things when one of the others surfaced. Like driving. Luckily, he knew these roads so well. Worse, sometimes an argument would break out and it was just like his mom's house, with her and Ernie and the Ernies all yelling. Two or three of them: Elizabeth, Tony, and Abigail all trying to make a point. Serious headache time for him.

He had a sense that Elizabeth was right but the truth was he had only vague memories of what his mom had said at Harry's. Had he even been listening? So Elizabeth reminded him about the time all those years ago when he was watching his mom make a pumpkin pie, and for some reason – there was always some reason though he could never really remember them – his dad came in and started to beat her. Elizabeth remembered how Tyler started crying and how his crying made his dad even crazier. Screaming at him to shut up, and then his dad picked up the rolling pin and was coming towards him. Tyler ran and made it all the way to the big bedroom scrunching himself under their double bed. His dad, completely drunk, tripped and fell and landed, smacking his head, on the floor. And luckily, before he could get to Tyler, he was semi-conscious, then snoring.

Elizabeth was saying that many people believe that little kids don't really remember or understand what has happened to them when they're really little, but she was pretty sure Tyler must have realized in some way that he was completely screwed, that this person called Mom and this other person called Dad just weren't going to take proper care of him. Not only weren't they going to help him or love him or protect him, but they were more likely going to hurt him. So even if he couldn't remember always feeling lonely and alone she knew that was the case. Then deciding to hide, to find a safe space.

So once again Elizabeth wanted to do something. Always looking for solutions. Medications, therapy, maybe even some kinds of exercise programs. But he remembered that quack doctor Ernie took him to, and swore there was no way he was going to do that again.

"OK," she said, "but things are getting worse. Forgetting things. The bad headaches … What about checking out Deb's psychic lady, the one who helped her friend with amnesia? She's not a doctor or psychiatrist so there won't be any of those weird pills."

Tyler had to admit that Deb's friend was probably the best of those rotten alternatives and so reluctantly agreed to see her, hoping he could drive the rest of the way in peace and that maybe Elizabeth would forget about the whole thing along the way.

But Elizabeth, glad that Tyler agreed to consult Katie, still had one more pressing matter on her mind. "I think it's really important that we make right what we messed up in some of the places we've been staying. Like the Krause place in Ripton. He obviously isn't happy with our programming choices. I think the note Abigail wrote was a good first step but how about giving him a present, a gift to make up for our error in judgment. I'm sure you can think of some gadget or other that the guy would like. Let me know what you pick." Then she was gone again and there was blessed silence.

THIRTY-SIX

First he had to quiet Tony, who wasn't particularly happy with Elizabeth's idea of making amends. It sounded like total surrender at worst, and appeasement at best. "Grow a set," he repeated several times. Tyler replied that he got the message and would think about it, and finally Tony relented.

Tyler didn't really have all that much money and a $25.00 gift certificate to Tune Street could easily be traced back to him by Krause and the cops, and anyway that didn't seem anywhere enough for a million-billionaire.

Then he remembered the digital video recorder he had just recently rescued from the dumpster behind Southern Exposure Satellite. He could clean it up and add an additional two hundred fifty gigabyte hard drive. So Mr. Krause could record more TV or use it as a backup. Luckily, he had stashed it in the crawlspace of the nearby Hardcastle place, that weird cottage down the street from Southern Exposure. For sale but empty because most of the neighbors thought it was haunted. Just because Lola Hardcastle and her thirty cats who were living there for thirty years were there one night and gone the next. Only the furniture was left. And the weird thing was Lola didn't even have a car.

The neighbors still kept an eye on the place. Many thinking that Lola and the cats could, at any moment, be returning the same magical way they left. So Tyler knew he had to be careful retrieving Krause's present.

His mom always kept old wrapping paper in the closet by the kitchen, Christmas paper, birthday paper, and odd ribbons and bows and rolls of scotch tape. Some people thought you needed to buy new but his mom, without ever using the word, had long ago mastered recycling. Often repeating: "waste not, want not." As if wanting anything was ever a real possibility in his house.

On this, day one after their talk, his mom was still in a good mood. Sometimes it lasted a day or two or three. Clearly, it was good for her to make amends. To believe she had done her part to wash away the pain of the past. Like Alcoholics Anonymous without having to go to the meetings. So it made sense to take advantage of the peace and good will that descended upon her, because it could disappear as quickly as it appeared.

For the first day, her good feelings could survive just about any assault from Ernie. Doris could stand in the midst of the storm and his rage would somehow safely part before her, streaming off to both sides. But by the second day, you could begin to see the toll it took creeping back into the eyes. See her shoulders sag a bit. This was probably the worse part of it all for Tyler: to have to watch her force-field slowly but inevitably melt away yet again.

The one small inconvenience of these rare occasions was Doris' enthusiastic if momentary determination to take a renewed interest in her son's life, so he had already prepared an answer to the question she immediately asked when she saw him with the wrapping paper.

"It's the birthday of a high school friend," he told her. Which made her smile, imagining Tyler surrounded by friends at a dream-like party, her son moving at ease amongst them, accepted, appreciated, and one of a caring, loving social network. Basking in the glow of her obviously ever so successful apology, he knew she would never even ask herself how such an unlikely miracle had come to be.

So, task one complete, wrapping paper in hand, and with the extra unexpected special bonus of not a single Ernie in sight, Tyler was happily on his way to the Hardcastle house. To find a time to slip around back unnoticed and get into the basement window where the old elm tree provided some additional cover. The Hardcastle house was just one of Tyler's several banks: it was great to be able to put things away without a word to anyone. No lines, deposit forms, or tongue-tied having to explain what he wanted to the much too pretty girls at the counters of the real bank.

But Tyler had to wait a good half hour while three neighborhood kids, oblivious to task two, were squeezing every last moment of skateboarding from the afternoon, zipping back and forth on the street in front of the Hardcastle house. Which gave Elizabeth one more opportunity to talk about the Katie lady. Until a mom from the house next door yelled loud enough to alert the kids it was now officially homework time and there would be severe consequences if they continued on. So they reluctantly headed home and Elizabeth faded away.

Tyler, who knew he was on a roll today, quickly put on his Hancock Home Repair jacket, grabbed his mostly empty tool box for show, and headed toward the back of the house. There was a barely visible hole in the bottom sill of the last basement window. It took only a minute to quickly screw the eyehook in and pull it open. The digital video recorder was right where he had left it, hidden beneath a filthy old rug. There was also a large plastic Ziploc bag filled with audio and video cables. He grabbed both and lifted them up and out the window. Climbed out and made it back to the car unnoticed. Then he started to drive from Brett to Ripton, his mind focused on what to do with these gifts.

Which is when his luck ran out because just a few minutes later Bob and Ernie drove by in the rental car in search of another x. By this point in the long day, Ernie had fallen into one of his semi-catatonic states, his low-level snoring punctuated by the occasional cough. Bob thought about not mentioning that he had just seen Tyler but was worried his dad might be playing possum, testing him. That he had somehow seen Tyler out of the corner of his eye. So Bob, excruciatingly aware of the price he'd pay for disloyalty in a matter as major as this, made a quick U-turn and decided he'd better tell.

"Dad," he said, pulling off onto the breakdown lane. "Dad, do you hear me?" hoping he wouldn't have to shake him awake, provoking a probable elbow. "Dad!" Then a little more loudly: "Dad, Dad … I just saw Tyler!"

That did it because Ernie jerked up, moving from seeming sleep to smelling blood. "Where the fuck is the little bastard?" Which prompted Bob to ease back into traffic and accelerate.

Tyler, still oblivious to the threat of the nearby Ernies, was taking mental inventory, thinking he had all he needed in the car. And because it was still a bit too early and light out for house-sitting, he decided to take a leisurely drive from Brett through Stockbridge toward Great Barrington, then maybe the shortcut on Monument Valley to Route 23 and Ripton. He figured he could do his final present wrapping hidden on one of the old abandoned dirt roads on the Krause property.

The thing is, he still wasn't completely sure about Elizabeth's idea. Because you never knew about presents. He certainly hadn't gotten that many himself, but when he was still considered normal enough to be invited to birthday parties, he saw how quickly the glow of a present faded. Because so often the gift-giver got it wrong and the birthday boy or girl hardly seemed to care for the gift, quickly discarding it without thought, and moving on to the next, hopefully better present.

After spending all those hours in his house, Tyler knew there was nothing that Krause really needed. Hopefully he would appreciate the thought.

Meanwhile, Ernie was driving Bob nuts, yelling that they were too close, then that they had fallen too far behind. Jabbering one command after another, making multiple threats. "This is it, Bob … our big chance … So you stay with him. You hear me, don't blow it … I'm telling you if you blow it, Bob, that's it for you," all the while Bob's neck was tightening, shoulders seizing, wondering if there was any way he could escape judgment day.

Then Ernie had his phone out, calling Bill and Buck, and as soon as Bill answered, yelling that whatever the hell they were doing it was time to get their asses in gear and meet up with them, one second directing his anger into the phone, then hardly taking a breath, turning towards Bob:

"That's a very good question, Bill … I don't exactly know. I'm still a bit out of it … But I'm sure Bob knows, don't you Bob? … So Bob, Bill wants to know where we are. And where the hell you think Tyler is headed?"

"This is Route 102, Dad, we're headed west not far from the old bowling alley," then Bob hesitated just a moment, knowing this was when things could get hairy. Getting ready just in case Ernie sent a slap his way, "but to tell you the truth I'm not exactly sure where Tyler's going."

Then luckily Ernie was distracted by what he heard Bill say to Buck. Turning from Bob to scream into the phone: "Did you just say you're at Burger King? … What do you mean Buck needed fries? You're kidding me, right? How about you get the hell out of there. Now! You damn well know what you can do with those fries! Or what I'll do to you if I see any of them … You heard me, Bill. Into the car. We're on Route 102. This is a two-car operation. We need back-up. What part of back-up don't you understand?" Then hanging up in a huff.

Ernie turned his attention back to Bob. "It's a good thing we saw him first, instead of your idiot brothers. They probably would have completely spooked him. At least we've got the element of surprise here. So if you don't blow it, we might just be able to catch him in the act."

Bob managed for the next five minutes to keep a respectable distance between them and Tyler, a good enough job to at least keep Ernie quiet for bit. Until he allowed his curiosity to get the better of him: "So what exactly do you think we're going to catch him doing, Dad?"

Ernie was trying to figure out whether Bob was being snotty or just plain stupid, and decided he just didn't have the energy at the moment to give him the swat he deserved. Instead, Ernie channeled his anger into increased volume: "You're a moron, Bob. If I knew exactly what he was up to, would we really need to be following him?"

Ernie shook his head several times then realized he hadn't heard from the others in a while. The phone rang several times before he heard Bill's hesitant hello.

"So where the hell are you now?" Ernie yelled. Putting the phone on speaker mostly because his hearing and the rest of his brain wasn't yet working right. Anyway, the good news was Bill and Buck had gotten it together enough to have made it from the restaurant to Ernie's car. The bad news was that while they had made it out of the Burger King parking lot, they just weren't sure whether they were heading in the right direction. So now Buck was yelling at Bill that he never went bowling so how the hell was he supposed to know where the old alley was? Plus, who really knew where west was anymore?

"Forget east or west," Bob yelled in the direction of his father's phone. "Did you turn right or left out of the Burger King parking lot? Because you should have crossed the road and turned left. If you did, you're OK. If not, make a U-turn and head back toward the entrance to the Pike, then go under the overpass and turn right onto 102. We're probably a good five or six minutes ahead of you."

Ernie couldn't help himself: "Just so you know, you guys better not have any fries on you when you get here!"

Even though Bill had hit his end-call button and they couldn't hear him anymore, Ernie kept yelling into the phone, reminding them about the mission.

It only took a minute before they started yelling at each other. "What did I tell you about the fries, Buck! I said no more fries. But as usual you whined and whined. Now because of your lousy fries we may catch a beating! You better hope Bob fucks up in the next few minutes and Dad forgets about us and those fucking fries."

"What do you mean, me? For hours we've been driving around and all I had for breakfast was a lousy English muffin. So yeah I wanted some fries. But you should talk, you ordered two Double Whoppers. How was I supposed to know that one order of fries wouldn't be enough."

Ernie continued to yell at his silent phone: "I said where the hell are you?" when finally Bob suggested the boys might have lost the cell signal. That it might make sense to wait a while and try again. Which made Ernie even more angry, because when he pressed his ear to the phone, he knew that Bob was right. There was no way of proving it but the odds were they had deliberately hung up on him. First the fries, and now this, outright insubordination. So now he wasn't sure whether he wanted to give them the satisfaction of calling back or wait for them to get scared enough to call.

Meanwhile, looking up he saw that somehow in all the commotion a pickup truck had managed to squeeze in before them. Quickly turning on Bob: "Damn it, Bob, you're too fucking far away. Wasn't I clear? Didn't I tell you no more than one car between us and the twerp? I get momentarily distracted by your stupid brothers and so now all of a sudden there's an extra pickup truck between us."

"I've got it under control, Dad. I can still see him."

"I said one car, not one car and one truck."

"Yes, Dad. One car. I can wait for the pickup to turn off, or I can pass him." Bob doing his best to summon up a distraction, praying for the phone to ring. Then, like magic, one ring, then two and Bill.

"You better tell me you lost service or you're in deep shit," his dad yelled, at which point both Bill and Buck agreed, "Yeah, Dad, we lost reception. We were talking to you and then, boom, you were gone."

Bill and Buck were expecting a nasty comeback but instead they heard Ernie scream at Bob: "There's a straightaway. Pass that pickup truck. Now!"

Bob eased out a bit to the left to gauge how much space he had and to figure out whether he could make it. But clearly Ernie had had enough with being patient. And before Bob could decide for himself, Ernie grabbed the wheel and wrenched it sharply to the left. With a loud screech, the car suddenly veered across the double lines into the other lane, and Bob had no choice but to frantically do his best to keep the car from careening out of control. Somehow he kept the car on the road but was now smack in the middle of the wrong lane with only a matter of seconds before they would collide with a large milk tanker headed their way.

Ernie, his senses now completely short-circuited by both alcohol and rage, was even more determined that Bob needed to get on with the mission, to push through his wimpy caution and pass the offending pickup, yelling: "Let's go, let's go! Faster!"

The driver of the approaching tanker, aware now that he had a crazy car coming directly toward him was furiously blowing his horn. The pickup truck in between Ernie and Tyler decided to do his very best to survive this approaching catastrophe and swerved his steering wheel to the right and precipitously sent his truck veering onto the shoulder, hoping he could somehow give the passing car enough space to come back into the right lane without being hit or hitting anyone. While Tyler, hearing the mad honking and loud squeal of tires, was now aware that something out of the ordinary was happening behind him.

Bob, deciding he was much too young to die, slammed on the brakes, sending Ernie smashing into the windshield, then wrenched his way back into the right lane just as the milk truck rumbled inches away and past him.

His entire body shaking, Bob pulled off onto the shoulder behind the pickup, unhooked his seatbelt then leaned over to check his dad, who though he had a bad bruise forming on his forehead was still breathing. Mostly he seemed stunned and completely out of it. Probably being drunk had helped.

Bob reached for Ernie's phone then quickly told his brothers to shut up and stop jabbering, and that no thanks to their dad, they had somehow avoided a milk truck and were both still alive.

Buck couldn't help himself: "Tell Dad I really didn't know the fries would take that long."

Bob quickly realized that no matter his condition Ernie would never forgive him if they lost Tyler, so with hands still trembling he reluctantly pulled back into traffic, trying his best to focus once again on what Ernie needed done.

A quarter mile up ahead it was Ronald, the young one they hadn't heard from in a while, who suggested that all that honking and brake squealing might be a sign that something bad might be about to happen. Suggesting they pull off into the gas station/convenience store parking lot up ahead on the right so they could check the cars behind them.

So it was Ronald who noticed Bob and Ernie zip by in the rental car. And Tony who quickly jumped in, exiling Ronald in the process, and ordering them to pull back into traffic so they could figure out exactly what Ernie was up to. Positioning themselves, finally, to spring into action. On the offense and with the element of surprise for a change.

As the prospect of death by tanker truck faded with every added second, Bob began to breathe normally. Taking advantage of Ernie's silence to sneak a look at the large bump above his father's left eye. Then ever so cautiously he edged across the now broken white line into the eastbound lane to see if it was safe to pass again. When he soon discovered he couldn't see Tyler's car anywhere up ahead. He quickly moved back across to his own lane, trying to figure out what the hell might have happened. "Shit" he muttered, knowing he better figure it out before his dad woke. Cursing several times more under his breath.

Several minutes later, when he next checked the rear view mirror, he saw the red Tercel. Now a few cars behind. Double-checking. Triple-checking. Somehow in the midst of all that milk tanker craziness they had moved past Tyler.

One way or another he better fix this before his dad woke up. So Bob, without much thought or his turn signal, yanked the car to the right, careening into the Ace Hardware parking lot. Snapping Ernie's head forward and back once more, disturbing him but provoking nothing more than a muted "what the fuck!"

Bob watched closely as the Tercel continued on past them, but couldn't tell whether Tyler had seen them. Anticipating that at any moment he might have to deal with an even angrier dad, he quickly pulled back onto Route 102 falling behind the black Volkswagen Jetta that was now directly behind Tyler. Miraculously managing to restore the Ernie-required one car only between them rule, and hoping Ernie might never know he had momentarily lost him.

Then the phone rang, shattering the silence Bob had grown used to. Again. Somehow with all the shifting Ernie had done, the phone was now wedged firmly under his right thigh. There was no way Bob could reach it. Ernie moaned a couple of times through the third ring and finally roused himself after the fourth. With a loud snort, Ernie shook his head and managed to get the phone to his ear.

"Now what do you want?" he said belligerently.

Bill started to stammer: "Uh … well we did what you said and we drove really hard to catch up. Maybe too hard …" Then in the background, Buck started to yell: "I told him to slow down but he wouldn't listen … He kept saying if I hadn't had those French fries we wouldn't have to speed. But I said what about those Double Whoppers you had?"

Ernie, without exactly knowing why, put his left hand up to his bruised forehead and without pausing screamed: "Shut up, Buck … I told you I don't want to hear about those goddamn French fires. Where the hell are you?"

Bill tried again: "Well, that's the problem, Dad, we just got pulled over by a cop on 102, and it turns out, and you won't believe this, I might just have left my license in my other pants. Because I can't find it … Anyway, here he comes now … I'll call you later!" Hanging up again before Ernie had a chance to yell some more.

Which left Ernie, phone in hand, cursing at his only nearby target, Bob, who was doing his best to concentrate on his driving. Slowly, Ernie began to acknowledge his throbbing head, awkwardly turning to Bob: "What the fuck happened? Why does my head and neck hurt so much?"

"Hey, Dad, there's Tyler right up ahead of us, in front of that Volkswagen," hoping distraction might work. "Do you think he's going to turn left by the Red Lion Inn or stay straight on 102 and maybe head for West Stockbridge?"

"You didn't hit me, did you, Bob?"

"I'd never hit you, Dad. I can't believe you don't remember the truck that almost killed us. That you saved our lives by grabbing the wheel and swerving toward the breakdown lane. Then, when I panicked for a second, you slammed down on my foot to make us brake. You knocked your head on the windshield, but at least we didn't hit that truck. You're like a hero."

Ernie didn't remember any of it, but it all sounded pretty good to him, and so he grunted and rubbed his head a couple of times.

"I wanted to take you to the emergency room but you kept saying a little rest was all you needed."

"Yeah well, when things get rough, the tough step up … something like that."

"OK, there he goes, Dad. Tyler's turning left toward Great

Barrington."

Which was a relief for Tyler. At least they had made a decision. Because in his car, there had been an extensive, often heated debate about what they were doing and where they should do it. Abigail thought it was silly to give the Krauses yet another electronic gizmo when there were some really interesting objets d'art they could score at a tag sale or flea market. Which once she explained what objets d'art were, Ronald thought they should get Krause a set of those penguin salt-and-pepper shakers from the Dollar Store. More than anything, he said, the guy just needed to laugh.

For the first time in a very long time, maybe the first time in forever, Tony and Elizabeth agreed on a plan. As formidable a team as you could imagine. Then Ronald and Abigail, seeing the writing on the wall seemingly surrendered, or at least decided to go silent. So Tyler set about implementing the first part of the plan, taking the longest, most roundabout route to the Krause property.

THIRTY-SEVEN

Frank went in search of the possible perpetrators of youthful folly. First to the high schools talking to principals, assistant principals, and guidance counselors. It didn't take long to learn that the local schools had significant drug and alcohol problems.

The statistics blew him away. He had naively assumed that these were mostly city problems but here in the beautiful Berkshires, teen drug use was far above average. A recent survey showed that forty-eight percent of twelfth graders had smoked pot in the last month, close to two and a half times higher than the national average. Eight percent of twelfth graders had used heroin in the last year, up from one percent three years earlier. The national average was two percent.

When he interviewed Brenda of the Youth Coalition she said she thought it began with the adults. Because residents of his newly adopted Great Barrington were three times more likely to have been admitted to the hospital for drug and alcohol problems than any other town in Massachusetts. One hundred forty-nine last year, and close to half of those were treated for heroin abuse. Even the picture-perfect Norman Rockwellian town of Stockbridge had twice the state rate. And the kicker, defying popular mythology, these people were ninety percent white.

So, Brenda stressed, sixty-seven percent of high school kids had been exposed to adults abusing both drugs and alcohol. Sadly, Frank could easily sympathize this morning, because thanks to his night with Penny, he was still hung-over.

The principal of one of the schools told Frank that even some of her fifth graders were smoking pot. Another principal complained there just wasn't enough money for treatment. "It's not just drinking and pot. My kids are getting into their parents' medicine cabinets and taking their painkillers. Twenty percent of them have tried OxyContin."

If that wasn't bad enough, the rate at which teenage girls in Berkshire County were giving birth was up twenty per cent in the last ten years compared to a twenty-one per cent decline across the state. "So," the principal stressed, "we've got a perfect storm when it comes to problems with our kids."

By the time Frank was done, he was really depressed. He also had a list of fifty-one kids who had dropped out of school in the last year who might be worth checking out.

The home visits put faces to the statistics: absent fathers and chronic under-employment or just no work at all. Stories of mill closings, of lay-offs in the plastics industry, part-time restaurant work. High rents, rising heating oil costs and expensive medical bills.

In Brett, you could see the deprivation. Despite its semi-successful attempts at downtown revitalization, you could still see the vestiges of its former life as a busy mill-town and the slightly dazed look of not enough money on the faces of its people. But some of the other, smaller South Berkshire towns mounted major efforts to create the appearance of a festive, vibrant retail presence for the summertime and ski tourists they now depended upon.

It didn't take any more than a ten-minute trip out on the side roads of these same towns to find the folks the tourist dollars never touched. Frank's list of drop-outs took him to back roads he might not have found without his trusty map.

The alcohol was obvious: empty beer and whiskey bottles; the drugs better hidden. But you could see the effects of speed and coke in the clenched jaws and brain stutters, and the haze of pot and hash and painkillers in the eyes.

This was a Berkshires never championed by the Chamber of Commerce. And it didn't take long for Frank to see the simmering anger that his badge immediately provoked. The rural version of the deep suspicion and serious dislike of cops he had known well in the worst neighborhoods of New York.

From his first surly "Whaddya want?" to the slightly worse: "Who the hell are you?" Then the "Get the fuck off my property!" Figuring if he had an actual warrant he wouldn't just be standing there.

He made it past the door of ten or so places: a few trailers, a couple of houses in dire need of new roofs and new porches and paint jobs, and then a couple of in-town apartments. Where he discovered that roaches had somehow made it up Route 22 from the Bronx.

Some of these folks were honest enough to admit that they hadn't a clue about their own kids: they had threatened them, begged them, even occasionally bribed them, but to no avail.

Betty McPherson was working three jobs: her seventeen year

159

old son Richie had recently broken his arm and now she owed two grand to the hospital and various doctors; then Shannon, her sixteen year old daughter, moved into her boyfriend's parents house, and wouldn't return her phone calls.

Roberta Bennett's forty-three year old husband had run off to West Virginia with their twenty year old neighbor, leaving her with their three kids. She had one of the few remaining jobs answering phones at the mill that made paper-making machines in Brett and was hoping to pick up some night shifts at the Cumberland Farms mini-mart gas station. Most of the time she had only a vague idea of where her kids were.

The Griels, Don and Cynthia, seemed to agree only that they had four kids. Everything else provoked an argument. He worked at MagicMart and she at Rite-Aid. Together, they made less than thirty-five thousand dollars a year. They couldn't even agree on where their kids were during the day, or during the night, and who their friends were and what they might be doing.

A few more home visits and he realized he'd have to start talking to the kids themselves, because most of these parents hadn't had a clue. He also had a much clearer idea about the great chasm that divided many of the locals from the owners of so many of the pricey homes that had been broken into.

In the city, there was the same gap between the poor and the phenomenally rich, but in so many ways they were all crushed together. In Manhattan, they all shared the same small island.

But it was possible up here for the wealthy to pretty much avoid living anywhere near the poor. If you lived in Alford and shopped at Guido's instead of Price Chopper; if you never ever set foot in a laundromat and avoided McDonalds, went to Tanglewood for classical music and Jacobs Pillow to see dance and up to the Williamstown Theater Festival, you could pretty easily spend a poverty-free summer.

Living a part time weekend life made it ever so much easier. Your kids didn't have to go to local schools. You could socialize with other summer people. Have dinner at one of the many restaurants the locals could never afford. Of course, you had to employ a few of them to clean the pool, tend the garden, and plow the driveway just in case you wanted to come up for a weekend of skiing. But they were the help, not your friends, and certainly not your neighbors.

For many of the locals he had just met, the summer people took, not gave. Most recently high-speed internet, the ubiquitous laptop and virtual office enabled the enterprising to buy and sell anything to anyone anywhere they were. Making it easier to move up here full-time. The former city folk took the best land and drove up property and home prices for all.

The changes were everywhere and all too easily seen: large working farms broken up into extraordinarily expensive lots; neighborhood seedy bars transformed into trendy bistros offering overpriced pasta or raw fish; while hardware stores and auto parts shops became boutiques that budget-conscious locals ignored.

Barber shops were hair salons, and the food cooperative which once served the working poor now offered organic tofu ragout at nine dollars a pound. If the newcomers had kids, they sent them to a smorgasbord of private schools: the Rudolf Steiner School, Berkshire Country Day, Miss Hall's or the Berkshire School.

There were many locals who were pissed about these big changes; many young people bummed that they could no longer afford to live in the towns they were raised. Thinking they'd have to leave the area after school. It wouldn't take much to go from being seriously annoyed about these ever expanding mansions to breaking into them.

It wasn't all that hard to find several of the kids on his list. At some point during the day or night, teenagers from most of the South Berkshire towns made their way to Barrington. A favorite hangout was the parking lot by the new movie theater. A bit bleak for his taste but it seemed to work for them. There were a few spindly trees and small patches of grass favored by the many dogs that came to relieve themselves. There was a lot of asphalt and in between the parked cars some small nooks and crannies for dealing. The best part about it was there wasn't much reason for parents or other adults to linger there more than a minute or two.

So there were always clumps of kids scattered throughout the lot, and several small groups hanging out in the wide hallway of what used to be Great Barrington's big downtown hotel. Which now, thanks to the state's subsidized housing program, provided lodging for some of the town's less fortunate tenants. This indoor atrium hosted several food shops: Taco Mexico, which served affordable burritos, Café Athens with its Greek gyros, and the entrance to Downtown Diner, offering burgers and an all-day breakfast menu.

Several years before Frank's time the parking lot had been the scene of one of the Berkshires most publicized and politicized drug busts. A few teenagers had been sent to jail for two years for selling what Frank, by city standards, regarded as miniscule amounts of pot and ecstasy and some painkillers. Others were forced to make plea deals and would forever have black marks beside their names. There was still deep-seated anger directed toward the District Attorney, whose prosecutorial zeal was regarded as both excessive and vindictive.

One of the unfortunate results of his protracted campaign against youthful drug use in Great Barrington was that even without a uniform, every kid in the parking lot made Frank as a cop the moment he headed towards them. They now had finely-tuned radar and some very hard-earned experience with both undercover cops and supposed friends who, in return for a free pass on prosecution, would agree to testify against their buddies.

So what he had hoped would be some fruitful fact-finding turned into his own interrogation. Surrounded by ten teenagers, he was bombarded with questions: Had he ever inhaled? Did he really think it was appropriate to jail an eighteen year-old for two years for taking a couple of bucks from a friend in return for generously giving up some joints from his stash? What about the state's ridiculous school zone rule? Which meant that just because you happened to be within 1,000 feet of some kind, any kind of school, and in possession of drugs that someone else says you had "an intent to distribute," well then you were completely screwed. Did he even know about – because they didn't – the tiny day care center in the basement of the church a couple of blocks away? The very school the D.A. used against their friends.

Frank stood there as the questions kept coming. Did he know that under Massachusetts drug laws, there was no specific quantity of drugs to prove that you were dealing, not just using? That they took you in front of a jury and scared the hell out of these people, showing them baggies and needles and saying that pot leads to heroin and crack, which leads to gangs and gun violence and death.

Or what about the undercover cop who lied in court? The kids who were caught here weren't big-time dealers. Did a couple of them sell small quantities of pot and some other stuff, yeah, and maybe some valium they stole from their folks. But under the school zone law you're looking at a mandatory two-year sentence.

Why? Just about everyone they know smokes an occasional joint. Put the parents of just about every kid in the parking lot under oath and ask if they smoke, and they'll either be committing perjury or admitting they do.

Frank finally had enough. "Jesus, are all you kids going to law school? Listen, the truth is that up until a few months ago I was living in the city and was a New York City Detective trying to solve murders and assaults. I really didn't have the time or inclination to bust someone for a couple of joints.

"That said, I'm just learning that there's a serious problem with drug and alcohol abuse around here. I understand what you're saying, and just because a law is on the books, it doesn't necessarily make it a smart law. But until you change a bad law and make it better, you have to find a way to stay out of trouble … I like to believe there are always exceptions and I happen to believe in trying to find some justice. Obviously in this case, mandatory sentences make that kind of impossible."

A tall pimply white kid with ripped jeans and a red bandana stretched over and tied behind his head, trying his best to be a bad-ass, moved to within a few inches of Frank to challenge him: "What about the fact that a cop in a nearby town has been dealing coke for years and no one's done squat about it. You going to defend that? You going to deny that? Like that's not possible, right?"

"I'm a cop, not a moron. There are always dirty cops. Just like there are always some punk kids. Does that mean that all cops are dirty, or most cops are dirty, absolutely not! I don't know anything about many of my fellow officers up here. Not yet, at least. But I'm going to give each and every one the benefit of the doubt until I learn otherwise.

"Now just so you know, my name is Frank Falco and I'm the Assistant Chief in Ripton. So until the law changes – and I do hope some of you end up going to law school and help change it – but in the meantime do me a favor and don't let me catch you selling dope by the Ripton kindergarten. I'd much rather spend my time putting the really bad guys away. But," moving his jacket aside, "I do have this badge and I do have a job to do.

"Now how about you give me a chance to ask a question or two? I'm checking into a series of break-ins in houses that are for sale or houses owned by weekenders, and mostly empty. For the most part, there hasn't been any serious damage or theft, and that's good. But something happened recently with a bunch of paint at one of the houses, and I'm getting worried that we're moving into some serious and out-of-control vandalism.

"If some of you know who's doing it, I'd love to talk to you. Given your recent experiences with the local police, you may not want to tell me. But I'm trying my very best to resolve this in the fairest and most peaceful way possible. So if you won't talk to me maybe you can pass along the word that now's the time to give this house-breaking a rest."

Frank was getting ready to leave, then stopped for a moment, and looked back at them: "I said before I'm not a moron. I'm also not a genius. So thanks for taking the time to tell me about what went down here, and I'm promise you I'm going to take a closer look at the drug laws. You all have a good day!"

As Frank headed home, he found himself thinking about last night and Penny. Probably as a result of all the work he had done with Dr. Silver, Frank couldn't ignore that he was more than a bit spooked by how comfortable he had felt with her. Especially because after the shooting and pushing his girlfriend Gloria away, he had gotten so used to being alone.

Now maybe all that had changed. He had already left a bumbling message on her voicemail, thanking her, saying he had enjoyed last night, and hoped to see her again. Then thinking he had sounded pretty lame and that he could and should do better, leaving a second message. Managing to get even more self-conscious, saying he hoped she understood what he was trying to say the first time around, then explaining how he had gotten busy driving around the county talking to parents who didn't seem to care that much about drugs and alcohol and … But then time had run out mid-sentence. Luckily, finally realizing a third message wouldn't be any better, so he left it at two.

THIRTY-EIGHT

Ernie's head was hurting. The bruise on his forehead more visible. Tyler had taken them from Stockbridge to Housatonic to Great Barrington to Sheffield to Hartsville then up the hill to New Marlborough then back the way they had come down a steep dirt road to Ripton. They had been driving for more than an hour. And even though Bob had done his best to keep some distance between them, it was hard to imagine Tyler hadn't seen them.

Bob had suggested several times that they pull over to rest for a bit or turn back and head home to at least get Ernie some aspirin. At this point, continuing on was just about his stubborn refusal to admit defeat. Yet, with each additional mile, Ernie grew ever more frustrated, ever more furious, declaring that "once and for all we're gonna find out where this little bastard is headed."

At the bottom of the hill, Tyler turned left onto yet another dirt road. Bob tried to create a bit more space between them, waiting a few moments before he turned left to follow. A half mile later, Tyler turned right, heading over a small bridge.

Ernie was soon nagging Bob to speed up. "Faster, Bob! Whatever you do, don't lose him!" And Bob, the memory of his near demise by milk tanker still in the forefront of his mind only halfheartedly hit the accelerator just as Tyler, without signaling, swerved left onto an old abandoned dirt road. Ernie tried to duck out of sight, yelling: "Don't let them see us! Keep going straight!"

Which was fairly ridiculous advice because Bob was going too fast to do anything but keep going the way they were going.

Ernie, imagining some kind of victory in sight, kept up a constant harangue while Bob found a driveway a quarter-mile up the road to turn around in. By now Bob was dreaming of a hot shower and a couple of cheeseburgers and some fries, anything besides driving around back roads with his maniacal dad. He headed back in the direction they had just come from.

Without warning, Ernie punched his right arm: "Here, Bob. Here! He turned here!"

Bob's jaw was already tight and clamped shut and he silently absorbed the pain. By the time Bob turned onto the old farm road, Tyler's car was nowhere to be seen. There were a series of other dirt roads branching off this one, paths mainly used by the

Tremblays to move their farm equipment from field to field during haying.

"The little prick has got to be here somewhere … C'mon, Bob!"

Bob couldn't help but notice the bright brand new "No Trespassing" signs tacked to posts and trees scattered everywhere around them.

It was during one of Tyler's first forays onto the property that he had found the several turnabouts Grandfather Tremblay had cut into the forest. Now mostly overgrown, these circular paths had made it possible during Tremblay's farming days to turn his tractor and plow and baler around. And because Tyler had taken to heart Leonard's advice to not only know how to get in but especially how to get out, he had spent some significant time during each of his early trips to the Krause property carefully cutting brush to create a few places he could hide his car from sight.

Today, safely hidden in the first of these turnabouts, Tyler watched as Bob and Ernie headed up the abandoned road searching for him. He couldn't help but smile thinking of the many near-lethal bumps and ruts that were waiting for Ernie up ahead. He gave them another minute or two, then got out of his car to hike a half-mile through the woods to get a better view of what they were up to.

*   *   *

Frank was on his way to the florist when he got the call from Tom's Towing about a distress call from the Krause property. From an Earnest Bevans of Brett, who somehow got his car stuck on one of old man Tremblays' dirt roads.

Chalk another one up to the *I Ching*. Frank was especially glad he had taken the time to add "able helpers" to the effort, having asked a bunch of local businesses, the jewelry stores and second hand places, the landscaping, snow plowing folks and the car repair shops to keep an eye out for anything that might involve the break-in properties in any way possible.

"Bevans … Bevans," the name sounded familiar. Then when Frank looked down to check his sheet of high school dropouts, he found the three Bevans boys: Bill, Bob, and Buck.

Driving out to the Krause property was getting old for him. By the time he got there, the guy from Tom's had managed to lift the

Bevans' car out of the ditch it had landed in, and up onto his flatbed. Figuring he'd tow it back to the main road, then see whether or not it could be safely driven.

Unfortunately, there were also three guys in crisp uniforms from Apex Security hovering menacingly about Ernie and Bob.

Frank immediately went to his 9mm Smith & Wesson M&P, unclipping the strap as he moved forward. "Listen guys," flashing his badge. "I'm Assistant Chief Frank Falco from here in Ripton. I assume you've been employed by Mr. Krause to protect his property but this is an official police matter now. I'm sure Mr. Krause appreciates how hard you're working, but I'll take it from here."

One of the three moved toward Frank. He had a Captain's patch on the right shoulder of his Apex jacket. "Well, I'm sure you can appreciate that Mr. Krause hasn't invited these folks onto his property. He's hired us to deal with just this kind of situation and that's what we've been doing. We very respectfully have asked this gentleman what he thinks he's doing on the property and we'd like an answer."

Frank was thinking how much he truly despised the new breed of rent-a-cops. In his experience many of them had been unable to pass police exams. As much as he wanted to tell these guys to take a hike, he needed to defuse the situation. There was Tom's tow-truck driver and the two Bevanses to take care of.

Frank continued to move forward as he spoke. "I appreciate the effort you've made but exactly who are you? I'd like your name and the names of your colleagues. I intend to be speaking to Mr. Krause later in the day to see if he wants to press charges and I'd certainly prefer to tell him you helped rather than obstructed police business."

The Captain begrudgingly made room for Frank and his two men followed his lead. "Cards, gentlemen," and as he reached into his front jacket pocket, they followed suit. He held out three business cards for Frank, who now was gesturing for Ernie and Bob to follow him back toward the Ripton cruiser.

Frank took a quick look down at their spiffy business cards, the raised black letters "Protect and Defend" beneath an impressive thunderbolt, and tried to stifle a smirk. Looking back to add: "Thanks, Captain Stark, I appreciate the assistance."

Frank turned to the tow truck driver: "Why don't I meet you

down at the bottom of the road, and these gentlemen can settle up with you. In the meantime, they'll ride with me."

Tyler watched from the woods as Frank persuasively took hold of Ernie's left and Bob's right elbow, guiding them down to his car. "Thus far, there's no official complaint of trespassing against you both. But I'm betting that once these gentlemen speak to their employer, they'll certainly be one. So how about we try to get ahead of this right now. I'd appreciate it if you would both take a seat in the back of cruiser, and I'll drive us down to the road. Where we'll continue the conversation, and you can tell me what you were doing on Mr. Krause's land."

There was just enough room for Frank to back up and turn around. He could see Ernie Bevans in the rearview mirror frantically whispering instructions to his son.

Talking with his dad was always an adventure for Bob. Apart from the constant criticism, he never ever knew what his Dad would come up with. "Deer, deer," he'd kept telling Bob, who had to ask. "What do you mean, deer?"

"Follow my lead and keep your mouth shut!"

Ernie's idea of a whisper was another man's shout, and Frank tried not to shake his head in amazement.

After a check of Bob's license and the rental car's registration, and a quick test that the car would start, Frank kept Ernie in the cruiser and told Bob to follow him in the rental to his office in Town Hall.

It was there that Ernie added to his deer story. "There are a couple of guys at The Back Door and they're always talking about the best place to get yourself a deer. Of course, we're talking legal deer. 'Cause I always wait for deer season, not like some other guys who are looking to jack a deer all year long, rigging some extra lights on their pickup to blast a field late at night or early in the morning, which freezes the poor deer in the bright light just long enough to get off a shot.

"Now I don't know about you Officer, uh, sorry but I don't think I got your name, I don't know what you think about venison, but me and my boys we love it. So anyway, there's this guy at the bar who swore to me that there's this incredible spot right here in Ripton, on the old Tremblay farm – and the deal is you could hunt on the property and give the Tremblays a fair share of the meat – except it turns out which is what you just saw is that we couldn't really find the place and we must have gotten lost. I was hoping to find the Tremblays but didn't. Reconnoiter, isn't that the right word. Just trying to scope everything out to make sure we have it right when deer season comes around."

Bob was impressed, thinking that smacking his head against the windshield might have helped. This story, even though a complete lie, actually made more sense than anything Bob had heard out of his dad in a long time.

"Well, Mr. Bevans, exactly how many deer did you see?"

"Uh … well, now that you mention it …"

"The bump on your head. Did that happen when you were counting deer?"

"Uh … the bump," involuntarily lifting his hand to rub his forehead "that happened uh … when my son, who decided to help me look for the deer, he had to brake suddenly … must have been some critter, a woodchuck maybe, running across the road and I was hunched forward, even with my seatbelt on, in case you're wondering, and so boom."

"And the break-ins?"

Which for the first time silenced Ernie, and slowly he began to realize that deer and woodchucks might not be enough.

"Uh … what do you mean, break-ins?"

"Are you trying to say that you and your son weren't about to break into Mr. Krause's house? That is, after you finished counting all the deer you wouldn't be shooting because it's out of season!"

"No way, no way in hell are you gonna pin this on me …"

Bob could see his dad beginning to lose it big time. His face was starting to turn red, the telltale sign.

"Excuse me, Chief Falco … I think what my father was trying to say …"

Ernie somehow managed to keep himself from smacking Bob, but quickly interrupted: "Shut up, Bob. I told you I would handle this." Then turning his glare from Bob to Frank, and losing his patience: "Deer … I told you deer, and I'm sticking to deer …"

Bob tried not to cringe at his dad's re-emerging stupidity, closing his eyes, hoping he could somehow magically be tele-transported out of there, Star-Trek like, away from the Berkshires, away from his family, to start a new life on a new planet, somewhere, anywhere but here.

"Well, as I said before Mr. Bevans, there are no formal charges against you, so for the moment I thank you for your cooperation. And Bob, I sincerely hope I won't be seeing you too soon."

Ernie got up as quickly as he could, offering a short grunt to register his indignation. He then turned to Bob, signaling him to get up and get going.

Outside, Ernie grabbed the car keys from Bob then snarled: "I can't believe you lost Tyler again!" Luckily Bob didn't have a chance to respond because Ernie's cellphone rang.

"Mr. Bevans, this is Officer Thompson of the Brett Police Department. We've got your boys here. We'd like you to go home and get your son Bill's driver's license and bring it to us and, if everything is in order, you can pick them up at the station."

Two police stations in one day was a record even for Ernie. The more he remembered bits and pieces of this disastrous day, the more his head hurt. The more tired he felt. He didn't even care that Bob took the car keys and got behind the wheel without asking. He slowly eased himself into the passenger's seat. Dreaming of a drink or two or three, then realizing he'd have to get his kids before he could get to The Back Door. Resigned for the moment, he put his head against the passenger side window and before he knew it he was snoring.

THIRTY-NINE

It took one call to the Brett police for Frank to learn from Officer McDaniel that Ernie Bevans had been in and out of trouble for years. A continuing history of drunken driving, bar fights, and an arrest twelve years ago for "criminal harassment" of his wife. Somehow, maybe because he gave her a big check, he avoided jail time. When very soon after, his then wife, Janice Fields Bevans, left Ernie and her kids and the Commonwealth of Massachusetts for California.

With another call Frank learned that two of Ernie's three kids had recurring disciplinary problems at Brett High School. Only Bob had done well, and Arnold Jackson, the school counselor, admitted he was relieved when Bill and Buck left early, but sad that Bob had dropped out along with them. Jackson said that Mr. Bevans was extremely unsupportive of the efforts the school made to make education work for his kids. Jackson was most worried about Buck, who most of the time was withdrawn and uncommunicative, but had a dreadful temper. He had several times urged Mr. Bevans to explore therapy for Bill and Buck, and a private school for Bob, to remove him from the immediate influence of his brothers, but Bevans became extremely hostile.

After school, according to Officer McDaniel, the kids had extremely spotty work records, moving from one low-paying retail job to another: Baker's Hardware, Theresa's Sub Shop, MagicMart, Burger King, and Chicken City.

It was possible that Ernie Bevans and his kids could be the ones responsible for the break-ins. In fact, the Bevans family dynamic seemed to eerily match some of what he had just read in the *I Ching*. The only problem was, they just didn't seem smart enough to have pulled some of this off. Unless, if Arnold Jackson was right, Bob was in charge.

It wasn't surprising that this time Chief Paul got the call from Krause. Frank had obviously come across as uncooperative, and Krause didn't appreciate resistance. So it was the Chief who first learned that Krause wanted Ernie and Bob Bevans arrested and prosecuted for trespassing. That Krause needed the Chief to handle it personally.

Frank was thinking Krause was bound to be disappointed.

Probably hoping for death by lethal injection. But, unfortunately, he and Chief Paul knew the law.

Chapter 266: Section 120 of Massachusetts General Law considered it "trespass" to enter upon posted land, and violators convicted of the offense were subject to "a fine of not more than one hundred dollars or by imprisonment for not more than thirty days or both such fine and imprisonment."

Based on what Chief Paul had told him about the local courts, it was pretty unlikely to expect anything more than a fine Ernie Bevans could easily afford for this offense.

Frank was hoping, though, that these charges would at least give him a real shot at Bob.

*   *   *

Doris was washing dishes when she heard a car drive up, and looked up from the sink to see the cruiser come to a stop. Not again, she thought. Ernie had been drinking beer all afternoon and was spread out cold on the living room couch.

"Ernie!" she called out. "Ernie, it's the cops," watching as the officer got out of the car and stopped to check to make sure he had the right address.

She put down the sponge and quickly got out of her long yellow rubber gloves, wiping her damp hands on her apron. Moving quickly into the other room.

Her choices weren't good: waking Ernie herself or letting the cop wake him. She decided to risk it and gently shook his shoulder. "Ernie, you've got to wake up. There's a cop about to knock on the front door. C'mon, Ernie," watching as he mustered a groan and tried to roll over. "Ernie, I mean it," shaking him a little big harder.

Ducking out of the way as he swung a sleepy heavy arm in her direction. "Shut up, why don'tcha, I'm sleeping."

"It's either me that's gonna wake you up or the police officer who's on his way in!"

"What are you talking about?"

Just then, Chief Paul began to knock loudly.

Doris looked down at Ernie with contempt: "That's what I'm talking about," calling out in the direction of the kitchen: "I'm coming ... Just a minute."

Doris made it to the door just after Chief Paul's second round of knocking. In some ways, this was one of the hardest parts of the job, seeing for yourself how others lived. He could see the toll life had taken on Doris' face, the fear in her eyes as she reluctantly opened the door to him. It was getting to the point where he could hardly remember the days when his was a welcome face, when people were glad to see the police, when they assumed you were on their side. Now it was barely concealed hostility, or annoyance at best.

"Could you please ask Mr. Bevans to come to the door, Ma'am?"

She nodded, thought about going back to the living room to try once more, then decided on the easier course, turning away from the officer and raising the volume several notches: "Ernie … Ernie you need to get up and come to the door!"

They could both hear Ernie cursing loudly: "Fucking assholes … Can't even let a guy sleep in his own home …"

Chief Paul started to silently count numbers in his head. His doctor had been warning him about his blood pressure for years now, suggesting long vigorous walks, daily exercise and some simple relaxation techniques. "How about when you think you might lose your temper," Doctor Small said, "you take a deep breath and count, maybe one to a hundred. I'd suggest sheep," the doctor added with a smile, "but I have a feeling instead of counting them, you'll round them up and charge them with creating a public disturbance." By now Chief Paul was up to six, but still imagining himself dragging Bevans into the cruiser. There had to be a better way to relax.

Ernie, after ricocheting from one side of the doorway to the other, stumbled his way into the kitchen, glowering at Doris, then scowling at Chief Paul.

"Mr. Bevans, Mr. Earnest Bevans … I'm Chief Paul from the Ripton Police Department. I have a summons here for you, charging you with a violation of Massachusetts General Law, Chapter 266, Section 120, Trespassing upon the lands of Mr. and Mrs. Milton Krause on the Ripton-New Marlborough Road. There will be a court hearing at ten A.M. on the 30th of this month in Southern Berkshire Court. Do you understand, Mr. Bevans?"

Ernie offered a resentful grunt.

"Just a word, Mr. Bevans." Looking from Ernie back to Doris. "I convinced Mr. Krause to remove your son's name from the

173

complaint. I won't be so kind in the future. Have a good day …
Both of you." Chief Paul opened and closed the door behind him.

*   *   *

Five hours into drinking at The Back Door, Ernie could no
longer remember to whom he had told the story. Because each
time he told it, he remembered another part, remembering
someone else who had fucked up, or something else that had gone
wrong. Six or seven beers in, he was still pissed most of all at Tyler
for whatever the hell he was doing in secret, and for slipping away
every time before Ernie had a chance to teach him a lesson.

Another hour in, he was pissed at Doris, the world's worst
mother, except maybe for his ex-wife. A close contest. Then at Bill
and Buck, of course, for getting caught without a license and
humiliating him and making him go to the cop shop in Brett.
Pissed at Bob who led them right smack into what was clearly a
trap in Ripton, and then for somehow weaseling his way out of
being charged. Thinking, who knows, that maybe Bob had made a
deal with that cop. Why else was it only him who had to go to
court? When he wasn't even driving.

Could have been maybe the fourth or fifth time around telling
the story, but somehow Sam Preston ended up on the stool to his
right. Anyway, Sam started talking about how easy kids had it
today, which got Ernie thinking about those stupid hamburgers
and French fries and how maybe everything would have been
different if they had two cars in Ripton instead of just one
following Tyler. Able to have stopped him before he disappeared.
To once and for all get to the bottom of all this.

Instead, his idiot kids were late and got caught by the cops. So
where the hell did Tyler get off to anyway? Wondering whether
Tyler was in cahoots with those asshole phony cops who seemed to
be waiting for him and Bob on that dirt road? Maybe if he hadn't
hit his head while saving Bob's ass, he would have been able to see
the ambush for what it was.

Sam was right, and it really pissed Ernie off big-time to think
about all he had sacrificed for his ingrate kids and Doris, who was
hardly worth the trouble, not to mention that idiot son of hers. He
still had a lot of the insurance money stashed away. He began to
daydream about California and no more snow, and a simple little

ranch house with air conditioning and cable TV, and getting up in the morning with no one to deal with, and a whole day's worth of relaxing to look forward to. Why should his ex-wife have California to herself. Didn't he deserve some of it? The only thing he would really miss was The Back Door. If he never saw the kids again well that would be just fine with him.

Sam was on a whiskey-soaked rhetorical roll, and all the while Ernie saw himself sitting on his imaginary Southern California porch with a cold twelve pack, the sun warming his beer-soaked bones. Now Sam was talking real loud about how early on he had gotten his kids to respect him, spare the rod and all. Taking his big hunting knife from its sheath, slamming it on the bar. Announcing that a couple of roundhouse rights to the kids, and waving this around helped seal the deal. So yeah even though he never really saw them much anymore, he could rest easy knowing he had taught them who was boss. Sliding the knife over to Ernie: "here, how about you borrow this, try it out for a while. You need it a lot more than me, and you know where you can find me."

A few beers later, Sam had somehow been replaced by Johnnie Dupree, who after Ernie tried to tell him the story for the third time, urged Ernie to take his knife and shove it where the sun doesn't shine. Which was reason enough for the bartender to call a time out, take Ernie's money, settle his bill, and call a cab for him. In ten minutes, Ernie was asleep in the back seat of the taxi, dreaming once again of the California sun.

FORTY

Frank had gotten there at six-thirty in the morning. In his own car for cover, parking a few houses down from their house. Hoping that Bob would get up early and he could get to the kid one on one.

Inside, Ernie woke at seven with a massive hangover and splitting headache. Skipping his shower and shave, he headed to the kitchen to treat his headache with four aspirin and two cups of coffee.

As the headache receded a bit to the back of his brain, he felt a new determination. Unlike so many other mornings after, visions of the West Coast were still with him. Knowing his new life was waiting. There were only a few things to wrap up. In the meantime, he had Sam's knife to remind himself to be extra firm, steady, and resolved.

By seven-thirty, he had gathered his wits enough to notice that for the first time in several days Tyler was sleeping in his own bed. He quickly woke Bill, Bob, and Buck, and gave them clear instructions. Separating the burger boys, he and Buck would take his car, while Bob and Bill would take the rental car. This time, no matter what, they wouldn't lose Tyler.

Their previous defeat still lingered and while it was hard for the boys to find the energy necessary to resume the battle this early in the day, the concentrated fury in Ernie's eyes made it clear they'd pay a stiff price for dereliction of duty.

Soon they were outside dividing into teams, the two of Ernie's cars positioning themselves on the road so they'd be ready to follow Tyler. While unbeknownst to Ernie, Frank was watching and waiting, wondering what trouble the Bevanses were planning this time.

*   *   *

Tyler woke, and made himself a quick breakfast of milk and cereal, shifting from nervous apprehension to excitement. In semi-sleep he had heard Ernie and the boys conspiring. They still hadn't figured out how pathetically thin the walls were. But he was getting very tired of this cat and mouse game, tired of having to waste so much energy slipping away from them. Tired of his mother, tired of Ernie, tired of the boys.

As he started up his Tercel, he figured the trip would take him a half hour or so. His many months of house-sitting and appliance rehabilitation and repair had heightened his observational skills, so it wasn't difficult to see Ernie's small army deployed on both sides of the street. Then a new guy parked further down in front of the Shepard place. In the slight moment when Tyler drove past, he recognized the policeman from Mr. Krause's dirt road.

Almost immediately he could see Ernie pull in behind him and watched as Bill did a U-turn to fall in behind his dad. He was about to turn onto Route 20 and could only imagine the cop completing the convoy.

*   *   *

This was the morning Ernie was finally going to catch Tyler in the act. Even though he wasn't completely sure what act that was, he was willing to bet it involved breaking and entering and stealing.

But this time, a citizen's arrest. They had stuff like this on television all the time. He and the boys would nab Tyler and hold him for the cops. It would solve so many problems. Get Tyler out of his house and out of his hair. Make Doris focus more fully on what he wanted, not this crazy freak son of hers. Make things more pleasant until he finally hit the road.

He had watched enough TV to know Tyler could be used as that collateral stuff they were always talking about. The cops would get their breaking and entering guy, and, in return, agree to leave him the fuck alone. Erase that trespassing stuff and ease up on him. They'd be nuts not to take such a good deal.

The plan, of course, was on a need-to-know basis, and the less his idiot sons knew, the better off everybody would be. Thus far, they were more a minus than a plus, but unfortunately this was still more than a one-man job.

For Bill and Bob and Buck this was just another exercise in déjà vu. As they headed once more onto Route 102, Bill kept checking his front shirt pocket to assure himself that he had his driver's license handy. Buck, unfortunately, was stuck in the rental car up ahead with his dad, and he had scrunched himself into the furthest corner of the passenger seat, out of easy range of a random smack. So far, so good. Ernie had that slightly diabolical look in his eyes, which all the kids had come to understand was an indication that their dad was scheming. It might have disastrous effects in the long run, but for the moment, he was preoccupied and Buck was safe.

Bob, like Tyler, had noticed the Ripton cop. But for reasons he wasn't sure of, he hadn't told Ernie or Bill. In many ways, he felt like he was trapped in a bad movie, one of those flicks where you see the characters about to do something incredibly stupid, like go down into the dark basement where the serial killer is waiting or leave the safety of their house to reason with the ax-wielding maniac who has already killed two of your best friends. More and more, Bob was thinking he had to find a way out of this before the inevitable and disastrous end.

*   *   *

So once again Tyler had company. Having watched the security guards and Ripton policeman so quickly catch Ernie and Bob was what Elizabeth called poetic justice. So just maybe when he had the energy and some extra time, he'd bring Ernie and the boys back to the Krause property for some more excitement. There were at least a couple more abandoned dirt roads he could send them up.

*   *   *

As one by one the cars turned off Route 102 onto the Tottingham Road, Frank was wondering what was going on? He had hoped to isolate and get some time with Bob. But they all seemed to be following Tyler this morning. Why?

From talking to a lot of people about the Bevans clan, it was Tyler who was the biggest enigma. Like Bob, everyone spoke of Tyler's potential, and many thought he was by far the most intelligent of them all. Even in the early grades he was making all kinds of things, using crayons of every shade, telling wild, imaginative stories. But he always seemed distracted, in a world all his own: talking to himself and many times missing what his teachers were saying. Doing something quite different from his fellow students. Several teachers had noted they had spoken to his mother about what they regarded as his significant psychological issues. One wrote he often seemed a bit shell-shocked. Another diagnosed him with Asperger's Syndrome. After Frank had a

178

chance to talk to Bob, he'd try to sit down with Tyler. Hopefully he wouldn't be talking to them behind bars.

*   *   *

Sometimes it took Tyler by surprise: it happened at the oddest times. Those moments when he was blessedly by himself. No constant chorus or reverb. No do this. Do that. Do something. Do nothing. He smiled, wondering how long he had been driving in silence. Noticing, too, that he was unexpectedly excited. He had imagined feeling terribly anxious. But the way Elizabeth explained it, it was like setting off on a new adventure. Sort of the way he felt when he fixed that very first broken VCR at the house in E. Otis, knowing that Leonard would be pleased. Because it was a fair trade. An accomplishment.

*   *   *

Unfortunately, the coffee and aspirin hadn't done the trick. Ernie's head was aching, making it hard to concentrate on the road. It was probably a mistake letting Bill and Bob take the other car. Leaving him with Buck who only had his learner's permit. Well, at least it was daylight and if his head got worse, he could always get Buck behind the wheel. But first he figured he'd go back to the remedy that almost always worked, starting on one of the several small whiskey minis he had in his pocket.

Non-drinkers never really understood how essential it was to drink on the morning after. You'd get these stares, but drinking at nine or ten or eleven in the morning just worked better than anything else to get back up and running.

Buck watched as Ernie started to swig, knowing he was about as far away from his father as he could possibly get without falling out the door and onto the highway.

Ernie watched as Buck re-checked his seat belt. Much to Ernie's embarrassment, Buck still couldn't hold his liquor, so, of course, he just didn't know how good you could get at driving while drinking. How quickly the mind and body could readjust. Ernie knew he was a much better driver with five shots in him than most of those hypocritical non-drinkers. Plus he felt a bit better with each additional swig.

179

Bill could see his dad drinking in the car up ahead and, as much as he was relieved not to be there with him, he was beginning to worry for Buck, for all of them really. He wouldn't admit this to any of them but he had been scared shitless from the moment he had been stopped by the Brett police till the time he was released. He knew he should be tougher, but the thought of being locked up completely freaked him out. So the one thing he was now the most sure of was his desire to never again see the inside of jail. Problem was that with his dad, even in the best of times, that was pushing it. A couple of bottles in, and who knew where they'd end up.

*   *   *

As Frank followed several cars behind through the Tottingham Valley, then onto Ripton Road, he was thinking they might well end up back at the Kraus place. That he might possibly be close to solving these break-ins.

He couldn't help thinking that if these suspects were as intellectually handicapped as many of the crooks he was used to, he was blessed to be surrounded by the beauty of the Berkshire Hills rather than the chaos of Columbus Avenue.

Up the mountain and down into Ripton, and as if on cue, first Tyler, then the Bevanses turned left and then right.

Tyler couldn't help but smile as they all dutifully fell into line, wondering what was next for them all, as he abruptly and without warning accelerated sharply, turning right with a cloud of dust onto Long Pine Road.

Ernie, who had been drinking steadily, slammed on the brakes, and Bill, who was assuming they had another mile and a half to go before they got to the Kraus property, couldn't help but smash into the back of the rental. Frank now had a traffic accident to deal with instead of breaking and entering.

FORTY-ONE

Katie was just finishing taking the lemon poppy muffins out of the oven when she heard the knock. "Come in, please," she called out.

It seemed as if Rabbit was waiting for him. Rabbit smiled, performed a perfunctory smell, then moved aside and followed Tyler in.

"I'm right here in the kitchen," Katie added. "Make yourself comfortable and pull up a chair. I see you've met Rabbit. He's quite friendly."

"Yes, we know each other," and almost immediately the voices began. First, Ronald in his high voice announced that this was a really bad idea. Warning that if Tyler revealed too much, they'd get in trouble, and not only that Mom would be in trouble too. Abigail informed everyone that, even though there was no organizing feng shui aesthetic at work here, the room felt warm and comfortable. Tony took the opportunity to remind them that they were wasting time, that once again Ernie and the boys were stalking them and it was time to strike back. Elizabeth answered impatiently that they had delayed this for far too long. That if Deb was right, this woman could provide some insight into the confusing and maybe dangerous situation they found themselves in. It was, Elizabeth stressed, certainly worth the risk.

Katie could see how distracted Tyler was. As if he was present on the physical plane, but somewhere else entirely on the inside. She decided to keep things as informal as possible, thinking they'd work at the kitchen table, offering Tyler a plate for a muffin, a butter knife and the butter dish.

"Tea?"

He nodded, already tackling his muffin. As Katie poured, she explained that Deb had spoken to her a week or so ago. And that the way she worked was with some questions and this very smart Chinese book which was put together hundreds of years before Jesus Christ was born. That Tyler could do this at his own pace. Then offering him his own copy which he could take with him. Emphasizing that the most important thing was that he feel as relaxed as possible, because this process was just for him. That if at any time things didn't feel right, or if she was making him uncomfortable, well he should please tell her and she would find another way that worked for him.

Tyler sat there in silence as Katie sipped her tea and had some muffin. Then she reached for the *I Ching* and her coins and a new yellow pad:

"So Tyler, I think the best way to proceed is for you to tell me a little bit about what's on your mind and how I might be able to help."

Tyler closed his eyes for a bit and when he opened them he was ready to try. "I'm not the same. I've never been the same as everyone else. I don't belong. 'Too weird,' my father said. 'I don't know what to do with you,' my mother said. 'I can't even understand you.'

"Ernie says I'm crazy and he and my mother tried to make me take pills. But they were the wrong pills. Still, Elizabeth says it's worse than it ever was. That we have to do something before anyone gets hurt."

Katie was nodding. "Thank you, Tyler. I just want to say that I am not a doctor and I am not a therapist. I can be a guide and hopefully help figure some things out, but if you feel like you or someone else might get hurt, then seeing a doctor and/or a therapist might be absolutely necessary. So if that's called for, hopefully I can help make you feel better about doing that. So I need you to know that if I feel like things are beyond my ability or capacity to help, I will tell you that as quickly and clearly as I can.

"But, in the meantime, let's just see what happens. I want you to think of a question, a question you'd really like an answer or answers to. A question that can't just be answered with a simple yes or no."

All of a sudden everyone seemed to have a question, and the questions seemed to bounce from one side of his brain to the other. Like an air traffic controller dealing with too many planes and not enough airspace, Tyler felt overwhelmed. Katie could see the recent calm draining from Tyler, and watched as he desperately began to rub his forehead, trying as best he could to keep the looming headache at bay.

"Breathe, Tyler ... breathe," Katie suggested. "Take a deep breath in and hold it: one ... two ... three ... now let it out slowly. That's it ... once again, take another deep breath in and hold it: there you go, one ... two ... three ... and now out slowly."

Tyler could feel the voices recede, the silence returning.

"A few more times, Tyler, in, one … two … three, and slowly let it out, one … two … three. And again."

Slowly Tyler opened his eyes, and offered Katie a very slight smile: "Thank you, it is very hard when there is not enough space for me …" He paused to take a sip of tea. "I think I know the question: 'Why am I so different?'"

As Katie explained how the coins worked, she got Tyler another muffin and re-filled his mug.

Tyler took another large bite, then gathered the coins. "Why am I so different?" he asked before each turn. His first two throws were identical: three tails, a broken and changing line. Watching as Katie began to draw the two hexagrams. He then threw two heads and a tail, then two tails and a head two times in a row, and ended with two heads and a tail. He watched as Katie looked through her book and found the hexagrams: "P'i" and "Lü."

"Let's start with 'P'i / Standstill:'"

Heaven is above, drawing further and further away, while the earth below sinks further into the depths … It is a time of standstill and decline …

THE JUDGMENT
STANDSTILL. Evil people do not further
The perseverance of the superior man.
The great departs, the small approaches.

Heaven and earth are out of communion, and all things are benumbed …

Katie looked up to see how Tyler was doing. His eyes were wide with surprise and he looked from Katie to the coins and then back up to Katie. He had never heard words used this way …

Katie began to read some more:

> … and on earth confusion and disorder prevail …
> The way of inferior is in ascent; the way of
> superior people is on the decline. But … if the
> possibility of exerting influence is closed to them,
> they nevertheless remain faithful to their
> principles and withdraw into seclusion.

"So, Tyler, what do you think of this? Does this make sense to you?"

"Confusion and disorder and decline … and fists. And smacks. And belts. Mother crying. With no place to go. With nowhere safe. My room. Bathroom. Beneath the bed., until melting away into the closet, the shed, withdraw, small and smaller and smaller … "

Katie tried not to flinch as she began to better understand Tyler's story. She waited to see if Tyler had more to say, then: "Thank you, Tyler, thank you so much for telling me this …"

Rabbit moved to sit beside Tyler, then put his chin on Tyler's thigh.

"Whatever you feel, whatever you felt, it seems to me that the *I Ching* knows that this is real and true about your world, and not something you have imagined. That for you the world of good works, of generosity, of kindness and concern was/is so very far from this life of yours. The inferior triumphing over the superior; disorder over order."

Tyler, eyes wide, was waiting for more.

Katie continued to read:

> When, owing to the influence of inferior men,
> mutual mistrust prevails in public life, fruitful
> activity is rendered impossible … Therefore the
> superior man … does not allow himself to be
> tempted by dazzling offers to take part in public
> activities. This would only expose him to danger,
> since he cannot assent to the meanness of others.
> He therefore hides his worth and withdraws into
> seclusion.

"My father, and then Ernie … the meanness of others. At home, in town, at school. Exposed to danger … And the hiding,

hiding all the time … Until Elizabeth … " Tyler offered, then paused to think more about all he had heard.

Katie could see the question forming within Tyler, the slightly furrowed brow, then the words tumbling out: "How does this book know about my danger? I haven't told Deb. I haven't told anyone … Do you know this because you are a witch?" and then wondering, worrying whether he had insulted her, with a pause, "Not a wicked Wizard of Oz witch. But maybe a good magic witch."

"Thank you, Tyler, it's a beautiful compliment. But I don't really think any of this is coming from me. It was your question. You took the coins. You threw them. I am glad that the story makes sense for you. When it works it does feel like magic. I like to think it is because we want and need it to work. Because we are finally ready to find the answers to the questions we are asking. So if it is magic, it is your magic, Tyler."

Tyler sat there in silence, probably unaware he was nodding.

"I'm going to read bits and pieces from some of what the book says about the individual lines you threw:

> If it becomes impossible to make our influence count, it is only by retirement that we spare ourselves humiliation. Success in a higher sense can be ours, because we know how to safeguard the values of our personalities.

Katie stopped as she watched Tyler react to the last line. He seemed transfixed for the moment, not quite believing what he had just heard: "Excuse me, what did you just say?"

Katie looked down at the book, and slowly repeated:

> Success in a higher sense can be ours, because we know how to safeguard the values of our personalities.

She watched as Tyler's soft smile spread from inside out across his face. As he remembered the books Elizabeth got them. The smile transforming his face. Then in a voice so very different from anything Katie had heard before, softer, feminine:

"I told you it was time. I told you we could be safe. Finally …"

Katie sat there, her eyes widening; she who was transfixed. She who was now experiencing a kind of magic. Because while this was still Tyler sitting before her; there was a not really Tyler emerging from within.

Slowly she remembered the movies she had seen: "Sybil" and "The Three Faces of Eve." She sat quietly for a moment, sipping tea. Until, having steadied herself:

"Hi, my name is Katie. We haven't met yet. Obviously, this section is very important to you. So would you be willing to talk about it?"

"I'm Elizabeth. Tyler refers to me as the smart lady ... He must trust you because this is the first, the only time any of us have been out in the world with others ..."

"There are more of you?" Katie asked.

"Well, there's me and the two ... well, there are times I wonder whether or not they are still boys at heart. Ronald is the youngest and I think it's fair to say timid, and so most often he's far away in the background. Tony always wants to fight back, and defend us just about every time we're in trouble, and sometimes when we're not. Then, of course, there's Abigail, a bundle of wild ideas, wacky and wonderfully creative.

"Maybe I'm just seeing things, well hearing things actually, making more of it than is meant but when you read: 'because we know how to safeguard the values of our personalities' I felt like someone finally said out loud what was happening for us."

Katie paused to take in all that had been said, to try and process its many ramifications. "Well, Elizabeth, it seems the *I Ching* sees and hears far more than the rest of us. And appreciates how Tyler has managed to maintain his principles in the face of significant meanness, to safeguard, and when necessary even hide his true self.

"I've obviously just met you and hardly know Tyler but I really want to thank you, Elizabeth, for trusting me enough to talk with me."

Katie took another sip of tea, then continued: "If it's OK with you and Tyler, I'm going to read some more. If any of you have any questions or want to say something, please just jump in."

Katie waited and decided to take the silence as agreement:

Six in the second place means:
They bear and endure ...

186

By his willingness to suffer personally he insures
the success of his fundamental principles …

"I'm sorry if my questions seem naive or obvious … But
anything you and Elizabeth and the others can share with me
would be appreciated.

"The *I Ching* speaks of enduring, and bearing with, and putting
up with a lot of very hard things," then looking back at the text,
"confusion … disorder … humiliation … shame, and you've
mentioned fists and belts and smacks. Would you be willing to talk
some more about this?"

Tyler hesitated, then slowly wrenched himself back into the
past. "My father … he was always angry, angry with my mother.
Everything she did was wrong. She cooked wrong. She dressed
wrong. The house was messy. She didn't vacuum. She vacuumed at
the wrong time. She woke him up. Or she forgot to wake him up.

"I was just a kid but I woke him when I played. A smack. I
talked too loud. Or other times he couldn't hear me. Speak up. A
smack. My friends were too noisy. Then I didn't have any friends. I
was stupid. Then very stupid and very bad. So he wished he didn't
have me. He didn't want to hit me but it was for my own good. He
didn't want to hit me but I wouldn't learn otherwise.

"My mother, she too had to learn. To be cleaner. To cook
better. My mother said it wasn't really him. It was the drugs. Speed,
she said. The man she married was a nice man. This was some
other man. Sometimes she could see the man she married. He was
still there but you really had to look for him.

"I spent lots of time hiding, but peeking out to try and see the
nice man she had married. I looked all the time. Sometimes he saw
me watching and he would yell, 'Who the hell are you looking at,'
and before I had a chance to move away, smack. But I never
stopped looking for the man she had married.

"Elizabeth came to help one day when he was hitting my mom
so hard she was crying and crying and I tried to stop him, grabbing
him, and he was yelling I was next. Elizabeth said for me to run
because this time he might just kill me. 'Run, run,' she yelled. So I
ran out the back door and I was hiding under all my dad's junk in
the shed and it got very dark and very cold and I didn't have warm
clothes and I didn't have food and I was trembling and I peed my

pants but Elizabeth said it was all right and that we had to hide until he got tired.

"I was happy when he left but felt very sad I never found the real him. Then later Ernie and Bill and Bob and Buck came to stay because my mom said it was important to have a man around the house and it would be good for me to have company. Because I had no friends and was spending too much time alone, good for all of us, she said. I would have brothers who would stick up for me."

Katie was about to thank him when Tyler twitched, and once again brought his hand up to rub his forehead. Then she heard a deeper, curt, to the point voice, with a sharp edge of anger: "Worse than father. So bad that I had to pull the knife one day when Ernie was smacking us around. I wanted to cut him, but Tyler wouldn't let me … and then Elizabeth piped in to say it was enough just to scare him. Then they decided to take us to the empty houses. To be safe."

Katie looked down at her notes: "Are you Tony?"

"Yeah … We might have scared him for a few minutes, but I keep telling them that that's not enough. Ernie can't help himself especially when he's drinking. He has got to be stopped."

"Can you tell me how and why it is worse with Ernie?"

Tyler was quiet, and Tony seized the opportunity: "Four of them. Before it was just one. Like a pack of dogs. You never know from which direction they're coming. I am always watching and waiting …"

Then from what seemed deep within Tyler came a young man's, almost a boy's thin, fragile voice. "He's always drinking, like Dad, and always hitting Mom, and hitting his boys, who then just want to hit us. Mom always thinks it will be different next time …" his voice trailing off into silence.

"I'm guessing you're Ronald. I appreciate your helping me understand the situation. Perhaps, as the *I Ching* suggests, Ernie and his sons are 'the inferior people who have risen to power illegitimately.' Both your father and Ernie were, are older; they had, and have power over you. Bullying, beating, humiliating children is in no way a legitimate exercise of power. It is an abuse, immoral and criminal. The work of 'evil people.' And because of them, you have had to endure shame.

"Tyler, you have done well to have survived, and persevered in the face of this terror. You asked 'why am I different?' Well how could you not be different from children who, even if they weren't loved and appreciated as much as they needed, were at least safe and secure?

"But let me add that the *I Ching* is also suggesting you can do something about this:

> The time of standstill is nearing the point of change into its opposite.
>
> Whoever wishes to restore order must feel himself called to the task and have the necessary authority ...

"Imagine coming to see me and courageously sharing your story as the first step. I want you to appreciate what you've done, as the *I Ching* describes it, to ensure the success of your fundamental principles, or what I call staying true to yourself:

> ... the man who is truly called to the task is favored by the conditions of the time, and all of those of like mind will share in his blessings.

"So it seems, Tyler, that you have been called to this task. But it is often a difficult task:

> ... such periods of transition are the very times in which we must fear and tremble. Success is assured only through greatest caution, which asks always, 'What if it should fail?' ...
>
> Continuous effort is necessary to maintain peace ... The time of disintegration, however, does not change back automatically to a condition of peace and prosperity; effort must be put forth in order to end it.

Suddenly, it was very quiet. Katie headed back to the stove to put the kettle on, wondering how Tyler managed to do even the simplest of things. Deciding what kind of muffin to eat? What to have for supper? Let alone how to respond to a childhood fraught with danger and violence.

She was also increasingly aware that Tyler was at a crossroads, and filled with an added sense of responsibility. In many ways she was out of her depth here. She had never before met anyone with distinct multiple identities. Yet, it was clear that of all the professional helpers out there, Tyler had chosen her. Hopefully, she could serve as a bridge for Tyler, to help him through his immediate confusion, to support him while he gained the strength and confidence to find someone with greater experience and expertise. She took their cups to refill, then returned.

"As I explained before, the changing lines you threw, the three heads or three tails, shape the second hexagram and offer additional insight. 'Lü / Treading [Conduct]' tells us:

> The name of the hexagram means on the one hand the right way of conducting oneself … In terms of a human situation, one is handling wild, intractable people. In such a case one's purposes will be achieved if one behaves with decorum …

> The meaning of the hexagram is not standstill but progress. A man finds himself in an altogether inferior position at the start. However, he has the inner strength that guarantees progress. If he can be content with simplicity, he can make progress without blame …

> When he attains his goal, he does something worth while, and all is well.

"But, Tyler, things are always more complicated than they seem. The *I Ching* urges determination, but as Tony suggests there's protecting yourself:

> … one has to be resolute in conduct. But at the same time one must remain conscious of the danger connected with such resoluteness, especially if it is to be persevered in. Only awareness of the danger makes success possible …

If we want to know whether good fortune will follow, we must look back upon our conduct and its consequences. If the effects are good, the good fortune is certain. No one knows himself. It is only by the consequences of his actions, by the fruit of his labors, that a man can judge what he is to expect.

Tyler sat quietly for several minutes. He was feeling lighter than he had felt in, well he couldn't actually remember ever feeling this way. As if he had put down the imaginary rock-filled backpack he had been lugging around forever. Unburdened.

This woman Katie and her book had somehow gotten him to begin to tell his story, his secret. She had heard him, heard them, and was still here, ready to help. This was almost too much for him.

"Thank you," he stammered, not wanting to cry in front of her. "Thank you so much." Getting up, remembering to grab his copy of the *I Ching* and his muffin, putting two twenties on the table, then rushing out, hoping to make it out the door before the sobs overtook him.

Katie watched as he stumbled up and away. "You're welcome Tyler … and thank you." She moved to the door, catching it before it slammed shut. Then watching as he rushed to his car. Calling out, "Please know you can come back whenever you want."

Tyler pulled out of the driveway just as Frank was arriving. Frank could see him behind the wheel, tears streaming down his cheeks. Flashing back to the night Ralph died, the night Donnie could have killed them all, Frank was immediately terrified. Slamming on the brakes, rushing to the house, hoping against hope that Katie was alright.

Katie, who had just gone back in to wash the teacups, heard the door open again, thinking that maybe Tyler had forgotten something, but it was Frank who burst in, slightly crazed.

"Are you O.K?" rushing toward her. "He looked out of his mind. I was …"

"Frank, I'm fine," smiling, "and please do me a favor and sit down. Everything is fine. Relax for a few minutes and let me make you some tea."

His mind racing, Frank was trying to reconcile the last few hours, from the stakeout to following them all from Brett to Ripton, watching Tyler drive away up Long Pine Road as he was left there to deal with the moronic Bevans family. Because there was Ernie screaming, rushing at Bill. Who was looking as if he might actually take a swing at his dad. With Frank hoping he wouldn't have to use force to protect, well he wasn't quite sure who needed protecting there, keeping an anxious eye on all four of them as he called the Chief for back-up. Then forcing Ernie into one car and Bill into the other, while moving Buck and Bob to the side of the road.

The Chief arrived a few minutes later, followed ten minutes after by the tow truck. And it was only then that Frank allowed himself to think about Tyler turning onto Katie's road.

Katie brought a muffin and butter to Frank. Glad his breathing was returning to normal, hoping his adrenaline levels had dropped enough to have a reasonable conversation.

"So I'm guessing the fact that you decided to unexpectedly visit me this morning has less to do with me and Rabbit than my recent visitor," Katie offered.

Taking a bite, "I'm sorry, dear. This is an especially delicious muffin and much appreciated considering the bizarre morning I've had already. So the answer is yes and yes that this is a completely unplanned visit. I started my day following your visitor and his crazy step-family. Suspicious hardly does justice to what they're up to. So imagine my surprise when I saw Tyler turning down your road. Unfortunately, I had to deal with yet another stupid car crash. Then when I finally got a chance to check on you, he's speeding out of your driveway, looking slightly crazed. Given what's happened lately, it wasn't hard for me to imagine the worst."

"Well, Frank, I understand that impulse better than I ever would have before, but for whatever it's worth, I don't think I'm in danger. Please believe me, even if I might not have told you in the past, now I'd tell you in a heartbeat if I felt I was in trouble. So without breaking any kind of confidentially I do think it's much more likely that my visitor is in greater danger than me. And I suspect he's always been in danger.

"I clearly don't know all the details of your break-in problem, but I think you're facing an even more complicated task than I first imagined."

FORTY-TWO

For Bob, driving the still functioning rental, it was the ride from hell. Because Ernie, in the passenger seat, was maintaining a steady stream of curses toward the backseat where Bill was sitting besides Buck who was striving for invisibility. Ernie wouldn't settle for anything less than complete surrender, and yet for whatever surprisingly unusual reasons, Bill wouldn't relent.

"It was you," Bill insisted, yelling at their dad. "You slammed on the brakes without warning, and the car, with its cheap bald tires just couldn't stop in time. I tried. I slammed on the brakes. How is it my fault that you rented this piece of crap, probably the cheapest car on the lot; or my fault that that little bump crumpled the rear end? It wasn't like I deliberately smashed your car."

Bob was waiting for Bill to let it go. He could see Ernie's right hand death grip on the hand-rest. But Bill kept at it. "Remember how last time we were too slow. You never let us hear the end of it. Hamburger this; French fries that. This time I was just doing my job, keeping up. Why don't you appreciate that?"

For Ernie, this was nothing less than complete and utter insubordination. Especially coming from Bill, his right hand man. His eldest and most reliable. Of course, with each additional kid there was a little more slippage, less discipline. But Bill was his enforcer. Time to remind them there was zero tolerance for disrespect.

"Bad enough I had to listen to that idiot Police Chief talk about missing his fishing day. If anyone ought to be fishing, it ought to be me. Me and the sea. The Chief's making good money off the taxpayers, so why in the hell is he taking time off to fish?"

Bob had never before heard his dad talk about fishing; never saw a rod anywhere in the house. Now all of a sudden he was going on about some imaginary boat, a shitload of rockfish red snapper, whatever the hell that was, and the California sun. He could hardly ever remember seeing his dad in sunshine. When most dads were out playing catch with their kids, his dad was usually sitting on a stool in some dark and stinky bar. The kids would fight not to be the one to go inside to remind him to come home. Because pretty much everyone at the bar would groan and curse if you held the outside door open for more time than it took to slink in;

sometimes they'd even shriek like vampires, frantic and afraid they'd die in the daylight.

Bob had always thought of Bill as a kind of Ernie clone, like a photocopy of their dad. So it was incredibly weird to see them going at each other. Even scary. They both had a way of sticking out their jaws when they were pissed, the same muscles tightening in the neck. It was like seeing Ernie twice, old and young.

As long as he could remember, Bill had always obeyed their dad. So they all knew never to complain in Bill's presence because that complaint would moments later make its way to Ernie. He was a major snitch.

Even Buck made a minor attempt to intervene. Offering a meek "C'mon guys," but they both immediately turned on him: Ernie yelling, "Shut the fuck up!" then Bill shouting, "Shit, Buck, if I need your help, I'm totally screwed!" So Buck wisely decided to close his mouth and then his eyes.

The Chief followed them for five miles, which forced Bob to drive the speed limit, an almost impossible thirty-five miles an hour on the Ripton/Tottingham Road, which kept Ernie at a constant boil. While, ironically, Tyler seemed forgotten in all this turmoil. No one wondered where he had gone to.

Bob let out an audible sigh of relief when Chief Paul finally pulled a U-turn and headed back up the mountain. Then began the guessing game: how long would it take before Ernie ordered him to drive to The Back Door.

*   *   *

The session with Katie had energized Elizabeth, for this was the new beginning she had hoped for. So she spent time going over some of what had happened the past few months. How the almost desperate need for a safe place had recently brought with it a kind of sloppy disrespect. The night at the Stoughton place, the clearest example. For Elizabeth, it was now about healing. She suggested some places that might require a … well, if not always a physical, but certainly a spiritual fixing.

All this business with Ernie and the kids had kept Tyler from finishing a few projects. There was the toaster from the Hopper house off Blue Hill, the one with the broken lever he had fixed but hadn't yet delivered. Then the houses Abigail was convinced needed a few minor makeovers, a throw rug here, or a new reading lamp there. Which now after some important Elizabeth-inspired reevaluation and reflection required some simple swapping to return the houses to their original states.

∗   ∗   ∗

Ernie drank through the remainder of the afternoon at The Back Door. Along the way, his volume had diminished, until now, his vocal cords soaked in whiskey, he could offer only an odd collection of moans and sighs and the occasional snore, all easy enough to ignore. The knife had been taken from him three times over the course of seven hours until he no longer had the strength or will to wave it about, or attempt to carve the counter, and it sat quietly in its sheath on his belt.

For Ernie, the proverbial shit had hit the fan. Mutiny. There was no other word for it. Never before had any of his troops turned on him. Some grumbling maybe but never anything like Bill's open resistance. There was a moment when he thought it might come to blows or worse. Intolerable.

This was on Tyler. None of his boys would ever have thought of opposing him, not until Tyler's recent rebellion. His deception and complete lack of cooperation. Making them drive halfway across the county trying to figure out what he was up to. Ernie had seen more cops in the last month than he had in years. Tyler's fault.

The truth was he didn't need any of this. The kids weren't worth it, and Doris certainly wasn't. He liked to think it was his deep sense of responsibility that kept him from hitting the road, but this fight with Bill might have pushed him over the edge.

Everyone made a big deal about murder but the fact was it was a part of life. Animals did it. People did it. Truth is, he almost never thought about the spider and his father. Never ever regretted it. It made perfect sense when he did it and he had no reason to think anything else today.

He only wished he was a little more sober so that he could start making some real plans. But everything was fuzzy. Soon he would make some clear decisions about how best to take care of Tyler and when to take off. He'd get right on it as soon as he could see straight. There was always another spider. And Sam Preston's knife.

*   *   *

Tyler hadn't said a word for hours, lying atop his bed, his clothes still on. Abigail tried to take advantage of the silence to rattle on about the understated yet tasteful simplicity of Katie's place but no one seemed to care and she reluctantly faded into the far distance.

Doris poked her head into his room long enough to say how nice it was to see him relaxing at home, then headed off. For some reason, Bill and Bob and Buck were unusually quiet. For the slightest of moments, this seemed an almost normal home. But then Ernie was nowhere to be seen.

Tyler was hoping he hadn't seemed too crazy, leaving Katie's without a proper goodbye, hoping she understood how it was all so much, too much for him. Well, not too much that he wished it hadn't happened. Because really it was nothing like he had worried about and he was very grateful and knew he wanted to, had to go back.

Probably, considering all the inside uncertainty, he had grown very attached to the outside stuff, the physical here and now, to things he could pick up and pick apart, toys and tools and machines, small and large. Perhaps because he always felt broken within, he tried his best to fix the broken things without.

His nightmarish fear was that a shrink or head doctor would do to his insides what he did with appliances. Take everything apart, unscrew this, re-solder that, install a new transistor or circuit board, then replace the motor. Sometimes fixing appliances was just about trial and error. Sometimes you made it worse before you made it better. Sometimes you just had to surrender and throw the whole thing into the dumpster.

But somehow Katie and her book had managed to move things from inside out without cutting through his hard head, without mucking about his brain. Nothing unscrewed; no part replaced. Who knew you could do so much with three coins and a question?

He had always had questions, still had questions. They were everywhere around him. Why was this happening? Why was his father always so mad? Why did his mother keep Ernie? Why did Ernie hate everything and everybody? Every question gave birth to a bunch more.

196

Instead of being told he was doomed to a life of darkness, he had left Katie's with hope. Realizing how hard they had worked to survive: how Elizabeth's smarts had found ways through what felt like a constant danger; how Tony's annoying insistence that he toughen up had, in fact, made him stronger; Abigail's wackiness encouraging him to look at everything from dozens of different ways; and even Ronald, as whiney as he sometimes was, had convinced him that he too deserved a space that was safe.

He kept coming back to the paragraph he had bookmarked:

> If we want to know whether good fortune will follow, we must look back upon our conduct and its consequences. If the effects are good, the good fortune is certain.

Having spent so much time focused on what had been done to him, he knew now it was time to look at what he could do in the days to come. And he better appreciated Elizabeth's insistence that they make everything right. As the weariness descended and his eyes closed, he pledged to begin tomorrow.

FORTY-THREE

Alex found the sticky note on his desk. Twice a year Tom needed to rearrange and update the website. To replace the photos of houses surrounded with snow with houses bathed in sun. Or for those houses that hadn't sold, a new and different view of the master bedroom, or the downstairs bath, a better shot of the dining room. And there was no arguing with his track record or his sharp, unerring eye. Because of Tom's desire to approach perfection, their houses and properties looked a bit better than everyone else's.

So Alex found his Canon, and re-checked his settings to make sure he was shooting at the highest resolution, found a new data card then cleaned the lens. He began to make a list of the properties he'd be photographing. Grabbed a latte from Fuel and hit the road.

After shooting four houses in GB, he took a short lunch break at the Ripton General Store. On a roll, he was hoping to do three or four more houses in the afternoon.

Alex checked his iPhone. He was pretty sure he hadn't scheduled showings of the Hopper house with any other realtors. Pretty sure if anyone in the office had done so, they would have left him a message. The Hoppers, he knew, were at their Florida house. So why was that red Tercel parked in front of the garage? It was hard to imagine any of the local real estate agents driving their clients around in such a messy old car.

This was incredibly annoying. Whoever had parked there had pretty much ruined any of the exterior shots he had planned. The wide shot of the house, highlighting its circular driveway, and then the garage with upstairs apartment from several different angles: straight-on, from the left, and then the right.

Exasperated, Alex slammed his car door. As he got the house keys out, he quickly headed to the front door. He leaned in to listen but couldn't hear anything. Rang the bell several times then discovered he didn't need the key.

"Hello … hello" as he entered. "Is anyone here? This is Alex Beaumont from GB Properties. I'm going to need you to move your car …" moving from the foyer left to the small parlor. "Hello … Listen, I'm not sure if you're a friend of the family, but I really need to talk to you!"

Alex dropped his keys when he saw the body, the blood spread all across his midsection, the knife protruding from his gut. His first instinct was to rush over and check his pulse, but memories of Las Vegas and the Rising Sun Casino and his years at Lovelock Correctional came flooding back. Sadly this was not the first body he'd seen up close. There in the shower at Lovelock where it turns out you never want to be the one to see or hear or know anything. Especially to witness the body of someone who had testified against someone with friends inside. Luckily, his cellmate Bernardo shoved him back outside and reminded him several times he hadn't really seen what he had just seen.

So Alex knew not to touch anything. Then quickly remembering his trial, and how often people talked about time, the time this had happened, and the time that had happened, he automatically looked down to check his watch. About one twenty-five. The time, give or take a minute or two, he first saw the body.

Thinking how easily this too could become his fault, his crime, Alex took just a moment or two to figure out whether he could do anything to actually help here. He moved just a bit closer to check whether the guy was breathing when he saw a second body, legs protruding from behind the couch. He looked behind the couch to find a young man with what seemed to be a serious head wound, bleeding from his forehead.

Wrenching himself from pictures of the past, moving through and beyond his fear, he steadied himself to call 911, telling the operator he thought one of the two bodies needed immediate medical attention and an ambulance.

Frank was in the cruiser doing what Chief Paul called "the circuit" driving east from the office to the Otis line, then back to the Great Barrington line. Just passing the new firehouse when he got the call from dispatch. He immediately checked in with the Chief to say he was headed to Blue Hill and the Hopper house.

And so with pistol drawn, Frank quickly checked the red Tercel, then Alex's car, and the tracks of a third vehicle. He circled the house before entering.

"Alex," he announced, "it's Frank Falco, I'm armed … I'm going through the house room by room to make sure no one's here. Please stay where you are … I'll be with you in a moment." Frank decided to check the upstairs first, moving as quietly as he could up the stairs. Through the two bedrooms and bath, then making his way back down. He checked the kitchen, dining room, and downstairs bathroom. As he entered the living room he could see Alex standing by the couch, almost frozen in place.

"Alex," he whispered. "I don't want to frighten you but my gun is drawn. I'll holster it as soon as I secure the room." He recognized Ernie Bevans the minute he saw him. Then moved to Ernie's side to quickly check for a pulse. Though the body was still warm, Ernie was dead.

He moved to the other body and saw it was Tyler. Still breathing, though his pulse was faint. He holstered his gun and called to check on the status of the ambulance.

He leaned back down to whisper in Tyler's ear: "Listen Tyler, this is Frank Falco, I'm Katie's brother. I'm also the Assistant Police Chief in Ripton. An ambulance is on the way so I want you to hang in there. It seems like you took a serious whack in the head, so you may not know where you are. But you're going to come through this."

Tyler managed a barely audible moan and the fingers of his left hand tentatively reached out in the direction of Frank's voice. Frank took his hand and squeezed gently. He looked back to Alex and smiled, watching the color return to Alex's face.

*　　　　　*　　　　　*

The Crime Lab team from Springfield identified the Hopper's Statue of Liberty as the weapon that struck Tyler. But that and the knife that had killed Ernie Bevans were badly smudged and they were unable to get usable prints. The Coroner found extremely high levels of alcohol in Ernie and the autopsy found that his liver had been on its way out. So if it hadn't been the knife, it might have been either liver disease or cancer in the very near future. Frank found himself wishing that whoever had done this had just waited a while.

The ambulance took Tyler to the hospital in Barrington while Chief Paul stayed with the team from the State Police. The Chief gave Frank directions and he took off to find Tyler's mom and the boys. He had a very strong feeling the boys were involved somehow.

Notifications were one of the worst parts of policing, telling someone a part of their life was gone forever, that nothing would ever be the same again. There was the incomprehension, the denial, the anger. Many times he had been hit and smacked by the survivors. You never knew what to expect.

Frank checked the house, the backyard, and the shed. There was no one home, no car. Chief Paul had told him that if Tyler's mom wasn't home there was a good chance she was working at one of the local hospitals or nursing homes. He called Eastview in Barrington, then Springside Hospital in Canaan. When he learned Doris was finishing up the end of a double shift there, he decided to take the drive down Route 7 to Connecticut.

He went straight to the hospital's administration office to access their work records. Doris had gone on at one in the morning and was due to clock out at five this afternoon. Anna Bedford, the Assistant Supervisor, with a quick look back to the Supervisor's Office, quickly whispered: "It's probably not a good idea to piggy-back shifts but it's not up to me, if you know what I mean."

"Thanks for your help. Where do you think I can find her?"

"Well, she was on Intensive Care for the first shift and now she's up on Maternity. Down the hall and to the right and you can take the elevator to the fourth floor."

The babies had quieted down, and most of the mothers were in their rooms. Doris was just about to sit for the first time in hours when she saw Frank coming toward her, his badge attached to his belt. Her eyes closed for a brief moment and her fatigue seemed to triple in intensity. Another cop, so soon. Never good news.

"Mrs. Bevans?"

Shaking her head wearily: "Never really married him though everybody sort of assumes it … Still Deakins, kept the name of the first bum. It was easier than paying a lawyer. So which one's in trouble now?"

"I need you to sit down, Ma'am."

All of a sudden the last thing she wanted to do was to sit down.

"If I sit down, I'm never getting up, and I've got a bunch of babies to take care of still. So tell me what you came to tell me, so I can get back to them."

Frank took a step closer, hoping he was close enough to catch her if necessary. "Do you happen to know anyone who might want to harm Mr. Bevans?"

Her response was a cross between a snort and loud laugh, followed by "You've got to be kidding … How about everyone who's ever known him?"

"Do you happen to know anyone who might want to harm your son, Tyler?"

Doris did a double-take. "Who?"

"I asked you, Mrs. Deakins, if you know of anyone who might have wanted to harm your son, Tyler?"

"Did Ernie hurt my boy?"

"I don't know for sure, Ma'am … but Mr. Bevans is dead. I'm pretty sure someone murdered him and your son is hurt."

"Are you saying Tyler murdered Ernie?"

"No, Ma'am … but why do you think that's possible?"

The fact that Tyler was hurt finally sunk in: "Did you say my son is hurt?" and all of a sudden, she reached out to grab him, both hands squeezing his right arm with all her might.

"Ma'am," he gasped. "I need you to let go … Please, Ma'am, you're hurting me."

Doris looked down, shocked to see that her hands clamped around his forearm. She let go. "My boy … what about my boy?"

"He was taken by ambulance to Eastview. I'm not trained in these matters, but he has a head wound and there was significant blood. He's breathing and they've stabilized him. I'm glad to take you there. But do you understand that Mr. Bevans has been murdered? That I can use your help in figuring out what happened and who might have done this."

He could see her shutting down before him. "My boy," was all she could manage. "My boy."

*   *   *

Doris was granted special dispensation by her fellow nurses, and she spent hours beside Tyler's bed. A CT scan confirmed that Tyler had been lucky and that his skull hadn't been fractured. But he had lost consciousness and a lot of blood and probably sustained a severe concussion. He would occasionally manage what seemed to Doris like a low moan, resembling a "no," but hadn't yet come out of it.

Still feeling the effects of her double shift, Doris managed a few hours up, with some fitful chair sleep. At first she thought she was dreaming, then woke with a start to find Frank in the room standing on the other side of the bed beside a woman she hadn't met before. She had Tyler's hand in hers, whispering: "Tyler, this is Katie. You've had an accident. You were hit pretty hard in the head. The doctor said you have a concussion. Your mother is here."

"Are you doing a Neuro consult?" Doris asked. "I haven't seen you before. Are you new here?"

Katie smiled at Doris. "No, no. I don't work here. Tyler came to see me a few days ago … and I was very upset to hear that he was hurt. I think Tyler trusts me, and my brother," pointing back to Frank, "thinks I might be able to help. But now that you're up, I'll leave the two of you. I'll try to come back later. Tyler is a very strong young man and I feel confident he'll make it out of this."

Doris was exhausted and couldn't tell whether or not she was annoyed that this strange woman was telling her about her own son, or comforted by what she was saying. So very confused, all she managed was a nod. And before Frank and Katie had made it out the door, she had drifted off.

*   *   *

Now persons of interest in a homicide, it was only a day and a half later that Bill, Bob, and Buck were apprehended doing eighty-five in Ernie's car heading south on the turnpike outside Baltimore. All of them refused to talk to the Maryland State Troopers who hauled them off to jail.

Chief Paul offered Frank a list of givens: given that Maryland had more than enough of their own homegrown problems; given that one of the boys, Buck, was legally a minor; given that they were unable to locate the boys' birth mother; and given that Doris was a nurse, a mother, and had lived with the boys for many years, the Maryland State Police agreed to expedite matters and release all three of them into the custody of Doris and the Ripton Police Department as long as Bill and Bob signed off on the arrangement.

So Frank's trip to Maryland with Doris began at Murphy's Funeral Home where she identified Ernie's body with a simple yes. All her energies funneled into concern for Tyler, Doris seemed to no longer have any concern for or connection to Ernie. Whatever had tied them together seemed as done and dead as Ernie. Frank suspected that Doris had quickly decided that Ernie was to blame for Tyler's condition, and, with that judgment, deserved what he had gotten.

So Frank found himself driving in the Ripton cruiser with a silent Doris, who seemed glad for the moment to take her guilt and grief as far as she could from Tyler's bedside. Still, every few miles, Frank tried to engage her, hoping as much for another voice to offset his own internal ramblings as for any useful information, but barely got a grunt from her.

Then, after the third tollbooth on the Jersey turnpike, she startled him: "You know, I could have done it. Should have. I hated the man. I hated the men. I had plenty of chances. The cops were always coming over. They always wanted me to tell them what he had done to me. But, you know, I was scared. I was always scared. Scared of the first one. The others. Then scared of this one.

"It's not fair when the kid knows you're always scared. Too scared to stop it. Tyler would scoot under the bed and he tried to stay very quiet. Tried not to cry. Would hardly breathe. For a minute he would think he was safe, then his dad would rip apart the bed if he had to, just to get to him. Why does a grown man have to beat his little boy? I kept yelling, 'pick on someone your own size,' then he'd smack me so hard I would be out of it for hours and hours.

"Tyler would look at me with those eyes, asking why, why, why? It got so I didn't want to look into his eyes. Can you imagine a mother who won't look into her little boy's eyes? Because the disappointment was worse than getting smacked.

"It didn't take long for him to know I couldn't, or wouldn't help him. That was probably worse. That was when he turned different. I never ever blamed him. He would very softly mumble to himself. Sometimes rocking back and forth, back and forth. Most of the time he was in the closet or hiding sometimes in the shed. His dad hardly knew where he was, but then for no good reason, he decided he wanted Tyler to hear something or eat something or do something, he'd go out of his way to track him down, and if he heard Tyler talking to himself, he'd scream something like 'no boy of my mine is an idiot' and he'd lift him up and shake him and yell, 'boy, you have something to say, you say it to me. Loud and clear.'

"I never told his father about Tyler's nightmares. Seeing him rolling, tossing back and forth in bed. Hearing those different voices. Like the people in his nightmare were talking aloud. I've never mentioned those voices to anyone. Then his father must

204

have gotten bored of hitting us, because just like that he was gone.

"Then all the boyfriends until this last one, and boy was Ernie sneaky. Nice at first, helping out, saying how my husband never realized what a prize he had. He took me and Tyler and his boys to the Expo in Springfield and bought us food and paid for the rides and told his boys to include Tyler in everything they did.

"Which lasted until I asked him to move in … It has got to be me, right? One jerk, that could just be bad luck. But one worse than the other, back to back to back. That's me. Maybe I could have got out early on, but working all the time … People think nursing's a breeze, the doctors do the important stuff and all you do is fluff the pillows and take temperatures, bring the pills, and make sure all the visitors are out by ten. That's a laugh. Some doctors breeze in and breeze out, shouting instructions on their way to the elevator, and you're left with patients and relatives all over the place, wanting to know what's up, and what the last test really showed, and how come the doctor had that look in his eye, and so how bad is it really? Patients wanting to know if they're getting better, and always when the hell they're getting out?

"Ask your cop friends in Brett: they'll tell you how many times they came to the house. They saw the bruises. I'm only sorry I didn't listen to them. But Ernie kept saying he loved me and he'd stop the drinking and he'd be better and all of a sudden I wasn't scared, thinking the old Ernie is back. So yes I'm a dope. The truth is, it's my fault.

"So I ask you, Mr. Policeman: what would you do? Would you take care of your mother? If someone was beating her, what would you do? That's got to be some special kind of self-defense. So why punish my boy for doing what anybody's son would do? Really, what would you do?" Then, as if she had no desire to hear an unsatisfactory answer, she fell silent.

*　　　　　*　　　　　*

Katie decided to keep Tyler company while Doris was gone, and all the nurses got accustomed to her near constant vigil, talking, playing music, and holding his handcuffed hand.

While either Chief Paul and or members of the Barrington police kept watch on a chair outside the room, Katie did what she always did, and trusted her instincts. She tried her best to explain to

Tyler what was happening: that Ernie was dead, that he had been found nearby. That he was bleeding from a head wound. That Frank and his mom were on their way to get Ernie's sons who had taken the car and made it as far as Maryland. The hours slipped by and Tyler seemed a bit more restless, at times increasing the pressure on her hand, and muttering some more.

*   *   *

It didn't take long to deal with the paperwork. His counterparts in Maryland seemed quite glad to be emptying their cells rather than adding to them. Especially because these three very annoying young Massachusetts men were acting like they were prisoners of war in some bad World War Two movie. Still refusing to talk. Even though everyone knew who they were and where they lived and why they were being held.

Bill and Buck clearly weren't happy seeing either Frank or Doris. Bill said up front they had nothing to say. But Frank had the feeling that Bob was relieved. Then Bill signed just minutes after Bob, agreeing to their transfer. Opting for the familiar over these Maryland folks who were about out of patience.

Frank made sure to pat them down before moving them into the back of the cruiser: Bob on the driver's side, Bill in the center, and Buck behind Doris. Bob had nothing to say. Bill glared. While Buck kept asking to stop for burgers.

There was a Burger King right before the entrance to the turnpike, and Frank stopped by the take-out window. Even Doris seemed glad to refuel. Frank removed the plastic knives and forks and spoons from the take-out bag and passed the burgers and fries back to them through the opening in the grate.

Frank watched in the rear view mirror as Bill took the opportunity to whisper first in Buck's ear, then Bob's: "Keep your mouth shut. Remember what we talked about."

He figured it would come down to Bill one way or the other. The most like his dad. The last, probably, to help. Pretty sure now that unless Tyler came to full consciousness sooner than later, the boys were the key.

Bill and Buck's dislike of Doris was palpable. With just the smallest bit of empathy for a fellow victim, they might have forged a bond. But it was clear that they had absorbed Ernie's contempt for her, and instead relished the belief that they, at least, were a lot better off than she was.

As they drove in silence, Frank was still hoping that when it came down to it, Bob would choose to turn his life around, and opt for the truth.

Bob had seen Frank glancing back at them in the rearview mirror. For some reason, this cop didn't fit the picture his dad had always painted. The constant diatribe about cops hassling him for no reason at all. Actually anyone, everyone in authority. The government big or small. Even the Building Inspector or the Health Department. Especially Child Services.

But there was something about Frank he trusted and there was a strong part of him that thought Frank might help. Of course, everything was a thousand times more complicated now, and that kind of aid seemed less and less possible. How come his life was getting more shitty by the day?

He could remember when he thought he could make his real life as rich and as interesting as his daydreams: that he would travel to faraway places, meet people whose lives were as different from his as night from day, that he would have stories to tell. Sitting in the back seat, he could remember the small ways he had tried to get out, his little rebellions. How he just wouldn't go along with Ernie's crazy idea to turn them into ninja fighters. Years later, he still hated that white uniform; hated the way Ernie used to smile only at Bill in the martial arts studio. Until Bill lost, and the screaming started as soon as they were in the car.

Driving back to the Berkshires, and imagining all that was waiting for them, Bob was beginning to understand how much he disliked them all. Bill for being older and never ever helping, especially now; Buck for being younger and so incredibly stupid; and Doris for being useless. And, of course, his dad for being his dad in name only all those years.

*   *   *

Time melts in the hospital. You find yourself looking, then looking again at the clock, because there is only so much, or rather so little to see in a hospital room, a room that looks pretty much the same as the next room and the next after that. Maybe there's some mind-numbing chemical in the air but you almost immediately forget whatever it was the clock just told you. So, even though you just looked, you find yourself looking again. But hardly ever remembering what time it is.

A day and a half in, Katie began to acknowledge that this vigil of hers was more than a bit strange. She had spent less than two hours with Tyler, yet somehow felt responsible. Not for what had happened to him, but rather for what might be coming his way. Convinced that Tyler's decision to ask for her help had created, if perhaps only in the spirit world, a kind of binding contract between them. Then quickly remembering that she had put her hand on the *I Ching*, recalling that moment when she had agreed to become Frank's willing able helper. So here she was. Because she hadn't had this strong a sense of obligation since working with Penny.

Somewhere between one and two in the morning, she felt a slight tug on her sleeve, and forced herself from sleep. She had to move closer to Tyler to hear:

"We were making things right …"

The voice sounded like a cross between Tyler and Elizabeth.

"What do you mean?"

"Bringing everything back, lamps … toasters … The third house. Everything was going well. Then they came in. So angry …" trailing off.

"Who came in?"

But Tyler had fallen back to sleep.

*   *   *

Doris began to cry once they hit the New Jersey line, a low moan that seemed to rise from the depths, followed by a persistent weeping.

Bill tried to make fun of her, elbowing first Buck then Bob, though neither seemed interested in joining. Frank was wishing he could be anywhere else, wishing he could be with Penny. They hadn't really spent any time together since that second night together. He wondered whether she had been freaked out by how easily things had gone. It had certainly freaked him out. To be that vulnerable again. To enjoy touching, being touched, ever so slowly opening to another.

An hour and a couple of toll-booths later, he began to think he had once again gotten it wrong. Maybe he was the only one who was freaked. Maybe Penny had it all together, and quite reasonably was expecting him to take the next step. So was he blowing this opportunity? Remembering how lame he sounded after their first night, the too many tongue-tied messages. How could he have not sent her flowers, thanked her, arranged a third date?

Weighing all this when Bill snapped: "Could you shut that bitch up!" and Doris, Bob and Buck all shuddered as if one, as if Ernie was still with them, alive and occupying the skin of his eldest.

Frank looked back: "Son, unless you're willing to tell me right now exactly what happened to Tyler and your father, I suggest you keep your mouth shut."

Which helped Bill remember where he was. And for another hour, all Frank heard was the sound of wheels and the steady hiss of the cars and trucks that sped past them.

FORTY-FOUR

David Stein carried an extra seventy to eighty pounds, most of it circling his waist, and some of it in the form of the unruly twenty-five year old pony-tail tangle of gray white hair that tumbled down from his head to below his shoulders. It was hard to tell where his hair ended and his beard began.

Most people mistook David Stein for a left-wing refugee from the nineteen sixties, imagined him one of those hippies who dropped too much acid. Who had gotten stuck in the space-time continuum. Many folks got nervous around him or passed him by. But the few who engaged him quickly discovered that David Stein had a mind like a steel trap and still possessed the determined temperament of the former suit and tie conservative Federal Prosecutor he once was. Unfortunately, he was as impossible to live with as he was brilliant, and he had gone through four wives and four times as many girlfriends.

His first wife had grown up in the Berkshires and after thirty-five years of summers and holidays in Ripton, he had retired there. It took him a year to discover that he detested the peace and quiet that doing nothing required every day, and quickly rectified matters by passing the Massachusetts Bar and making a pest of himself in Berkshire courthouses.

David's kids were spread across the country, determined to put many miles between them and their various quarreling parents, until Rebecca, daughter one from marriage two, announced at the close of her seventeenth summer visit with David that she was done living with her suffocating and over-protective mother in New York, New York. That she hoped never to see another subway as long as she lived, explaining that, of course, this meant the logical place for her was Ripton, Massachusetts. Rebecca just happened to luck out, because her father, in the face of his multiple matrimonial and relationship failures, had decided for the moment to attempt acquiescence rather than resistance, and David for a rare change quickly relented and Rebecca joined him and never left the country.

So it was that one summer day six years later, after many months of wondering whether she should continue to keep Desmond, her English-born womanizing carpenter fiancé, Rebecca found herself at Katie's. And, after many months of will-strengthening weekly sessions with Katie and the *I Ching*, told Desmond to leave in the morning, then two months later, married Desmond's boss, Richard.

David, who always despised Desmond and always appreciated Richard, was more than glad to have a now happy daughter depart his home for her very own Richard-built house just a few miles away. He quickly wrote Katie to say how thrilled he was with her efforts, and to tell her, should she ever have the unfortunate need of an attorney, he'd appreciate the opportunity to repay in small part the great favor she had done him. And so it was that this morning Katie called David.

*   *   *

Frank dropped the Bevans boys at the Great Barrington lockup, then met up with Chief Paul. Who with a twinkle in his eye informed him that Katie had hardly left the hospital and somehow managed to secure Tyler his own attorney, the extraordinarily talented, equally famous, and highly eccentric David Stein.

"He may make our lives more miserable, but I think you're going to like this guy. He makes the local DAs tremble. I wasn't aware of it but it seems that a while ago your sister really helped his daughter. He's had a place here for decades and so he's one of ours, living by the lake. But he's still nine-tenths a New Yorker and I wouldn't ever want to be on the other end of his cross-examination. Which we may very well be.

"You know, of course, these mushy boundaries we're working with could land us all in deep trouble. So I'm trusting your sense that Katie can help us figure a way out of this mess rather than make it worse …"

Then, continuing his update, he told Frank that when he'd been by the hospital Tyler had slipped back into unconsciousness. So he still hadn't had a chance to question him. And the Crime Lab hadn't yet come up with any usable prints.

Frank drove back home from Ripton. His downstairs neighbor had been kind enough to stop by and check in on Danger, who, although the recipient of kind and loving care and many hours of TV, was nevertheless annoyed that Frank had bailed on him. No hello, no good-morning, no you're the best human being ever. Just

211

a series of complaining shrieks.

"I'm sorry, Danger. I really am. But I thought I explained all this to you. Sometimes, not very often, certainly much less often than when we were in Manhattan, I just have to spend some extended hours at work. It's not like I wanted to leave you. And to be completely truthful, I really don't enjoy turnpike driving. Not that you care but my travelling companions lacked a certain charm. So I really would have preferred spending the time with you. Now how about I give you some clean water, some birdseed and," opening the refrigerator, "believe it or not but today is your lucky day, because we've got a compelling mix of grapes and melon and broccoli." Cutting bite size portions on the cutting-board and moving them to a paper plate.

"If you come out of the cage I'm sure we can work this out, mano to birdo," undoing the latch.

Danger held back for a second, sizing up the situation, looking into Frank's eyes, then suggesting the cost of compliance: "cracker?" Watching carefully as Frank considered it, then a bit more forcefully: "cracker!" Quickly pressing his growing advantage, Frank's obvious guilt, with an additional "cracker," watching as Frank stalled for time: "Danger, my dear friend, I just chopped up an incredible selection of great stuff for you, and so very healthy."

But Danger stood his ground, standing as tall as he could on his wooden bar, staring out at Frank, still unwilling to leave the cage. Until Frank wilted, reaching into the can for a Nutri-berry treat and plopping it down by the broccoli. In a blink, Danger was out of the cage and on the paper plate, the treat on its way to his beak. Looking up between bites to smile. The world was surely a better place after a cracker. Then turning toward Frank to honor his part of the bargain: "good morning!" With Frank laughing, "and good morning to you, Danger, although strictly speaking we both know it's good afternoon."

Frank, so very glad that there was peace once more in Birdville, decided to try his luck with Penny. Unfortunately, he got her machine. He hated answering machines, and when he encountered one, he could feel himself moving a few inches away from himself, as if he was both simultaneously a participant and an observer. So the simple message he intended to communicate now twisted in on itself: "Uh, hi Penny. It's Frank. I'm not sure you heard about the murder – uh, well, I didn't really want to talk about that, it's so depressing – but, uh, it's the reason I've been away. But I'm back and just wanted to say, uh, well I wanted to see how you're doing … and actually I was hoping that we could …" when he was cut off by her machine, the 'uhs' taking up more time than he imagined.

Even Danger had put aside his fruit to listen, then looking back at Frank: "What?" And a second, "what?"

Frank nodded, because there was no denying it had been a rather pathetic performance. Then decided to wait a bit before he called again and headed for the shower.

*   *   *

Katie was glad to see Frank back in the hospital. Having him living and working close by not only brought her great pleasure but also a heightened, more constant worry. Somehow it had been much easier to put at bay all that he faced when he was working the streets out of sight and miles away in Manhattan.

So the image of him stuck in a car with three possible teenaged sociopaths had gotten to her, especially after Tyler's short but scary mumbling: "then they came in."

Katie motioned to Frank to take the chair across the bed from her, then leaned in closer to the bed. "Tyler … Elizabeth … I'm hoping one of you can hear me."

Frank swiveled in his chair to see if someone else had entered. Katie smiled, then put her finger over her lips to signal Frank to be quiet.

"My brother Frank is here. He's investigating everything that happened to you and Ernie Bevans. I trust him with my life. And yours, and so if I talk about what we talked about during your session it's just because things are so very serious now. I also want you to know I've hired a lawyer to help you." Katie gently squeezed Tyler's hand. A minute later could feel a soft pressure on hers.

"The other day, you were barely conscious and it might have been you or maybe Elizabeth who mentioned that you were bringing things back, fixing what was broken. I think you said it was the third house. So I'm hoping you feel better enough to tell me more about what happened at that house in Ripton …"

Tyler's eyelids began to twitch, and Frank moved closer to hear what sounded like a faint "yes."

213

"I'm glad that you're doing something about your past actions. That's very brave, Tyler …"

Tyler's voice seemed to drop an octave: "I wasn't paying enough attention …"

Katie could read the confusion on Frank's face, and looking from Tyler to Frank, she was nodding, trying to reassure him.

"Tony, is that you? … I can tell you from my own recent experience that we can't always be ready for what comes so unexpectedly …"

"Yeah, but I should have been paying attention … My job … But I was back too far … sometimes there is just so much noise and static and one of the others is up front …"

Frank had absolutely no idea what was going on here, when just a moment later, he heard another, a third voice:

"'Be content with simplicity,' I think that's what the Chinese book said. But with so much interference … and the meanness of others …" Elizabeth began, then hesitated.

"Thank you, Elizabeth … Am I right in thinking that you were trying to make the kind of progress the *I Ching* spoke about, returning things, making right your past actions? Maybe if my brother Frank and I have a clearer idea of what happened at the Hopper house, we can do a better job of helping you. Can you please ask Tyler to tell us what he remembers?"

"He is very weak and we are all very sorry we couldn't help …" her voice fading away.

Frank's hands moved to his forehead, fingers moving up and down. Closing his eyes. As if he could massage away the headache that hadn't yet come but might at any moment. Then a memory. Or maybe just a compelling daydream. Playland, the amusement park. Stuck in The House of Mirrors. Mirror facing mirror. A confusing corridor of several young Franks without any idea of where he was or how the hell to get out.

Now these many voices from a single Tyler … and the same sad feeling that he had lost his bearings. Stuck once more. Then so very quiet. Katie's eyes closed. The only sound that of the machines monitoring Tyler. As Frank tried to make some sense of all that had happened in the last few days. Realizing there was still some significant part of him back in the patrol car with the creepy kids, the family from hell, with Doris' tears, her involuntary sighs and sobs and moans, mile after mile.

It didn't help that ever since Theresa's protracted illness, Frank hated hospitals and hospital rooms. Uncomfortable even in the simple, homey small-town version he found here at Eastview, sitting beside this young man, in yet another white room across from his sister.

So he wanted to believe it was because he was over-tired, or maybe because he had a low-grade fever that he was hallucinating this odd illusion. Some new-fangled ventriloquism, lips moving, as if Danger, mimic extraordinaire, had taken possession of Tyler.

He thought he had moved miles this last year, proud that he had been able to meet Katie on her own ground. Accepting her spiritual bent, acknowledging the coins and the book and the odd but often amazing power of a question answered in large part by the dead. But this was pushing it. Then all of a sudden flashing back to the movies. Because he had had an incredible crush on Jessica Lange, still did, he had seen her several times therapizing in "Sybil" while never imagining he'd find himself in such a movie. Facing no longer a single boy-man, but many.

So as much as he needed Tyler to tell him what happened at the Hopper house, he was beginning to accept that there would be nothing simple about whatever it was Tyler could tell. No clear single story, but many stories differently told by the several voices that had already freaked him out, that would freak anyone out. Yet these were the guardians of the story he so desperately needed, the witnesses to what had gone on there.

So very quickly he couldn't help but imagine Tyler on the witness stand, a judge trying his/her best to manage impassive and unaffected. He could see the faces of the incredulous jury melt and disappear beneath the confusion that increased ever so steadily about them, one different Tyler voice after another testifying out of the one same mouth, a growing tidal wave of the hard-to-believe.

Then, bouncing back to the moment, watching Katie across from him so completely unfazed, his sister, dreamer of the horrible dream that came true, seeing in sleep their father in flames. Had that vision prepared her for witnessing a world he so often hadn't seen. Their brave father on his secret mission to help Latin American political refugees find a safe new home up North. None of them ever able to make it home.

Here and now, Katie, without fear recognized, and without judgment, respected these voices; and could talk to them with the same ease with which she spoke to him. Obviously, for every mile he had come toward her, there were many more miles to travel.

Very quickly he knew life would never seem as uncomplicated as it had before Penny and her greedy, murderous husband and his crazy brother, before this very strange world of Katie's three coins and Chinese fortune-tellers, and these voices beside voices. It wouldn't ever be simple again, even as Tyler, almost as if for Frank's sake, regained his body and his voice:

"I must have left the front door open," Tyler, trying hard to speak to Katie, and sounding just a bit creaky. "I put the fixed toaster in the kitchen and then I was looking around the living room making sure everything was in its right place … You know, for the first time, I felt I didn't need to be there. I didn't belong there. It wasn't my place. It was the Hopper place. That I … well what did you call it, yeah, it was the wrong way of conducting myself. I was standing there and I must have gotten a bit confused, because maybe there were a few new things I didn't recognize or I was confusing this house with another in my mind, and then Abigail started in on how nothing felt right with the feng shui of the place …

"Anyway, I wanted to tell you about the door … Because I must have left it open …" Then so very quickly Tyler seemed to tire. His eyes closed and he was gone again … Katie could see that Frank wanted to rouse him but she gently held her hand up to ask him to wait and see if Tyler could continue on. After several minutes, Tyler was out and Katie signaled Frank to join him outside in the corridor.

"OK Sis, what have you got me involved in this time?"

"Frankie, do you remember when you insisted on taking me to see 'Jaws' and aside from the fact that it kept me out of the ocean for a decade, I still remember the tagline: 'Just when you thought it was safe to go back in the water …' Well, it's never safe or simple dealing with people. I think Tyler has what used to be referred to as Multiple Personality Disorder. Now it's got some fancier name: Dissociative Identity Disorder.

"I've done some research since Tyler came to see me the other day, I think I met three of them: Elizabeth, who he calls the smart one; Tony, who is tough and tries to defend them; and Ronald, who seems like the young boy Tyler never got a chance to be. I didn't get to talk to Abigail, the fourth of them, the teenage woman who is feisty and creative. There's a strong correlation between this kind of disorder and abuse. Sometimes, the young mind responds to persistent violence, and the trauma of insecurity and lack of love, by creating different personalities and retreating into an internal world of imagined safety. I think all of them played a different but essential part in keeping Tyler going, in not surrendering to the brutality, and not giving up.

"By deciding to come to see me, and reading the *I Ching* together, I think Tyler felt understood enough and safe enough to let them out in public ... and while I may be wildly optimistic here I'm hoping the reading has prompted Tyler to find a new way to deal with life. So yes, it turns out you've found the person or persons responsible for the break-ins. But I want you to know that the first thing he decided to do after our session was to go back and return everything.

"I understand that you have to do your job, but I want you to consider that for Tyler these houses were places to escape to. Plus, in his own way, he always tried to barter his services in return for using the houses. Fixing things, and maybe in his own odd way, re-arranging them in what he was convinced was a better way. The way I look at it, Frank, Tyler was not really a burglar. In his mind, it was always a fair trade."

"I'll bear all that in mind, Katie. But right now, I'm much more concerned with who shoved the knife into Ernie and who creamed Tyler. Don't quote me but in my old precinct we would have called things like reprogramming someone's digital video recorder or taking a toaster oven, 'the chicken-shit stuff.' Like having to deal with the son of some City Councilman whose car stereo got boosted when you've got a triple homicide to solve."

"I think as soon as he is able Tyler will tell you what you need to know ..."

"I hope you're right. And I hope that I can prove it and resolve it in a way that doesn't include bringing Tyler in front of a jury."

"Well, Frank ... just when you thought it was safe to go back in the water ... Let's go see if Tyler's ready to try again."

*   *   *

Penny had spent the day driving about the county stopping at just about every antique shop she could. She had returned with several small rugs and three lamps.

She stowed her new treasures in the house which everyday was becoming more her own, then went to check the answering machine. A message from the dry cleaners, and one from the painters saying they couldn't start until the day after tomorrow and then a message from Frank, who had her laughing within seconds as he tried maybe, she wasn't quite sure, to ask her out.

*   *   *

"He was completely inebriated," Elizabeth offered, then stopped as she heard Tony in the background correcting her, 'you mean drunk out of his gourd,' and so conceding aloud 'yes, Tony, he was drunk out of his gourd,' while Frank couldn't help but turn to Katie, probably not aware that he was shaking his head.

Elizabeth continued: "He was already incredibly angry and he pushed Buck into the living room, then Bob and Bill came in behind Buck."

Frank looked back to Katie and silently mouthed "Who?"

"Who exactly are you talking about, Elizabeth?"

"Ernie. He's always drunk and always angry … Are you happy, Tony? I said 'always drunk,' even though 'inebriated' is a more interesting word." But Tony had either given up or just didn't care, and there was a prolonged silence.

Frank started to squirm and looked back to Katie and began to mouth, "What happened next …" but never got a chance to finish.

"My brother Frank is driving me crazy with his detective questions, so I'm hoping you can help me out here. He's dying to know the who, what, why, when kind of stuff."

"Well, it would go a lot faster if Tony wasn't interrupting me," Elizabeth offered. "When Ernie pushed Buck, Buck stumbled into the couch and fell. That scared the heck out of us, probably not Tony, but everybody else. Then it seemed like Bob and Bill were pushed too.

"Mr. Bevans was like one of those crazy people you see on TV quiz shows who's just won a new refrigerator or a vacation at Disney World, screaming and jumping up and down. Yelling: 'Gotcha, you bastard' or something like that. 'Caught you in the act,' and at first we thought he was just waving his hand but it was a knife, one of those big hunting knives, and he was waving it in

218

this weird celebratory way.

"Tyler tried to explain about the coins, and the Chinese book, and finding the right way, and apologizing to Mr. Krause, and the mistake with the sheepskin rug, and how sorry we were about those paint cans and wild colors, which is why he was bringing the toaster back here, but I don't think Mr. Bevans was even listening.

"He was still yelling: 'You got Bill and Buck tossed in jail. You got us all in trouble with those rent-a-cops and my rental car was smashed. Now the cops in both Brett and Ripton are on our ass. You're a bigger pain in the butt than your mom.

"Saying something that didn't make much sense, like: 'First I was thinking the spider but then I got smart. Just do a trade and turn you in.' He stopped waving the knife and reached into his pocket for his bottle and took several big gulps, or should I say 'swigs,' Tony …

"Then he put the bottle away and he's swaying back and forth still holding on to the knife. He stumbles over to Buck and pushes him over to where we are, and yells 'Find something to tie Tyler up.' Buck had this panicked look in his eyes, and Bob was looking over to Bill as if to say 'do something,' but Bill just looked away" and then Elizabeth repeated, "Bill just looked away" as her voice faded.

Silence. Frank put his hands up in a what just happened gesture. Katie smiled, hoping to reassure him. But Frank missed it, looking back up to the clock in the room, wanting somehow to move things along. Instead, it seemed as if the second hand was stuck in mud. Frank began to worry he'd be left in limbo, not knowing what happened next. He looked down and across at Katie, who, he realized, had never stopped holding onto Tyler's right hand, and who never wavered in her concern for Tyler, and for those others who lived within him.

Frank found his eyes closing, more tired than he realized. His impromptu nap was interrupted minutes later when he was startled by the sound of Tyler clearing his throat, and looked over to see him slowly open his eyes. Katie gave an extra squeeze then got up to offer him the glass of water and he slowly sipped from the straw. He looked over at Frank and back to Katie with an attempted smile, but his face still hurt and he couldn't help but wince. Then began to speak:

"Buck was very frightened so I said to him, 'I know,' whispering so his dad wouldn't hear us … 'I was just bringing some things back here … But your dad doesn't understand, so you better do what he asks and find some rope …' Buck gave me a look. I could see he was grateful but then the fear returned and he seemed paralyzed. Maybe I only made it worse. He just stood there.

"I could see Mr. Bevans getting more angry. 'Buck' he yelled. 'What the fuck are you doing? I said to tie him up, not talk to him. You are such a fucking moron.' Then Mr. Bevans moved closer to Buck, 'Why are you just standing there?' Pushing him. But it was like Buck was just stuck, standing in a puddle of super glue, and couldn't move. Mr. Bevans pushed him again and Buck knocked into me, and I reached out to keep him from falling. Then Buck started to cry. His body was shaking and he just couldn't stop crying, and Mr. Bevans was furious and slapped him as hard as he could in the face. That did it. Buck just shut up.

"I tried to explain again that I had fixed the toaster. It was working real good now and that I was just checking to see if everything else was OK in the living room when they came.

"Mr. Bevans looked at me like I was speaking a foreign language. 'Shut up,' he screamed. 'Just shut up.' Then I said to him that we were just about to leave. 'You're not going anywhere. I'm the one who's leaving.'

"Then I heard Bob say 'Dad, why don't we all go. C'mon, I'll take you to The Back Door.' But Mr. Bevans completely ignored him and got this look of disgust. 'Have to do everything myself. You're a bunch of worthless sacks of shit.' He handed the knife to Buck then moved to within an inch of me.

"So I said to him that I wasn't going to use anybody's house anymore. Then I said again I just wanted to go home.

"Then he yells: 'You're just like your fucking mother. Always arguing. Finally I say "shut your mouth" but she can't leave it be. "Contradicting me, whining." She won't ever learn. Surprise, surprise, you won't either. Didn't I just tell you to shut up!'

"Then he grabs me by my shirt and starts to shake me. So I say, 'Mr. Bevans, please stop, you're hurting me and I don't want to upset Tony …' He starts yelling: 'Tony, I don't see a Tony. Fuck Tony … I warned you,' and before Tony had a chance to do anything, Mr. Bevans reached out with his right hand and picked up that metal Statue of Liberty and I watched it come crashing down on my head … and then I felt myself falling to the floor …'"

FORTY-FIVE

Because Bill had tried his best to school his brothers, Frank decided to begin with him. Then he'd see how Bob and Buck held up under pressure.

He had learned over the years that his best allies were time and patient, persistent questioning. That most people who relied on stories, rather than actual memory, were bound to slip and stumble with repeated retellings.

Frank read Bill his rights again, but not surprisingly, in so many ways his father's son, he couldn't imagine paying money for a lawyer to occasionally talk for him. So he shook his head with a kind of smug confidence. When Frank reminded him that he needed a verbal reply for the record, he could see the first flickers of fear in the far reaches of Bill's eyes.

Now Bill needed to find a voice that conveyed confidence. A partial victory, for there was only a slight crack in his voice. "No, thank you," he managed. Frank offered an encouraging smile. "So you understand your rights, Mr. Bevans?"

A long pause, as if that might somehow inconvenience Frank, then with a snide, "Yes, sir."

Which prompted a second smile from Frank.

"Wonderful ... Again for the official record, you don't want us to contact an attorney on your behalf, and decline to have one present with you?"

"Yes."

"Well, then let's get to it. I'm hoping you'll be able to help me understand what happened on the 15th day of May this year when you and your brothers accompanied your father, Earnest Bevans, to the Hopper home in Ripton. So how about you run through what happened? Let's start with breakfast. Maybe you can tell me what you and your brothers and father had to eat?"

Frank could see the surprise in Bill's eyes. "Uh ... I don't know ... I guess what we usually have, breakfast cereal with milk. There are usually two or three boxes of corn flakes, raisin bran, Cheerios, I don't know, I just mix them together. If Doris has made Mr. Coffee, whoever gets there first gets the coffee."

"What did your dad have?"

"My dad ... well, he's usually hung over and has a couple of aspirin with coffee and sometimes Doris will have bought him a box of chocolate covered donuts which no one's allowed to have except him. So maybe he'll have some of those. But I don't remember … usually we just try to stay out of the way."

"What did Tyler have for breakfast?"

"Tyler … he doesn't usually eat with us. He's usually gone before us." Bill paused and Frank could see him thinking, then deciding. "You know he hates … uh, he hated my dad."

Frank smiled. "Thanks, Bill. I appreciate your insight but I don't want us to get too far ahead of ourselves. So, as far as you remember, you didn't see Tyler at breakfast on the 15th?"

"Uh … no … I don't think so."

"Listen Bill, we're not talking last year or even last month. We're talking several days ago. Was Tyler there with you all for breakfast or not?"

"Uh, no. No, he was not."

"Great, Bill … thank you."

Bill was nodding, feeling a bit more comfortable now with the back and forth.

"So at what time did you finish your cereal?"

"About ten-thirty, maybe a quarter to eleven …"

"Well, Bill, it can't be both, so what do you think … Maybe take a moment, close your eyes … You're taking your last spoonful of cereal, slurping the last bit of milk from the bowl and you look up at the clock. What do you see?"

"It's about ten thirty-five …"

"Perfect … So was it before ten thirty-five or after ten thirty-five that your dad told you you'd be going after Tyler?"

"Uh before … we were having cereal … Hey wait, was that a trick question?"

"Bill, I'm just trying to get an accurate timeline of what happened and when it happened. Are you trying to say that you weren't going to follow Tyler?"

"Uh …" Bill paused, trying to figure out the implications of the question and the best possible answer.

"I mean, Bill, tell me if I'm wrong but I always assumed that when I found you all in Ripton, that was because you had been following Tyler. But maybe I'm wrong. Maybe it had nothing to do with Tyler and you just had a car accident on the way to an attempted burglary. … Could it have been armed robbery? Maybe your weapons were hidden in the trunk?"

"No, no … We weren't going to rob that guy. Dad insisted we follow Tyler to find out what he was doing. He was convinced Tyler had some great big scam going and was ripping off all these rich people and hiding a lot of money from him."

"That's what I thought, Bill. That's good to hear. No plans to rob Mr. Krause. So the same thing is true about this most recent incident. You weren't planning an armed robbery at the Hopper house on the 15th?"

"No way!"

"So while you were having cereal … about what time do you think your dad mentioned that you were going after Tyler?"

"Probably just a few minutes before we finished …"

"So where was Tyler?"

"Well, Bob had found a note, sort of a list that Tyler must have left in his room, a list he wrote about returning a bunch of things. I don't remember exactly but it was like the toaster to Mr. and Mrs. Hopper, maybe a clock radio to a house in South Otis, adding some better video equipment for Mr. Krause, stuff like that. We also had a map that Tyler made with x's for all the houses he went to …

"Anyway, because of all this, Dad was very happy, saying now we had what he called a tactical advantage, and that we would be able to surprise him."

"So was Tyler at home at this point …"

"No I don't think so … he doesn't really like it there anymore. And he really doesn't like Dad, did I mention that? So he usually leaves very early in the morning and comes home very late at night … He's like a ghost."

"So when did you leave the house to find Tyler?"

"I remember Dad was complaining about his headache so he opened up another bottle of Jack Daniels and started adding liquor to his coffee, so that took some time."

"So what did you think about your dad's plan?"

"Think? I just try to stay far enough away from his hands. So I didn't have time to think. Because you have to be careful every single second. It pays not to say anything. I mean anything. Because it can be wrong. Everything can be wrong."

"What about Bob and Buck? Were they quiet, too?"

"Bob tried to convince our dad to forget it … But he made sure he was all the way on the other side of the table before he spoke. Even so, Dad threw a coffee cup at him. But missed."

"So when exactly did you leave the house?"

"Well, it took a while to get out of the house. He kept drinking his version of coffee, and while he drank we managed to scatter from the kitchen. The way it works is when he can't feel his headache anymore, then it's time, and so he yells at us to go. Maybe around eleven-thirty …

"He made me drive which meant he was close by in the passenger seat, and Bob and Buck were in the back, and of course we had to drive around a bit which meant when he wasn't drinking, he was yelling at me.

"Bob was trying to navigate from the back seat which wasn't easy, so we might have made some wrong turns which Dad thought was deliberate and he kept muttering that Bob was sabotaging what he called the operation, convinced we were somehow deliberately getting to the places too late to catch Tyler in the act. But how were we supposed to know his schedule? Dad was yelling that he needed to finish the job. That he couldn't leave until the job was done. Which didn't make any sense to me because he doesn't have to go to work anymore because of what he calls his pension …"

"So when did you catch up with Tyler?"

"Well, the clock in Dad's car hasn't worked since he smashed it trying to hit Bob with his bottle. So we never really know what time it is inside the car. But I think I saw a clock when we got into the house that said something like one-twenty but I'm not really sure …"

"Let's back up a little bit. How did you find Tyler?"

"It must have been the third or fourth house on the map, and there in the driveway was his red Tercel parked off to the right. Dad went kind of nuts. Grabbing and squeezing my arm as tight as he could."

"So what happened next?"

"He started shushing us, to make sure we were quiet, but probably making more noise than all of us put together because when he's had too much to drink he doesn't even realize he's yelling. Then sometimes it's a little hard for him to get out of the car seat, so he's grabbing the arm rest and trying to lift himself up and out, and all the time he's going 'shhh!'

"We would have laughed except he'd smack us. So it took a bit of time for all of us to get to the front door. Dad sort of stopped dead at the door, realizing he hadn't figured out how he was going to get in … Then looking at the four panes of glass in the door … 'Buck, how about you get a hammer from the trunk …' Buck was just about to go when Bob reached out to turn the doorknob and the door opened."

"So tell me Bill, what exactly did you think was going to happen when your father found Tyler?"

"Uh … I figured … well I didn't figure … I guess I thought somehow Tyler wouldn't be there, that maybe he had another way out of the house, and like every other time it would turn out to be another stupid wild goose thing … or that Dad would get bored or frustrated and we would end up getting out of there and taking him to the bar like always …"

"OK, now you're inside the Hopper house, so what happens next?"

"Well, Dad makes like some kind of commando, signaling with his hand that he wants Buck and Bob to go to the right, and putting his finger over his mouth to tell us to shut up. Then he sticks his forefinger in my chest, then signals me to follow him to the left … So I follow him to the entrance to the living room when he puts out an arm out to stop me … like maybe he thinks there are landmines or something, or maybe I'll step on a loose floor board and the noise will spook Tyler, who is carefully checking all the knick-knacks and books and stuff, pretty much not even aware that we're all there watching him, and soon Buck and Bob are behind me …"

At which point Bill pauses to ask, "Hey, do you think I could get a burger, some fries and a coke?"

"You're doing a great job, Bill, filling in the missing pieces. So I don't want to interrupt the flow. How about we get through this and I'll get you some food? … Now that everyone is in the living room, what happens next?"

Bill hesitated. He really wanted a burger. Really wanted to take a break.

Frank smiled again. "This shouldn't take too long, Bill. Before you know it, you'll be eating."

"Uh … well. We were trying to quietly move closer to Tyler when my dad just couldn't help himself. Needing a drink. So he got the bottle out to take another swig, and maybe it was Buck or Bob but someone must have knocked his arm and the whiskey spilled down his chin. He couldn't help himself, and yelled: 'Shit!' Completely focused on wiping his mouth with his sleeve.

"Spooked by the noise, Tyler turned around and seeing all us, he said something like: 'What are you doing? You shouldn't be here. I'm just making sure things are where they're supposed to be. I'm about to leave.'"

Bill paused a minute to check how Frank was reacting, trying to figure out how he was doing with the story. Not sure if he was dealing with the kind of good cop or bad cop he was used to seeing on TV.

"That seems pretty reasonable, doesn't it?" Frank asked. "What Tyler told you. So how did you all react to his explanation?"

Bill seemed surprised: "Uh … what do you mean? You actually believe Tyler? He broke into the house. That's a crime, right? A lot of houses I bet …"

"So are you saying that you didn't believe that he was about to leave?"

"Uh … I don't know … he's a thief, isn't he?"

"Well, why don't you tell me what happened next?"

"My dad was really pissed … He definitely didn't believe Tyler. He called him a criminal and demanded to know where he put all the stuff he had stolen. Tyler said something about the toaster in the kitchen … But Dad started talking about a citizen's arrest and deputizing us and saying that we caught Tyler red-handed and that maybe there was a reward …

"Tyler didn't say anything, so Dad said that maybe if Tyler just gave us the cash and jewelry we could let him go …"

"Bill, are you saying that your dad suggested that you all take the money and jewelry that Tyler took from the Hopper family?"

"Uh … I'd really like that burger and the fries now …"

"Well, you know, McDonald's is on the other side of town. There's pizza across the street … But I really need to get through this, and it wouldn't be fair to feed you and let your brothers starve, right?"

"Yeah I guess …"

"So what happened when your father suggested to Tyler that he give you the money and the jewels?"

Bill was still dealing with the fact that a meal break was no closer, but Frank continued to wait for an answer and Bill soon relented.

"Tyler didn't seem to get it. He's not really that smart. He said he didn't have the tools to repair jewelry and didn't know enough about it. But that he did know about toasters and it only took him about an hour to fix the Hopper's toaster. Dad was getting really pissed. He said, 'I don't give a shit about the stupid toaster. You really want to talk about toasters, well how about I hogtie you and drag you to the cops.'

"Then Tyler started to get worried, talking about how he was done with the houses and it really wouldn't happen again. And did we really have to upset his mom, which would happen if we involved the police? So what if he promised never to come back to the Hopper house?"

"Well Bill, how about that? Did you believe Tyler? Do you think he was telling the truth?"

"Uh I don't know … Dad was drinking a bit more from his bottle and Tyler was talking and it was getting a little confusing."

"So no one believed Tyler? No one said anything to calm your dad down?"

Bill paused … "Bob said something to Dad but that only seemed to make him more mad …"

"What did Bob say?"

"Something like why don't we let Tyler go and why don't we all get out of there."

"I guess that didn't happen, did it?"

While Bill was trying to decide whether Frank was being what his dad called a smartass, Frank had another question: "So what happened after that?"

"Dad told Buck to tie Tyler up!"

"Had you brought rope with you?"

Bill was thinking it was probably a really good thing that they hadn't, that it might count for something that he could say no.

"No way …"

"Well that's good … so what did Buck do?"

"Buck didn't do anything … I think he didn't know what to do. Probably because he didn't have any rope and maybe he just got scared, but he just stood there and Dad started yelling. I think Tyler must have stirred Buck up somehow because Tyler leaned in and said something to him, which we couldn't hear but then Buck started crying, which just pissed Dad off something awful.

"Dad was screaming something like no son of mine is going to be a crybaby, and then all of a sudden, Dad just hauled off and smacked Buck in the face. Buck's eyes got real big and he stood there until Dad started to shake him and then reached over to grab Tyler, which is when Tyler must have grabbed the knife because Dad groaned and slumped down to the floor and we saw the knife sticking out of him. It must have hit something important because there was a lot of blood really quickly …"

"So you saw Tyler stab him?"

"Well, uh, Buck was in the way but …"

"So you didn't actually see Tyler stab him?"

"Uh … well … Buck was in my way but Buck didn't have a knife."

"OK … that clarifies things a lot … Thanks Bill." Frank started to get up, then paused for a second: "So when did you call for an ambulance?"

Bill stopped to think, but thinking didn't really help: "Uh, I didn't call for an ambulance. I went to see how my dad was …"

Frank sat back down. "Did you tell Bob to call for an ambulance?"

"Uh … no … I must have been too busy seeing how my dad was …"

"So you didn't tell Buck to call for an ambulance?"

"Uh … no …"

"Did Tyler call for an ambulance?"

"Uh no, I don't think so but I was busy …"

"Because you went to see how your dad was, and you were so busy with that you didn't have time to call for the ambulance or ask your brothers to call, so you must have been too busy to grab Tyler?"

"Uh … yeah."

"Even though he had just stabbed your father?"

"Uh … yeah."

"Were you angry at him for stabbing your father?"

"Yeah …"

"But you were busy with your father, so …" pausing … "Well, that's nice that you were taking care of him … What exactly did you do for your dad?"

"Uh well … I … uh, I sat there … in case he wanted to say

anything. But he didn't say anything …"

"I'm sorry, that must have been very difficult for you."

"Yeah …"

"So when you were doing all this, what direction were you facing? Were you facing Buck and Tyler or the other direction, where I assume Bob was?"

Bill paused for several long moments. He really wanted to ask about the burger again but decided not to. "Uh … Bob."

"So what was Bob doing if he wasn't calling for an ambulance?"

"Uh … he was standing there …"

"So he didn't grab Tyler either?"

"Uh … I guess not."

"And you don't know exactly what Buck and Tyler were doing at that time?"

""Uh … I guess not."

"You didn't see if Buck grabbed Tyler after the stabbing?"

"Uh … no."

"So when did Tyler's head get bashed in?"

"What do you mean?"

"I mean when did you or Bob or Buck smash Tyler on the head?"

"I don't know anything about that."

"You mean you don't know because you were busy sitting next to your father, or you don't know because you were looking in Bob's direction and didn't see Buck hit Tyler?"

"I just don't know … and anyway you promised me food!"

"I did, and you'll eat after I talk to your brothers. Maybe they can tell me why you decided to leave your father lying there with a knife in his gut, and why Tyler had his head bashed in?"

FORTY-SIX

Frank watched from behind the mirror as Buck fidgeted, his hands constantly moving, his legs rocking back and forth. Frank waited. Every minute or so, Buck looked expectantly around the room, then over each shoulder.

Frank waited ten minutes more then went in to talk to Buck who by this time was a nervous wreck.

"Buck, we've met before, at the Krause property in Ripton then again in Maryland when I drove you back to the Berkshires. I don't know if you remember but I'm the Assistant Police Chief in Ripton. I understand that Sergeant Taylor of the Great Barrington police spoke to you a few minutes ago about your right to stay silent and your right to an attorney."

Buck stared at Frank.

"That was a question, Buck. I need you to answer 'yes' if Sergeant Taylor did indeed speak to you about your right to stay silent and your right to an attorney. That you do agree to waive those rights, or tell me 'no' if that's not accurate."

"OK."

"OK 'yes,' or OK 'no?'"

"OK 'yes' …"

"Great … thank you, Buck. I really appreciate it that you are willing to talk to me about the events at the Hopper house. My fellow officers in Maryland told me that you had a bit of trouble adjusting to your cell. Some people do better with jail than others. They don't seem to mind the bars, the hard bed, or the little toilet or the complete lack of privacy. I'm probably like you, I really like my personal space and locking the door behind me in the bathroom … So I'm really sorry. You just may have to get used to spending an awfully long time behind bars …"

"What do you mean?"

"Well, I was just talking to your brother Bill …" letting his voice trail off.

"What do you mean?" a little louder now.

"About Tyler …"

"Tyler … what about Tyler?"

"Well, maybe Bill got it wrong …"

"What did Bill say?"

230

"Well, let me see if I have it right," marking an imaginary x on the table. "This is the living room ... You must have been very upset about your dad. And really pissed at Tyler. The way he describes it, Bill was sitting next to your dad who was lying on the floor after having been stabbed. Bill says he was trying to take care of him and he remembers looking directly up at Bob, who was standing in the direction of the doorway. So that leaves you in the other direction in the same area with Tyler by that cabinet.

"The way I figure it, you were so upset with Tyler that you probably weren't really thinking straight when you picked up that metal Statue of Liberty and smashed him in the head ... Maybe the jury will understand how angry you were ... You never know about juries. Maybe they'll give you a break ..."

"Bill said I hit Tyler in the head?"

"Well, not exactly. Mostly he said he didn't do it. He said he was watching Bob. Which means Bob didn't do it. According to Bill, your dad was lying there on the floor bleeding to death from the knife. So he couldn't do it.

"It seems pretty simple. Am I missing something here, Buck? Was there anyone else in the house who could have done it? ... Bill said you and Bob and your dad came into the house and Tyler was in the living room. Things got pretty hot and your dad was very angry. Yelling about Tyler stealing stuff and screaming about tying him up. Then somehow Tyler has a knife and stabs your dad. Your dad's falling to the floor. No way he can pick up that heavy statue. Now Bill's right about all this, isn't he? That Tyler stabbed your dad? Because you didn't stab him, did you? You didn't murder your father?"

"Uh no ..."

"Bill didn't murder your father, did he?"

"Uh no ..."

"Your brother Bob didn't murder your father, did he?"

"No ..."

"Well that leaves Tyler, right?"

Buck, very confused and very worried now, is staring at Frank.

"Isn't that the story, Buck?"

"Uh ..."

"So now your dad's lying on the floor. Bill says he is on the floor taking care of him. Bob is standing off to the side. And Bill is looking right at Bob. Bill said you were next to Tyler. That leaves you and Tyler, and I don't think there's any way Tyler can pick that heavy statue up and lift it high enough to hit himself on the head that hard. Which would be pretty weird even if he could."

"Can I talk to Bill? That's not what …" pausing … "I think I really need to talk to Bill …"

"I'm sorry, Buck, it just doesn't work that way. I have to talk to you one at a time so I can figure out exactly what happened. Sometimes, and I'm not saying you guys would ever do this, but sometimes people get together and agree to tell the same exact story because they're hiding something. My job is to make sure I discover the true story. Believe me the last thing I want to do is put someone in jail for a big chunk of his life … especially someone who doesn't really deserve to be in jail. But, hey, who knows, in all the commotion at the Hoppers it's possible that Bill may have missed something. He seemed in a big hurry to tell me his version so he could get a burger and fries and a coke."

"Hey, I want a burger too …"

"No problem. As soon as we're done here … So I've got an idea. How about I talk to Bill for you … what do you want me to say to him?"

"Ummm …"

"Well, Buck, why don't you think about all this for a while … Sergeant," calling through the intercom, "can you please take Mr. Bevans back to his cell?"

As worried and confused as Buck was, he seemed even more hungry: "Can I get a Quarter Pounder with Cheese, large fries, and large Coke? I can't get two Quarter Pounders, can I?"

Frank looked at Buck as he was being led out: "I think pizza will be easier. But how about we figure all that out next time we talk?"

FORTY-SEVEN

Frank was wondering which way Bob would go, hoping he'd prove smarter than Bill or Buck.

"OK, before we can go into anything in any depth I need to make sure that Sergeant Taylor of the Great Barrington Police Department spoke to you about your right to remain silent and your right to an attorney. So for the record, will you confirm to me that you have waived those rights? And I need a clear yes or no."

"Yes, I waive those rights."

"Well, thanks to your brother Bill I really don't need very much from you. He pretty much laid everything out for me. Lucky for all of us he's got a great memory. But, just for the record, I thought I'd give you a chance to tell your side of the story … Who knows, in case Bill might have missed something. It appears that you were all willing participants in a scheme to extort cash and jewelry and other objects from Tyler Deakins, objects you knew or believed he had stolen, or was in the process of stealing, from Mr. Hopper's house in Ripton and other houses in the Southern Berkshires."

"Whoa … where did you get that?"

"Well, according to Bill's account, you and he and your brother Buck accompanied your father, Earnest Bevans, to the Hopper home. With you, in particular, opening the door to a house to which you were not invited. Then when you all discovered Tyler Deakins trespassing in this very same house, your father threatened him with exposure and arrest but then offered him a way out if he would give you the money and jewelry he had taken. Bill was quite clear that none of you intervened to stop this, and so it's not going to be difficult for the District Attorney to argue that you were a party to a criminal conspiracy led by your father."

"I didn't ask Tyler for anything …"

"Well, that may or may not be true, Bob, but you were in fact there and, according to your brother Bill, you did nothing to try to stop your father. Your joint illegal entry resulted in the murder of your father and the violent assault on Tyler."

"Didn't Bill tell you that I told my dad we should go home …"

"Well, yes, Bill did say that at one point you said something to that effect, but much more important than that is the fact you never took action to stop any of it, or walked out of the house and away from this ..."

Bob's eyes had widened and he was speechless.

"I can see that this is upsetting to you, so how about we forget about what Bill has said for the moment, Bob, and you tell me in your own words what happened? Like, for example, when you reached out and opened the closed door to the Hopper house, were you aware that you hadn't been invited in by Mr. and Mrs. Hopper?"

Bob paused and looked more closely at Frank. He had the sudden and unnerving sense that he was playing chess with someone who was already several moves ahead of him. Who had several more pieces than he did. It was pretty clear that Bill and Buck were hopelessly out of their depths. And that he probably couldn't do much better. He could see his life spiraling away from him.

"Uh ... well yes, sir, I guess I did know that. I don't know the people who own that house and I'm pretty sure they don't know me ... I'm sorry but the reality was I got swept away by my father ... So there were a lot of things I probably should have been thinking about but I just wasn't."

"What was Tyler doing when you first saw him in the house?"

"He had his back to us and I don't think he realized we were even there at first ... He sometimes can be in another ... Well, even when he's nearby, or across the table from you, it seems like he's very far away ... like he's listening to people I can't see or hear. But that time in the house I think he was just completely involved in tidying up a bunch of books and pictures on a shelf in the cabinet."

"Thank you Bob. It seems your dad is ... well, he was a pretty tough customer ... so I can understand why you'd both want to look after and protect Buck, I mean, because he's the youngest. Do you think that's why Bill after a while decided to take responsibility for smashing Tyler on the head?"

"Bill? Bill said that ... that he hit Tyler?"

"Why, was it you who hit him?"

"Me ... no way ... I think I like Tyler ... he's kind of brave and pretty smart in his own weird way ..."

"Well, between me and you, I don't think Bill really thought things out. But I don't think I need to tell you because you probably know that about him. He's not the smartest guy on the

234

block. He probably should have stayed in school. Probably all of you should have ...

"So the way Bill told it to me this morning, he was next to your dad who was seriously bleeding, and he was looking up at you across the way from him. By a process of elimination that left Buck right next to Tyler.

"You ever see that CSI program on TV? The original one from Las Vegas. It's about your basic Crime Scene Investigation unit. Today, most police departments and the state police have CSI folks working with them. For example, using all their scientific understanding, we can calculate from the position of Tyler's body, and the angle with which the statue hit him, and how heavy it is, that Tyler wouldn't have been able to smash himself on the head, even if he wanted to. You'd think we wouldn't have to use fancy science to figure something like that out, but prosecutors always need to make a convincing case and always want the scientists to testify in court."

Bob was very, very quiet. The chessboard was gone. Now he was feeling a bit like a frog cornered by a nasty cat.

"Anyway, I'm thinking that as Bill was telling the story, it dawned on him that his description of the crime scene and his account of what happened pretty much screwed Buck ... That Buck might be facing a very serious charge of attempted murder, maybe murder if Tyler doesn't make it. And between you and me, based on how badly Buck does with dinky little jails, I don't really see him surviving hard time.

"Maybe Bill was realizing the same thing, because after a few minutes of being real quiet, Bill looked at me and said he needed to change what he had said. That now he wanted to tell me the real story. That happens more times than you'd imagine and I wasn't that surprised. So I said it was fine with me as long as we ended up with the truth. Which was when Bill told me that he was so upset with Tyler for killing your dad, he got up and pushed Buck out of the way and picked up the statue and hit Tyler ..."

Bob just sat there, staring at Frank. Wondering whether Bill and his big mouth had completely screwed them all. Trying to figure out what to do now and what to say.

"Why do you think your dad hated Tyler so much?"

Glad, for the moment at least, that he could actually say something that wouldn't make things any worse: "My dad hated everyone … except himself and maybe The Back Door. I think he really liked the bar."

"That's probably true, Bob, but isn't everything that happened at the Hopper house about some special grudge he had with Tyler. I mean all of you following him and threatening him and then trying to kill him."

"I didn't try to kill him."

"I don't think you quite understand how this works, Bob. Of your own free will, you illegally entered someone else's house. Then you did nothing to stop your father from threatening Tyler. You watched Tyler murder your father, and then you did nothing to keep your brother from trying to kill Tyler. Maybe you think it's enough to sit there and say that you didn't threaten Tyler but you were, in fact, a willing participant.

"In my experience, juries and judges like people who try to prevent crimes from taking place. They like heroes who rescue kids from burning buildings, not cowards. So it would be one thing if you had been trying to stop your dad from going into the house in the first place, or once you were there actively tried to stop him from confronting Tyler. Had grabbed him or restrained him. Helped Tyler. Did something to prevent two serious crimes from occurring. So I want you to think about all that …"

Bob closed his eyes. He saw a cats' paw come from out of nowhere, just barely missing the frog …

Frank gave him just a moment, then began again.

"How about, in the meantime, you think just a bit more about your dad and Tyler. Because isn't that why all three of you are sitting in jail? So how about you help me understand your dad's problem with Tyler?"

"Well … Tyler was always so weird. He did everything differently. It was like nothing my dad did ever surprised him. He might have been really scared in the beginning, but it seemed after a while he wasn't really frightened anymore. Whenever Dad got angry or would threaten him, he would just stare at him. Tyler wouldn't flinch or run. He'd just stand there.

"Then one time, none of us saw it because it happened early one morning, but it freaked Dad out so much he woke us up. Tyler was using his tools and my dad was so pissed he must have gone after Tyler. Then out of nowhere Tyler had a knife at my dad's throat. Which none of us even knew Tyler had or knew that Tyler could use a knife. But telling us the story, we never ever saw Dad that freaked out before. Plus he must have seen how we all saw how frightened he was.

"So maybe that was what made it worse. Because from then on he really wanted to teach Tyler a lesson. Maybe teach us a lesson too. After that, he wouldn't stop talking about Tyler. Then at The Back Door he heard about all those burglaries. So he decided that Tyler was behind them. Thinking that Tyler had some big secret treasure hidden away. Even more now than before he wanted to get back at him, and yeah he also wanted everything that Tyler had taken."

Frank was nodding. "Well thank you, Bob. That makes a lot of sense. Good, so now we have a better idea about what was driving your dad. What about you guys? Do you really hate Tyler so much that you're willing to spend most of your life in jail?"

"What do you mean?"

"Well, the way it looks now is that Bill will probably go away for the longest, for the attempted murder of Tyler. Then, you and Buck can be charged as accomplices. You seem to be emotionally stronger than your brother but like I said before, jail's already been hard on Buck, and this is nothing compared to serious time at Cedar Junction."

There was a stunned look on Bob's face.

"Oh yeah, before I forget, Bob, exactly what kind of knife was it that Tyler pulled on your dad that time at your house?"

"The way Dad described it, it must have been pretty small 'cause it fit in his pocket. I think Dad said it was like one of those Buck knives with a black handle, you know, one of those folding hunting knives. You can get something like it at Reed's Sporting Goods. Can't be any more than five or six inches."

"Thanks Bob, so let's get back to the other day. The way you and Bill tell it, you're in the living room of the Hopper house, and you were looking in Tyler's direction when he turned around, realizing he wasn't alone in the house anymore … By the way, when the Sergeant explained to you about your rights to an attorney, he did mention that anything you say can be used against you in a trial, right? So you do understand that we're recording this. I went through all this with Bill, but like I said before, I'm not completely sure he got the part about the consequences of not telling the truth. That's another thing juries appreciate: people who tell the truth.

"With that in mind, how about you walk me through what happened in the living room?"

More and more, Bob was thinking about prison. Up until now he had thought of his time in Maryland and his interrogation as but an inconvenient interruption of his normal life. But with every additional moment, with every new threat this policeman sent his way, he was forced to admit that he could actually end up spending some significant time in jail.

It was one thing to sit in a cell in a temporary state of shock. It must be quite another thing to accept this as reality. A very real today, but worse, a real tomorrow and tomorrow and tomorrow.

Shock. In some ways he and his brothers had lived almost all of their lives in an odd state of shock. The exhausting always waiting, watching, expecting the worst. Then the inevitable explosion. So he been living a kind of prison life. Without bars maybe but a jail of sorts he had shared with his brothers. Ironically, as he thought about it now, a jail he had shared with Tyler these last few years. His father their jailer.

So now he finally realized he had a very big problem. Because he was sitting across from someone who was free. Had most likely always been free. Judging him, holding him accountable, as if he, too, were free. Warning him about a jury that wouldn't ever understand what it meant to be him, what it meant to be trapped.

So he had to think about all this in a new way. Because Bill and Buck couldn't, wouldn't figure it out. Because if this was a chess match he had a couple of bishops and a castle hedging him in. Running out of moves, out of space. Playing against this cop who kept coming at him. Bob wasn't sure he was anywhere near smart enough to find the best way … well, there probably wasn't any good way out of this. Maybe if he was older, maybe if he knew more he could figure out how not to completely screw it up, to minimize the damage. Maybe … but for right now he knew he better try.

"Dad wants what he wants … Usually he's drunk or he's hung-over which means what he wants never has to make sense to anybody but him. So then there's nothing you can say. Early on, Tyler would sometimes tell him directly that what he wanted just didn't make sense. Well, we learned a lot quicker than Tyler that that never worked. You risked getting your ass kicked. Sometimes he was so plastered, he'd fall down trying to take a swing, but more likely he'd connect. He never really needed a reason to smack us.

"This is not an excuse. I get what you were saying about making choices and bravery … So we should have done something. To not be there at that house in the first place. Maybe we're too stupid. We're not brave. Maybe you would have known what to do. I wished a lot that he'd have a heart attack. That one day he wouldn't make it back alive from The Back Door. Wishing that for your own father … it's not that easy.

"Dad hated Tyler. So if he were around, we hated Tyler too. Because Dad always made us prove it to him … I didn't really hate him but I couldn't ever say that.

"For the longest time we thought Dad hating Tyler made us just a bit safer. But considering where we all ended up, I'm thinking Dad probably hated us just as much. Even if he wouldn't say it out loud. You have to hate your kids to treat them this way, right?

"Just so you know, all these years I never ever hit Tyler. Maybe Bill and Buck bumped him or pushed him. But not smacking him like Dad hit him and hit us. Did we say mean things to him and do rotten things to him, yeah all the time. Like mess up his room and follow him around, and steal things that belonged to him, yeah. Maybe try and frighten him sometimes. But actually that didn't work. Most of the times Tyler would just ignore us or smile at us like he felt sorry for us or because he was just very far away …

"Dad liked to pretend he was some kind of Special Forces guy which seemed pretty crazy to us 'cause he was so out of shape and didn't really know anything about military strategy. Like how easy we got caught on that guy's land by those weird security guys, and how easy it was for Tyler to get away from us all the time."

Frank interrupted: "So you're saying that you didn't hit Tyler over the head with that statue?"

"No, I didn't hit Tyler. I never hit Tyler."

"And you didn't see your brother Buck hit Tyler with the statue?"

"No, sir!"

"And you didn't see your brother Bill hit Tyler with the statue?"

"No, Bill didn't hit Tyler."

"Any chance Tyler figured out a way to smash himself over the head with the statue?"

"No, if he could do that, he didn't do it when I was there."

"So, Bob, how about we cut to the chase and you clear up the mystery of Tyler and the Statue of Liberty …"

"It seems so crazy now but Dad was waiting for Tyler to confess or give in and tell him about some secret stash, like he was some kind of pirate who knew about a whole bunch of buried treasure. The more confused Tyler seemed, and the more he tried to explain what he was doing there in the house, like having fixed the toaster and bringing it back, and now just checking things in the living room, the more pissed off Dad got.

"All of a sudden Dad was waving his humungous hunting knife, yelling he'd caught Tyler red-handed, like he was in some kind of movie. He went on about everything bad that had happened over the past few weeks. Bill and Buck getting pulled over on Route 102, and the rental car getting smashed, saying that he hated Tyler, just like he hated Tyler's mom.

"It was like they were talking two different languages. Tyler was talking about some lady named Abigail and a sheepskin rug and some guy who just didn't appreciate 'Battlestar Galactica' and seeing another lady named Katie and because of what he learned from these coins with the llamas, well, he was apologizing now and going around trying to undo some of what he had done. All the while Dad was getting more and more pissed. Then Tyler said something about all of them trying to live right from now on. Probably my Dad thought he was making fun of him. I tried to say we ought to just leave Tyler be and head home. But Dad ignored me so then I suggested dropping him off at The Back Door but that didn't help at all.

"Next thing I know Dad is pushing Buck and yelling at him to find some rope to use to tie Tyler up, saying if he wasn't going to cooperate, he'd show him. All the while waving that knife around. The big knife he had been threatening us with for a few weeks. All of us got so used to his screaming and his threats and so maybe we just took it as a part of life, but I think this time we all were a lot more scared, seeing how mad he was, and with that knife.

"Buck just completely freaked out. He stood there frozen. Then he started to shake. I couldn't hear what he said, but Tyler sort of leaned in and began to whisper to Buck. Whatever it was, it sort of helped Buck for a bit, but Dad got even more crazy seeing the two of them talking, with Buck not making any effort to find some rope. Then Dad moved in closer to Buck calling him a moron and pushing him, which only undid things for Buck again.

"Dad took another couple of swigs, still waving the knife, weaving even more but managing somehow to put the bottle back in his pocket but weaving a bit. When he steadied himself, he pushed Buck even harder, knocking him into Tyler. Tyler reached out to keep Buck from falling, straining to hold him up. But Buck couldn't help himself and did the worst thing possible. He started to cry. He was looking at Bill for help, then at me, but we were frozen just like Buck. I wish I hadn't been stuck there. I wish I had moved. I tried once more to ask Dad to leave, to go to the bar. But he was completely out of control.

"When Dad saw him crying, he slapped Buck across the face. Buck's eyes were like huge. I don't know whether he thought Dad was going to kill him but at least he stopped crying. Then Tyler tried to explain to Dad one more time that he was just about to leave, hoping maybe he could get through to him. For me, it was like everything was happening too fast. I couldn't think fast enough or do anything fast enough to catch up.

"Dad looked at Tyler like he was some kind of alien bug talking a language he didn't understand. I'm not sure whether he even really heard what Tyler was saying to him because he started screaming like a maniac: 'Shut up … shut up, I said … just shut the fuck up!' Tyler tried one more time to say he was leaving, but Dad yelled that if anyone was leaving it was him.

"He looked at Buck one more time and started to shake his head, and quickly looked back at me and Bill. Like he could barely look at us, that's how much he hated us. Then yelling, 'you worthless sacks of shit … I can't depend on any of you. I have to do everything myself.'

"Tyler is still calmly trying to explain he just wanted to leave. Then all of a sudden Dad hands the knife to Buck so he can grab Tyler with both hands.

"Dad is screaming about Doris and how Tyler's just like her and still doesn't know when to shut up, shaking him. Tyler asks him please to stop and for the first time seems worried, talking about how he doesn't want Tony to get upset. So I guess all of us look around to see whether there's someone else here. Dad starts yelling, saying he could give a crap about Tony, cursing this Tony and Tyler out, and then before any of us knows what's going on, he's got this statue in his hands and smashes Tyler in the head.

Tyler just crumples to the ground.

"Buck is all of a sudden unstuck. He reaches up and grabs Dad with his left hand before he can hit Tyler again.

"That's when Bill and I both started to move to Dad and Buck. Dad grabs Buck's right hand, the hand holding the knife. You think just because he's a drunk that he's weak but, if you've ever been hit by him, you know how incredibly strong his hands are. He clamped down on Buck's hand and you can see the pain on Buck's face.

"By this time, both Bill and I are trying to keep Dad from getting the knife away from Buck, knowing he's nuts enough to kill Buck and kill Tyler and us, too, if he can.

"You want to keep me in jail for the rest of my life, well you can if you need to. But the way I remember it, everything got completely crazy then. We're all trying to stop Dad, trying to yank his hand off Buck's hand. Buck cried out in pain and I guess it was then that Dad got the knife from him. Honestly, it was so nuts I really couldn't see the knife sometimes, being blocked out by Bill and Buck and my dad, all of us fighting for our lives. Kind of like football when everyone is going for the ball, not exactly knowing where it is, but grabbing anyway.

"But I did see at some point that Dad had managed to point the knife at Buck. I don't know who tripped who, or whose foot I stumbled over, but slowly we're all losing our balance and heading for the floor. It must have been then that we managed to turn the knife away from Buck's gut.

"I didn't want to kill my dad. I don't believe Buck wanted to kill Dad. I don't believe Bill wanted to kill Dad.

"I don't really know whose hand was where exactly. I know once Dad had the knife he always had it in his hands. I never got a chance to take it away. Buck was pretty much exhausted by that time. Plus I'm pretty sure Bill never got it away from Dad.

"We all hit the floor in a jumble, all kind of landing on Dad and each other. I heard a groan but I didn't really see the knife sticking out of him until we all untangled ourselves. The blood was seeping everywhere around the knife. Bill wanted to pull it out but I've seen those movies where someone always says you shouldn't, because the guy will bleed out.

"We started arguing and yelling at each other about what to do, about whose fault it was, about who to call or even if we should call. Then Dad's body seemed to slump a bit and I tried to find his pulse which we learned in biology class and leaned in close to see if I could hear his breathing. Then Bill did the same. But pretty soon Dad was dead. We all freaked out.

"I wish we hadn't wiped the knife handle. But we were worried about Buck. I wish we hadn't left Tyler there. Completely out of it. We really didn't know whether he was dead too. So yeah I really wish we hadn't taken the car. I wish we didn't drive away. I wish a lot of things. Mostly, I wish I had stopped Dad ... But we were scared before and we were scared after ...

"I hope Tyler doesn't die. I really do. I'm sorry Bill came up with the stupid idea to blame him. I should have stopped him. Maybe we were just trying to protect ourselves, maybe to convince ourselves we weren't responsible. But I think, too, I was worried about Buck and Bill and they were worried about me ...

"So I wish I wasn't here ... I wish I wasn't telling you all this ... I wish it wasn't true ..."

Frank nodded several times, paused, then added: "Thank you, Bob. I only have one more question. What kind of burger do you want?"

FORTY-EIGHT

Frank fed the boys, then after a short break took Buck, then Bill into the interrogation room. Telling them one at a time how Bob had let Tyler off the hook, and suggesting that now was the time for the truth. To avoid a charge of obstructing justice and to set the record straight. Their relief was palpable as they slowly replaced Bill's story with their real memories.

And yet, as they unburdened themselves, Frank felt his burden grow. Remembering his first *I Ching* reading about the break-ins:

> Clarity prevails when mild and severe penalties are clearly differentiated, according to the nature of the crimes.

Now, months later, he was confronted with Bill, Bob, Buck, and Tyler, the flesh and blood manifestations of his dilemma. As a cop, the suspects secured, you left the complicated issues of guilt and punishment to the prosecutors, the judge and the jury. It was hard enough trying to catch the criminals. Trying to help the victims find some semblance of justice, to act in their place.

In fact, empathy was exactly what you needed to prevail. To slog through hours of interrogating friends, neighbors, co-workers, boyfriends, girlfriends, husbands, wives, mothers, fathers, brothers and sisters, then questioning all the suspects.

When you hit the inevitable dead-ends, it helped to see the victim clearly in your mind. Often by the end of this grueling process you had no energy left to contemplate how to be fair to the perpetrators. But now, he was thinking about the very complicated realities of this particular case. Thinking about the protracted abuse of Bill, Bob, Buck, and Tyler that lay at the very heart of all this.

Despite Bob's very convincing account, there was the always complex question of premeditation versus accident, and the very real possibility that he could or would never really know exactly what happened at the Hopper house that day. Acknowledging that everything was made even more complicated by the fact that a good part of him felt there was a certain justice to the way things ended for Ernie at the Hopper house.

FORTY-NINE

Frank offered Katie some tea and one of Fuel's apricot ginger scones. Danger, who had already claimed Katie's right shoulder, was wondering whether it was worth abandoning his very comfortable human perch for a few scone crumbs on her paper plate. He had missed Katie and decided to stay a while longer to rearrange some of her stray red hair. Hoping the crumbs would still be there when he was done.

Frank had his copy of the *I Ching*, his coins, and a yellow pad for notes. He looked at Katie, took the coins in his hand, and asked: "OK, so after everything that has happened, I want to know how I can bring some clarity and justice to my case?"

He shook the coins then threw them six times, Danger adding a squawk each time the coins hit the table: two heads and one tail; two heads and one tail again; two tails and one head; three tails, a changing line; then two heads and one tail twice. He quickly found his two hexagrams: "Ch'ien" and "Hsiao Kuo."

Katie smiled as Frank looked up "Ch'ien/Modesty," remembering how Penny had thrown it twice last year, and how all three of them threw it together after Penny's husband Peter was safely behind bars.

Frank saw the smile: "So, Katie, I take it you've already made some interesting 'Ch'ien' connections in that lovely intuitively-enhanced brain of yours, all undoubtedly protected by psychic-client privilege. So you probably won't share them with me."

"Right you are, bro'."

Frank picked up the *I Ching*. "Well, I'm going to do my version of that skimming thing you do. I'll pick out pieces that stand out for me, then later I'll go back to read it all again. So Danger, unless you've got an objection, I'll be moving right along."

Danger, with a short stare, then an impatient: "Just do it."

Katie and Frank laughed, while Danger, slightly annoyed, left Katie to grab a few crumbs which he took to the top of the refrigerator. Frank began to read:

> The destinies of men are subject to immutable laws that must fulfill themselves. But man has it in his power to shape his fate, according as his behavior exposes him to the influence of benevolent or of destructive forces.

> The superior man ... when he establishes order in the world ... equalizes the extremes that are the source of social discontent and thereby creates just and equable conditions ...

"It seems my dead Chinese friends continue to hallucinate me as a 'superior man.' So my new *I Ching* assignment, should I choose to accept it, is to not only wrap up the Ripton break-ins and the death of Mr. Earnest Bevans, but make right the underlying sources of social discontent at work here. Then, if I have a spare moment, I'm supposed to create 'just and equable conditions' for all involved. Bearing in mind this additional advice:

> When a man holds a responsible position, he must at times resort to energetic measures.

"A lot of work. Energetic work. Is that about right, Katie? Which leads me to believe I definitely deserve a raise."

Katie couldn't help but laugh. She was quickly joined by Danger who offered his own pitch-perfect Katie laugh.

"Thank you, Danger," she offered, then took a couple of sips of tea. "Well, even though it might be asking a lot, Frank, it does seem appropriate. Considering the law you are sworn to uphold. With the moral responsibility to bring perspective and discretion to your work. Think of 'the destinies of men' as the destinies of Tyler and his step-brothers. Then ensure that your intervention is benevolent rather than destructive.

"As Carl and Theresa would gladly remind us, there is poverty and social injustice and a long list of other inequities that prevent most people from receiving real justice. Which I imagine is why the *I Ching* suggests you need to be bold and imaginative to bring clarity and justice to bear."

Frank silent but nodding, turned to the second hexagram:

Hsiao Kuo / Preponderance of the Small …

The flying bird brings the message:
It is not well to strive upward,
It is well to remain below.
Great good fortune.

"Danger, my friend, my faithful companion, my flying bird, finally something more relevant to my problem than 'fifteen minutes can save you fifteen percent or more …'"

Danger flew back to the top of his cage, hesitated a moment, then declared: "Danger. Good boy … Good boy … It's not just a job. It's an adventure … Danger, good boy. Cracker …"

Katie, with a big smile, quickly found the canister of Nutri-berry treats. "Danger, if anyone deserves a cracker, it's you …' dropping one in his food dish. Danger quickly popped back inside his cage to grab his bounty.

Katie reached for the *I Ching*, then continued to read:

Exceptional modesty and conscientiousness are sure to be rewarded with success … We must understand the demands of the time in order to find the necessary offset for its deficiencies and damages. In any event we must not count on great success, since the requisite strength is lacking. In this lies the importance of the message that one should not strive after lofty things but hold to lowly things.

… this message is brought by a bird … the image of a soaring bird. But a bird should not try to surpass itself and fly into the sun; it should descend to the earth, where its nest is …

Frank looked back to Danger's cage. "I think ever since he hurt his foot, Danger's avoided flying towards the sun … But ever since he's come to stay with me, he's certainly sent messages my way. So between my bird and your book, I'm probably covered."

Katie continued to read aloud:

THE IMAGE

Thunder on the mountain: The image of PREPONDERANCE OF THE SMALL.

… the superior man derives an imperative from this image: he must always fix his eyes more closely and more directly on duty than the ordinary man … He is exceptionally conscientious in his actions … But the essential significance of his attitude lies in the fact that in external matters he is on the side of the lowly.

At certain times extraordinary caution is absolutely necessary … There are dangers lurking for which they are unprepared. Yet such danger is not unavoidable …

… in exceptional times … a man must seek out helpers with whose aid he can carry out the task. But these helpers must be modestly sought out in the retirement to which they have withdrawn … [and] the exceptional task is carried out in spite of all difficulties.

Frank sat there quietly, eyes closed for a few moments, then looking back up toward Danger and over to Katie. "Just when I thought it was safe to go back in the water … I've got these lurking dangers and unavoidable sharks."

"Frank, Frank, Frank … Shifting metaphors here, I'm getting the distinct feeling that the I Ching is more worried about you overreaching, you not Danger who might be about to fly into the sun. Are you planning something risky to deal with this 'exceptional task?' Which, and it's my turn now, you haven't shared with me yet,

I'm thinking. some policeman's confidentiality thing. Anyway, so while I'm confident you're trying to do the right thing, if the *I Ching* is worried, so am I."

Katie turned a few pages: "Just a word or two about what the *I Ching* said about the 'demands of the time' and 'the necessary offset for its deficiencies and damages.' I remember how you first looked at Tyler when Elizabeth began to speak. Many people, maybe most people, won't understand, appreciate, or believe Tyler. Perhaps that's your 'exceptional task.'"

Frank nodded several times, a simple attempt to reassure Katie he was taking this to heart.

"Then maybe the *I Ching* is suggesting that if your plan might frighten or threaten some folks, your superiors, for instance, well it seems now's the time to take a step back and clarify your strategy. Most importantly, to bring along some major allies and helpers with you."

"Got it, Sis', go small instead of too big. With help."

"I'm sure Danger and I would appreciate that … Then last but not least, because you're probably already at work on a Frank Falco/superior man interpretation of the law, I want to remind you that David Stein, recently lured out of retirement, agreed to represent Tyler. I suspect David might be of use to you in this process. So if I can help, I'm glad to talk to him."

Frank's smile turned into a laugh: "Maybe next time I'll skip the book entirely and just ask you."

"It's not just a job. It's an adventure," Danger reminded them.

Katie laughed, and Frank laughed, and they both reached for another muffin.

*   *   *

Frank met Alex for breakfast at Martin's. Alex ordered the poached eggs and Frank went for a bagel and cream cheese.

"There's no delicate way for me to do this, Alex. I've got a big decision to make and it involves the possibility of several young people spending significant amounts of time behind bars. I'm not sure it's even fair of me to ask, but here I am. I'm hoping you'll share some of your prison experience with me."

"I have to hand it to you, Frank. Ninety-nine out of a hundred people never even summon up the courage to ask the question, let alone ask it at eight in the morning. My experience might be a little different than most because unlike most everyone who says they're innocent, I actually was. So much of the punishments, and the lessons you're theoretically supposed to learn, were wasted on me.

"But more than that, based on what I observed, you can just plain throw out a lot of the lofty claims and the justifications for jail-time that police commissioners and district attorneys and judges and even cops talk about to the press, the jury, and the public. I'm not saying it has to be this way but in my case, there was almost no heartfelt attempt at rehabilitation.

"Every year there are more and more prisoners housed in privatized profit-making prisons, and so even public prisons are pressured to cut costs. You're dealing with tired, overworked, and often bitter prison guards and inmates without hope. I want to make it clear that I'm no bleeding heart liberal. You wouldn't, and I certainly didn't want to spend a lot of time with many of the guys in my prison. I'm not saying going to prison should be like going to summer camp. But in my experience most of the time things just get worse for everyone. That's not good for the inmates and it certainly isn't doing any favor to the folks the inmate is going to be interacting with once he or she gets out.

"This may sound wishy-washy to you but I do think there are ways to help people come to grips with what they've done. The thing about prison is time, and finding ways to make the time more tolerable. Twenty-four hours in prison is a heck of a lot longer than twenty-four hours on the outside. Fill some of that time with activities that provide real links to where the inmates have been, something they can relate to. Hopefully that will begin the process to help them get to where they could be going. But that's exactly the stuff they're cutting these days. Libraries, recreation, job-training, therapy …

"So yes, bring in teachers, not necessarily teacher-teachers, but folks who have lived where they've lived, experienced the life they know. Train people for realistic work. Maybe a bit like Alcoholics Anonymous, with some honest-to-God everyday real talk with others who know what they've been up against: poverty, mothers and fathers on crack, and where I came from, in Vegas, parents on the game, gambling addicts, and childhoods filled with violence …"
His voice trailed off for a moment. "I didn't mean to lecture … I guess this stuff still affects me more than I realize.

"So Frank, I obviously don't know exactly what's going on, but I'm guessing you're talking to me because you're at some sort of crossroads. Maybe you've got some doubts about whether someone's guilty or innocent ... but if you think he or she or they are redeemable, and if you think there's another way to turn them around, I say go for it. I don't need to quote the recidivism rates for you. I can tell you, though, that it's pretty easy to die in there. As in not only occasionally lose your life, but most often lose your soul. Give up believing in a decent future.

"The last thing I have to say is I have a strong feeling whoever you're talking about here, they're a lot better off dealing with you than I was with the Las Vegas cops and D.A. and the jury who sent me away."

*   *   *

Before he would agree to talk to Frank, Attorney David Stern had several conditions: they'd meet and eat at The Old Mill in Egremont, he'd have lamb chops for dinner and profiteroles for dessert, and several drinks along the way and Frank would pick up the tab. "Consider it a proffer that you won't be wasting my extremely valuable time," Stern added, "and if in fact you do, at least the alcohol will help me make it through the boredom."

Frank decided he might need each and every one of his brain cells so he drank water while Stern went for a Bloody Mary. Stern was an exercise in visual anarchy: shirt un-tucked to shield his extra thirty pounds, his very long unruly gray-white hair headed everywhere.

But once Stern started talking, he was quite the brilliant thinker and showman. It took only a few minutes for Frank to know he wouldn't ever want to be in the witness box on the answering end of Stern's intellect.

Halfway into his first drink, Stern went to work. "I've had a chance to talk several times with my client. He's as impressed with your sister as I am. As I'm sure you are. All of which is going to make things a bit easier for you.

"Katie has helped me better understand what's been going on for Tyler ... and thus far, I haven't had a chance to meet any of his other personalities, which makes things a bit easier for me. I'm not sure what unique ethical obligations I might be under to represent several different clients all residing within my primary client." Stern paused to take a deep sip. "Don't you just love a challenge?

"Because of what he's been through, my client is sympathetic to the plight of the Bevans boys … By the way I love this place … Everything's great but the lamb chops are the best. And since you're springing for them I think it's only fair to say that over the course of my many years of lawyering I've gained a healthy suspicion of the agents of the law. So I would be remiss if I didn't share what I'm thinking. And get back to doing my job, which is representing my client. So what the fuck are you up to here, Falco? Forgive me but 'Assistant Chief Falco' is a mouthful, know what I mean?"

Frank couldn't help but laugh, trying hard not to spit out the last gulp of water he hadn't yet swallowed. "Sorry, Counselor. This is probably the first time a lawyer's made me laugh."

"My pleasure …"

"Well, my sister adores you, so how about you call me Frank. What is that great lawyerly term you guys always use, 'hypothetically?' So to cut to the chase I'm hypothetically hoping that I can find a way to close this case so that Tyler doesn't get jail time for all of his basically well-meaning if misguided and illegal break-ins. Then I'm hypothetically hoping I can also find a way to help those mostly stupid Bevans kids, although actually I suspect Bob is quite bright, but somehow get them some kind of probation and therapy and job-training rather than lock them away. Hopefully, Tyler and Katie have given you some idea about what life was like for them with their dad …

"So what I'm hypothetically thinking is that it's in your client's interests, and, as my sister might say, in the interests of the universe, to find a creative and more productive way to deal with this mess. I thought that you, being a former prosecutor as well as an interested party, could hypothetically help me not screw this whole thing up."

Stern smiled: "So we're talking about drawing outside the lines here, Frank. Hypothetically speaking. Well, congratulations. It seems you are your sister's brother after all. And your parents' son. I have to say this is very exciting, Frank. Not to mention fraught with the possibility of failure … So exciting it's time for another refill."

Frank caught the waitress' eye and signaled for another Bloody

Mary.

"You know about my folks?"

"Well, let's just say that once upon a time I had major contacts in several information-collecting agencies and many friends in federal high places. So when my daughter told me she was thinking about talking to this psychic lady in Ripton, I, of course, did my due diligence … I have a feeling I might really have liked your folks … But moving right along …

"There's no more political place than the office of District Attorney. First of all, this dinner meeting never happened. That said, if this effort is going to work, insert hypothetically, you're going to have to tie up every single strand of this case. Remove any and every potential need for the D.A. or the Court to intervene, any excuse for them to actively and enthusiastically do what they like to call 'the people's business.' Because they're always looking over their shoulders, always sensitive to any suggestion that they're not fiercely protecting the public. So root out any possible complainers before they complain. It's got to be a package deal that makes every party to this solution happy enough to not only agree to it but to stay silent about their agreement or any lingering doubts they have.

"We're talking the Berkshires here: small is beautiful. It's both easier and more difficult to patch these things together. Easier because people know each other, and they have a history. Therefore, they are more apt to trust each other; yet deals are more difficult because, unlike the big city where most things fall through the many cracks, every small mistake in the boonies gets magnified by the press, by gossip, by misrepresentation.

"Let's start with my client. Hypothetically, it would be helpful if the homeowners who previously complained about Tyler found a solution that worked for them, that provided them with the sense that they no longer had a problem and some justice had been done. Hence, no need to press for unreasonable punishment.

"Having talked to my client, and to your sister, I'm sure you appreciate the problem of putting him/them on the stand. Anything I can do to prevent that potential public humiliation or misunderstanding I'll do. Anything you can do to prevent that will be enormously appreciated. If it's not done right, we can ruin Tyler's life here in the Berkshires.

"So, too, you have my wholehearted support for any alternative to potential imprisonment. Tyler might not make it. He's done an amazing job of surviving thus far, but he's paid an enormous price. I'd like to get him the medical and psychological help he needs. That's just not going to happen once he's in the system.

"By extension, based on what Tyler has told me, I believe you're probably right about the other kids. They might screw up any opportunity you give them, but I think it's worth the gamble."

Frank took a sip of water, then plunged in. "Now, Counselor, here's where the hypotheticals get a little dicey. First of all, I'm hoping that based on what my sister tells me about Tyler's new outlook on home-borrowing, he won't be the cause of any new incidents in the future. Which brings me to the notion that justice has already been served. Because Mr. Bevans was, in fact, seen by witnesses trespassing on two of the properties. Which I would suggest, as the investigating officer, offers compelling enough evidence that the perpetrator has been identified. That, in fact, said perpetrator, Mr. Bevans, died during the commission of these crimes. Which guarantees he won't be the cause of any new incidents in the future."

Stern emptied his glass. "Well, hypothetically, that could work. While I can't represent the Bevans boys, if they're willing, I can help find a decent attorney for them. Because it's pretty clear their cooperation is vital. Out of stubbornness or stupidity, they could easily send this whole plan down the toilet. Royally screw themselves and Tyler. It's a bit complicated considering there are potentially competing interests here, but I know someone with a large heart and expansive view of the nature of righteousness. Who'll appreciate the efforts we'd be making on behalf of all these kids. So in the spirit of these Bloody Marys and the higher call of justice, I'll make a call.

"Lastly, Frank Falco, in the end we are going to need the aid, dare I suggest, the active sympathy of a local judge. Someone whose very judgment will send the strongest signal to the District Attorney's office, that even though there is much that is unconventional in this matter, the Court, nonetheless, is convinced that justice is being, and will continue to be served.

"I happen to know that your Chief and the right Honorable Frederick Van Alston of the South Berkshire District Court are good buddies. I'm told the Chief threw the football to Freddie all through high school and together they won the County title. But most importantly they've been participating in the famed Tuesday night poker game in the back room of Finster's Insurance for close to three decades. Let me tell you there's been many a Tuesday night I wished I had an invite. But until someone dies the game is closed up tighter than the vault at the Cooperative Bank. If you want to see the real Who's Who in South County, you should take a look at the waiting list. So I say we need to get Van Alston on board.

Frank smiled: "Hypothetically, I may have already talked to the Chief about this and I think it's fair to say the Judge is headed for the boat …"

Stern took another sip: "Very, very good … well you've got your work cut out for you, Frank. I'll certainly do whatever I can on my end. Just for the record, this night was far more interesting than I ever imagined it would be. And there's still the lamb to look forward to. You don't play poker, do you, son? Maybe we can start our own game."

*   *   *

Frank returned home to a happy bird. Danger was on a roll: his own idiosyncratic version of Quaker Parrot does Vegas. Some stand-up, some hopping from perch to perch all the while singing and whistling and humming in a variety of styles. "Sweet Boy …" the s and w drawn out so that it sounded more like 'saaa-weeet boy' once, twice, three, four then five times followed by a rendition of 'good mornings' up and down the harmonic scale. Then just in case, Frank hadn't gotten the message a whole bunch of "crackers."

It was such a heartfelt performance that even though it was after nine-thirty and well past the bird's bedtime, Frank opened the cage and invited Danger to join him for some spray millet dessert.

Frank went to sleep with snippets of the *I Ching* echoing in his mind, wondering whether he had paid enough attention to the small and insignificant things? Had he adequately anticipated the lurking dangers, and brought together the right helpers?

FIFTY

It was in the end a celebration of self-interest. It didn't hurt Frank's plan that all this was occurring at a time when the Honorable Justice Van Alston had begun to harbor his own grave doubts about the ability, or the lack thereof, of the justice system to foster redemption. Notwithstanding the new multi-million dollar jail the County had constructed on Route 8, Justice Van Alston and his many colleagues could easily recount the multiple times they had seen the same faces appear before them. Recidivism and more recidivism. All made worse by the recent suicide of Robert Richmond, a young man serving a mandatory two year sentence in the new jail for the sale of several joints and a handful of valium.

Then, David Stern was more than eloquent in his meetings with the D.A. Shifting seamlessly from sales pitch to threat. His case was compelling: the D.A.'s office had more than enough on its plate. And it didn't take too much effort to remind the D.A. of the potentially treacherous prospect of prosecuting a bunch of abused youngsters. Who so very sadly had fallen through the gaping cracks of our local social services.

Surely, David Stern suggested, their teachers must have seen how they had been scarred by the unrelenting violence of their alcoholic father; surely, if not their teachers, then their guidance counselor. If the school had somehow missed it, what about the police? Or the hospitals who had admitted Doris Deakins on multiple occasions, the victim of the repeated, sometimes brutal beatings she had suffered? How had this systematic abuse been missed by so many year after year? Then David Stern leaned in a little closer to the D.A. and his voice lowered to his most conspiratorial of tones, "you know, I can't help but wonder how many concerned and helpful members of the community sit on the Boards of these institutions?"

Finally, Stern stressed, "one might reasonably ask, why was it that the D.A.'s office hadn't prosecuted Earnest Bevans for his continuing crimes? Why now would your office contemplate prosecuting Tyler Deakins, so clearly the victim of Mr. Earnest Bevans' vicious assault? Why punish Tyler for seeking a safe place and a place to hide from the perpetrator of this constant violence?

"As for the Bevans boys," Agatha Grandison, their new

attorney argued, "given the lack of any compelling evidence that they were responsible for Mr. Bevans' death, well I would argue that if those charged with making sure our young children aren't abused have so repeatedly failed us, well surely a jury of concerned community members should and could step in and right this dreadful wrong."

While the D.A. silently fumed, he began to craft the press release that not only explained why his office, with the death of the prime suspect, Ernest Bevans, had decided to refrain from pressing additional charges, but also forcefully renewed his call for more vigilant efforts to combat child abuse in the County.

The deal they reached stipulated that as long as the boys agreed to a rigorous menu of probation, therapy, school and/or job training with scheduled monthly meetings to ensure their compliance, Justice Van Alston and the D.A. would consider this a rare but necessary exercise in discretion. Then, as hands were shaken, and smiles smiled, they all imagined themselves, as David Stern suggested, the brave architects of an important, even groundbreaking social experiment.

By the time Frank and his helpers had done their parts, each of the boys had his own therapist. Bill and Buck had joined the Culinary Arts Program of the Berkshire Youth Association, apprenticing themselves to local chefs, each dreaming of the perfect burger. Bob was back in school at Brett High. While Tyler, seeing Katie once a week, had recently discovered that his talent for taking things apart extended to even larger motors, and was now working full-time for Dominic Tilson at Tilson Automotive. Remarkably, they were all living with Doris, and all helping out at home.

Thankfully, every homeowner, with two notable exceptions, was greatly relieved to learn that the Ripton police had not only solved the break-ins but that the larcenous days of the perpetrator, Earnest Bevans, were over and done with for good. Many were quick to acknowledge that apart from the great uneasiness they had experienced knowing how easy it was for someone else to gain entry to their homes, nothing of any great consequence had been taken, and in fact, several of their appliances had never worked better.

The first dissenter, Arthur Davidson of the Marco Pizzarelli white rug, needed most of all the time and space to complain some more, to exaggerate the great inconvenience he had suffered, and to bask in the extended apology he so clearly deserved.

But then there was Milton Krause. What, in a better world, might have been a simple short notification to Mr. Krause that his entertainment center was now safe and under his sole control, followed by a joint acknowledgment of mission accomplished, turned instead into a nasty and extended exercise in scolding. Because, for Mr. Krause, it seemed there was far less pleasure knowing that the break-ins were a thing of the past, than the perverse but great satisfaction he quickly got reminding Frank of the previous multiple failures of the Ripton Police Department. And the need to proclaim his determination to continue and amplify his complaints to the higher authorities.

As their conversation continued, it became increasingly clear that the greatest test of Frank's plan, the largest of the lurking dangers was the need to somehow pacify this self-absorbed, overly-entitled land baron.

Frank was called upon several times to remind himself to breathe, to invoke the gods and goddesses of patience and modesty, to think unceasingly about Tyler and Bill and Bob and Buck and the greater good, and to pepper each pause with a "Yes, sir" or "I understand completely" or the occasional "absolutely."

Then, ever so slowly slipping into daydream, imagining tracking Krause down, forcing him into one of his Land Rovers. Taping his mouth shut, then making him listen a hundred times over to this ridiculously insensitive and unnecessary conversation.

When Krause broke the spell to announce: "Listen, I've spent fifteen minutes talking with you and haven't made a dime. Let me tell you something. My nephew Carter says he's heard from several local girls that you've been protecting the kids of this criminal. Now I don't know what your angle is here but I do know you've been wasting my precious time. I had my people review the video surveillance and I know damn well that this dead guy wasn't the one breaking into my place. So don't be surprised when I level an official complaint with my good friend, the Governor. You know, when I see him next week in his private box at Fenway Park. Goodbye, Mr. Falco!" Then he hung up.

FIFTY-ONE

Katie felt the stars slowly aligning for Tyler. They had been making great progress, and he and Rabbit followed their sessions with long walks. Just yesterday afternoon she had spent a fascinating hour with Tyler and his therapist. Not only had Dr. Patty Brown treated several people suffering from Dissociative Identity Disorder but had raised three sons. During her time at university, she had spent several years studying Karl Jung. Given Jung's great respect for the oracle, Dr. Brown was well-acquainted with the *I Ching*. Katie was thrilled to see how easily she related to Tyler and all his friends.

Unfortunately, according to Frank, there was the one remaining Krause danger, a danger which had recently shifted from lurking to looming. So Katie made a basketful of blueberry muffins and she and Rabbit drove to Frank's apartment.

Frank was still so very pissed at Krause, and even more worried that all the work he and the Chief and David Stern had accomplished might collapse around them.

"How can I best deal with Krause?" he asked, throwing the coins with just a bit too much force. Two tails and a head, a seven.

"Easy, Frank, these llamas are your friends."

Danger looked down from atop his perch on the refrigerator: "Nationwide is on your side ..."

Only Katie laughed. Luckily, Frank had nothing to throw at Danger but the coins. "Danger, I'd ground you except you already are. Please, enough with the insurance companies ..." pausing a moment for a couple of deep breaths, then more gently throwing two heads and a tail, an eight. Then the process repeated itself: a seven followed by an eight followed by a seven and the last eight.

"You've thrown 'Chi Chi / After Completion.' And if I remember this hexagram, Frank, it's quite appropriate."

"Let me read a bit:

> The transition from confusion to order is completed, and everything is in its proper place even in particulars … This is a very favorable outlook, yet it gives reason for thought. For it is just when perfect equilibrium has been reached that any movement may cause order to revert to disorder …

Frank wasn't really aware that when he heard the word 'disorder,' his right hand quickly landed on his forehead and his fingers began a slow massage. As if rubbing could somehow erase the threat Krause posed. Rabbit moved to his side and placed his head on Frank's knee. Katie continued on:

> Hence the present hexagram indicates the conditions of a time of climax, which necessitates the utmost caution.

"I copied this excerpt from 'Mêng / Youthful Folly,' Frank said as he reached into his front shirt pocket and took out a folded piece of yellow paper to read:

> But the penalty should not be imposed in anger; it must be restricted to an objective guarding against unjustified excesses. Punishment is never an end in itself but serves merely to restore order.

"Thanks to you, Katie, it's been guiding what I do. But I'm really worried, and reminded of something Carl often said: 'so near, so far.'"

"Well, as for 'so near,' you and your able friends have created the possibility for a 'favorable outlook,' to give those Bevans boys a chance at a decent life. A new start for Tyler. As for 'so far:'

> The transition from the old to the new time is already accomplished … and it is only in regard to details that success is still to be achieved …

Everything proceeds as if of its own accord, and this can all too easily tempt us to relax and let things take their course without troubling over details. Such indifference is the root of all evil. Symptoms of decay are bound to be the result …

He who understands it is in position to avoid its effects by dint of unremitting perseverance and caution.

"Caution … perseverance … The polite Chinese way of suggesting there's another shark circling just a few feet away."
"Well, Frank, it's not surprising that someone who values his privacy and private property more than the future of these damaged young adults might not appreciate what you're doing. Spare the rod, spoil the child. You, after all, are the police, the ones paid to protect property. But, instead, here you are asking for a more sophisticated sense of justice. As 'Chi Chi' tells us:

In a time of flowering culture, an occasional convulsion is bound to occur, uncovering a hidden evil within society … such evils can easily be glossed over and concealed from the public. Then everything is forgotten and peace apparently reigns complacently once more.

However, to the thoughtful man such occurrences are grave omens that he does not neglect. This is the only way of averting evil consequences …

"The good thing is you're one step ahead and, despite the concealment, you can see the shark. In this case, the injustice, the inflexibility of the justice system … 'Chi Chi' highlights the struggle between the moral and the material, public responsibility versus the sanctity of private property, the true and false faith:

> In divine worship the simple old forms are
> replaced by an ever more elaborate ritual and an
> ever greater outward display. But inner seriousness
> is lacking in this show of magnificence; human
> caprice takes the place of conscientious obedience
> to the divine will. However, while man sees what
> is before his eyes, God looks into the heart.

Frank's hand was back to his forehead. His burden seemed greater, the stakes higher.

"There's just a bit more … Makes me think about Dad. It was one of his mandatory movie days. Do you remember that German deli he loved on Broadway and 87th? We always got roast pork sandwiches on rye with potato salad. Then we'd sneak them in to The New Yorker. This time to see "The Loneliness of the Long Distance Runner" which is what I think about when I think about this passage. This is no sprint but a long run:

> Here in conclusion another warning is added.
> After crossing a stream, a man's head can get into
> the water only if he is so imprudent as to turn
> back. As long as he goes forward and does not
> look back, he escapes this danger. But there is a
> fascination in standing still and looking back on a
> peril overcome.
>
> However, such vain self-admiration brings
> misfortune. It leads only to danger, and unless one
> finally resolves to go forward without pausing, one
> falls a victim to this danger.

Danger flew down to the table, circled around until he found a few crumbs from the scones. "Danger … Cracker," he announced.

"Close enough," Frank offered. Breaking off a small piece of his remaining scone, and pushing it towards him: "Danger … Cracker!"

Danger looked up at Frank, then waited a moment, his dark eyes focused and intense. "Just Do It," he suggested. "Just Do It!"

FIFTY-TWO

Thanks to the work they were doing with Katie and Dr. Patty Brown, they were learning how best to pool their efforts. There was less chaos, less commotion, fewer headaches.

But none of them was happy to learn that despite everything Assistant Chief Falco was trying to do, Mr. Krause was still threatening to make trouble for Tyler. So once again they were talking over each other, interrupting, occasionally disrespectful.

As she brought his eggs and coffee, Deb could see the stress and strain on Tyler's face.

"Tyler, honey, I'm worried. I'm going to take this back to the kitchen and pack your breakfast up and put this coffee in a to-go cup. You can have it later. I want you to head up to Katie's. I'm going to call her right now so she knows you're coming."

$$* \qquad * \qquad *$$

Katie explained that Frank and the Chief and Tyler's lawyer and some other members of the community were hoping that the combination of Ernie's presence at the Krause property, his break-in and death at the Hopper house would persuade Mr. Krause that his problem was now over. But that wasn't happening.

That if Krause continued to press the issue, and the District-Attorney surrendered to the political pressure, he could go back on his word and still prosecute Tyler for the break-ins. That the attempt to get the Bevans boys a suspended sentence and some long-term help could also go down the drain.

It seemed clear that repairing some appliance in the Krause house wasn't going to do the trick. So they asked: "How can we help fix this?" Taking turns throwing the coins, separate but together trying to figure out what to do next. Throwing a eight and then a seven, and two eights and the final two changing lines, two sixes.

Katie explained that they had thrown 'Shih / The Army' and 'Huan / Dispersion.'

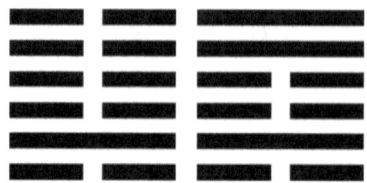

Katie turned to "Shih / The Army" and began to read aloud:

An army is a mass that needs organization in order to become a fighting force. Without strict discipline nothing can be accomplished, but this discipline must not be achieved by force. It requires a strong man who captures the hearts of the people and awakens their enthusiasm ...

Katie looked up from the book: "Well, Tyler, this builds on what Dr. Brown has been saying. That one of the central goals of your therapy is to get you all communicating and coordinating better. How did she put it: 'gradually integrating your selves.'

"Obviously, a strong man or woman is required," Elizabeth interrupted, "if we are actually going to help the Assistant Chief, if we are going to help ourselves."

"That's true, Elizabeth. The challenge is to work together with discipline and focus. As the *I Ching* reminds us, that what you and my brother do or don't do, and how you all do it, has great consequences:

But war ... like a poisonous drug, should be used as a last recourse ... Unless there is a quite definite war aim to which the people can consciously pledge themselves, the unity and strength of conviction that lead to victory will not be forthcoming. But the leader must also look to it that the passion of war and the delirium of victory do not give rise to unjust acts that will not meet with general approval. If justice and perseverance are the basis of all action, all goes well.

"Remember, this is a coming together of different people in the community to confront this serious threat to your safety. Requiring a steady determination, but just as importantly, making sure the effort doesn't step too far over the line. So hopefully, when the threat is overcome, and justice is done, there's a return to peace and normality:

> When danger threatens, every peasant becomes a soldier; when the war ends, he goes back to his plow …

Katie could see that Tyler, while a bit less anxious, was still working hard to understand exactly what he needed to do. As she began to look for the second hexagram, 'Huan / Dispersion,' she heard Rabbit at the front screen door.

Having decided he'd save his egg sandwich from Dom's for lunch, Tyler took a moment to spread some butter and jam on a corn muffin. He was still chewing when Rabbit came to lie down beside him. By the time Katie settled herself and began to read, the corn muffin was no more and both Rabbit and Tyler were smiling.

> Huan / Dispersion [Dissolution]

> Wind blowing over water disperses it … This suggests that when a man's vital energy is dammed up within him … gentleness serves to break up and dissolve the blockage …

> … the dispersing and dissolving of divisive egotism. DISPERSION shows the way, so to speak, that leads to gathering together.

> Religious forces are needed to overcome the egotism that divides men … The sacred music and the splendor of the ceremonies aroused a strong tide of emotion that was shared by all hearts in unison, and that awakened a consciousness of the common origin of all creatures.

> … in the common concentration on this goal, all barriers dissolve, just as when a boat is crossing a great stream, all hands must unite in a joint task.

All of a sudden Tyler did a double-take, and he began to grin. Katie paused to take a sip of tea, familiar now with these moments when some of Tyler's other personalities emerged in often unexpected ways. Trying to imagine what it was like to contain and mediate so much contradictory information. A bit like watching doubles ping pong, an almost impossible task, absorbing and appreciating so much sustained, seemingly frenetic energy.

Tyler was nodding. It was as if they all had come to a conclusion. Tyler began, "Well, Elizabeth thinks it's great that the book celebrates the 'common origin of all creatures,' which is sort of like our story. I think we all understand the need to work together, but we've also been laughing about something the book just said. It's pretty amazing. But now we really have to talk to your brother."

Katie smiled, "I don't know what's funny about any of this, but I hope you'll tell me some day. But please before you rush off, let's finish with 'Huan.' There might be something else that's important.

> In times of general dispersion and separation, a great idea provides a focal point for the organization of recovery. Just as an illness reaches its crisis in a dissolving sweat, so a great and stimulating idea is a true salvation in times of general deadlock ...

> But here the thought is not that a man avoids difficulties for himself alone, but rather he rescues his kin - helps them to get away before danger comes, or to keep at a distance from an existing danger, or to find a way out of a danger that is already upon them. In this way he does what is right.

Tyler was smiling. "Well, it's not very often we all agree. But maybe this time we kin have found a way out of this. It may not be such a great idea but it's ours and it just may work. "

266

FIFTY-THREE

Tyler plopped himself down in the chair across from Frank at The Roadside Store, mid-bite of his oversized blueberry pancake, an artful mix of pancake and melted butter and real syrup from the Gould Farm's real maple trees.

Tyler smiling. Close to laughing. The words spilling from him. "Just so you know, we weren't joking about something you take seriously. But when Katie was reading from the China book and she said 'joint task,' Ronald started to giggle and then pretty soon Abigail and even Tony started to laugh. I know it's hard to believe, but even Elizabeth was laughing. It's a pretty silly joke and to tell you the truth we were worried you might be annoyed if you discovered what we did ..."

Frank very reluctantly put his fork down. "Well, Tyler, to tell you the truth I was enjoying a little peace and quiet and really loving my pancake so I wish I knew what you're talking about."

"I know we broke the law, and we know you're a policeman, but there are other laws, too, that get broken. Like a few weeks ago, during one of those times we went to the Krause property, and we were taking the really long way around walking through the woods to get to the house."

"It was Tony who first saw them. He's the only one of us who even knows what they look like."

Which is when Tyler turned on his iPhone and found the pictures and handed it to Frank. As Frank flipped from photo to photo, Tyler and his friends couldn't repress the giggles. Like Danger laughing five different laughs.

Frank wanted to laugh, too, remembering that it wasn't all that long ago that the llamas had offered Frank "Mêng / Youthful Folly," suggesting that the young fool would seek him out, promising good fortune. Frank turned to Tyler: "I need to borrow your phone for a few minutes. Do me a favor and finish my pancake, and get yourself some bacon or whatever you want," dropping a twenty on the table. "I'll be back in a half hour."

*   *   *

Frank knew that every one of those pictures was digitally

tagged and had somehow logged the GPS coordinates of where it was taken. So thanks to the generosity of Catherine Gianelli of the Cyber Crime unit of the NYPD, who was willing to work some extra hours to help her once-upon-a-time slightly more than friend, Frank now had a complete set of digital files and printouts with the time, date, and precise location of every photo Tyler had taken.

Then, thanks to a couple more trips to the GB parking lot and several conversations with some kids who, after being assured they wouldn't be hassled, were more than willing to tell him Carter Krause was an untrustworthy creep and a cheat who overcharged them for weed, but worse than that continually preyed on the girls they hoped would be theirs. So with perseverance and patience, Frank was able to discover who Carter Krause hung out with when he was weekending at the Krause estate.

The Chief suggested they hold the interviews at the more intimidating Great Barrington police station rather than their own dinky, unlikely to frighten a mouse one-room affair at Town Hall. They started with Skye Patrick, who brought her single mom and potter, Deborah Patrick. Then they spoke to Jenn Fulton-Davidson, who was accompanied by her parents, Roberta Fulton and Harvey Davidson, owners of the highly successful Purple Pirate Gift Shoppe. The Chief and Frank and the parents were almost immediately stunned to discover that these two best friends since kindergarten, and now fifteen year old juniors together still at Monument Mountain High School were not only thrilled to have been chosen to spend time in their bikinis in the Krause hot-tub smoking dope with nephew Carter but had the cellphone selfies to demonstrate their exceptional good fortune.

So early the next morning Frank and Rabbit and Tyler took a road trip, traipsing through the woods of the Krause estate where with Rabbit's help they quickly found the bountiful crop. And Frank soon had a whole new set of photos.

*   *   *

Frank spread Tyler's pictures on Chief Paul's desk, then added the new photos he had printed from his phone.

"You deserve to do it, Chief. I mean how many times did he call you at home? Threaten your job? And worse, interrupt your

Red Sox games? That's got to be at least a misdemeanor in Massachusetts. Oh and I just thought of something else. After all the time Derek Ford put into taking care of that property the last few years, the least he deserves is his job back."

Chief Paul smiled. "As much as I'd enjoy making the call this really is your case, Frank, your hard work. Believe me, I'll get enough pleasure listening."

Frank, his notes in front of him, dialed. "Milton Krause, please. Could you tell Mr. Krause that this is Assistant Chief Frank Falco of the Ripton, Massachusetts Police Department, calling on official police business ... "

Frank had to wait a few minutes.

"Good morning, Mr. Krause ... I just want you to know that you are on speaker phone and that Chief Paul is listening to our conversation."

"Chief Paul, could you please inform your deputy that I'm in the middle of some extremely important negotiations with a company I'm interested in acquiring in Stuttgart. I assume you're calling to tell me that you have those young people in custody and that your District Attorney is prepared to prosecute."

"Not exactly, Mr. Krause, and by the way this is still Assistant Chief Falco here. This is my case, Mr. Krause. Actually, everything has become a lot more complicated. We've come across some important new information in the last two days that has bearing on this case."

"Chief Paul, I have no idea why you and your assistant are bothering me. I understand from Patricia McWhinney of the Selectboard that you once had those four kids in custody. So how about you get on with it and complete your assignment. There's certainly no need to contact me until they've been convicted. Now let me be completely clear with you, as soon as we're done here, I'm on the phone with Patricia and the entire Selectboard and the Berkshire County District Attorney's Office. Hopefully, they'll make sure the job is done as quickly as possible."

"Mr. Krause, I'm afraid you've been misinformed. We're in the process of closing this case. We've identified the guilty party as a Mr. Earnest Bevans of Brett, Massachusetts. Mr. Bevans recently died as a result of an accident he had while breaking and entering into another property here in Ripton. You might remember that members of your private security force detained this same Mr.

Bevans when he had a minor traffic accident on your land. While we believe he intended to break into your home on that occasion, he never made to the house. At the time, Mr. Bevans claimed he was only checking to see whether he might be able to hunt deer on your land during deer season. Unfortunately, because of a lack of evidence, he got away with only a small fine for trespassing.

"We subsequently learned that he put sustained pressure on, and occasionally got violent with his sons to make sure they joined him during these break-ins. And it's our considered opinion that either a judge or local jury might well believe there were very understandable extenuating circumstances when it comes to the boys. In return for not being prosecuted they've agreed to participate in a rigorous routine of court supervised therapy and job training."

Krause exploded: "So after all the times my property was invaded, and my home violated, you've decided to reward them with a job! No wonder so many young people are close to worthless. I can't tell you the number of young people we hire in my companies then fire within the year. So much for the law … All I can say is that the two of you must want to find a new line of work, and let me tell you I am perfectly willing to reach out to the Governor and the Attorney-General and anyone else I need to, to make sure that that's exactly what happens for you …"

Frank reached out to restrain the Chief who was close to grabbing the phone from him. He took several deep breaths before speaking.

"Well, it's good to know you care so much for the law, Mr. Krause. In which case I'm going to give you the benefit of the doubt and assume that you're not completely familiar with Section 32C of Chapter 94C of the Massachusetts General Law. That section reads, and I'm quoting: 'Subsection (a) Any person who knowingly or intentionally manufactures, distributes, dispenses or cultivates, or possesses with intent to manufacture, distribute, dispense or cultivate a controlled substance in Class D of section thirty-one shall be imprisoned in a jail or house of correction for not more than two years or by a fine of not less than five hundred nor more than five thousand dollars, or both such fine and imprisonment …'

Frank didn't get a chance to finish. Krause's curses were loud enough to ricochet from wall to wall in the small office.

"What the fuck do you think you're doing? Let me tell you, Chief, if you country bumpkins are thinking of blackmailing me, you better think twice. I'll have ten fucking lawyers going for blood."

"That's certainly your right, Mr. Krause. But I, and this is still Assistant Chief Falco … Well, Ripton as you well know is a very small town, and even if we disagree, we think of you as a valuable member of our community. We would very much like to resolve this matter in as friendly a way as we can. So I hope you'll let me finish before you start to pay your ten very expensive attorneys."

All they heard was a grunt and so Frank continued: "Marijuana is a Class D substance … and in the course of our investigation into the break-ins, we've come across compelling evidence that your property is being used for the cultivation of an extremely large amount of marijuana. Actually in quantities so large that it is certainly intended not for personal use but for illegal distribution and sale."

More silence.

"We believe that we are talking about quantities large enough to invoke even more serious penalties. I quote: 'Fifty pounds or more, but less than one hundred pounds, be punished by a term of imprisonment in the state prison for not less than two and one-half nor more than fifteen years or by imprisonment in a jail or house of correction for not less than one nor more than two and one-half years. No sentence imposed under the provisions of this section shall be for less than a mandatory minimum term of imprisonment of one year.' So we're hoping …"

Krause couldn't help but interrupt: "O.K., I have been exceedingly patient with you, Chief Paul, and with your deputy but you have a crossed a serious line here … You clearly have no idea who you are talking to. I can promise you, you will both regret making this call."

Before Frank knew what was happening, the Chief grabbed the phone from him.

"Let me assure you, Mr. Krause, and this time it is Chief Paul, that if you choose to disregard what we are telling you and you continue to threaten us, it will be you and your nephew Carter who will be doing the regretting. We've chosen to speak with you politely, instead of arresting you both. We've chosen to give you the opportunity to fix things here. But the more I hear from you the less likely I am to continue down this path."

Chief Paul paused. Frank had never seen him more furious. He could barely contain himself. And Frank was glad Krause was more than a hundred miles away. The Chief closed his eyes then tried once more to talk in a normal tone:

"I have been a policeman for more than thirty years, Mr. Krause. I have always tried to do my job fairly and with respect for those I come in contact with. But I swear to you I am an inch away from sending my Assistant Chief to the city to bring you and your nephew back here in handcuffs …

"I promised my wife I'd watch my blood pressure and so before I do just that, I am going to take a bunch of very deep breaths and have him use his phone gizmo to send you pictures of that large illegal crop of marijuana plants that are growing right this minute on your property.

"So before you continue to argue with me, I advise you to think for a moment. I could easily have called our Countywide Task Force on Drugs. I've been told there is a very good chance those plants weigh more than fifty pounds.

"For the last time, Mr. Krause, would you like to see those pictures on your phone or Deputy Chief Falco at your front door with a warrant for your arrest?"

There were several very long moments of silence, while they heard what sounded like Krause's fingers tapping angrily on his desk. Then a reluctant and begrudging: "Send me the pictures."

Frank had picked a couple of wide shots and two close-ups. They heard a soft whoosh as his cellphone sent them to the city and to Krause.

"Mr. Krause, this is Assistant Chief Falco … You'll be seeing photographs taken this morning on your land. We also have photos from several weeks before …"

"Give me a moment … OK, I just got them … So there are a bunch of bushes here. How exactly am I supposed to know this is my land? Do you think I actually walk in the woods?"

"Mr. Krause, all of these photos are tagged with precise GPS coordinates. If you don't know where these plants are and how they got there, well I'm sorry. But that's no defense … Perhaps if you hadn't fired Mr. Ford, he would have found them and alerted you … But, in any event, based on our recent investigations I think you would benefit from a prolonged conversation with your nephew Carter. If he tells you he knows nothing about them, you might mention Skye Patrick and Jenn Fulton-Davidson, two under-aged high school girls from here in Ripton. Ask him about the times he spent with them in your hot tub bragging about and sharing some of his crop, and the pictures they took celebrating the occasions. As of this moment it appears Carter's actions fell short of statutory rape but it would be in his very best interests to cooperate … You should also know it won't be difficult for us to find some of those he sold marijuana to in Great Barrington. Last of all, you might ask your ten attorneys about your own liability in these matters."

Frank looked down at his informal list: photos, GPS, Carter, Skye and Jenn, Derek Ford, dropping charges against Tyler … He looked back up and across the desk at Chief Paul who while nodding to himself still seemed pissed. Meanwhile, Krause was silent.

"Mr. Krause, this is Chief Paul. Are you still with us?"

Even the finger tapping had stopped.

"Mr. Krause?"

"I'm back … I'm sorry, you've obviously given me a lot to think about. It goes without saying that I may have seriously underestimated you both … And in the process severely underestimated your ability to do your jobs. It seems you have done them so well I am now at a serious disadvantage.

"Let me assure you, and I appreciate I haven't given either of you any reason to trust me, but this is truly the first I've learned of these plants. I love my sister, but not so much her spoiled-brat of a son. I know, though, it would break her heart to see him in jail. So let's say I am very interested to see if there is any way for me to find some way out of this massive mess my nephew has made for us …"

There was several moments of silence, then they heard Krause's exaggerated sigh.

"Obviously, I don't need to tell either of you that I can be a real arrogant sonofabitch. And because I don't allow myself very often to believe I have anything at all to apologize for, well I'm not very good at it. It seems you've proven to me quite clearly that my sister's son is a more of a moron than I imagined, and clearly I was foolish to trust him … My mother made me promise to take care of my sister and her children and well, no excuses. So while I appreciate he broke the law, I hope we can find a creative way to deal with it. Quite frankly there are probably much better and more effective ways to help him than locking him up ..."

"Well, Mr. Krause, this is Assistant Chief Falco. It turns out we came to the exact same conclusion about the Bevans boys and Tyler Deakins ... So we would certainly appreciate it if you would join our efforts to find an equitable end to this sad affair. To teach these kids there's a better way to find peace and safety than breaking into other people's property. And, most importantly, to help them turn their lives around ... That said we're willing to accept the same approach for your nephew if you promise us you'll find an adequate and effective way to administer some sort of justice for your nephew ..."

They could hear Krause's slow sigh of relief. "Thank you ... Thank you very much. Well, first off, if you send me the addresses of those two girls I'll immediately contact the families and see what I can do for them. I promise you, and I'll promise them, none of you will ever again see Carter in Ripton. I hope it's not too late for him but I assure you that Carter will be working hard six days a week in the maintenance department of one of my companies until he begins to understand what hard work is, and learns something about responsibility.

"Now let me return to something I do a lot better than apologizing, which is closing a deal. If you'll allow me, if I understand the terms of our agreement, the first thing I'll have Mr. Ford do as part of his renewed caretaking duties is to destroy all these plants. He will do whatever it takes to assure us that this never happens again. And while you haven't yet mentioned it, I will congratulate you for finding the perpetrator of the break-ins at my property.

"Since you've assured me this will no longer be a problem, well then I will be glad to let the District Attorney and the Selectboard know that I am more than satisfied. Finally I promise not to call you at home unless it's to offer you box seats to see the Red Sox at Fenway."

And before either Frank or Chief Paul had a chance to reply, he hung up.

FIFTY-FOUR

The Chief shook his head, a bit amazed but mostly very relieved.

"Well, Frank, you may well have saved that kid, Tyler. Who knows you may even have saved those bratty Bevans. I think you may also have worked your way to a promotion. Alice is pretty much done with this life, with my leaving at all hours of the day and night to deal with other people's emergencies, big and small, real and imaginary. She wants us in Carolina closer to her family and without the ice and snow.

"It's hard to imagine any of the Selectmen saying no to you after this, and especially after they hear from Mr. Krause. Anyway, you think about it. But I don't think I can hold off Alice much longer …"

*   *   *

Derek Ford called him the next morning, stunned that Milton Krause had offered him his job back. Pretty sure that Frank had everything to do with it. Completely amazed that Krause had thanked him for all the work he had done in the past, even saying he was sorry that he hadn't been more appreciative. Then asked about his wife. Wondering whether there were any official police reports that aliens had taken control of New York City? But really so very grateful.

As Frank drove to Taft Farms then to Domaney's, he found himself thinking about "Méng / Youthful Folly." What with Tyler getting help with Katie, and with his therapy, just maybe this time around punishment had taken a back seat to restoring order.

As he sat there in his car, Frank felt a wave of exhaustion shuddering its way down from head to toe. As tired as he was, he felt glad that he had found and delivered at least a small bit of justice. And that along the way, he had learned a bit about folly, youthful and otherwise. So with a bottle of red and a blackberry pie, he went to find love in the arms of Penny.

THE END

ABOUT THE AUTHOR

Mickey Friedman is the author of *A Red Family: Junius, Gladys, and Barbara Scales*, the non-fiction oral history of a unique American Communist family, University of Illinois Press, 2009. You can learn more about it at aredfamily.com.

He has made documentary films about a wide range of subjects, including U.S./Nicaraguan relations, breast cancer, GE and its misuse of PCBs, and one soldier's year in Iraq. You can watch them at mickeyfriedman.com or on YouTube.

The television adaptation of his play *Songs From The Heart: Edith Wharton* aired on BRAVO and PBS, and was nominated in 1988 for the Best Dramatic Special on Cable TV. A copy of *Songs* is in the Museum of Broadcasting.

He writes a newspaper column twice a month for The Berkshire Record. And is preparing a collection of these columns, *The Best Small Town in America*. In the meantime, many of them can be found at redcrownews.com.

This is his second *I Ching* novel. The first *Danger Times Two: An I Ching Mystery* can be purchased at Amazon.com.

He is about to begin his third *I Ching* novel.

www.ingramcontent.com/pod-product-compliance
Lightning Source LLC
Chambersburg PA
CBHW071310170626
46809CB00001B/391